When artfully attempting to land a lord, a lady must always remain highly mysterious… and make ***him*** *chase* ***her.***

"Why were you hiding from me?"

"I should think that would be rather clear." When Nicholas did not respond, Isabel continued, eager to fill the silence. "I was surprised by our . . . moment. I had not expected to be so . . ."

Nicholas was suddenly aware of their location—in the darkened attic, the rain outside muffling all sounds, the warm, small space closing in around them. It was the perfect place for a clandestine tryst.

He took a step closer; they were scant inches from one another. "So . . . ?"

She sighed, resigned. "So . . . drawn to you."

He watched embarrassment flood her cheeks, fierce and red. She spoke, the words coming fast. "I am sure it is just a passing phase. I think it is best for you to leave. I shall find another way—"

He reached out, his touch stemming the flow of her words.

He should not kiss her. He knew it.

But she was like no woman he had ever known—and he wanted to discover her secrets. More than that, he wanted her.

He settled his lips to hers, and she was his.

By Sarah MacLean

Ten Ways to Be Adored When Landing a Lord
Nine Rules to Break When Romancing a Rake
The Season

SARAH MACLEAN

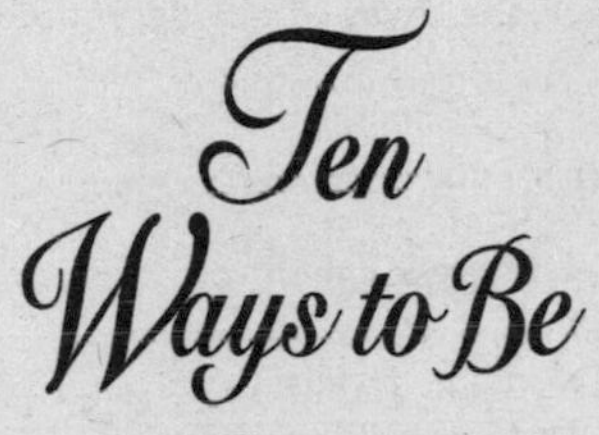

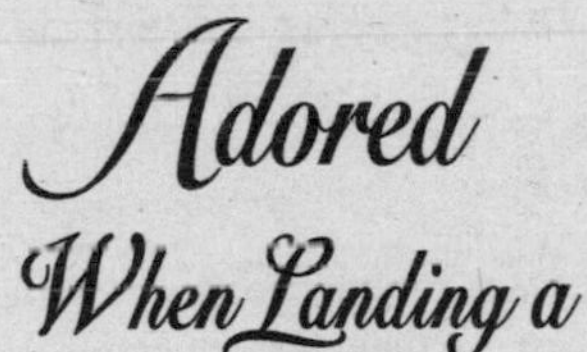

When Landing a

AVON

An Imprint of HarperCollins*Publishers*

This is a work of fiction. Names, characters, places, and incidents are products of the author's imagination or are used fictitiously and are not to be construed as real. Any resemblance to actual events, locales, organizations, or persons, living or dead, is entirely coincidental.

AVON BOOKS
An Imprint of HarperCollins*Publishers*
10 East 53rd Street
New York, New York 10022–5299

ISBN 978-0-06-185206-0
www.avonromance.com

First Avon Books paperback printing: November 2010

Printed in the U.S.A.

10 9 8 7 6 5 4 3 2 1

For Chiara,
who went off to college
and didn't mind that
I stole her books.
And her cat.

Prologue

It cannot be denied that there is a veritable epidemic spreading among the young ladies of London—a tragic reality that ends in nothing but the very worst possible scenario.

We refer, of course, to spinsterhood.

With so many unmarried ladies in our fair city so unfortunately shaded from the brilliant sunshine of wedded bliss, 'tis nothing short of criminal that these promising young buds might never have the opportunity to blossom!

And so, Dear Reader, it is in the interest of public service that we have compiled a list of time-tested solutions, oft proven to simplify the most daunting of tasks—that of securing a husband.

We humbly present, Lessons in Landing a Lord.

Pearls and Pelisses
June 1823

Townsend Park
Dunscroft, Yorkshire

Lady Isabel Townsend stood in the shabby receiving room of the only home she had ever known, and willed the roaring in her ears to subside. She narrowed her gaze on the pale, reedy man standing before her.

"My father sent you."

"Precisely."

"And would you mind repeating that last bit?" Surely she had misunderstood the words that had tripped from the tongue of this most unwelcome visitor.

He smiled, the expression empty and unattractive. Isabel's stomach flipped. "Indeed," he drawled, the word coiling between them in the suddenly too-small room. "We are betrothed."

"And by *we* . . . I take it that you mean . . ."

"You. And I. Are to be married."

Isabel shook her head. "I am sorry, you are . . . ?"

He paused, clearly unhappy with the idea that she had not been paying attention. "Asperton. Lionel Asperton."

Isabel made a mental note to savor the unfortunate name at a later time. For now, she must deal with the man. Who did not appear to be very clever. Of course, she had learned long ago that the men of her father's acquaintance were rarely men of intellect.

"And how is it that we became betrothed, Mr. Asperton?"

"I won you."

Isabel closed her eyes, willing herself to remain steady. To hide the anger and hurt that surged at the words. That *always* surged at the words. She met his pale gaze once more. "You won me."

He did not even have the grace to feign embarrassment. "Yes. Your father wagered you."

"Of course he did." Isabel exhaled her frustration on a little puff of breath. "Against?"

"One hundred pounds."

"Well. That's more than usual."

Asperton waved off the cryptic words, taking a step closer to her. His smile was cocksure. "I won the round. You are mine. By rights." He reached out a hand, tracing one finger down her cheek. He lowered his voice to a whisper. "I think we shall both enjoy it."

She remained still, sheer will keeping the shudder that threatened at bay. "I am not so sure."

He leaned in, and Isabel became transfixed by the man's lips—red and waxy. She edged away, desperate to maintain a distance, as he said, "Then I shall have to convince you otherwise."

She twisted from beneath his touch and their uncomfortable proximity, placing an old, fraying chair between them. A gleam flashed in the man's eyes as he followed her, moving closer.

He liked the chase.

Isabel was going to have to end this. Now.

"I am afraid you have traveled a very long way for nothing, Mr. Asperton. You see, I am well past the age of majority. My father"—she paused, the word foul-tasting—"should have known better than to wager me. It has never worked before. It certainly will not work now."

He stopped his stalking, eyes widening. "He has done this before?"

Too many times. "I see that gambling away one's only daughter once is fair play, but to do it multiple times, that somehow offends your sensibilities?"

Asperton gaped. "Of course!"

Isabel narrowed her gaze on her would-be betrothed. "Why?"

"Because he knew he would ultimately renege on the wager!"

The man was most definitely an acquaintance of her father.

"Yes. That is obviously the reason for this situation's untenable offense," Isabel said wryly, turning abruptly and opening the door to the room wide. "I am afraid, Mr. Asperton, that you are the seventh man who has come to claim me as his bride." She could not help a smile at his surprise.

"And, as it is, you shall also be the seventh man who shall leave Townsend Park unmarried."

Asperton's mouth opened and closed in quick succession—his fleshy lips reminding Isabel of a codfish.

She counted to five.

They always exploded before she could reach five.

"This will not stand! I was promised a wife! The daughter of an earl!" His voice had gone high and nasal—the tone that Isabel had always associated with the idle unpleasants who fraternized with her father.

Not that she had seen her father in half a dozen years.

She crossed her arms, bestowing the man with her best sympathetic look. "I imagine he hinted at a substantial dowry, as well?"

His eyes lit as though he was finally understood. "Precisely."

She almost felt sorry for him. *Almost.*

"Well, I am afraid that there isn't one of those, either." His brow furrowed. "Would you care for tea?"

Isabel watched as the slow-moving wheel of Asperton's brain completed its rotation and he announced, "No! I do not care for tea! I came for a wife and by God I shall leave with one! With you!"

Attempting to retain an air of calm, she sighed and said, "I had very much hoped that it would not come to this."

His chest puffed out at the words, misunderstanding her meaning. "I am sure that you did. But I will not be leaving this house without the wife I was promised! You belong to me! By rights!"

He lunged for her then. *They always did.* She stepped to the side, and he plunged through the open doorway and into the entryway beyond.

Where the women were waiting.

Isabel followed him into the foyer, watching as he straightened, as he took in the three women standing there like well-trained soldiers, a wall of defense between him and the door to the house. Certainly he'd never seen any women like this before.

Of course, he would never realize that he was looking at three women.

Isabel had always found that men tended to see only what they wanted to see.

She watched as his gaze shifted from the cook, to the stable master, to the butler.

He turned on Isabel. "What's this, then?"

The stable master slapped her coiled horsewhip against one thigh, the *thwack* of the leather causing Asperton to flinch. "We do not like you raising your voice to a lady, sir."

Isabel watched as the angled notch at his thin throat quivered. "I—I am . . ."

"Well, one thing you are *not* is a gentleman, if the way you came lunging out of that room is any indication." The cook indicated the receiving room with her large, heavy rolling pin.

He looked to Isabel again, and she gave a little feminine shrug.

"Surely you were not lunging after Lady Isabel in such a manner." This from the butler, who, perfectly pressed and cravatted, lazily investigated the edge of the sabre she held. Isabel did her best not to look at the empty spot on the wall from which the ancient—and likely very dull, indeed—sword had come.

They really did have a flair for the dramatic.

"I—no!"

There was a long moment of silence as Isabel waited for a sheen of perspiration to take up residence on Mr. Asperton's brow. She watched as the rise and fall of his chest quickened, and only then decided to intervene.

"Mr. Asperton was just leaving," she said, her tone infused with helpfulness. "Were you not, sir?"

He nodded nervously, mesmerized by Kate's horsewhip, moving in slow, threatening circles. "I—I was."

"I don't think he'll be returning. Will you, sir?"

He did not reply for a long moment. Kate dropped the soft leather of the whip to the ground, and the sudden movement shook him from his trance. He snapped to attention and shook his head firmly. "No. I shouldn't think so."

The tip of Jane's sabre hit the marble floor, sending a powerful clang through the large, empty space.

Isabel's eyes widened, her voice lowering to a whisper. "I should think you would want to *know* such a thing, sir."

He cleared his throat quickly, "Yes. Of course. I mean—no. I shan't be back."

Isabel smiled then, wide and friendly. "Excellent. I shall bid you adieu, then. I feel confident that you are able to find your own way out?" She indicated the door, now flanked by the three women. "Farewell."

She returned to the receiving room then, closing the door firmly behind her and moving to the window just in time to see the maypole of a man hurry down the steps of the Park and clamber onto his horse, riding away as though the hounds of hell were upon him.

She released a long breath.

Only then did she allow the tears to come.

Her father had wagered her away.

Again.

The first time had hurt the most. One would think she would be used to such treatment by now, but the truth of it surprised her, nonetheless.

As though, someday, it all might be different. As though, someday, he might be other than the Wastrearl.

As though, someday, he might care for her.

As though, someday, *anyone* might care for her.

For a moment, she allowed herself to consider her father. The Wastrearl. A man who had left his children and his wife tucked away in the country and returned to London to live a profligate, scandalous life. A man who had never cared: not when his wife had died; not when his servants, unwilling to go another day without pay, had left their positions en masse; not when his daughter had sent letter after letter asking for him to return to Townsend Park and restore the country house to some semblance of its former glory—if not for her, then for his heir.

The one time he had returned. . .

No. She would not think on it.

Her father. The man who stole her mother's sprit. Who had robbed her brother, an infant, of a father.

Had he not deserted them, Isabel would never have taken responsibility for the estate. She had risen to the challenge, doing her best to keep the house standing and food on the table. While not fruitful, the estate had been able to just barely sustain its inhabitants and tenants while her father had spent every last penny of the income from its lands on his scandalous activities.

There had been enough to eat, and the Wastrearl's black reputation had kept curious visitors from arriving on the steps of Townsend Park, allowing Isabel to populate the house and its servants' quarters however she wished, away from the prying eyes of the *ton*.

But it did not stop her from wishing that it had all been different.

Wishing that she had had the chance to be everything daughters of earls were born to be. Wishing that she'd been raised without a care in the world. Without a doubt in her head that it would someday be her day to sparkle; that she would one day be courted properly—by a man who wanted her for *her*, not as a spoil from a game of chance.

Wishing that she were not so very alone.

Not that wishing had ever helped.

The door to the room opened and shut quietly, and Isabel gave a little self-deprecating laugh, wiping the tears from her cheeks. Finally, she turned, meeting Jane's knowing, serious gaze.

"You should not have threatened him."

"He deserved it," the butler said.

Isabel nodded. Asperton had taken the place of her father

in those final minutes. Tears pricked once more; she kept them at bay. "I hate him," she whispered.

"I know," the butler said, not moving from her place in the doorway.

"If he were here, I would happily kill him."

Jane nodded once. "Well, it seems that such a thing will not be necessary." She lifted one hand, revealing a square of parchment. "Isabel. The earl . . . he is dead."

One

And what would these lessons be, Dear Reader, without a prospective lord to land? The gentleman for whom you have so diligently studied? The answer, of course, is that they would be nigh on useless.

Are we not, then, the very luckiest of ladies, that our fair city boasts the best and the brightest, the charmed and the charming, a veritable treasure trove of bachelors—wealthy, willing, and wandering lonely through our streets, wanting only for a wife!

Finding these paragons of gentlemanliness is a daunting task, but never fear, Dear Reader! We have assumed the job for you—scoured the city for the lords most worthy of your invaluable, unbridled attention.

Consider, if you will, the first on our list of eminently landable lords . . .

Pearls and Pelisses
June 1823

When the blonde by the door winked at him, it was the very last straw.

Lord Nicholas St. John sank further into his seat, cursing

under his breath. Who would have imagined that a superlative doled out by an inane ladies' magazine was enough to transform London's female population into clamoring fools?

At first, he'd found it amusing—a welcome entertainment. Then the invitations had begun to arrive. And when the clock in his St. James town house had barely struck two, Lady Ponsonby had joined them, claiming to have business to discuss—something to do with a statue she had recently acquired from Southern Italy. Nick knew better. There was only one reason for a viper like Lady Ponsonby to come calling at a bachelor's home—a reason Nick was certain Lord Ponsonby would not find at all reasonable.

So he had escaped, first to the Royal Society of Antiquities, where he had sequestered himself in the library, far from anyone who had ever heard of ladies' magazines, let alone read one. Unfortunately, the journalist—Nick flinched at the liberal use of the term—had done his research, and within the hour, the head footman had announced the arrival of four separate women, ranging in age and station, all in dire need of a consultation regarding their marbles—all of whom insisted that none but Lord Nicholas would do.

Nick snorted into his drink at the memory. *Marbles, indeed.*

He had paid the footman handsomely for his discretion and fled once more, this time with little dignity, through the rear entrance to the Society and into a narrow, sordid alleyway that did little to enliven his disposition. Tilting the brim of his hat down to shield his identity, he'd made his way to sanctuary—to the Dog and Dove, where he had been ensconced in a dark corner for the last several hours.

Well and truly trapped.

Ordinarily, when a voluptuous barmaid made eyes at him, he was more than willing to consider her ample charms. But this particular woman was the fourteenth of her sex to have overtly considered *his* charms that day, and he had had quite enough. He scowled, first at the girl, then into his ale, feeling darker and more irritated by the minute. "I've got to get out of this damned city."

The deep, rumbling laugh from across the table did not improve his mood.

"Do not doubt for one moment that I could have you shipped back to Turkey," Nick said, his voice a low growl.

"I do hope you will not. I should hate to miss the conclusion of this entertaining theatre." His companion, Durukhan, turned and looked over his shoulder, dark eyes passing lazily over the comely young woman. "Pity. She will not even consider me."

"Clever girl."

"More likely, she simply believes everything she reads in her magazines." Rock laughed as Nick's scowl deepened. "Come, Nick, how awful can it be? So the women of London have been publicly apprised of your—eligibility."

Nick recalled the stack of invitations that awaited his return—every one from a family with an unmarried daughter—and took a long drink of ale. Setting the pewter mug down, he muttered, "How awful, indeed."

"I should take advantage of it if I were you. Now you may have any woman you want."

Nick leveled his friend with cool blue gaze. "I did perfectly well without the damned magazine, thank you."

Rock's response was a noncommittal grunt as he turned to wave the young barmaid over. An arrow shot from a bow, she arrived at their table with speed and purpose. Leaning low over Nick to best display her voluptuous curves, she spoke in a low whisper. "My lord? Do you have . . . needs?"

"Do we, indeed," Rock said.

The brazen female seated herself in Nick's lap, leaning close. "I'll be anythin' you want, luv," she said, low and sultry, as she pressed her breasts against his chest. "Anythin' you want."

He extracted her arm from its place around his neck and fished a crown from his pocket. "A tempting offer, to be sure," he said, pressing the coin into her hand and lifting her to her feet. "But I am afraid that I want only for more ale. You had best look elsewhere for companionship this evening."

Her face fell for a split second before she redirected her attention to Rock, considering his wide chest, brown skin, and thick arms with an appreciative gaze. "Care for a go? Some girls don't like 'em dark, but I think you'll do just fine."

Rock did not move, but Nick noticed the tensing of his friend's shoulders at the blatant reference to his heritage. "Farther elsewhere," the Turk said, flatly turning away from the barmaid.

She turned up her nose at their combined rebuff and left—to fetch more ale, Nick hoped. As he watched her make her way across the room, he felt the keen attention of the other women in the tavern. "They are predators. Every last one of them."

"It seems only right that the *bulan* finally know what it is to be hunted."

Nick grimaced at the Turkish name and the long history that came with it. It had been years since anyone had called him the *bulan*—the hunter. The name meant nothing now; it was a leftover of his days in the East, deep in the Ottoman Empire, when he'd been someone else—someone without a name—with only a skill that would ultimately be his downfall.

The irony was not lost on him. His time in Turkey had ended harshly when a woman had set her sights upon him and he had made the mistake of allowing himself to be caught, quite literally.

He had spent twenty-two days in a Turkish prison before he had been rescued by Rock and ferreted to Greece—where he had vowed to put the *bulan* to rest.

Most of the time, he was happy to have done so . . . appeased by the world of London, the business of his estate, and his antiquities. But there were days when he missed the life.

He much preferred being hunter to hunted.

"Women are always like this around you," Rock pointed

out, returning Nick to the present. "You are merely better attuned to it today. Not that I have ever understood their interest. You are something of an ugly bas—"

"Angling for a pounding, are you?"

The Turk's face split in a wide grin. "Sparring with me in a public house would not be the appropriate behavior for such a paragon of gentlemanliness."

Nick's gaze narrowed on his friend. "I shall risk it for the pleasure of wiping that smile from your face."

Rock laughed again. "All this feminine interest has addled your brain if you think you could take me down." He leaned forward, resting his arms on the table between them, underscoring his bulk. "What has happened to your sense of humor? You would have found this vastly amusing if it had happened to me. Or to your brother."

"Nevertheless, it has happened to me." Nick surveyed the rest of the room and groaned as the door to the pub opened and a tall, dark-haired man entered. The newcomer paused just inside the room, scanning the heavy crowd, his blue eyes finally settling on Nick. One lone brow rose in amusement and he began to weave his way through the throngs of people toward them.

Nick turned an accusing gaze on Rock. "You are asking to be returned to Turkey. Begging for it."

Rock looked over his shoulder at the newcomer and grinned. "It would have been rather unfriendly of me not to invite him to join in the amusement."

"What an immense stroke of good luck. I confess, I had not thought I would be able to get near London's Lord to Land," a low, amused voice drawled, and Nick looked up to find his twin brother, Gabriel St. John, the Marquess of Ralston, towering above them. Rock stood and clapped Gabriel on the back, motioning that he should join them. Once seated, Ralston continued, "Though I should have expected to find you here . . ." He paused. "In hiding. Coward."

Nick's brows knit together as Rock laughed. "I was just pointing out that had *you* been named one of London's

Lords to Land, Nick would have taken immense pleasure in your pain."

Gabriel sat back in his chair, grinning foolishly. "Indeed, he would have. And yet your mood seems less than cheery, brother. Whatever for?"

"I suppose you are here to revel in my discomfort," Nick said, "But surely you have better things to do. You do still have a new wife to entertain, do you not?"

"Indeed, I do," Gabriel said, his smile softening. "Though, to be honest, she nearly pushed me out the door in her eagerness to find you. She is hosting a dinner on Thursday evening and is reserving a seat for you both. She does not want Lord Nicholas wandering wistfully through the streets that evening, wanting for a wife."

Rock smirked. "It is entirely possible that he would have been doing just that without the invitation."

Nick ignored his friend. "Callie reads the damned thing?" He had hoped his sister-in-law was above such things. If she had read it, there was no escape.

Gabriel leaned forward. "This week? We have all read it. You've brought respectability to the St. John name, Nick. Finally. Well done."

The barmaid returned then, setting another round of drinks on the table; surprise flashed in her eyes, followed quickly by pleasure as she looked to Nick, then Gabriel, then back again. Twins were rare enough that strangers tended to stare when the St. John brothers ventured into public together; Nick found he had no patience for her curiosity. He looked away as Gabriel paid the girl handsomely, saying, "Of course, those women who coveted me must be thrilled to have a second chance of sorts—title or no, you at least share my good looks. If a younger, lesser version of them."

Nick's blue gaze narrowed on his brother and friend, now guffawing like idiots. Lifting his ale, he toasted the duo. "May you both go straight to hell."

His brother lifted his own tankard. "I do believe it would be worth it to see you so put out. You know, it is not the worst of things to be labeled an eligible bachelor, Nick. I can attest to the fact that marriage is not the prison I once believed it to be. It is quite enjoyable, I find."

Nick leaned back in his chair. "Callie's turned you soft, Gabriel. Do you not recall the pain caused by clamoring mamas and cloying daughters, all hoping to secure your attention?"

"Not remotely."

"That is because Callie was the only woman willing to have you with your history of wickedness and vice," Nick pointed out. "My reputation is rather less tarnished than yours was—I am a far more valuable catch, Lord help me."

"Marriage might do you well, you know."

Nick considered his ale long enough for his companions to think that he might not reply. "I think we all know that marriage is not for me."

Gabriel offered a small, noncommittal grunt. "I might remind you that the same was true for me. Not all women are like the cold bitch who saw you nearly killed, Nick," Gabriel said firmly.

"She was merely one of a long line of them," Nick pointed out, drinking deep. "Thank you, but I have learned to keep my women to the best of encounters—brief and unemotional."

"I wouldn't brag about brevity if I were you, St. John," Rock said, flashing a wide grin at Gabriel before he continued. "Your problem is not the women who choose you, but those whom you choose. If you were not so easily wiled by those who play the victim, you might have better luck with the fairer sex."

Rock had not said anything Nick did not already know. Since his youth, he'd had a soft spot for women in need. And while he understood it to be one of his biggest weaknesses—having brought more trouble than fortune upon him in his lifetime—he seemed unable to resist the trait.

So he kept his women at arm's length. His rules were clear. No mistresses. No regular assignations. And, most definitely, no wife.

"Well, either way," Gabriel said, returning lightness to the conversation, "I shall enjoy myself immensely while you run the gauntlet of this impressive superlative."

Nick paused, drinking deep before finally leaning back and placing his hands flat on the table. "I am afraid I am going to have to disappoint you. I do not plan to run the gauntlet at all."

"Oh? How do you expect to avoid the women of London? They are huntresses of the highest caliber."

"They cannot hunt if their prey has gone to ground," Nick announced.

"You are leaving?" Gabriel did not look pleased. "To where?"

Nick shrugged. "I have clearly overstayed London's welcome. The Continent. The Orient. The Americas. Rock? You've been itching for an adventure for months. Where would you like to go?"

Rock considered the options. "Not the Orient. A repeat of the last time we were there is not tempting. I would rather steer clear of it."

"Fair enough," Nick conceded. "The Americas, then."

Gabriel shook his head. "You would be gone for a year at least. Have you forgotten that we have a sister just out and in need of a match? You will not leave me to deal with that sure-to-be-disastrous event simply because you fear the attention of a handful of ladies."

"A handful!" Nick protested, "They are a swarm." He paused, considering his options. "I don't really care where I go . . . as long as there are no women there."

Rock looked alarmed. "None whatsoever?"

Nick laughed for the first time that evening. "Well, not *none*, obviously. But would it be too much to ask that there be no women who have read that ridiculous magazine?"

Gabriel raised a dark brow. "Very likely so."

"St. John."

All three gentlemen turned at the sound of Nick's name to find the Duke of Leighton beside the table. Tall and broad, if Leighton hadn't been a duke, the man would have made an excellent Viking—fair-haired and stone-faced, he rarely smiled. But today, Nick noted that the duke seemed even more stoic than usual.

"Leighton! Join us." Nick used one foot to capture a nearby seat and drag it to the table. "Save me from these two."

"I'm afraid I cannot stay." The duke's words were clipped. "I came looking for you."

"You and the female population of London," Gabriel said with a laugh.

The duke ignored him, folding his giant frame into the seat and setting his gloves on the scarred wooden table. Turning to face Nick, nearly blocking Rock and Gabriel from the conversation, he said, "I'm afraid that you are not going to like what it is I have to ask of you."

Nick waved the barmaid over with a tumbler of whisky, keenly aware of the distress in his friend's gaze.

"Does it involve marrying him off?" Gabriel asked dryly.

Leighton looked surprised. "No."

"Then I would think that Nick would welcome your request."

The duke took a large gulp of whisky and met Nick's interest. "I'm not so sure. You see, I am not here for Nick. I am here for the *bulan*."

There was a long silence as the words sank in around the table. Rock and Gabriel stiffened, but did not speak, watching Nick carefully. Nick leaned forward, placed his forearms on the scarred wood, and tented his fingers. He spoke quietly, his eyes not leaving Leighton.

"I do not do that any longer."

"I know. And I would not ask if I did not need you."

"Who?"

"My sister. She's gone."

Nick sat back in his chair. "I don't chase after runaways, Leighton. You should call Bow Street."

Leighton's frustration brought him forward in a rush of movement. "For Christ's sake, St. John. You know I can't do that. It will be in the papers yesterday. I need the *bulan*."

Nick recoiled from the word. He did not care for being the hunter once again. "I don't do it any longer. You know that."

"I'll pay you whatever you ask."

Ralston laughed at that, drawing a growl from the duke. "What's so amusing about that?"

"Only the idea that my brother would take payment. I don't imagine you've endeared him to your cause with that offer, Leighton."

The duke scowled. "You know, Ralston, you were never the twin I preferred."

"Most people feel that way," Ralston said. "I assure you I am not overwrought at the idea. Indeed, I confess a modicum of surprise that you are even here, deigning to speak with us, what with our 'questionable stock'—isn't that how you refer to it?"

"Gabriel, enough." Nick stopped his brother from going too far into the past.

Leighton at least had the grace to be embarrassed.

For many years, the St. John twins, though aristocracy themselves, had been a primary outlet for young Leighton's disdain. The scandal that had fallen on the house of Ralston when the twins were young—their mother's desertion of her husband and family—had made them ideal prey for the more pristine families of the *ton*, and Leighton, in their class at Eton, had never failed to remind them of their mother's disreputable actions.

Until one day, Leighton went too far, and Nick had put him into a wall.

Pounding a duke was not something that the second son of a marquess could get away with at Eton; Nick would have almost certainly been dismissed had he not been a twin—and Gabriel had taken responsibility for the event. The future Marquess of Ralston had been sent home from term early, and Leighton and Nick had come to a tentative truce, no one the wiser.

The truce had become a friendship of sorts—one that had

blossomed in the upper years of Eton, and withered during the years when Nick cut a swath across the Continent. Leighton had already ascended to the dukedom, and his fortune had, in no small part, funded Nick and Rock's expeditions into the dark recesses of the Orient.

Leighton had played an important role in making the *bulan.*

But Nick was not that man any longer.

"What do you know?"

"Nick . . ." Rock spoke for the first time since the duke had arrived, but Nick raised one hand.

"Mere curiosity."

"I know she's gone. I know she's taken money and a handful of things she considers invaluable."

"Why did she leave?"

Leighton shook his head. "I don't know."

"There's always a reason."

"That may be . . . but I don't know it."

"When?"

"Two weeks ago."

"And you only come to me now?"

"She had planned a trip to see a cousin in Bath. It was ten days before I realized she lied to me."

"Her maid?"

"I terrified her into confessing that Georgiana went north. She knew nothing else. My sister was very careful to cover her tracks."

Nick sat back in his chair, mind racing, energy coursing through him. Someone had helped the girl. Was still helping her if she'd not given up and returned to her brother. It had been years since he had tracked someone—he'd forgotten the pleasure that came with a new search.

But this was no longer his life.

He met the duke's worried gaze. "She's my sister, Nick. You must know that I wouldn't ask you if there were another way."

The words struck Nick to his core. He had a sister, too. And he would do whatever it took to keep her safe.

Damn.

"My lord?"

Nick turned at the tentative, feminine voice, to find two young women standing nearby, watching him eagerly. Nick spoke, wary. "Yes?"

"We—" one of them began to speak, then stopped, uncertain. The other nudged her toward him.

"Yes?"

"We are fans."

Nick blinked. "Of?"

"Of yours."

"Of mine."

"Indeed!" The second girl smiled broadly and stepped closer, holding out what looked suspiciously like—

Nick swore under his breath.

"Would you be willing to autograph our magazine?"

Nick held up a hand. "I would, girls, but you've got the wrong brother." He pointed to Gabriel. "*That* is Lord Nicholas."

Rock snorted as the two shifted their attention to the Marquess of Ralston, a dazzlingly handsome copy of their prey, and tittered their excitement.

Gabriel instantly eased into his role, turning a brilliant smile on the girls. "I would be happy to autograph your magazine." He took the journal and the pen they proffered and said, "You know, I must confess, this is the first time I've ever drawn the attention of ladies when in the company of my brother. Ralston has always been considered the more handsome of us."

"No!" the girls protested.

Nick rolled his eyes.

"Indeed. Ask anyone. They'll tell you it's the marquess who is the best specimen. Surely you've heard that." He looked up at them with a winning smile. "You can admit it, girls. My feelings shan't be hurt."

Gabriel held up the magazine, displaying the cover, which boasted: *Inside! London's Lords to Land!* "Yes . . . there's no question that this is going to do wonders for my reputation. I'm so happy to see that it's getting around that I'm on the hunt for a wife!"

The girls nearly expired from delight.

Unamused, Nick looked to Leighton, "North, you said?"

"Yes."

"*North* is an enormous place. It could take us weeks to find her," Rock warned.

Nick looked to the pair of females waiting excitedly at Gabriel's elbow, then back to the men at the table.

"I find myself willing to make the trek."

Two

Townsend Park
Dunscroft, Yorkshire

Isabel considered the pale, exhausted girl who sat before her on a low, narrow cot. She was barely old enough to be out, let alone old enough to have traveled four days by mail coach to arrive on a strange doorstep in the dead of night.

Eyes wide with fear, the young woman stood, clutching a small traveling bag to her.

Isabel smiled. "You are Georgiana."

The girl did not move. Her expression did not change.

"I am Isabel."

Recognition flared in Georgiana's blue eyes. "Lady Isabel?"

Isabel came closer, warm and welcoming. "The very same."

"I thought . . ."

The smile turned into a grin. "Let me guess. You thought I would be old? Wizened?"

The girl half smiled. A good sign. "Perhaps."

"In that case, I shall take your surprise as a great compliment."

The girl set down her bag and dropped into a curtsy.

Isabel stopped her. "Oh, please don't. That will make me feel old and wizened. Sit." Isabel pulled over a small wooden stool to join her. "We don't stand on ceremony here. And if we did, I would be the one deferring to you. After all, I am a mere earl's daughter and you . . ."

Georgiana shook her head, sadness in her expression. "Not anymore."

The girl missed home.

Not many girls who landed at Townsend Park missed where they came from.

"How did you find us?"

"My . . . a friend. She said you took in girls. Said you could help." Isabel nodded, encouraging. "My brother. I couldn't tell him . . ." Her voice cracked, making speech impossible.

Isabel leaned forward, taking the girl's cold, shaking hands in her own. "You don't need to tell me, either. Not until you are ready."

I know that sometimes it is easier not to tell.

Georgiana looked up, eyes wide and filled with tears. "My friend . . . she said you would take care of us."

Isabel nodded. "And we shall." The girl slumped with relief. "I think you have come a long way. May I suggest that you try to sleep? We shall have breakfast in the morning, and you can tell me anything you wish."

Within minutes, Georgiana had slipped between the crisp, clean sheets of the narrow bed, a bed Isabel imagined was likely far less grand than any in which the sister of the Duke of Leighton previously had slept. Isabel watched for a few long moments to ensure that the girl was, indeed, asleep, and slipped from the room.

To find a collection of curious onlookers had assembled in the hallway beyond.

"Is she asleep?" Isabel's cousin and closest friend, Lara, asked in a whisper.

Isabel nodded, waiting for the latch to click before turning back to her audience. "Why isn't this hallway properly lit?"

"Because you cannot afford the candles."

Of course.

"The sister of a duke, Isabel?" Jane whispered the rhetorical question.

"It shouldn't matter who she is," Gwen, the cook, argued. "She needs us! We take in girls who need us."

"She cannot stay," Kate announced flatly, looking to the others for support.

"Perhaps we could move this conversation away from the poor girl?" Isabel whispered, motioning the whole group back down the hallway.

"She cannot stay!" Kate whispered again as they walked.

"Yes, I believe you've made your position clear on the subject," Isabel said dryly.

"It's an enormous risk, Isabel," Jane said when they were back at the top of the stairs, as though Isabel had not thought of it herself.

As though her heart were not pounding with dread.

Of course, it was a risk. One did not simply open one's doors and offer board to the sister of a duke—one of the most powerful men in England—without his knowledge.

This could end James.

Her brother was only ten years old, a new earl, and he would struggle to escape their father's reputation. If the Duke of Leighton discovered his sister here—discovered the women who were hidden here under the protection of the Earl of Reddich—James would never survive the scandal.

The others were right. She should turn the girl out.

It would be the responsible thing to do. It would protect them all.

She looked from one woman to the next, each of whom had come to Townsend Park under similar circumstances to the young woman she had just left. She could have turned them all away. But she hadn't. Settling on her cousin, she asked, "Lara?"

There was a beat, as Lara considered her words. "I know the rules, Isabel. I know what we say. But . . . a duke. It will bring suspicion upon all of us. She . . . What if someone comes looking for her? What if we are found?"

Isabel looked in the direction of the room where she had left the sleeping girl. "I imagine that it is more a question of what shall happen *when* someone comes looking for her. Sisters of dukes are not often allowed to go missing." She paused, then, "She is increasing."

Jane let out a low whistle.

"Did she tell you that?" Gwen asked.

"She did not have to."

"Well," Lara said, "obviously we cannot turn her out, then."

Kate disagreed. "She's no merchant's daughter. No barkeep's wife. Not even from landed gentry. She's an aristocrat, for heaven's sake. She could be two aristocrats! We should send the girl home to her aristocratic family."

"An aristocratic family is not always the solution, Kate. I know that better than anyone." Isabel thought of the deep, dark circles beneath the frail girl's closed eyes, the hollow cheeks that spoke volumes of this small, mysterious woman.

This girl who was lost and alone.

It was enough for Isabel.

"I've never turned a girl away. I shan't start now. She has a place here for as long as she needs one. We shall put her to work. James is in need of a new governess. I am certain that she will do quite well."

Kate snorted. "Did you see her? I'd wager she's never done a day's work in her life."

Isabel smiled then. "Neither had you when I took you in. And now you're the finest stable master this side of London."

Kate looked away, wiping one hand down her breeches. "Sister to a duke," she whispered.

Isabel looked at the women crowded around her—to Jane, her butler, who ran a house with the ease of any male servant trained for years; to Gwen, a cook who could have been trained in the best kitchens in London for the pride she took in her work; to Kate, who had a way with horses that rivaled that of the jockeys at Ascot. Each of them had come to Townsend Park under similar circumstances to that of the sleeping girl, each of them had been given room, board, and a chance for a future.

And they had believed that Isabel could face any challenge.

Little did they know.

She was just as scared. Just as uncertain.

She took a deep, steadying breath, and when she spoke, she did her best to infuse her tone with confidence—prayed that the others would believe it. "She needs Minerva House. And Minerva House shall rise to this challenge."

I hope.

Isabel opened her eyes and shot straight up in her chair.

Her cousin Lara was standing on the other side of the earl's desk. "Good morning."

Isabel squinted at the windows, where a brilliant blue sky announced that she had slept well into the morning. She looked back at Lara. "I fell asleep."

"Yes. I see that. Why did you not attempt such a feat in your bed?"

Isabel tilted her head back, the muscles of her neck and shoulders screaming at the movement. "Too much to do." She placed one hand to her cheek, removing a small slip of paper from where it had become stuck in the night.

Lara set a teacup down on the desk and seated herself across from Isabel. "What could you possibly have had to do that required you to forgo sleep?" She paused, distracted. "You have ink on your face."

Isabel wiped her palm across her stained cheek, her gaze falling to the paper she had removed from the same location. She considered the list she had drafted the night before.

The *immense* list she had drafted the night before.

Her stomach flipped.

She brushed a stray auburn lock back from her face and returned it to its tight, practical home. Guilt washed over her as she was consumed with the myriad of things that she had meant to do the previous night—after taking a quick nap.

She should have come up with a plan to secure the girls' safety. She should have drafted a letter to her father's solicitor to confirm that there were no funds set aside for James's education. She should have written to the real estate office in Dunscroft to begin the search for a new house. She should have begun reading the book on roof repair that was soon to be an emergency text.

She hadn't done any of that, however. Instead, she'd slept.

"You need rest."

"I've had plenty of rest." Isabel started to organize the papers on the desk, taking note of a new pile of envelopes there. "Where did these come from?" She lifted the letters, revealing a ladies' magazine that had come for the girls. She registered the headline: *Inside! London's Lords to Land!* and rolled her eyes before returning the envelopes to their place.

"With the post this morning. Before you open them—"

Isabel lifted a letter opener and looked at Lara. "Yes?"

"We should talk about James."

"What now?"

"He has been hiding from his lessons."

"I am not surprised. I shall talk to him. Has he even met the new governess?"

"Not exactly."

The words were a signal. "How, exactly, Lara?"

"Well, Kate found him watching her in her bath."

Isabel leaned forward. "I don't suppose you mean he was watching Kate in her bath?"

Lara laughed. "Can you imagine how that would have gone? She would have skinned him."

"I just might skin him myself! He's an earl now! He shall have to behave as one! Watching the new girl in her bath? What on earth? What would possess him—"

"He may be an earl, Isabel, but he is a boy first. You think he is not curious?"

"He grew up in a house full of women. No. I would think he would be entirely disinterested."

"Well, he isn't. In fact, I think there's no question that James is interested. He needs someone with whom to discuss such interests."

"He can speak to me!"

Lara gave Isabel a disbelieving look. "Isabel."

"He can!"

"You are a marvelous sister. But he cannot discuss such interests with you."

There was silence as Isabel considered the words. Of course he couldn't. He was a ten-year-old boy with no one to help him understand his world and he needed a man with whom he could discuss such . . . male . . . things.

She sighed. "I must find a way to get James to school. I plan to send a letter to my father's solicitor about that very thing today. Not that there will be money to arrange it." She paused. "Alternatively, perhaps the new guardian of the estate will arrive bearing knowledge only those of his gender can impart."

They had been waiting for word of Oliver, Lord Densmore, the mysterious and missing guardian named in her father's will, since they had learned of the earl's death. It had been just over a week now, and every day that went by without news, Isabel breathed a bit easier.

His specter loomed nonetheless, for if the Wastrearl had appointed him, it seemed that Lord Densmore would very likely be precisely the sort of guardian they would all prefer not to have.

"There is something else."

There always was.

Isabel winced at the thought. "About James?"

"No. About you." Lara leaned forward in her chair. "I know why you fell asleep here instead of taking yourself to bed. I know you are concerned about our future. About finances. About James. About Minerva House." Isabel started to shake her head. "Do not insult me by feigning ignorance. I have known you for your entire life. Lived with you for six years. I know you are worried."

Isabel opened her mouth to speak, then closed it. Lara was, of course, right. Isabel was worried. She was worried that the dire financial straits of the estate would keep James from going to school, from learning to be an earl, from restoring some semblance of honor to the earldom. She was terrified that his new guardian would never show his face—and his finances. Almost as terrified as she was that he would arrive and close Minerva House—casting out the women she had worked so hard to keep safe.

The women who needed her.

The roof was leaking, they'd lost seven sheep through the fence at the western edge of the Park that week, and Isabel hadn't a farthing to her name. She was going to have to send some of the girls away if she could not find a solution.

"I don't suppose the earl left *any* money," Lara said softly. It was the first time any of the other residents of the Park had spoken of their combined situation.

Isabel shook her head, feeling frustration surge at the question. "Everything is gone."

Everything that had not been entailed to the future Earl of Reddich.

Her father had not even cared enough to ensure that his children were cared for—that his *heir* would be cared for. It had taken her half an hour to convince the solicitor who had arrived a day after the news of her father's death that she could understand the finances of the estate well enough for him to explain their situation to her.

As though being impoverished were a complicated state of affairs.

The Wastrearl had gambled everything away—the house in town, the carriages, the furniture, the horses . . . *his daughter.* There was nothing left. Nothing but what was now James's by right. . .

And what was Isabel's to sell.

A pang of sadness flared in her chest.

Her brother had not had the father or the mother or the upbringing that the earldom should have promised him—

but he would have an earldom. And she would do what she could to keep it afloat.

A dead earl.

A child heir.

A crumbling estate.

Two dozen mouths to feed, all of which were required to remain well hidden.

She had never felt so panicked in her life.

If only she hadn't slept the night before, she might have already devised a plan for them all to be saved.

She just needed time.

Closing her eyes, Isabel took a deep, steadying breath. "It is not your concern, Lara," she said firmly, refusing to show her thoughts, "I shall make certain that we are well taken care of."

Lara's gaze softened. "Of course you shall. None of us have doubted such for a moment."

Of course they hadn't. No one ever doubted Isabel's strength. Not even when they should. Not even when she was holding the whole thing together by a thread.

She stood and went to the window, looking out at the once-lush and fertile Townsend land. Now the fields were overgrown and untilled, and the livestock had dwindled to a pittance.

"Are the girls worried?"

"No. I do not think that it has crossed their minds that they might all be tossed out on their ears."

Isabel's heart raced at the words. "They shan't be tossed out. Never say such things again."

Lara had followed her. "Of course they shan't."

They might be. Isabel heard the words as though they had been spoken aloud.

Isabel turned quickly, her skirts swirling around her ankles as she raised a finger, wagging it in front of Lara's nose. "I shall think of something. We shall find some money. I shall move them all to another house. It is not as though this one is any kind of prize."

"Minerva House the second," Lara said.

"Precisely."

"A capital idea."

Isabel huffed at her cousin's tone. "You needn't agree simply to appease me."

"Fair enough," Lara said. "Do you have a stash of money stored somewhere? Because last I'd heard, houses that accommodated two dozen women required funds."

"Yes. Well. That is the part of the plan that I have not quite worked out." Isabel crossed the room to the door, then turned back, pacing to her desk. She sat there, staring at the papers strewn across the enormous tabletop, where three generations of Reddich earls had sat. After a long silence, she said, "There is only one way to ensure that we've the funds to stay afloat."

"Which is?"

She took a deep breath.

"I will sell the marbles." There was a roaring in her ears as she spoke the words—as though, if she did not hear them, they had not been said.

"Isabel . . ." Lara shook her head.

Please don't fight this, Lara. I do not have the strength. "It's silly to keep them. No one is enjoying them."

"*You* enjoy them."

"They are a luxury I can no longer afford."

"No. They are the only luxury you've ever had."

As if she didn't know that.

"Do you have a better solution?"

"Maybe," Lara hedged. "Maybe you should consider . . . maybe you should think about marriage."

"Are you suggesting that I should have accepted one of the myriad of oafs who has passed through over the years after having won me in a game of chance?"

Lara's eyes widened. "Oh, my, no! Not one of them. Never one of them. No one who knew your father. I'm suggesting someone else. Someone . . . good. And if he is wealthy, well then, all the better."

Isabel lifted the magazine she had seen earlier. "Are you suggesting I try my hand at landing a lord, cousin?"

Color flared on Lara's cheeks. "You cannot deny that a smart match is not the worst thing that could happen to you."

Isabel shook her head. Marriage was not the answer. She was willing to swallow a bitter pill or two to save this house, and the women in it, but she would not sacrifice her freedom, her sanity, or her person for them. She did not care if it was a solution or not.

Selfish.

The word burned, echoing in her head as though it had been spoken seconds rather than years ago. Isabel knew that if she closed her eyes, she would see her mother, face contorted in anguish, flinging it like a dagger.

You should have let him marry you off, you selfish beast. He would have stayed if you had. And you would have gone.

She shook her head, refusing the image and clearing her throat, suddenly tight and painful.

"Marriage is not the answer, Lara. Do you really think anyone with the means to help us would consider marrying the twenty-four-year-old, never-seen-the-inside-of-a-London-ballroom daughter of the Wastrearl?"

"Of course they would!"

"No. They would not. I've no skills, no training, no dowry, nothing but a houseful of women, most of whom are in hiding, a handful of them *illegally*. How do you propose explaining such a thing to a prospective suitor?" Lara opened her mouth to answer, but Isabel pressed on. "I'll tell you. It's impossible. No man in his right mind would marry me and take on the burdens that I carry. And, frankly, I am rather thankful for it. No. We shall just have to try a different tack."

"He would marry you if you told him the truth, Isabel. If you explained it all."

Silence fell between them and Isabel allowed herself to consider, fleetingly, what it would be like to have someone with whom she could share all her secrets. Someone to help her protect the girls . . . and rear James. Someone who would help her to shoulder her burden.

She pushed the thought aside, immediately. Sharing the burden of Minerva House would require sharing its secrets. Trusting someone to keep them.

"Must I remind you of the horrid creatures that Minerva House has shown to us? The ham-fisted husbands? The villainous brothers and uncles? The men so deep in their cups they could not find time to put food on the table for their children? And let us not forget my own father—willing to sell his children for funds enough for another night on the town, unable to support his estate, entirely willing to leave it penniless and without reputation for his child-heir." She shook her head firmly. "If I have learned one thing in my lifetime, Lara, it is that the lion's share of men are anything but good. And those who are tend not to be out searching the Yorkshire countryside for spinsters like me."

"They cannot all be bad . . ." Lara pointed out. "You must admit, Isabel, the girls who come to Minerva House—well—their tables must be the worst of the lot. Perhaps men like the ones in there"—she indicated the magazine—"perhaps they are different."

"While I doubt it, I shall give you the benefit of the doubt . . . but let us at least be honest with ourselves. I am not exactly the type of woman who could land a lord. Let alone a lord deserving of a magazine article to tout his exceptional qualities."

"Nonsense. You are lovely and smart. And incredibly competent. And the sister to an earl—even better, an earl who hasn't ruined his name yet," Lara said emphatically. "I am certain London's Lords to Land would be quite enamored."

"Yes, well, I am also two hundred miles north of London. I imagine that these particular lords have already been landed—by a collection of lucky young ladies with subscriptions that do not travel by mail coach."

It was Lara's turn to sigh. "Perhaps not *these* lords. Perhaps the magazine is merely a sign."

"A sign."

Lara nodded.

"You think"—she paused to check the name of the magazine—"*Pearls and Pelisses* . . . is a sign. Why do we even receive this rubbish?"

Lara waved a hand dismissively. "The girls like it. And yes. I think it is a sign that you should consider marriage. To a good man. One of means."

Isabel softened. "Lara, marriage would only bring more trouble upon us. And even if it would not, do you really think good men of means are lining up in Dunscroft waiting for me to sally into town?"

She opened the magazine, considering the description of Lord Nicholas St. John, the first of London's Lords to Land. "I mean, really. This man is the twin brother to one of the wealthiest peers in Britain, rich in his own right, an exceptional equestrian, an unmatched swordsman, and, it seems, handsome enough to send the ladies of the *ton* running for their smelling salts." She paused, looking impishly at Lara, "One wonders how the female population of London remains conscious when he and his twin appear together in public."

Lara giggled. "Perhaps they are kind enough to maintain a certain distance from each other, for the safety and virtue of society."

"Well, that would be the right and proper thing for this 'paragon of manhood' to do."

"Paragon of manhood?"

Isabel read aloud, "*Lord Nicholas is a veritable paragon of manhood—handsome and charming, with an air of mystery about him that sets fans and eyelashes fluttering. And the eyes, Dear Reader! So blue!* Tell me again why this magazine is so supremely edifying?"

"Well, not this particular article, obviously. What else does it say?" Lara craned her neck to read along.

"But this lord is even more of a catch, Dear Reader! Why, his legendary travels across not merely the Continent but also deep into the Orient have both bronzed his skin and expanded his mind—no simpering misses will do for Lord Nicholas, ladies, he will want a companion with whom he can converse! La!"

"It does not say *La!*" Lara reached for the magazine in disbelief.

"It does!" Isabel held it away. "*La! Did we not profess to have found the very best of London's gentlemen for your consideration?*"

"Well, I suppose that if he is that incredible a man, *la* is as appropriate as any other exclamation."

"Mmm." Isabel was reading on silently now.

"Isabel?" Lara leaned over to see what had captured her cousin's attention. "What is it?"

At the fervent question, Isabel's head snapped up. "Lara, you are right."

"I am?"

"This silly magazine *is* a sign!"

"It is?" Lara was confused now.

"It is!" Isabel stopped reading and reached for a fresh piece of paper on which to write her letter.

"But I thought . . ."

"So did I. Nevertheless, it is."

"But . . ." She paused, bemused, then said the first thing that came to mind. "But . . . what about two hundred miles between here and London?"

Isabel looked up at that. She was quiet for a long while, tilting her head as she considered the words.

"Well then, I shall have to make a very convincing argument."

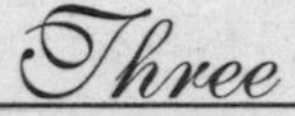

Three

Lesson Number One

Do not attempt to make too strong of a first impression.

To land your lord, you must be seen, but barely heard. Do not overdo with conversation at first—you would not like to overwhelm him with your thoughts. While this might seem challenging, do not fret, Dear Reader. Your quiet grace shall be more than enough to land your lord.

Pearls and Pelisses
June 1823

Nick had traveled extensively, and he prided himself on his ability to see the value in even the most uninspiring of locations. He had spent years crossing the Continent—not in Vienna or Prague or Paris or Rome—but in the unsung villages of Europe. Afterward, he had traveled east, found gems in dingy Ottoman bazaars, embraced the simple pleasure of the tiny communities of the remotest parts of the Orient.

When he and Rock had hiked slowly from Turkey through

the mountain passes of Greece with nothing but the clothes on their backs, Nick had spent weeks without hot food, without a bed, without a single luxury, and he had still discovered his passion for antiquities. There had never been a place in which he could not find a redeeming characteristic or two.

But he was very near giving up on the village of Dunscroft. There appeared to be little about the place that was worthy of note.

Nick and Rock stood together in the courtyard of the town's only inn, waiting for their horses to be delivered. They had been waiting for nearly a half an hour, and the village's early bustle had given way to a quiet, mid-morning laziness. Nick shifted his weight as he watched the door to the butcher's shop open and a gangly boy emerge. The boy's arms were piled high with packages and he dropped one awkwardly shaped parcel to the dusty ground almost immediately. When he turned back to retrieve it, his pile tilted precariously.

It was the most interesting thing that had happened since they had arrived in the little Yorkshire village two evenings earlier.

"A crown says he drops another before he reaches the haberdasher," Nick said.

"Make it a sovereign," Rock agreed.

The boy passed the shop without incident.

"Are you ready to return to London yet?" Rock asked, pocketing his winnings.

"No."

"Will you at least consider leaving Yorkshire?"

"Not unless we have reason to believe she left Yorkshire."

Rock took a deep breath, rocking back on his heels. After a long moment, he said, "It occurs to me that *you* are the one who is committed to finding the girl. There is nothing in this place that is keeping me. Ankara was more accommodating than this town."

Nick raised one dark eyebrow. "Ankara? I think that's a

bit extreme, considering our accommodations when last we visited Turkey."

"Also your doing," Rock grumbled. "We could at least move to York. This inn—and I use the term loosely—is awful."

Nick smiled at that. "You know, for a Turk, you really have become something of a dandy."

"It is called The Stuck Pig, for God's sake!"

"Do you think we would find a more interestingly named establishment in York?"

"I think we might well find a *finer* establishment there."

"Perhaps, but the last we heard, she was headed here," Nick said. "Where is your sense of adventure?"

Rock huffed in irritation, looking toward the stables. "Lost, along with our horses. Where do you think this place is keeping them? Bath? The only excuse for taking so much time to fetch a horse is death."

"Death of the horse?"

"I was leaning toward death of the groomsman who went looking for it," Rock said, and he was off, heading for the stables, leaving Nick to turn his attention to the village of Dunscroft.

They were close.

They had tracked Lady Georgiana across England to Yorkshire, where her course seemed to disappear. They'd ridden north for a day, questioning anyone who might have had a chance to witness a young woman traveling alone, and found nothing past Dunscroft, where a boy who worked at the post remembered seeing a "lady like an angel" come off the mail coach. He could not remember what happened to the angel in question, but Nick had quickly decided that she hadn't gone far. She was in Dunscroft. Or close to it.

He was certain of it.

With a deep breath, he considered the little village that lined a single main street, where a church, an inn, and a simple row of shops marked civilization. Across from the inn was the village commons, a small patch of green that still bore an empty maypole from the May Day celebration that likely marked the most exciting night of the year in Dunscroft. As he took in the commons, Nick's attention was drawn to a lone woman crossing them.

She read as she walked, transfixed by the stack of papers she carried, and the first thing Nick noticed was her ability to keep a straight line despite her obvious lack of awareness of her surroundings.

She was in mourning, clad in a simple black day dress, a common enough design, if slightly out of fashion, but such a thing was to be expected, considering their location. The dress indicated that she was very likely the daughter of some local landed gentry, but her movements were unselfconscious enough to suggest that she was no society miss.

He watched her carefully, taking in her uncommon height—he didn't think he'd ever met a woman as tall as she was. Her quick, purposeful strides were entirely the opposite of the mincing little steps that young ladies were taught to believe graceful. He could not resist focusing on her skirts, which clung to her shapely legs with each long step. As she walked, the hem of her dress kicked up, revealing plain walking boots—footwear chosen for function rather than fashion.

Her black bonnet sat low over her face, shielding her eyes from the sun. Between the low brim of her hat and the placement of her reading material, Nick could not make out anything more than the tip of what looked to be a very straight, very pert nose. Idly, he wondered at the color of her eyes.

She had nearly reached the street now, having crossed the entire greensward without looking up once. He watched as she turned over a page, missing neither a step of her journey nor a word of her correspondence. Her singular focus was fascinating—he could not help but wonder what it might be like to be the object of such undivided attention. Would she bring such purpose to everything that she did?

He straightened, turning to look for Rock. Nick had been too long without a woman if he was musing about a nameless, faceless female who had simply happened into his line of vision.

And then all hell broke loose.

The loud crack sounded from nearby, followed by a combination of men shouting, horses screaming, and a banging that Nick could not immediately place. He turned in the direction of the sound and initially saw nothing, barely registering that the noise had come from farther down the main street, around a bend in the road, before the seriousness of the situation came into clear, horrifying view.

Tearing up the road was a team of enormous workhorses, hooves pounding as their muscled haunches moved with unbridled force. Behind them, they pulled a large workman's cart that had lost two wheels and was dragging on one side. The cart was losing its cargo of flagstones, and the sound of the rocks tumbling off the wooden cart was unnerving the horses, who were now running at breakneck speed. Their driver had been lost along with the wheels, and there was no one in control of the massive vehicle; the horses cared nothing for what was in their path.

And the girl from the commons was about to put herself squarely in their path.

She remained engrossed in her reading even as Nick called out to her. She took her final, fateful step onto the main street, and it was then that he knew he would have no other choice but to save her.

Dammit.

He took off, running across the courtyard of the inn. A quick glance confirmed that he could get to her barely in time, presuming that he did not miss a step, and that she did not suddenly decide to become aware of her surroundings.

Not that the latter appeared likely to happen.

He felt the hardened earth vibrating with the thunder of the horses' strides beneath his riding boots as he tore across the street, headed for her even as he felt the enormous animals bearing down upon them.

This was idiocy.

Whether from the cacophony surrounding her or a latent sense of self-preservation, she looked up.

Her eyes were brown.

And wide as saucers.

Her jaw dropped and she stopped short, frozen with surprise and uncertainty, and all Nick could hope for was that she would not move out of his path, or both of them would be in extremely dire straits.

Had he not learned his lesson regarding saving young women from impending doom?

Apparently not.

He was on her then, the momentum of his large body propelling her backward, his arms wrapping tightly around her as they were lifted off the ground with the force of the collision. Her papers went flying.

Instinctively, he twisted in midair, protecting her from the impact that would almost certainly rob him of breath—and quite possibly of working limbs.

When they landed, it was just off center enough to send a shooting pain down Nick's arm; he gritted his teeth before they tumbled several feet farther in the thick grass. As they came to a halt, Nick felt the horses pass, the earth trembling beneath them as they left scarred earth in their wake.

He lay still for a long moment, his left shoulder and right knee throbbing in pain familiar enough not to be worrisome. It was then that he registered his position, wrapped around a warm, feminine body.

He was curved around her, his arms having instinctively protected her head and neck from injury. He lifted his head carefully, looking down at her cradled in his embrace; her eyes squeezed shut, her lips pressed into a thin, firm line. He could feel the wild rhythm of her breathing against his chest. She had lost her bonnet in the fall, and one thick auburn curl lay across her face. He flexed one hand, moving it from where it cradled her head, and, without considering the action, brushed the hair aside.

She opened her eyes at the touch, blinking up at him.

Her eyes were no mere brown. They were a mosaic of honeys and golds and mahoganies magnified by a sheen of tears, the product of fear and confusion and surprise and relief.

There was something soft and tempting about this woman.

Then she began to struggle.

"Sir! Remove yourself from my person!" She found use of her hands again, pounding against his chest and arms. "Immediately!" One of her blows landed just so on his wounded arm, and he winced at the pain that shot through his shoulder.

He had been wrong. There was nothing soft about her. She was a harridan.

"Stop." The word stayed her movement.

She went rigid beneath him and he was instantly, keenly aware of their position—the press of her body against his, the feel of her breasts against his chest as she struggled for deep, calming breath. The place where his thigh rested, cradled between her own, tangled in her skirts. And, suddenly, the throbbing in his knee was not nearly as distracting as the throbbing of entirely different parts of him.

That would not do at all.

He lifted his body from hers gently, wincing as his wounded shoulder protested the weight. He hissed at the discomfort, one side of his mouth kicking up. "I hope your letters were worth nearly killing us both."

Her eyes widened at the words. "Surely you are not blaming me for our current position. You attacked me!" She pressed her hands to his chest and shoved against him with all the strength she had—a surprising amount, considering their recent near-death experience.

He raised an eyebrow at the words, but lifted off her, standing and making a show of adjusting his coat, taking a moment to consider its ruined sleeve, half torn at the elbow, before he took hold of its cuff and, with a firm tug, ripped the entire lower portion off completely.

He turned his attention back to her, still on the ground, now seated, ramrod-straight, peering up at him from beneath a mass of escaped auburn curls, transfixed by his billowing white shirtsleeve now flapping loosely in the breeze.

"Well, it is not as though there was any amount of mending that might have made the thing wearable again," he pointed out, reaching the arm in question out to her.

She leaned away slightly, as though uncertain of his motives.

"A lesser man would take offense, you know," he said. "Saving your life should have proven my good faith."

She blinked, and for a fleeting moment, he was certain that he saw something flicker in her eyes—amusement, perhaps? She reached up, accepted his hand, and stood. "You did not save my life. I was perfectly fine until you—" She winced as she tested her weight on one foot—he might not have even noticed if he had not been so fascinated by her.

"Easy," he said, slipping one long arm behind her. "You've had quite a tumble." Their position brought their faces mere inches from each other. He lowered his voice. "Are you well? Can I help you home?"

When she looked up, he saw the flash of awareness in her gaze. *She was warming to him.* It was gone before he could consider it further, shuttered away. She stepped away from his touch, removing her hand from his, a pink wash spreading across her face, incongruous with the wide smudge of dirt that marred one high cheekbone. "No. I am quite well, my lord. I do not require your assistance. You need not trouble yourself any longer."

He was taken aback. "It is no trouble at all, miss. I was happy to play the knight to your damsel in distress."

Her tone turned defensive. "I can see how you might have thought that I was in trouble, my lord, but I assure you, I was completely aware of my surroundings."

One brow rose. "You were, were you?"

She nodded once. "Quite."

"And when were you planning to get out of the way of the horses that were barreling toward you?"

She opened her mouth to respond, then closed it. She took another step back and turned to fetch the papers she had lost in their fall, now strewn across the grass around them. She was embarrassed, and he was immediately chagrined. He watched her for a moment, then helped, chasing down several of the letters that had blown particularly far afield. Surreptitiously, he looked at the contents of these materials that had so engrossed her and noticed that they were bills—which surprised him. Why would an attractive young woman be handling financial matters?

Returning to her, he bowed low and presented her with the papers. When she reached to take them, he recaptured her hand, running one thumb over her grass-stained knuckles as he straightened. "My lady, I do apologize. May I introduce myself? I am Lord Nicholas St. John."

She froze at the words, searching his face, and he resisted the urge to straighten his cravat. Extracting her hand from his grasp, she repeated, "Did you say St. John?"

There was a hint of recognition in her words, and Nick paused, uncertain of what to make of it. "Yes."

"Lord *Nicholas* St. John?"

She knew him.

The damned magazine.

When he spoke, his tone was filled with dread. "Yes."

She was after him. Just like all the others.

Of course, the others had not been so life-threatening.

Or so beautiful.

He shook his head to clear it of the thought—beautiful or no, the woman was a viper—and looked over his shoulder, searching for the most immediate escape route.

"Lord. Nicholas. St. John. The *antiquarian*."

And it was Nicholas's turn to be surprised. The question was entirely unexpected. He had been prepared for *Nicholas St. John, brother to the Marquess of Ralston?* Or *Lord to Land, Nicholas St. John?* Or even *London's most eligible bachelor, Nicholas St. John?* But to be identified as an expert in antiquities—this seemed an entirely different approach than that he would expect from most women.

Perhaps he had found the one woman on the island of Britain who did not read *Pearls and Pelisses.*

"The very same."

She laughed then, the sound bright and welcome. She grew more beautiful in that moment, and Nick could not help but return her smile. "I cannot believe it. You are very far from home, my lord."

Not so far, as long as she was smiling.

Nick shook off the ridiculous thought.

"It seems unfair that I have come so far and you have the better of me. On a number of levels."

"I confess, I thought you would be . . . different." She laughed then. "Of course, I hadn't thought much about you at all. But now you're here. In Dunscroft! What excellent good luck!"

Nick struggled to clear his mind of the confusion she had wrought. "I am afraid I don't understand."

"Of course you don't! But you will! What brings you to Dunscroft?" He opened his mouth to speak, but she waved a hand. "Never mind. It doesn't matter! What matters is that you are here at all!"

Nick's brows snapped together. "I beg your pardon?"

"You are a sign."

"A sign?"

"Yes. You are. But not of what Lara thought you were a sign of."

"No." The whole conversation was making him wonder if he had suffered a blow to the head when they fell.

She shook her head. "No. You are a sign that I must sell the marbles."

"The marbles."

She tilted her head. "Lord Nicholas, are you quite well?"

He blinked. "Yes. I believe so."

"Because you've been repeating me more than actually

responding." He did not respond. "Are you certain you are Lord Nicholas St. John? The antiquarian?"

Yes. That was one of the few things he was sure of in the face of this perplexing female. "Quite."

She considered him for a long moment. "Well, I suppose you'll have to do."

"I beg your pardon?"

"Forgive me, but you don't seem the most . . . alert . . . of scholars."

Now he was offended. "My lady. I assure you . . . if you are in need of an antiquarian, you couldn't do much better than me."

"You needn't sound so affronted," she said. "It's not as though I've a selection of antiquarians from which to choose." She grinned, and it was like a blow to the head. Again.

Who was this woman?

As though she'd read his thoughts, she spoke. "I am Lady Isabel Townsend. And I must thank you for making this so very easy."

Nick's brows snapped together. "I beg your pardon?"

But the perplexing woman did not reply. Instead, she turned away, looking down at the ground around them until, with a cry of triumph, she limped several feet and retrieved a rather sad-looking reticule. Nick watched as she ransacked its contents, finally emerging with a small square of paper, which she promptly extended in his direction.

He cast a doubtful look at the offering and said, "What is it?"

"It's for you," she said simply, as though such a thing were perfectly reasonable to assume.

"For me?"

She nodded. "Well, it was for the Royal Society of Antiquities at large." She smiled at his confusion. "But as you are already here . . . I think you'll do just fine, indeed."

It was not every day that Isabel was catapulted through the air out of the way of a team of galloping horses. But if that was what it took to bring a member of London's premiere antiquarian society to Yorkshire, she would accept the bruises she had almost certainly received in the tumble.

Yes, Lord Nicholas St. John was most definitely a sign.

The man was an antiquarian—an expert in the history and, more importantly, the value of Grecian marbles. And she just so happened to have a collection of Grecian marbles in need of valuing. And selling. As quickly as possible.

She pushed aside the tiny ache that consumed her each time she considered the plan. *This was the only possible solution.* She needed money. Quickly. Lord Nicholas could just as easily have been the highly questionable Lord Densmore.

And if he had been, Isabel—and the rest of the women at the Park—would be in serious trouble.

But he wasn't. She took a deep breath at the thought.

No, he was the answer to their problems.

If her father had left her ten thousand pounds, she couldn't have been happier.

Well, ten thousand pounds would have made her slightly happier.

But the marbles were worth something—enough to rent a new house and get the girls out of trouble. With any luck, she would have a second Minerva House ready within the week.

She never thought she'd say it, but that magazine was something of a godsend.

She watched as Lord Nicholas read the letter she had drafted that morning. It was really no wonder he had been named a Lord to Land. He was rather a remarkable specimen of manhood. Empirically, of course. He was tall and broad-shouldered, and Isabel knew firsthand that his decimated topcoat hid a muscled bulk that dwarfed most men in Yorkshire, and likely in all of Britain.

But it was not his size that was so clearly his draw. It was his face, lean and handsome. His lips, now set in a firm, strong line, were easy to smile, and his eyes were a lovely blue, a stark contrast to the rest of him, his dark hair and tanned skin. She'd never seen eyes so blue—they were almost stunning enough to make one miss the scar.

And then there was the scar.

It was several inches long, extending from above his right eyebrow diagonally across the upper half of his cheek—a thin, white line that had faded with time. Isabel winced as she imagined the pain it must have brought with it. It ran dangerously close to the corner of one glittering blue eye, so close that he was lucky he hadn't lost it.

It should have been wicked—a warning—a sign that this man was dangerous and not to be trifled with. And there was a part of Isabel that saw the scar as a manifestation of the intensity that she had seen in Lord Nicholas before he'd tackled her in the street and landed them both out of the way of the horses. But she did not feel fear as she looked at it. Instead, she was desperately curious. Where had he received it? How? When?

"Lady Isabel." She was shaken from her musings by the sound of her name.

How long had he been waiting for her to respond?

Willing herself not to blush, she met his gaze. "My lord?"

"You are daughter to the Earl of Reddich?"

"Sister to the current one."

His gaze turned sympathetic. "I had not heard the news of your father. Please accept my condolences."

Isabel's eyes narrowed. "Were you acquainted with him?"

He shook his head. "I am afraid we did not move in the same circles."

She released a breath she had not known she was holding. "No. I don't imagine you did."

If he understood her meaning, he did not show it. He lifted the missive she had written. "I am to believe you have a collection of antiquities?"

"There is no collection finer." She could not keep the pride from her voice. One dark eyebrow rose at the words, and she blushed. "Well, no *private* collection finer."

His smile was there, then gone. "I've never heard of it."

"It was my mother's," she said quickly, as though that made everything clear. "I assure you, it is well worth your time."

He gave a little nod. "If that is the case, my lady, then I accept your offer to have a look. I've something to do this afternoon, but perhaps I could come tomorrow?"

So quickly?

"Tomorrow?" The word came out on a hitch of breath. She had not expected to welcome an appraiser for at least a week—likely more. After all, who would have expected one to be milling about in Dunscroft? What were the odds?

The estate was in no condition to be visited by a man, much less a Londoner. The girls would have to be prepared for his arrival; they would have to be on their best, most discreet behavior when he arrived. A day was not much time. "Tomorrow," she hedged.

How could she postpone his visit?

"By all means. In fact," he added with a glance toward the inn, "my man is on his way with our horses. Depending upon the speed of our errand, we might make it this afternoon."

This afternoon.

"Your man." She looked over her shoulder in the direction of his gaze, where she saw an enormous man leading a gray and a black toward them. Her eyes widened at his sheer bulk. He was a good six inches taller and several inches broader than the village blacksmith. She'd never seen anyone so large. Or so imposing.

She had to get home. The girls would need fair warning.

Turning back to St. John, Isabel hedged. "My lord—I—I am certain that you have much better things to do with your afternoon than to come and have a look at my marbles. You clearly had plans before I—"

"Nearly got us both killed, yes," he finished for her. "Well, as luck would have it, we have nothing at all better to do. We would likely have spent the afternoon in search of excitement, but, since you've already provided me with quite enough of that, I should very much like to visit your statues." He paused, registering the trepidation in her eyes. "You are not afraid of Rock, are you? He's a kitten."

The giant's name was Rock?

Of course it was.

"Certainly not," Isabel said a touch too quickly. "I am quite sure that Mr. Rock is entirely a gentleman."

"Excellent. Then it is decided."

"What is decided?"

"We shall come to Townsend Park this afternoon—tomorrow at the latest. I hesitate not to escort you home, frankly. I should like to ensure that, should you become distracted, you have someone there to save you from runaway horses."

She blushed again as she realized he was teasing her. "You exaggerate, sir. I would have been quite all right."

His expression grew serious. "No, Lady Isabel, you would not have been. You would have been killed."

"Nonsense."

His eyes narrowed on her. "I can see that you are a difficult sort."

"I am not!" She considered his words. "At least, no more difficult than most ladies."

"I do appreciate your honesty; however, most ladies would have thanked me for saving their lives by now."

"I—" She stopped, uncertain of how to respond. *Was he teasing her?*

"No, no," he said, interrupting whatever silly string of words she was about to speak. "Do not say anything now. It shall just seem as though I forced you into expressing your gratitude."

He was definitely teasing her.

He leaned close. "You may thank me another time."

Isabel did not like the way the low, dark promise in his voice made her stomach tumble.

Before she could reply, he had turned to greet his friend and take the reins of the large gray horse. Turning back, he said, "Lady Isabel, may I introduce my friend and companion, Durukhan?"

The man was immense up close, nearly as tall as the black stallion that stood at his shoulder. Isabel offered her hand, and he executed a perfect bow.

"Mr. Durukhan," she said. "It is a pleasure to meet you."

He straightened, his curiosity evident. "The pleasure is entirely mine."

Looking into the man's dark eyes, she felt compelled to explain. "Lord Nicholas—he was gracious enough to—push me out of the way of"—she waved one hand in the direction of the long disappeared cart—"some horses."

"Was he?" A look passed between the two men that she could not read.

It was gone in a flash as St. John changed the subject. "Lady Isabel has invited us to visit her collection of antiquities, Rock."

"Ah," Rock said, considering Isabel. "Are we leaving now?"

Isabel's heart began to pound as she imagined these two men arriving unexpectedly on the steps of Minerva House. "No!" she said, far too loudly.

The men looked to each other, then to her. Isabel gave a nervous laugh. "I have much to do here in town. And much to do at home. And the collection is not ready for you. After all, I did not expect you to be here. You were a sign, remember?"

Shut up, Isabel. You sound like a ninny.

He gave a small smile that made her stomach flip in a not altogether unpleasant way. "And you were not prepared for a sign."

"Precisely!" She paused. "At any rate, I am certain you understand."

St. John nodded. "Indeed. You have much to do."

"Quite." She ignored the amused gleam in his eyes, patting at her hair nervously before looking about for her bonnet. It had settled several yards away after flying from her grasp during their collision. She strode toward it—as well as one could stride with a throbbing ankle—and retrieved it, turning back to the two men who were staring after her.

If she weren't so uneasy, she would have been amused by their dumbfounded looks.

Instead, she backed away from the two imposing men, "So you see, Lord Nicholas, I cannot begin to show you the antiquities now . . . but tomorrow . . . tomorrow sounds fine. In the afternoon? Three o'clock?"

He dipped his head in assent. "Tomorrow it is."

"Tomorrow afternoon," she repeated.

"Fair enough."

"Excellent. I shall—look forward to it." With a too-bright smile and a too-eager nod, Isabel turned and hurried away, leaving the pair behind.

After a few long moments, Rock turned to Nick, who was still staring after her. "We are not waiting until tomorrow, are we?"

Nick shook his head. "No."

"She is hiding something."

Nick gave a single curt nod. "And not very well." He watched her, noting the slight limp in her gait as she rushed across the street and into a nearby building.

"It has been years since I've seen that."

Nick did not shift his attention from Isabel. "Seen what?"

"The face of the *bulan*."

Several long moments passed before Nick turned to Rock. "A hundred pounds says we've found her."

Rock shook his head. "I'm not taking that bet."

Four

Several hours later, Nick and Rock stood in the wide circular drive of Townsend Park. The country seat of the Earl of Reddich was a large and stately home, three stories high, with tall, arching windows and a façade that spoke of the earldom's rather more impressive past than its current situation indicated.

There was a quiet stillness to the house that Nick found intriguing—it was either the product of a sleepy country house that rarely saw visitors, or something not at all sleepy and infinitely more interesting. If the mistress of Townsend Park was any indication, Nick's wager was on the latter option. If his suspicions were correct, he was about to find both the women for whom he was looking.

That is, assuming that he was ever allowed inside the house.

He and Rock had been standing at the foot of the steps leading up to the manor, reins in hand, waiting for a groomsman or a footman to acknowledge their arrival for several minutes.

At this point, neither seemed very likely.

"You realize that we look like fools." Rock said dryly,

leading his horse to the edge of the drive, where he could lean against the side of the wide stone steps to the door of the house. The black seemed to sense his master's disapproval, pawing at the ground once with an impatient snort.

"We cannot look like fools if we do not have an audience to label us as such. She did not want us here today. She likely doesn't have servants posted."

Rock leveled Nick with a frank look. "I see that your insistence upon saving women who are capable of taking care of themselves remains fully intact."

Nick ignored the words, tossing his reins to the Turk and starting up the stairs, two steps at a time.

Rock followed his movements, curiosity getting the better of him. "What do you mean to do?"

Nick turned from his position in front of the wide oak door with a wry smile. "Why, I mean to do what any good gentleman would do in this situation. I mean to knock."

Rock crossed his arms over his chest. "This should be entertaining, if nothing else."

Nick raised the large metal doorknocker and let it fall with an ominous clang, trying to recall the last time he had used a doorknocker.

Before he could entertain the question, however, the door opened. For a very brief moment Nick thought it had done so on its own, until he looked down into a pair of familiar brown eyes, set in the face of a young boy. A young boy with a face covered in what looked suspiciously like strawberry jam.

Nick was not entirely certain how to proceed under such circumstances, but, before he could say anything at all, the child took matters into his own hands.

The door slammed shut as quickly as it had opened.

"THERE'S A MAN AT THE DOOR!"

The screech was loud enough to carry clearly through the thick oak, and Nick, surprised, turned to look back at Rock to confirm that it had all taken place as he thought.

His friend was quaking with deep, rumbling laughter.

"I see you are going to be a great help."

With a final chuckle, Rock raised one hand in solidarity. "I assure you, once you have breached the castle defenses, I shall throw my full support behind you."

Nick turned back to the door and, after a long moment of consideration, pressed his ear to the oak, as though he might be able to hear what was going on behind it. Rock let out a bark of laughter at the action, and Nick waved him silent, almost positive that he could hear frenzied whispers coming from inside the house.

Stepping back, he reached once more for the knocker, but was interrupted before he could use it. "Milord?"

He turned to find a tall, lanky boy in wool breeches, white shirtsleeves, and a dirty green waistcoat turning the corner from the side of the house. The boy wore a cap low on his brow, and Nick had a brief moment of questioning why the servant had not removed the hat before he realized that nothing about this estate seemed to operate normally.

"We are here at the invitation of Lady Isabel."

The boy had reached the foot of the steps, and he paused. "Weren't you supposed to come tomorrow?"

Ignoring the insolent behavior—when had he ever been questioned by a servant?—Nick replied, "We are here now."

"You won't find her inside."

"Is she not at home?"

The boy leaned back on his heels, considering his words. "She is at home . . . but not inside."

Nick began to feel his temper fray. "Boy, I am not interested in playing games. Is your lady in? Or not?"

The servant smiled then, a wide grin that seemed entirely unservantlike. "She is not in. She is out. On top of, more like." The boy pointed up. "She is on the roof."

"She is on the roof." Surely Nick had misunderstood.

"Just so," the groom said. "Shall I call her?"

The question was so bizarre that it took Nick several seconds to process its meaning.

Not so Rock. Unable to contain his own wide smile, the Turk said, "Yes, please. We should very much like you to call her."

The boy stepped back to the opposite edge of the drive, cupped his hands around his mouth, and called, "Lady Isabel! You have visitors!"

Nick stepped back from the house himself then, Rock at his side, horses in tow. He stared upward, uncertain of what might come next, unwilling to accept the possibility that the lady he had met earlier in the day would have any reason to be on the roof of her ancestral home, three stories above the ground.

Far above, a head poked over the edge of the house.

It seemed Lady Isabel was, indeed, on the roof.

Dear God. The woman had a death wish.

The head disappeared for a moment, and Nick wondered if perhaps he was hallucinating. When it reappeared, he found himself disappointed that the whole afternoon was not a figment of his imagination.

"You were not supposed to arrive until tomorrow." The words carried down to him. "I am not receiving."

Rock gave a little bark of laughter and offered, "It appears we have found a woman who does not consider you so irresistible."

Nick cast a sidelong glance in the direction of his friend. "You are not helping." Turning resolutely away from Rock, he called up, "It seems a good thing I came today, Lady Isabel. It appears you may need saving again."

The smile she offered was angelic—and entirely false. "I have survived twenty-four years without a keeper, my lord. I need not acquire one today."

He had an intense desire to fetch the infuriating woman down and show her precisely how dire her need for a keeper was. The thought had barely formed in his mind before it was chased away by a vision of the soft, beautiful woman in his arms that afternoon—entirely at his mercy. For a fleeting moment, he allowed the fantasy to run its natural course; she was lush and naked at his whim.

He pushed the image away. There was nothing about this woman that was at his whim.

"Considering you were nearly run down this morning and you are dangerously close to toppling off your roof now, forgive me if I do not share your certainty."

"I was nowhere near the edge before you arrived, Lord Nicholas. Should I fall, it will be entirely on your head." She cocked her head thoughtfully. "Perhaps quite literally."

She disappeared again, and the groom actually *snickered.* Nick gave him a look of lordly disdain, which in no way served to intimidate the insolent pup.

Rock laughed again, tossing the reins of both horses to the boy. "You might as well take them. I think we might be here for a while."

The servant did not move, too fascinated by the unfolding scene to leave.

Nick turned a scowl on his friend. "The woman would try the patience of a saint. Do you think that she has forgotten that it was *she* who invited *me* to the damned house?"

She peeked her head over the edge of the house once more. "You would do well to remember that sound carries *up*, my lord. Language, please."

"My apologies." He offered an exaggerated bow. "I am not used to conversing with ladies on roofs. The rules of etiquette for the situation have escaped me."

She narrowed her gaze on him. "Even from three stories up, I can tell that you are being facetious."

He ignored that. "Perhaps you would like to tell us why you are on your roof?"

"I am learning," she said, as though it were a perfectly normal response.

"Learning to nearly kill yourself again?"

"How many times am I going to have to tell you that I did not nearly kill myself!"

"I stand corrected. Again. What are you learning?"

"The fundamentals of roof repair. Fascinating, really." She smiled again; this time, she meant it.

He sucked in a breath. Would he ever grow used to her smiles?

Roof repair?

"I beg your pardon, did you say you are repairing the roof?"

"Well, it certainly will not repair itself, my lord."

Lovely or not, she was mad. It was the only answer.

He looked to Rock, who was smiling like a buffoon. "She has a point, Nick."

And her madness was clearly infectious.

"Lady Isabel, I must insist that you come down." She watched him for a long moment, as though assessing the likelihood of his leaving the estate if she remained roof-bound. "I should very like to see your marbles, and will be happy to value them. I should think you would find my offer generous enough to accept?"

She looked to Rock, then to the stable boy, before heaving an impressive sigh. "Very well. I shall come down."

Nick could not help the wave of triumph that coursed through him at the words. He had restored normalcy to this tiny corner of Britain.

At least for as long as it would take her to concoct her next mad scheme.

"Lara!"

Isabel tumbled through the tiny attic window that led to the top of the Park, her breeches covered in dirt acquired during her foray into roof repair. Tossing the book she had been using aside, she blew an errant lock of hair back from her face and headed for the narrow stairs leading from the top of the house into the servants' quarters. Jane, who had been on the roof with her, followed closely behind.

"Jane, you must—"

"All will be ready by the time you are," interrupted the butler, as they hurried down the long, dark passageway leading to the house's central staircase and the family wing.

Isabel nodded as Jane peeled away, heading for the stairs,

not pausing as Lara topped them, out of breath from the speed of her climb. Throwing open her bedchamber door, Isabel rushed in to retrieve a fresh dress from her wardrobe. She spoke from half inside the furniture, assuming that Lara had followed her.

"I told the infuriating man not to come until tomorrow!"

"It appears he did not listen."

"No! He did not! Did you see him out there? Affronted! As though I should have been doing nothing but shoving a needle through an embroidery hoop and waiting for him to arrive!"

Isabel held up a yellow day dress that she had always felt rather flattered her figure.

Not that she was interested in Lord Nicholas seeing her in a flattering frock.

Not at all.

"I did not see him," Lara said, adding, "You're in mourning, Isabel."

Isabel grumbled and turned back to the wardrobe, her voice rising. "I've half a mind to go down there dressed as I am! It would serve him—and his gentlemanly sensibilities—right!" She gave a vicious yank on a gray walking dress and turned back to Lara. "Of course, that would not do at all, as I am in mourning. As you insist upon reminding me."

The corner of Lara's mouth twitched. "You are, of course, right. If you were to go downstairs in trousers, it would be your breach of mourning etiquette that would undoubtedly cause Lord Nicholas alarm."

Isabel raised one dirty finger at her cousin. "You are not amusing."

"I am more amusing than you are clean." She stood and moved to pour some water into a washbasin. "I think you should send him away. We'll find another way to make money."

"No. You were the one who started this sign business. The man is about the boldest sign I've ever had. I'm selling the marbles. He's the answer."

Isabel tossed the dress onto the bed and moved to wash.

Lord Nicholas St. John was their only hope, and she had been on the *roof* when he arrived, for heaven's sake. Ladies did not go traipsing about on rooftops.

And certainly gentlemen did not frequent the homes of those ladies who did traipse about on rooftops.

It did not matter if the rooftop in question was in dire need of repair.

Or that the lady in question had no choice.

"It shall be a miracle if he has not discovered all of our secrets by now. Kate was out there, rubbing elbows with the man. I'm sure that he and his giant have already discovered that she is . . ." She trailed off, waving one hand in the air before splashing water on her face.

"Nonsense. If you have taught me one thing in my years here, it is that people see what they wish to see." Lara watched as Isabel scrubbed at the dirt from her face. "What is important is that Lord Nicholas see a lady in you—which could be difficult at this point."

Isabel paused in her ablutions. "How am I to convince him that he should stay?"

"Well, it is entirely possible that he found you fascinating."

Isabel looked up at her cousin, water running down her face in rivulets. "No, it is entirely possible that he found me addlepated."

"That is also a likely possibility, yes."

"Lara! You are supposed to make me feel *better* about the situation." Isabel reached for a long piece of linen and dried her face; mid-wipe, she lifted her head and turned horrified eyes on her cousin. "The girls. Their livery."

"Jane is arranging everything." Lara lifted the gray dress from the bed, tossing it over Isabel's head. "You haven't time for stays."

Turning her back to allow her cousin to secure the fastenings of the dress, Isabel reached under her skirts to untie her breeches and slip them off. Throwing the wad of brown wool aside, she moved across the room to her dressing table, dragging Lara along with her.

Once there, Isabel unraveled her long hair, brushing at it violently, attempting to tame the curls that had escaped during her time outside.

When Lara finished with the dress, she took the brush from Isabel's hand and began to restore her hair to its normal state. "You need a lady's maid."

"I do not. I could have dressed perfectly well without you. Just not as quickly."

"Precisely why you need a lady's maid," Lara said. "You've a houseful of girls at your disposal, Isabel, why not select one to be your girl?"

Isabel shook her head as she watched Lara work in the mirror, "Nothing fancy—we haven't the time." After a short pause, she answered the question. "I cannot do it. As it is, they share in the running of the house. They cook, they clean, they help with James. They feel a part of something larger—a community—one most of them have never had before Minerva House. If one were to be my personal servant . . . that . . . well, it would not feel right."

"That is utterly ridiculous. You're daughter to an earl. No one would begrudge you a servant or two, Isabel."

"I have servants. I simply don't have a lady's maid. And I do not need one. When was the last time I was rushing to meet a dashing gentleman?"

"Dashing, is he?"

Yes. Very.

"No. Not at all. He is a man who appears to have little understanding of both dates and invitations. He was not supposed to be here until tomorrow!" Isabel watched as her cousin shoved a pin into the tight mass of hair at the back of her head. "That's fine. I cannot linger any more." She stood, turning to her cousin and smoothing her skirts. "How do I look?"

"Quite staid. Not at all like a lady who was recently repairing the roof."

Isabel took a deep breath. "Excellent."

"You don't have to do this, you know."

"Whatever do you mean?"

Lara gave a little sigh. "You don't have to sell the marbles. We can find another way."

Isabel looked away for a moment as she took a deep breath. "We have no need for them. They serve no purpose here."

"They serve no purpose anywhere. But they're yours, Isabel."

As though she needed reminding.

Isabel forced a smile, refusing to allow herself to think too carefully on her decision. "They are our last hope. They are the last hope of Minerva House. I am selling them."

She squared her shoulders, and she was off, across the room and into the hallway, where James, Jane, and Gwen were waiting for her.

"Isabel!" James crowed, rushing toward her, "There was a man at the door!"

Isabel could not help the smile that tugged at one corner of her mouth at the surprise on the boy's face. "Yes, I saw that."

"He is very tall." The observation tugged at Isabel's heart. Of course James would have noted such a thing—men were a strange and uncommon occurrence at Minerva House. Of course the ten-year-old would have collected as much information about male visitors as quickly and voraciously as he could.

James needs a man.

Isabel pushed the thought aside.

"He is a very tall man, yes," she agreed, ruffling her brother's silky blond hair. "More than uncommon tall. As is his friend."

"There are *two* of them?" James's mouth fell open. So did Gwen's. "What are they *doing* here?"

"I invited them here," Isabel replied, moving past the group toward the stairs.

"Why?" James's question echoed the curiosity of the older inhabitants of the hallway.

She turned back. "Well, one of them is very clever, with a talent for Greek statues. I thought we could use him."

"I see," James said with a nod that indicated an understanding Isabel felt certain he did not have. "So they are not here to take you."

"Goodness! No!" She looked in the direction of the stairs. *Lord Nicholas could wait another minute.* "No one is going to take me anywhere."

"You do not need me to step in?"

Isabel had to swallow a smile at the seriousness in his tone. "No. I am quite safe."

"And the others?"

Isabel blinked at James's concern. "No one needs rescuing, love. Not today."

"But we are very happy to have you to protect us," Gwen said with a smile. "You are an excellent protector."

"Indeed," Jane agreed readily. "We are lucky to live with you, my lord."

James's chest puffed out and Isabel almost laughed at the boy's pride. Almost. But the imposing lord in her sitting room did put a damper on the moment. "And now, I must go and convince the man at the door that, while it might appear at first blush as though it were so, we are not in a state of bedlam."

"Excellent plan," Lara said with a grin.

"Yes, I thought so." Isabel set off for the stairs before she stopped and turned back to the group. "Georgiana," she said, referencing the newest resident of the manor. "Where is she?"

"In the library. She will not be seen." Jane had, indeed, considered everything.

Isabel gave a little nod. "Excellent. I shall go see to our visitor."

"Did someone let him in? After James slammed the door in his face, that is?" Gwen asked.

Isabel paled. "Oh, no." She looked from one face to the next, her mouth open in shock. "Oh, no!"

She was off, tearing down the stairs, ignoring the dull ache in her ankle.

Dear God. He was going to be livid.

If he was even there.

He had to be there. He was her only hope.

"She called him dashing," Lara offered in a too-loud whisper as they clattered down the stairs.

"I did *not*."

"Did she, now?" Jane asked.

"I was referring to dashing men in the broader sense."

"Well, that *would* be the case," Jane said dryly, "Considering the legions of dashing men who come along daily out here in the middle of nowhere."

Lara laughed. Isabel considered pushing them all down the next flight of stairs.

"It is too bad that all hope for lesson number one is out the window," Gwen said wistfully.

Isabel turned back as she hit the ground floor. "What does that mean?"

Gwen shook her head. "Nothing really, simply that the latest issue of *Pearls and Pelisses* had suggestions for just this situation—"

Jane snorted her disbelief.

"Stop." Isabel raised a hand. "I haven't time for this, Gwen."

"But it says—"

"No. I must somehow repair the damage that I have done and get Lord Nicholas to have a look at those marbles."

Isabel turned to the door, and Regina, one of the footmen, reached for the handle. With a deep breath, Isabel said, flustered, "Is he still there? Go ahead. Open it." Then: "Wait." She turned back to Gwen. "On second thought, I need as much help as I can get at this point. What is this ridiculous lesson?"

Gwen recited from memory, "*Lesson Number One: Do not attempt to make too strong of a first impression.*"

Isabel paused, considering the advice, and her first meeting with Lord Nicholas. And her second meeting with Lord Nicholas. "Well. I have certainly made a hash of that one."

As the door began to open, she shooed them all away.

"Hide."

Five

The last time Nick had been kept waiting by a female, he had ended up in a Turkish prison. He doubted he was in for a similar fate in Yorkshire, but nevertheless, he would prefer not to be kept waiting.

Outside.

For a madwoman.

No matter how lovely.

The groom had disappeared, along with the horses, and Nick and Rock had been left, summarily, on the doorstep of the manor house for far longer than was acceptable. Not that Nick had any lingering expectations of propriety at Townsend Park. Apparently, while the earl had been causing any number of scandals in London, his family had been left to rusticate in the country. Quite possibly in the care of wolves.

Ultimately, the pair had thrown manners to the wind and seated themselves on the wide stone steps, waiting for someone to come and fetch them.

And, as Nick fumed, Rock became more and more entertained.

"I retract my earlier statements on Yorkshire," the Turk said, leaning casually against the stone balustrade, twirling a piece of grass in his hand. "It has taken a turn for the better, don't you think?"

"Perhaps you would like to live here, then? In a parish full of oddities?"

Rock laughed at Nick's surly tone. "Unfortunately, Yorkshire seems to have robbed you of your good humor."

"Yes, well, sitting outside for half an age waiting for a woman who has, quite likely, dreamed up her fantastic collection of antiquities, does not help. I've a mind to leave."

"Five pounds says it's real."

Nick leveled his friend with a cool blue gaze. "Make it ten."

"Ten pounds says we stay to catalogue it."

As if on cue, the door opened, to reveal a mildly flushed Lady Isabel in a gray muslin day dress. Her hair had been returned to perfect smoothness and she was the portrait of calm and utter ladylikeness.

Nick looked up at her, instantly appreciating her long, willowy frame. She was tall and lithe and stunning.

It no longer seemed to matter that he had been sitting on these wretched steps for half the day.

He rose, Rock beside him, as she spoke. "My lords," she said with a welcoming smile as a young footman in full livery opened the door wide. "Please forgive me for keeping you waiting."

She was utterly poised, her tone and demeanor so even that one would never guess that they had just conducted an entire conversation with her roofbound.

She stepped aside, making room for their entrance.

Once inside, Nick registered the quietness of the house—the foyer was dimly lit, the front of the manor having been shaded from the late afternoon sun.

There was no sign of the boy who had been at the door earlier—he had been replaced, it seemed, by the woman who stood at the foot of a wide stone staircase, also dressed in mourning attire. Nick paused briefly, considering her. She was blond and willowy, with a serene smile and downcast eyes—entirely different from Lady Isabel.

Was it possible she was another Townsend sibling?

Noting Nick's attention, Isabel stepped back and said, "Lara, may I present Lord Nicholas St. John and Mr. Durukhan? Lord Nicholas, Mr. Durukhan, my cousin, Miss Lara Caldwell."

"Miss Caldwell." Nick bowed low before Rock stepped forward.

Lara's eyes went wide at the Turk's sheer size, even as he offered her a warm smile and reached for her hand to greet her, "Miss Caldwell, it is a pleasure to meet you." The Turk's eyes lingered on Lara's face as Nick turned back to Isabel.

"Where is the boy?"

"My lord?"

"The boy. Who answered my earlier knock."

"You mean James . . . my brother . . . the earl . . . Lord Reddich, I suppose I should start calling him." He watched as color flooded her cheeks. "He is . . . with his governess. I do apologize, again, for our somewhat . . . unorthodox . . . treatment. You see, the house was not expecting guests—we so rarely have them—and you startled James . . ."

Rock turned at her flustered explanation, meeting Nick's eyes. The woman was not comfortable with them in the house, that much was clear.

" . . . and several of the servants have the afternoon free," she hurried to finish.

"While you learn the fundamentals of roof repair."

"Precisely." She smiled shyly, and he was struck once again by the change that came over her. *She was beautiful.*

When he returned her smile, hers was gone in a flash, as quickly as it had come. "Shall I show you the collection, my lord? I should hate to keep you here for too long—particularly when you must be planning to leave Yorkshire at any moment."

Her words were a clear foray for information—one to which Nick was unwilling to respond. "Not at all. In fact, Rock was just pointing out how very engaging the area is—we may well stay awhile. So we have plenty of time this afternoon."

"Oh," she said, and he did not miss the disappointment in her tone.

She wanted him gone.

Why?

He was becoming intrigued.

Out of the corner of his eye, Nick noticed a nearby door slightly ajar and guarded by two liveried footmen, one tall and thin, one short and squat. He considered the sliver of space between the door and its seat, running his gaze along it. Sure enough, there, four feet from the ground, a little face peered out at him, wide-eyed. It was the boy from earlier.

He couldn't help himself. He winked at the child and was rewarded with a gasp that sliced through the quiet, open space before he was gone, yanked from the door in a cry of young outrage.

Isabel did not flinch as the door slammed shut, instead spinning on her heel to lead them toward the stairs. "Please follow me. I am happy to show you the marbles."

They climbed the wide stone stairs to the next floor in silence, Nick taking in the quiet dignity of the house that had not seen new decor in more than a decade. Lights were kept to a minimum, the darkened halls were bereft of servants, and all but a handful of doors were closed, indicating that the rooms behind them were rarely in use.

As she led them down a long, narrow corridor, Nick asked, "Lady Isabel, why you were repairing the roof?"

She was ahead of him, and her head turned slightly as she registered the question. After a long pause, she said, "It leaks."

The woman would try the patience of a saint. Truly.

He waited for her to elaborate. When she did not, he said, "I imagine that is the most likely reason for a roof to be in need of repair."

He ignored the sound that came from Rock, a cross between laughter and strangulation.

As they reached a far corner of the house, Nick registered a familiar, not-unpleasant odor—a musty smell that he had long associated with the very best of discoveries. When she opened a door near the end of the hallway and indicated that they should enter, the wash of golden sunlight that spilled through the doorway surprised him.

Isabel stepped back, allowing him access to the large room, a perfectly symmetrical space, with tall ceilings and a wall of high windows that looked out onto the vast manor lands. The windows did nothing to hide the late afternoon sun that shone directly into the large, open space filled with dozens of statues, each a different size and shape, covered in dusty muslin sheets.

Excitement coursed through Nick as he took in the contents of the room, his hands itching to remove the shrouds—to view the treasures they hid. He stopped several feet inside, turning back to Isabel. "You were not exaggerating."

A small smile played at her lips, and, when she spoke, he could hear the pride in her voice. "There is another room, identical to this one, across the hall. You will no doubt wish to see that, as well."

Nick's surprise was clear. "Perhaps Miss Caldwell could open that room for Rock while you tell me more about the statues?"

After a moment's hesitation, Isabel nodded her assent to her cousin, and the two exited the room, leaving the door wide. She uncovered a nearby statue, and Nick watched, tracking her movements as she pulled the fabric aside, revealing a tall marble nude.

He approached the piece, considering it for a long moment before running one hand down the curve of the statue's arm. When he spoke, there was reverence in his voice. "She is stunning."

Isabel tilted her head to one side, assessing the marble. "She is, isn't she?"

Her reverent words shook him from his inspection. He turned to her, noting the way she looked at the statue—with something akin to longing. "More importantly, she is real."

She looked up sharply, "You doubted as much?"

"It is not every day that I stumble across a woman who professes to have a collection of marbles such as this." He lifted one corner of a nearby cloth, "May I?" When she nodded her assent, he tugged on the fabric, revealing another statue, this one a warrior, spear in hand, on the hunt. He shook his head slowly. "It is not every *lifetime* that I stumble across a woman who is actually in possession of such a collection."

She smiled as she unveiled a cherub. "I am happy that our meeting has resulted in such excitement for you."

He paused in uncovering another statue, capturing her gaze. "Even without such a collection, Lady Isabel, I think it would be difficult to forget such a meeting."

Her blush sent a wave of pleasure through him. "I suppose I should admit defeat, my lord. You did, indeed, save my life. I owe you a debt of gratitude."

He ran his hand over a marble bust of Dionysius, perfectly wrought, his fingers tracing the intricate lines of the grape leaves that encircled the head of the statue. "Allowing me access to such a collection is an excellent start at repaying that debt." He looked to her again. "It is a tragedy that it is hidden away."

She paused, and when she spoke, her voice held a tension that he did not like. "That will soon be remedied, thanks to you," Isabel said with a small, sad smile. "Once you have identified them, the marbles must be sold."

His eyes widened. "You cannot sell them."

She busied herself with unveiling a large statue in particularly excellent condition. "I can, my lord. As you can see, it does me little good here, collecting dust. It must be sold."

"It means more to you than its monetary value." He could see it in her pride, in her obvious passion for the collection.

Her shoulders squared at his words. When she turned back, he noted that her eyes were shiny with tears. She took a deep breath. "I assure you, Lord Nicholas, I would not sell if—" He sensed a world in the silence. "If I felt that they were well shown here." She traced the line of the statue's foot. "How long do you think it will take?"

If he had thought the task she asked of him would take

any less than a week, he would have lied to her to give her more time—to consider her actions. But falsehoods were unnecessary.

"Some of the marbles will be easier to identify than others," he said carefully, making a show at looking around the room. "Two weeks at the minimum. Perhaps longer."

"Two weeks!" Her eyes went wide with despair.

"I see you would prefer to be rid of me sooner."

Her gaze flew to his, and she seemed to relax slightly at his smile. "It is not that . . . only the time. I had hoped to have the stones sold in less than two weeks."

"Impossible. Even the best antiquarian could not meet that goal."

"I do apologize, my lord. I was under the impression that *you* were the best antiquarian."

The bold words startled him, and he grinned, surprised and delighted by her teasing, so unexpected from a woman who appeared to have an untold weight upon her shoulders.

He was coming to see, however, that there was much about Lady Isabel that was unexpected.

"And it will take at least a month for you to get a reasonable price for it."

"I don't have a month."

"More likely, six weeks."

"I definitely do not have six weeks." Isabel sounded desolate.

The situation was growing more and more curious.

The collection would have been enough to sway him—but now, as he watched worry flood her gaze, he knew that it was not simply the collection that was keeping him in Yorkshire.

He wanted to know all her secrets.

And she had given him the perfect way to uncover them.

They were very close now, and Nick purposely took another step toward her, crowding her nearer to the statue. Her eyes widened, and he found that he enjoyed surprising her. "Two weeks," he said, his voice low. "And when I am done, I shall help you to sell the marbles."

"Thank you." Her relief was palpable. "I am only sorry that I have no way of repaying you the favor."

"I'm sure we could come up with some form of payment for my services."

The words were low and meant to be teasing, but Isabel was instantly guarded. "Could we?"

Someone had hurt her.

The thought set him on edge, the muscles of his back stiffening as he wondered who. And how.

He turned away, attempting a playful note. "May I propose a game?"

"A game?"

"For each statue I identify, you shall tell me something of Townsend Park. And your life here."

There was silence as she considered his offer—a silence that stretched out long enough for him to believe that she might not answer at all. He heard her take a deep breath, and looked back at her, meeting her eyes. He considered their dark, mahogany depths, so private and uncertain. So many secrets hidden there—so much that he wanted to discover. The legacy of the *bulan*—he could not leave a mystery unsolved.

What would it take to unlock those secrets? To see her with her guard down?

An image flashed, quick and intense—Isabel, her head thrown back in passion, open and unguarded, her long, lithe body spread across his bed, waiting for him. The force of the vision pushed him back, away from her, to a safer distance.

He indicated a nearby bust. "That is Medusa."

She gave a short burst of laughter. "Of course it is. Even I could have identified her. You can't really expect me to share my secrets for *that*."

"I never said they had to be secrets," he teased, "but if you are offering information of such value, the bust is Medusa, in black marble, likely from Livadeia. More importantly, it is Medusa after she was decapitated by Perseus, but before her head was seated at the center of Athena's shield."

"How do you know that?"

He indicated that she should move closer to the statue. Pointing to a small indentation where the head of one asp was consuming the tail of another, he said, "Look carefully. What do you see?"

She leaned closer, peering into the shadowy nook. "A feather!"

"Not just any feather. A feather from the wings of Pegasus. Who was spawned from the blood that spilled from Perseus's blade."

She turned wide eyes on him, and he resisted the urge to preen. "I've looked at this statue dozens of times and never seen it. You *are* the best."

He bowed exaggeratedly. "As such, you owe me payment, my lady."

Isabel nibbled carefully on her lower lip. "All right. I shall tell you about the collection."

"An excellent beginning."

She paused a long moment, and Nick thought she might change her mind. When she finally spoke, the words came from far away as she looked from statue to statue, lost in her thoughts. "My father won them from a French smuggler in a game of chance."

Years of practice kept him from replying—and she filled the silence with more of her thoughts. "In the early days of the war. He had always been an inveterate gambler. He wagered on everything, money, servants, houses . . ." She paused for a moment, lost in thought, then caught herself, and continued. "We would go weeks without seeing him, and then one day, he would arrive on the doorstep, a basketful of puppies in hand, or a new curricle in the drive. He gave these to my mother as a gift three days after I turned seven."

There was more to the story. He was certain of it.

"And she gave them to you," he prompted.

She nodded, stiffly, her lips pressed into a thin line. "She did. They are mine."

There was something in that word, *mine*, that called to

Nick. Here was a woman who cared deeply for that which was hers.

"You do not want to sell them," he said. That much was obvious.

His words pulled her back from wherever she had been. Silence stretched between them, and he thought she might not reply. When she did, there was little emotion in her tone. "No."

"Then . . . why?"

She gave a small, humorless laugh. "Sometimes, my lord, we must do things we do not want to do."

She breathed deeply and he noted the pull of her bodice across her breasts. Feeling guilty for the awareness that pulsed through him at the movement, he looked away, his gaze landing on a nearby statue, towering above them. Recognition flared, and he gave a short, hoarse laugh.

"What is so amusing?"

"That statue. Do you know who she is?"

Isabel turned, considering the nude, one hand at her breast as though she could hide her embarrassment at the statue's state of undress. Taking in the curve of the marble spine, the serene pleasure on the statue's face, the garland of roses that wound up one leg, Isabel shook her head. "No."

"She is Voluptas. The daughter of Cupid and Psyche."

"How do you know that? She looks like every other female statue here."

He gave her a frank look. "I know because I am the best."

She smiled, and he felt a supreme satisfaction in her amusement. When she was not wary of him, she was exquisite.

The air between them became heavy, the room suddenly warmer, the musty air thick with the clean scent of her—a mix of orange blossom and something fresh and welcome that he could not place.

He noted the flush of her skin, the hollow at the base of her neck where the column of her throat met her shoulder, and he was struck with want—quick and intense—more than he had felt in a long while.

He watched as the moment hit her, as well—his nearness catching her breath. Their gazes collided, and he was keenly aware of their position, so close, pressed between two statues, on the brink of touching. They were alone, with none but the marbles to see them.

Desire moved him forward.

He reached for her, one hand nearly brushing her cheek before he realized the mistake that touching her would be. He took in her wide brown eyes, rich and liquid with emotion, a heady mix of curiosity and excitement and fear that brightened her whole face, turning her into an innocent siren—flesh and blood, surrounded by her marble sisters.

Isabel closed her eyes against his nearness, and he considered her lovely face—high, strong cheekbones, lush mouth, brow clear of worry. Her beauty was generous when it had time to be.

She released the breath she had been holding in a rattling, unsteady sound, and her lips parted, marking the moment with an elegant pink sigh.

There wasn't a man on earth who could resist that sigh.

He leaned in, even as he knew it was wrong.

Nothing good could come of kissing this innocent country miss.

His lips were a hairsbreadth from hers when the sound came from outside the room.

He snapped back, straightening, and cursed briefly under his breath. He took a long step back, immediately wishing he had not gone anywhere near this woman, who seemed to have an inexplicable negative effect on his good sense.

Her eyes flew open, a mix of emotions in their depths, and for a moment, he wanted nothing but to pull her into his arms and damn everyone else.

And then Miss Caldwell and Rock returned and Nick was too busy moving to place a safe distance between him and

Isabel, who pressed herself into the statue of Voluptas so firmly that Nick worried, fleetingly, if she might push the thing off its pedestal.

That certainly would distract from their activities.

"What did you find?" Nick asked, hoping to cover the energy that remained between them.

Rock looked from Nick to Isabel, then back again. One dark brow rose. Nick matched it, daring the Turk to draw attention to the situation inside the room.

After a pause, Rock spoke. "I've not seen anything like it outside of Greece." He went on to describe the scope of the marbles in the second room, and Nick watched from the corner of his eye as Lara crossed to her cousin. Isabel smiled a too-bright smile, one that betrayed everything.

She had wanted him.

He shook himself from the thought. He should be grateful for the interruption that prevented the immense mistake that kiss would have been. This girl was everything he did not seek out in his women. She was innocent and alone and precisely the kind of female he avoided—the kind who would want more from him than he was able to give. He'd wager she'd barely ever been satisfactorily kissed, out here in the countryside with no one but the stable boys to toy with.

He did not deny that he would very much like to show Isabel how satisfying kissing could be.

"You owe me ten pounds."

Rock's words pulled Nick back to the present.

The collection was real. Its owner, a mystery.

They were staying.

Ignoring his friend's smirk, Nick slid his gaze back to Isabel, who was watching them, curiosity in her eyes. When she noticed his attention, she blushed, patting her hair nervously.

"Lady Isabel," he said, enjoying the sound of her name on his tongue. "If it suits you, we will begin our work on the collection tomorrow morning."

He saw the uncertainty in her eyes, followed immediately

by the recognition that she had taken them too far down this particular path to turn him away.

She patted her hair in a movement that he was quickly coming to recognize as nerves. “By all means. Tomorrow would be . . . fine.” She edged around them, heading for the door. “And . . . Lara will see you out today . . . I am . . . I must . . .” She paused, and Nick waited, a half smile on his face, for her to finish. “I must go.”

And she was gone, the skirts of her drab gray dress the last thing he saw as she fled the room.

Six

Lesson Number Two

Do your best to remain in your lord's mind. And in his eye.
While absence may make the heart grow fonder, only nearness will result in a sound match. Remember, if your lord is to recognize his desire for a wife, he must be reminded of the existence of such a woman! Do your best to stay in his sight; pass near to him at balls; learn his preferences for promenading in the park; and encourage your servants to befriend his own. Knowledge of his schedule is the very best tool for ensnaring a true gentleman.

Pearls and Pelisses
June 1823

Wellington might have said that the hardest thing of all for a soldier was to retreat, but that course of action was far easier for Isabel than remaining in the statuary—and in the company of Lord Nicholas St. John.

Indeed, she had escaped the room at as near to a run as a lady could reasonably get.

At least, a lady in full mourning attire.

She'd wanted him to kiss her.

Quite desperately.

Which would have been a mistake of mythic proportions.

Thank goodness for Lara and Mr. Durukhan, or who knew what might have happened.

What, indeed.

Isabel hurried through the maze of servants' passages that led to the kitchen of Townsend Park, knowing that she was in the middle of, quite possibly, the most craven afternoon of her life.

But what other choice had she had? She'd had to leave the room, to clear her mind, to . . . chastise herself.

What had she been thinking?

Inviting a strange man into Minerva House was one thing—one very unintelligent, risky thing. But allowing herself to consider him anything more than a means to a vital and important end? That was unacceptable.

She needed Nicholas St. John to value her marbles and to see them sold. No more.

If a lifetime around men and the women who were hurt by them had taught Isabel anything, it was that they were not to be trifled with. She'd seen enough women ruined by their hearts and their bodies, enough women—her own mother—fall victim to charming smiles and compelling touches. And she had vowed never to let it happen to her.

She was not about to allow one Londoner to change all that—no matter who thought him one of the most eligible bachelors in Britain.

She took a deep breath as she turned the final corner to the kitchen, newly prepared to ignore the presence of Lord Nicholas in her house. How difficult could it be? The man was an antiquarian. He would certainly be interested only in antiquities. It would be easy enough to avoid him.

Besides . . . she had a house to feed.

A house to *purchase.*

A houseful of people to care for.

"You cannot make me go to school. I am an earl now. No one tells earls what to do."

At the words, Isabel came up short, just outside the kitchen. Peering around the corner, she watched James reach across the scarred wooden table for a biscuit and plop it carelessly into his tea, splashing the brown liquid over the rim of his cup. He pouted into the tea for a moment before returning his gaze to Georgiana, who was seated on the opposite side of the table.

Isabel fell back on her heels, eavesdropping. She had asked Georgiana to begin suggesting school to James, in the hopes that he would warm to the idea.

Apparently he had not done so as of yet.

"Unfortunately, James, there is always someone who can tell us what to do. Even earls." Georgiana poured herself a cup of the warm brew.

"I hate being told what to do."

"Yes, well, I don't much enjoy it, either."

"I'm clever," James said defensively.

Georgiana gave him a little smile, taking a biscuit for herself. "You are exceedingly clever. I never denied that."

"I can read. And I know my sums. And I am learning Latin. You are teaching me."

"You most certainly are. It's very impressive. But young men . . . young *earls* . . . go to school."

"What will school teach me that you cannot?"

"All sorts of things. Things that are reserved for earls."

He watched as she considered her biscuit. "You should dip it in your tea. It's better that way."

Isabel smiled. She would wager that Georgiana had never in her life soaked a biscuit in her tea.

"Like this," James added, plopping a second biscuit into his teacup before fishing out the first, several fingers submerged to the knuckle in the liquid. When he produced the treat and held it high, half of the cookie dropped back into the tea, splattering it across the table. Georgiana made a show of grimacing at the action; James laughed.

Isabel wrapped her arms around herself and leaned back against the wall. Earl or no, she was not ready to lose James to his title.

"Do you think the men from earlier go to school?" James's question was rife with curiosity.

"Oh, I am sure of it," Georgiana said. "They seemed like fine gentlemen. And fine gentlemen go to school."

There was silence then, as James considered the truth of the statement.

"I have a brother, you know," Georgiana added softly, and Isabel leaned closer to the doorway. In the three weeks that she had been here, the girl had not spoken of the life she left in London.

"Really? Does he go to school?"

"He did do. In fact, he is very bright because of it. One of the brightest men in Britain."

And one of the most powerful, Isabel added silently.

"You must have learned from him," James said matter-of-factly, "or else how would a girl know to speak Latin?"

"I beg your pardon, Lord Reddich," Georgiana said pertly. "*Girls* know plenty of things . . . not only Latin."

Isabel couldn't stop herself from peering around the corner again. James's nose was wrinkled—he clearly wasn't sure that girls did know plenty of things. "You're the cleverest girl I know."

Isabel raised her brows at the reverence she heard in his tone. She would ignore the insult to her own intelligence in light of her brother's obvious infatuation with his governess—certainly the prettiest one he'd ever had—but she could not resist interrupting their cozy chat.

Pasting a bright smile upon her face, she entered the room with a cheerful "Is it time for tea already?"

James turned eager eyes on her. "Isabel! What happened to the men? One of them was very large! Did you notice?"

Yes. And one of them was very handsome. I nearly made a cabbagehead of myself.

Isabel moved to pour herself a cup of tea. "I certainly did."

"Where are they? Will they stay here?"

"They are still abovestairs, in the statuary."

"May I go and see them?" His eager face was almost impossible to resist.

"You may not."

"Why? I am the earl now, you know. It is my job to keep the residents of Townsend Park safe—I think they should meet me."

James's reference to safety—so soon after his concern for her earlier—surprised Isabel. They had always done everything they could to keep the seriousness of the girls' situations from James, but he was growing older, and more astute, and Isabel sensed that this conversation required more care than usual. "I appreciate that," she said with a nod, "and I agree that your role as earl is critical to the safety of the manor. But these gentlemen shall be very busy when they are here and we cannot afford to have them distracted." Isabel considered James's determined look. "Perhaps we shall have them to dinner one evening. How does that sound?"

James considered the option seriously. "I should think it would be the right and gracious thing for us to do."

Isabel popped a piece of biscuit into her mouth. "I am so happy you agree," she said with a wink to Georgiana, who hid her smile in her teacup. "Now . . . off with you."

James considered the two women before obviously deciding that there were more interesting adventures to be had beyond the kitchen. Stealing an extra biscuit, he hopped down from his chair and left, into the darkened corridor from which Isabel had come.

Isabel assumed her brother's seat, reaching for another biscuit herself. With a sigh, she looked to the young woman across the table and said, "Thank you for speaking with him about school."

"I am happy to. An earl needs a proper education, Lady Isabel."

"You know you may dispense with the formalities, Georgiana."

The other woman smiled. "On the contrary. I am your servant."

"Nonsense," Isabel scoffed. "We both know you are of a higher rank than I. Please. It would make me feel better for you to call me Isabel."

A flicker of sadness passed in the girl's gaze. "My rank is that of governess now. I am lucky to have such a valued position as that."

Isabel knew she was getting nowhere, and changed the course of the conversation. "Do you know the men who arrived today?"

Georgiana shook her head. "I was working on the afternoon's lessons for James and did not hear that they had arrived until after you had shown them to the statuary."

"They are Londoners."

"Aristocracy?" An edge crept into Georgiana's tone.

"Not entirely. Lord Nicholas St. John. Brother to the Marquess of Ralston—the antiquar—" Isabel stopped as Georgiana's eyes widened to saucers. "Georgiana?"

"Lord Nicholas and my brother—they are—acquainted." She lowered her voice to a whisper. "I have not met him, but—"

Of course they would know each other. One more thing that made the whole situation a challenge.

"Georgiana." Isabel's voice was firm and smooth. "You will be all right. When I took you in, I told you that Minerva House would care for you, did I not?"

The younger woman swallowed and took a deep breath. "Yes."

"Then care for you it shall," Isabel said calmly. "We shall simply keep you well hidden. 'Tis a large house. And you are James's governess—there is little reason why a guest should see you."

"Why is he here? In Yorkshire?"

"I do not know. I was led to believe that he was simply on a summer journey." She paused, considering the girl's fear. "You are safe under the protection of the Earl of Reddich."

As safe as any of us can be.

Isabel rejected the small, contrary voice in her head.

They were safe. She would make sure of it.

Georgiana remained silent in the face of Isabel's words. Eventually, she nodded once, placing her trust in Isabel—in the house.

"Good." Isabel poured more tea for them both, hoping to reinforce the girl's calm before she added, "When you are ready to discuss your reasons for coming here, I am ready to hear them. You know that, do you not?"

Georgiana nodded again. "I do. I simply— I am not— What if—"

"When and if you are ready, Georgiana, I shall be here." Isabel's words were simple and direct. She had years of experience coaxing young women out from their fear. Sisters of dukes or barmaids from Cheapside, girls were not that much different from one another.

Not that different from her.

If she had had another choice, she would never have allowed Lord Nicholas St. John into her house.

But the threat of the other choice—of turning Georgiana, and the others, out into the world with nothing but the clothes on their backs—was unthinkable. And so Isabel was taking a calculated risk.

Lord Nicholas.

The irony was not lost on Isabel that she was placing the future of a houseful of women into the hands of one of the most dangerously compelling men she'd ever met. But as she looked at Georgiana, small and uncertain, both hands wrapped around her teacup, her gaze fixed on the liquid inside, Isabel knew that he was their best chance at success. Their best hope for a future.

They would simply have to keep him confined to the statuary.

That would not be so difficult.

* * *

The next afternoon, Isabel was feeling exceedingly proud of herself.

All her worrying about Lord Nicholas had been for naught.

He was no trouble at all.

In fact, since he and Mr. Durukhan had arrived that morning and she had closeted them in the statuary and delivered careful instructions that they were not to be disturbed, Isabel had effectively avoided the pair.

Hidden from the pair, more like.

Nonsense. Isabel shook the thought away. So she was on the roof once more. The roof was still leaking. And, if the clouds careening toward them from the east were any indication, the repairs were going to be particularly welcome that evening.

So she was in breeches and shirtsleeves with Jane, and they were on their knees carefully applying a wicked-smelling paste to the underside of the clay tiles that seemed to have come loose all across the roof. It had been seven years since the first of the Townsend Park servants had left, including the skilled men—those who were most marketable to other large estates across the county. With them had gone any knowledge of the craft of roof repair, stone and woodworking, and several other skills that came in particularly handy on a country estate.

Isabel sighed at the memory. She supposed they had been lucky to have gone so many years without needing to take on major structural repairs of the house. Thank goodness for the manor's library, and its collection of titles on architecture and building practices. She smiled wryly. Roof repair was not the preferred reading of most young ladies, but it would do if she could remove the chamber pot currently perched on the end of her bed to capture the rain that seeped regularly through the poorly tarred roof.

"Would you like to tell me what happened yesterday to send you into hiding from Lord Nicholas?"

Jane had never been one to beat about the bush.

Isabel dipped a brush into the bucket of vile roof tar and said, "Nothing happened."

"Nothing whatsoever."

Nothing I'd like to revisit.

"No. He agreed to identify and value the collection. I thought I would let him get on with it. If all goes well, Minerva House shall have a new home within the month." She tried to keep her voice light. Confident.

Jane was quiet as she laid several newly repaired tiles back down upon the roof. "And Lord Nicholas?"

"What about him?"

"Precisely."

"I would prefer that he were not necessary to the endeavor," Isabel said, deliberately misunderstanding Jane's question. A strong gust of wind blew then, sending Isabel's shirtsleeves flapping like sails in a storm. She braced herself against the cool breeze, choosing her next words carefully. "But I think that we do not have much of an alternative."

"You have alternatives, Isabel."

"None that I can see."

Jane placed several more tiles in the silence that stretched between them before turning back to Isabel. "You have cared for us for a long time. You have made Minerva House a thing of legend for girls across London. The ones who come to us now . . . they can barely credit our existence. All that is because of you." Isabel stopped tarring her tiles, meeting Jane's cool green gaze. "But you cannot allow the legend to overtake you."

"It is not a legend for me, Jane. It is real."

"But you could have more. You are the daughter of an earl."

"An earl with morals best described as questionable."

"The sister to a new earl, then," Jane rephrased. "You could marry. Live the life you were meant to live."

The life she was meant to live. The words seemed so simple—as though it were clearly mapped out—and perhaps it was. Other wellborn girls seemed to have no trouble following the well-worn path.

Other girls had not had her father. Her mother.

She shook her head. "No. *This* is the life I was meant to have. No smart marriage, no amount of tea with the ladies of the *ton*, no London seasons would have changed my course. And look at where my course has taken me. Look at the difference I have made for you. For the others."

"But you should not sacrifice yourself for us. Would that not defeat the purpose of the house? Have you not taught us that our happiness and our lives are infinitely more important than the sacrifices we made before we arrived here?"

The words were soft, their aim true. Isabel considered her butler, the bracing wind turning Jane's cheeks a ruddy pink, her warm brown hair slipping out from beneath her cap. Jane had been the first to come to Isabel, a working girl who had barely escaped a drunken beating at the hands of a customer and somehow found the courage to leave London for Scotland, where she had hoped to start a new life. She had made it as far as Yorkshire with a handful of stolen coins—not enough on which to live, but enough to send her to prison for thievery for the rest of her life. When she had run out of money, she had been dropped, literally, onto the side of the road with nothing but the clothes on her back. Isabel had found her asleep in an unused stall in the stables, the day after her last remaining servants had left their posts.

Isabel had been barely seventeen, alone in the house with James, just shy of three years old, and her mother—close to death. One look at Jane, too weak to run, too broken to fight, and Isabel had understood the desperation that had driven the girl to take the most extreme of risks—bedding down in a stable not her own, clearly a part of an estate.

It had not been kindness that had driven Isabel to welcome Jane in—it had been panic. The countess was slipping away, mad with sadness and desperation, the servants were gone, James needed love and nurturing, and Isabel had nothing. She had offered Jane work and gained the most loyal of servants. The most trusted of friends.

Jane had been the only one to witness the countess in her

last days, as she railed against Isabel; against smiling, toddling James; against God and Britain—blaming them all for her isolation. For her devastation. When the countess had died—even as the other threads of Isabel's life were coming unraveled—helping Jane had kept Isabel from falling apart.

Within weeks, Isabel had made her decision to bring others to Townsend Park. If she could not be a good daughter or a good woman, she could ensure that other women on the edges of society would have a place to live and flourish. A few well-placed letters had brought her Gwen and Kate, and after that, there was little need to advertise their location. Girls found them. Townsend Park was renamed Minerva House in hushed whispers across Britain, and girls in trouble knew that if they could reach its doors, they would find safety.

In those girls, Isabel had found a purpose—a way to protect these ill-treated, ill-fated women, and to give them a fresh opportunity at life.

A way to prove that she was more than what others saw.

A way to feel needed.

Not all the girls had remained—in the seven years since Jane's arrival, they had seen dozens of girls arrive and leave in the dead of night, unable to keep from returning to the life from which they had come. Still more had left to build their own lives, Isabel welcoming the chance to help them realize their dreams. They were seamstresses, innkeepers, and even a vicar's wife in the North Country.

They were proof that she was not alone. That she had purpose. That she was more than the unwanted daughter of a notorious scoundrel. That she was not the selfish child her mother had accused her of being during those final weeks.

And when she was thinking of them—of Minerva House—she was not thinking of all that she had never had an opportunity to experience.

All the things she would have deserved—would have had—if she were born to a different earl.

No.

"It is not a sacrifice to continue Minerva House," she said finally, the words almost too quiet to be heard on the wind. "I would repair a hundred roofs to make sure this one held above the girls' heads."

Jane quirked a smile. "Need I remind you that you are not alone atop this house? I shall never be able to remove the smell of this muck from my person."

"Well then, we shall stink together." Isabel laughed.

"Your lord shan't enjoy that."

Isabel did not pretend to misunderstand. "He is not my lord."

"Gwen and Lara would have it differently."

Isabel's brows snapped together. "Gwen and Lara have cowslips between their ears. I won't be thrust at him, Jane. You might as well tell them as much."

Jane laughed then, the sound musical and merry. "You think *I* hold more sway than that ridiculous magazine?"

"I think you should," Isabel said with a sigh. "He is only here for two weeks. All I need do is keep the girls from the statuary."

"And what of you, Lady He-Is-Not-My-Lord?"

Isabel ignored Jane's teasing, a vision of Lord Nicholas's handsome face flashing. The way his teeth flashed white against his sun-warmed skin, how his full, soft lips turned upward in bold, promising smiles. The way his blue eyes tempted her to tell him everything.

He was very dangerous, indeed.

"I shall do the same. It shan't be that difficult. After all, I have a roof to repair."

The words were barely out of Isabel's mouth when a familiar masculine voice sounded. "I should have guessed I would find you here."

Isabel's heart leapt into her throat at the words. Eyes filled with dread, Isabel looked to Jane, who immediately put her head down, as any good servant would, focusing entirely on the task at hand.

She was on her own, or they were discovered. With little

other option, she turned to Lord Nicholas, who was climbing out of the attic window.

Who had let him up here?

She watched as one enormous Hessian boot took a tentative step toward her, landing precariously on the clay tile.

If the man wasn't careful, he'd damage more of the damned roof.

"Wait!"

To his credit, he waited.

"I—" Isabel looked to Jane, who shook her head in a manner indicating that she would be absolutely no help, then pressed on. "I shall come to you, my lord!" Scrambling to her feet, she scurried across the roof as carefully as possible. When she reached him, she smiled a too-bright smile.

Which he did not return.

"My lord! What brings you to the roof? Was there something that you needed?"

"No," he said, the one syllable drawn out into many as he raked his gaze over her, taking in her attire.

Dear God. She was dressed in men's clothing. Not at all the thing. *Of course, ladies on roofs were not precisely the thing, either.* Nonetheless, her attire was a problem. And leaping from the roof seemed like a not so sound solution. She'd simply have to brazen it through.

She crossed her arms over her breasts, ignoring the flood of heat that spread over her cheeks. "I was not expecting you to join me, Lord Nicholas," she said pointedly.

"I can see that. Although I do admit a modicum of surprise that you would dress so in front of your servants." He indicated Jane, who remained head down, setting a roof tile.

"Oh." *How was she going to escape this?* "Yes. Well. Jan—" *Careful, Isabel.* "Janney has been with the family for many years. *He* is aware of all of my—eccentricities." She laughed, wincing at the sound, loud and uncomfortable.

"I see." His tone said he did not, in fact, see.

"Shall we go inside? Perhaps you would like some tea?"

she said quickly, as though she could rush him off the roof, out of the house, and, indeed, out of Yorkshire.

"No, I don't think so."

"My lord?"

"I should like to see this roof that has so captured your attention."

"I— Oh."

Was it she? Or did he seem *pleased* with her discomfort?

"Will you give me a tour of the repair site, my lady?"

He was most definitely teasing her.

He was a wretched man. Not at all worthy of kissing.

"Certainly." Isabel turned to Jane—she had to get the other woman off the roof. "That is enough for today, Janney. You may go."

Jane was up like a shot, heading for the attic window like it was salvation itself.

Which, of course, it was.

But as she passed them, St. John stayed her with "You should be more protective of your mistress."

Jane paused, head down, and nodded once.

"I see you take my meaning."

Isabel held her breath for a long moment, waiting for him to continue. When he did not, she said, "That is all, Janney," and Jane scrambled through the window, disappearing into the attic.

Watching her disappear, Isabel considered her options. While she had never received formal training in deportment and proper conversation, she was fairly certain that roofs were not appropriate locales for conversations between members of the opposite sex.

"I do not like you on the roof."

The words, so imperious, as though she were placed on the earth at his whim, took Isabel aback. She met his gaze, and took pleasure in matching his irritation with her own. *It wasn't as if she'd asked him to join her up here, for goodness' sake.* "Well, considering it is both my roof and my person . . . I do not see how my location impacts your life in the slightest."

"If you were to fall . . ."

She lifted one foot, showing him her slippers. "I have an excellent tread."

His gaze tracked the limb, from the leg of her breeches down the curving slope of her stockinged calf, to her foot, and the perusal made her instantly nervous. She set her foot down firmly, the clank of the roof tiles punctuating the movement. One hand flew nervously to her hair, pulled back into a tight knot. "I think we should go inside."

He moved to sit on the peak of the roof. Surveying the work that she and Jane had completed, he asked, "Why did you leave me in the statuary yesterday?"

It was not a question shc had expected. "My lord?"

"*Leave* is not really the appropriate word, is it? *Flee* is more apt."

"I prefer *escape*, actually."

Her frankness surprised them both. He inclined his head. "A palpable hit, Lady Isabel."

She blushed at his words, embarrassed by her statement, but refused to back down. "I haven't time to languish in the statuary with you, Lord Nicholas. I have far too much to do."

"Need I remind you that it is you who asked me to attend your marbles?"

The color on her cheeks flared higher. He was calling her rude. *And he was not entirely incorrect.* "You needn't. I am very grateful for your help, my lord."

His eyes narrowed on her. "I am happy to give it, but you must admit, our time together has been rather . . . unorthodox."

She smiled crookedly. "I suppose our current location does not remedy that."

"Nor your clothing, Lady Isabel." He matched her smile with his own before he asked again, "Why did you flee the statuary?"

"I—I did not have a choice."

She thought he would press her further, but there must have been something in her tone that stayed the line of questioning.

There was a long silence before he changed tack. "I think you should tell me why you are repairing the roof."

She gave a little shrug. "I told you already, my lord. It leaks. Which makes it quite unpleasant when it rains. As this is Britain, it rains a great deal."

He draped one long arm over a bent knee and looked out over the lands, ignoring her tone. "You deliberately misunderstand me. I see I have no choice but to use my only currency." He sighed, then recited, "Voluptas, the daughter of Cupid and Psyche, is made of pink marble from Mergozzo, an area in the Alps known for it."

"That statue isn't pink. And it isn't Italian."

He shot her a look, and she was lost in the glittering blue of his eyes before she noted the twitch in the muscle of his cheek. She wondered what the movement meant.

"The statue is made of pink *marble* from Mergozzo," he repeated slowly, as though she were simpleminded. "Pink marble is not always pink. And the piece is not Italian. It is Roman. She is a Roman goddess."

She knew what he was doing—he was forcing her to answer his question about the roof with his information about the statue.

If he was right, she was laid bare.

"You must be mistaken," Isabel said, unconcerned by the insult that the words carried.

"I assure you, I am not. Voluptas is nearly always portrayed wrapped in roses. If that were not enough, her face confirms her identity."

"You cannot tell a goddess from a face carved in marble," she scoffed.

"You can tell Voluptas by her face."

"I've never even heard of this goddess, and you know what she looks like?"

"She is the goddess of sensual pleasure."

Isabel's mouth fell open at the words. She could not think of a single thing to say in response. "Oh."

"Her face reflects as much. Pleasure, bliss, passion, ecsta—"

"Yes, I see," Isabel interrupted, noting the amusement in his eyes. "You are enjoying yourself, aren't you?"

"Immensely." He grinned then, and she had to catch herself from returning it. She scowled at him, and he laughed; the sound was more welcoming than she was willing to admit. "Come, Lady Isabel, sit with me and tell me tales of a manor roof in need of mending."

She could not resist. She did as he asked.

Once she was seated, he did not look at her, instead looking out at the front gardens of the house, in the direction of the road. After a long silence, he asked quietly, "Why are you repairing the roof? With none but your butler to help you?"

She breathed deep, the warm summer wind swirling around them, unfettered by trees or buildings high atop the roof. Registering the dampness in the air that signaled an impending summer storm, Isabel felt a pang of regret that the clouds had not yet come, and she was out of ways to avoid answering his question. Only the truth was left.

"I cannot afford a roofer," she said simply, looking down and brushing imaginary dust from one of the warm brown tiles beneath them. "I cannot afford to hire a man with the skill. I do not have a man I can trust besides—Janney."

"What of the footmen?"

Well, to start with, my lord, they are footwomen.

"They are busy doing the things that footmen do," she said, her shoulders rising in an almost imperceptible shrug. "I can learn to roof as well as the next person."

He was silent for a long moment, until she finally looked at him, registering the understanding in his eyes—eyes the color of a brilliant summer sky. That silly magazine had been right. They were a distractingly beautiful shade of blue. "Most ladies of your standing do *not* learn to roof as well as the next person, however."

She smiled at his words, self-conscious. "That is true. But most ladies of my standing do not do many of the things that I do."

He considered her, and she imagined admiration in his look. "That, I would believe." He shook his head. "Certainly there is not another earl's daughter in the kingdom with your fearlessness."

She looked away, out at the grounds. *Not fearlessness. Desperation.* "Well, I would guess that if there were another earl like my father, there might be another earl's daughter like me. You may thank any one of the gods in the statuary that they broke the mold for the Wastrearl."

"You knew then of your father's pursuits."

"Not of their specifics, but even tucked away in Yorkshire, a child hears things."

"I am sorry."

She shook her head. "Do not be. He left seven years ago; James barely knew him and I have not seen him since."

"I am even more sorry for that, then. I know what it is to lose a parent to something less than death."

She met his eyes at that. Saw that he was telling the truth. Wondered, fleetingly, what the story might have been. "The loss of my father was not much of a loss at all. We were certainly better off without his setting an example here." He watched her closely for a long moment, until she became uncomfortable under his too-knowing gaze and she returned her attention to the darkening sky. "I will not deny that a shilling or two would have been appreciated."

"He left you nothing?"

She shuttered at the question; she was willing to admit her dire financial straits, but not to discuss them. She would not accept his pity. He seemed the type of man who would press for more. Who would want to help.

And she could not afford to allow him in.

She traced the curve of one roof tile, feeling the ache in her shoulders. The prick of worry that had been gone for the last few moments returned. There had been a brief moment when she had shared her burden—when it had felt good and right.

But this was not a burden to be shared. This was hers. It had been from the day her father had left, when she had taken responsibility for the estate and its people. She had done her best with no help from anyone else, regardless of how often she asked. And so she had learned her lesson—that an impoverished estate and a houseful of misfits was not something of which aristocratic gentlemen cared to be a part.

Particularly not wealthy, successful lords who happened to be passing through Yorkshire.

"The collection is worth a great deal, Isabel."

She took several seconds to comprehend the meaning of his words, so disconnected from her thoughts. "It is?"

"Without doubt."

"Enough to–" She stopped. There were so many ways to end the sentence . . . too many ways. Enough to buy a house? To care for the girls? To send James to school? To restore the Townsend name after years of profligacy had ruined it?

She could not say any of those things, of course, without revealing her secrets. And so she said nothing.

"Enough to repair this roof and much more."

She exhaled, her relief nearly unbearable.

"Thank God."

The whisper was barely sound, lost in a wicked clap of thunder that sent a jolt of shock through her, pressing her closer to the bulk of him there on the high peak of Townsend Park. Feeling his heat next to her, she turned to look at him. He was staring down at her, an intoxicating mix of danger and curiosity and inspection in his gaze. It was the last that made her pulse race, as though he might be able to look deep into her and discover everything that she had been hiding for so long.

Perhaps that would not be so terrible.

She knew it was a sign of weakness, but she could not look away. His eyes were so blue, the understanding there so tempting—almost enough to make her forget all her rules.

She had no chance to act on the temptation.

Instead, the skies opened, and the universe intervened.

Seven

Rain did not come lightly to the summers of Yorkshire—it came with a vengeance, as though the entire county had done something to deserve it. But in the case of this particular afternoon, Nick knew precisely who had brought the wrath of the heavens down upon them.

He had.

When, like an utter cad, he had seriously considered kissing Lady Isabel Townsend on her roof, on the heels of her rather raw confession of poverty.

She had looked at him with those enormous brown eyes, and he had known that she would let him kiss her. But not for any reason other than her obvious gratitude for his help.

And gratitude was not a viable reason for a rooftop liaison.

So, when the skies opened above them, for every ounce of him that wanted to shout his frustration to the heavens, there was an equal amount that was thankful for the interruption.

Until the lightning flashed, wicked and green, and he realized that if they remained atop the manor house, they were not only going to be soaked, but they would also very likely be killed.

The thought spurred him into action, and he wrapped

an arm around Isabel's shoulders, shepherding her up and through the downpour, toward the attic window. Just as they reached the entryway, she turned, ducking under his arm with alarming speed and heading across the roof to the spot where she had been working earlier.

"Our roof paste!"

Between the wet tile roof and the torrential rain and the real risk of a lightning strike, the last of his patience evaporated. "Isabel!" Her name carried across the roof, as ominous as the thunder that crashed around them, and she froze, turning back, eyes wide and uncertain. "Leave it!"

"I cannot!" She shook her head and turned away, down the slope of the roof, her words carrying back to him on the wind that stung his face. "It took us hours to make it!"

"You can and you will!" He said.

She looked over her shoulder at the demand, eyes flashing. "You are not my keeper, my lord."

She did not check her footing as she continued on her path.

Which was a mistake.

Her slipper dislodged a loose clay tile, sending it skidding down the pitched roof and over the edge, the movement knocking Isabel off balance. He registered the fear in her eyes as she began to fall, and he was already moving toward her.

She reached out to catch herself, the force of the impact dislodging more tiles and sending them crashing to the ground far below. She scrambled then, fear making her desperate, the movement only serving to increase her instability.

He was there, capturing her hand in a firm grasp, staying her movement. He said nothing when their eyes met, the anger in his gaze chasing away the desperation in hers.

He said nothing as she steadied herself and regained her footing, allowing him to help her up and hold her steady, as she took deep, calming breaths to settle her racing pulse.

He said nothing as he lifted her into his arms and carried her the several feet to the attic window.

Only when he set her down at the open entrance did he

speak. "I may not be your keeper, Isabel, but if you cannot take responsibility for your own safety, someone must do it for you." He pointed to the attic window. "Inside. Now."

Whether because of his tone or the rain or some innate sense of self-preservation, she did as she was told. Miraculously.

Nick watched as she climbed into the attic, ensured that she was safely inside, and went back to fetch the damned roof paste she so valued.

Pail in hand, he looked out across the lands to the stables, where the boy he'd met earlier in the day was closing the door to the stables, using his entire weight to do so. He ran toward the manor house then, wind and rain pelting his young face. The boy put his head down, protecting his face from the wind, and the movement took the cap from his head, releasing his hair to the elements.

His very long hair.

Nick stiffened, watching as the stable boy turned to fetch the cap as it rolled over the ground, spun on the invisible fingers of the Yorkshire wind. His hair flew out behind him in long red ribbons, immediately soaked with rain. And when the boy turned back, facing the house once more, there was no question of what the secret of Townsend Park was.

He played over the servants in his mind: the stable boy; the effeminate butler; the motley collection of diminutive, unmatched footmen.

She had a houseful of women.

That was why she was on the roof, nearly killing herself.

Because there was no one else to do it for her.

He swore harshly at the thought, the word lost in the howl of the wind whipping over the edge of the roof. Houseful of women or no, there was no excuse for her complete and utter carelessness. She should be locked in a room for sanity's sake. His sanity.

Thunder cracked high above him, sending him back to the entrance to the attic, where she peered out at him, rivulets of water coursing down her face. He thrust the pail of muck at her.

She took it and backed away from the window as he followed her inside.

He took a long moment to close the window behind him, latching it tight against the sheets of rain that pounded the glass before he turned back to her, soaked to the bone and not at all happy.

Setting the pail down carefully, she hesitated, then spoke in an agitated whisper. "I would have been perfectly fine—"

He thrust both his hands through his wet hair in frustration, and the movement stayed her words. Thank God. Because he might well have strangled her if she had continued.

She was the single most infuriating female he had ever met. She was a danger to herself and others. She could have gotten them both killed, for heaven's sake.

He'd had enough.

"You are not to go on the roof again." His words were quiet, but spoken in a tone that had stopped killers in their tracks.

And seemed only to incense Isabel. "I beg your pardon?"

"Evidently, years of being trapped in Yorkshire with the run of the estate failed to teach you an ounce of sense. You will stay off the roof from now on."

"Of all the imperious, condescending, arrogant things—"

"You may call it whatever you like. I call it ensuring your safety. And the safety of those around you." He paused briefly, tamping down the urge to shake her. "Did it even cross your mind that I might have been killed right along with you?"

"I didn't ask to be rescued, Lord Nicholas," she said, her voice rising.

"Yes, well, considering I have saved your life twice in the two days that I have known you, I might suggest that next time, you do ask."

She pulled herself up to her full height and let loose, apparently unconcerned with the fact that anyone near the entrance to the attic might hear them. "I was perfectly safe on the roof until *you* arrived! And did you even *consider* the idea that I was only *on* the roof because I was hiding from you?"

The confession was out before she could stop it, surprising them both.

"Hiding from *me*?"

She did not reply, deliberately looking away from him with a huff.

"You *invited* me here!"

"Well, suffice to say that I am beginning to regret it," she muttered.

"Why were you hiding from me?"

"I should think that would be rather clear." When he did not respond, she continued, eager to fill the silence. "I was surprised by our . . . moment . . . in the statuary. I had not expected . . ."

He tracked the nervous movements of her hands, smoothing over her breeches before she crossed her arms, and the white cambric of her shirt pulled tightly across her breasts, torturing him with their weight—with their lovely, shadowed peaks. He was suddenly aware of their location, in the darkened attic of her home, the rain outside muffling all sounds, the warm, small space closing in around them. It was the perfect place for a clandestine tryst.

She took a deep breath, looking up at the ceiling for a long moment. A raindrop moved slowly down her neck; he watched as it turned down the slope of her breast to disappear inside the collar of her shirt.

He was seriously contemplating becoming jealous of a droplet of water. Yorkshire was obviously damaging to his sanity.

"I had not expected to be so . . ." she tried again, meeting his gaze before her words trailed off.

He took a step closer; they were scant inches from each other. "So . . . ?" He knew he should not push her, but he could not help himself.

She sighed, resigned. "So . . . drawn to you."

Another step. "You are drawn to me?"

He'd never known a lady to admit such a thing. There was something overwhelming in the honesty of her confession.

She backed up then, and he watched embarrassment flood her cheeks, fierce and red. She spoke, the words coming fast. "I am sure it is just a passing phase. I think it best for you to leave. I shall find another way to sell the collection—"

Her nervousness was intoxicating.

He reached out, his fingertips brushing the soft skin at her temple, stemming the flow of her words. He pushed one long, wet lock back from her face, tucking it behind her ear before running the backs of his fingers down her cheek, soothing the heated flesh they left with his thumb.

Her eyes went wide at the touch, and he smiled, briefly, at her surprise. His free hand lifted, and his hands were cupping her face, tilting it upward to afford him a better look at her in the quiet, dimly lit space.

He should not kiss her. He knew it.

But she was like no woman he had ever known—and he wanted to know her secrets. More than that, he wanted her.

He settled his lips to hers, and she was his.

As was the case with the rest of the man, there was nothing tentative about Nicholas St. John's kisses. One moment, Isabel was battling a series of strange, unsettling emotions about the arrogant man, and the next, he had claimed her mouth in a searing kiss, robbing her of breath and thought and sanity.

She froze for a moment, savoring the feel of his lips on hers, of his hands cradling her face, of his fingers trailing down to her neck as his thumbs stroked the skin of her cheeks, setting her aflame. He held her firmly against him, his mouth playing over hers, sending wave after wave of sensation rocketing through her. The caress gentled. He lifted his mouth until it was just barely touching hers and licked her bottom lip, his tongue warm and rough against the soft skin there, and she gasped at the sensation, so foreign, so wicked.

So *magnificent.*

He captured her mouth once more, stroking until she opened for him, uncertain. She wasn't sure what to do—she was afraid to touch him, to move, to do anything that might end the caress and the pleasure that it brought.

He seemed to read her thoughts, and with a soft slide, his lips chased the path of one thumb across her cheek to her ear, where he caught the lobe between his teeth, sending a shiver of pleasure through her. "Touch me, Isabel."

This was why women turned silly for men. This heady mix of power . . . and powerlessness.

She shouldn't touch him. She knew that. But the words, combined with the sensual caress at the curve of her ear, unlocked her, and she set her hands to his chest, running them up and over his shoulders. The movement spurred him on, and he wrapped his arms around her, pulling her closer to his firmness, his heat. He pulled back, met her heavy-lidded gaze as if to confirm that she wanted it as much as he, and claimed her mouth once more.

Isabel was overwhelmed with sensation, with the stroke of his tongue, the press of his body, the scent of him. She met his caresses with her own, returning the kiss with an innocent passion that only encouraged him. She tangled her fingers in the damp hair at his neck and stood up on her toes to gain better access to his mouth. He let her explore, increasing the intensity of the kiss, then pulling back to allow her to take the lead. She ran the tip of her tongue over his full bottom lip tentatively, and his groan gave her a sense of satisfaction like nothing she'd ever felt.

He broke off the kiss then, regaining control, trailing his lips down the column of her throat and inhaling deeply at the place where her neck and shoulder met before he nipped lightly at the skin there, sending another ripple of pleasure through her. She gasped at the sensation and felt the curve of his lips against her skin in a smile that she did not have to see to know was filled with wicked promise.

He lifted his head, his blue eyes dark with heat. His mouth

opened slightly and she was transfixed by it, waiting for his next move.

"Isabel?"

The sound of her name was foreign to her, and for a fleeting moment, she was not certain from where it had come. She was too focused on the fact that Nick had released her and stepped back, away from her, putting as much distance between them as he could. She felt cold all of a sudden, the missing heat of him an intense loss. One hand flew to her lips as if to confirm that they had, in fact, been in an embrace mere seconds earlier.

"Isabel!"

The second time James called her name, realization came crashing down around her. She became acutely aware of their location, their situation, their *actions*, and she was overcome with an intense desire to escape back out the window to the roof. And to live there. For some time.

At least until Lord Nicholas left.

Instead, she looked to him, wide-eyed, and whispered, "It's my brother!"

"I gathered as much," he said dryly. "Don't you think you should answer?"

"I . . ." He was right, of course. "James!" she called, hurrying to the top of the stairs. "I am up here!"

"Izzy! Kate is looking for you!"

The mention of the stable master—who was entirely the wrong gender for a stable master—set Isabel on edge. She looked back at Nick, keenly aware of everything that had just transpired between them, and of the secrets that she had no choice but to keep from him.

Everything had just become infinitely more complicated.

Uncertain of what to say, of how one ended such an assignation, she said the first thing that came to her mind . . . the only thing that would make their situation easier. "You must leave."

"And how do you suggest I do that? Over the edge of the roof?"

She took a deep breath, desperate to regain some of the calm that she so prided herself upon. "Of course not. You may use the front door."

"How very magnanimous of you," he said, and she ignored his teasing, starting down the stairs. She had not even reached the second step when his words stopped her. "You cannot go down there looking as you do."

She waved off his words. "They've all seen me in men's clothing. It shall be fine."

"It is not your clothing to which I refer, Isabel."

She looked back at the words, meeting the glittering blue gaze that seemed to see so much. *Too much.* "What, then?"

"It is the look of you."

She raised one hand to her hair in a nervous gesture. "What do you mean? How do I look?"

"Like someone who has been thoroughly kissed."

She blushed then, the heat coming high and fast. She pressed a hand to her face, willing it away before she straightened and in her very coolest tone said, "You must leave. Immediately."

And, with that, she hurried down the stairs to deal with whatever new challenge was to be thrust in her direction.

"What do you mean, 'They cannot leave'?!"

Kate made a show of wringing out her long wet hair and leaned against the stall door of one of the two remaining horses in the Townsend Park stables. "Just what I've said. They cannot leave. The rain has flooded the post road. There is no route into town."

"They haven't a choice! They've got to leave!"

Kate's brow furrowed at Isabel's high-pitched squeak. "Isabel. I'm not sure what you would like me to do about it. I cannot direct the weather."

"We shall just have to keep the girls hidden," Jane, ever practical, said from her place just inside the stables. "We've done it before."

Isabel turned away in a fit of frustration, placing her fisted hands against her forehead and taking several deep breaths.

Turning back, she leveled the women with a stern look. "Lord Nicholas is no fool. He shall know immediately that something about Townsend Park is not what it seems. His friend shall do the same. They shall notice the lack of men."

"Not if they are too busy noticing the lack of servants," Gwen pointed out, running one finger along the curve of a saddle that had been slung over an unused stable door. "They've not seen many of us . . . we could just hide the girls and . . . well, hope for the best!" She punctuated the sentence with a grin that did nothing to comfort Isabel.

"Seven years of protecting you girls and the existence of Minerva House, and your solution is to hope for the best?" Gwen nodded happily, and Isabel's eyes narrowed suspiciously. "What has you so pleased?"

Gwen opened her mouth to speak, but before she could get a word out, Kate let out a mighty—and obviously false—cough, and Gwen's mouth closed. She shook her head and looked away. Jane moved to stroke the long muzzle of the horse nearest to her. Lara seemed transfixed by the edge of one of her kidskin gloves. Kate considered the ceiling of the stables.

Something was amiss.

Isabel looked from one woman to the next. "What is it?"

When no one answered, she tried again. "The four of you have never been able to keep something from me in your lives. What is it?"

Gwen could not keep the words in any longer. "Only that the universe appears to support our plan."

"Gwen . . ." Jane said, warning in her tone.

"Your plan?"

"Quite. You see," the cook said, looking to Lara for support, "*Pearls and Pelisses*—"

"Of course," Isabel said. "I should have known this would have something to do with that ridiculous magazine."

"*Pearls and Pelisses*," Gwen repeated emphatically, "tells us that the very best way to secure the interest of a lord is to keep him near! And what better way to keep him near than a rainstorm that does not look as though it is letting up any time soon? Why, we do not even have to fabricate a reason to keep you in his thoughts! Nature has done it for us!"

Isabel's brows shot up. "You assume that I have a desire to secure the man's interest! The only thing I want him taking an interest in is the statuary!" Returning her attention to Kate, she said, "There really is no way to get them back to Dunscroft?"

Kate shook her head. "None whatsoever. I expect the road will be passable in the morning, assuming the rain stops sometime during the night, but I would not send horses into this weather—nor strangers to the area."

"I assume that you are telling me the truth and not fabricating some issue to aid in Gwen's lunacy?"

Kate looked at Isabel as though she'd grown a second head. "Do you really think I would support anything related to that magazine?"

Isabel threw her hands up and looked to Lara. "What am I to do?"

"We shall have to soldier on and consider this cloud's silver lining." Lara paused, entertained by her pun.

"There is no silver lining in this cloud, Lara. Only a flooded road and a man who is far too observant for his own good."

"Nonsense!" Lara said. "This means he will have additional time to work in the statuary! Perhaps this turn of events will speed his process!"

Isabel doubted it.

"And you forget the most important part," Jane added.

"Which is?"

"As long as the road is flooded, we are free of Viscount Densmore."

Isabel considered the words. Jane wasn't incorrect. There were not many worse things than Lord Nicholas being trapped at Townsend Park . . . but Densmore's arrival was one of them.

"Perhaps Lord Nicholas can provide us with information on the viscount?" Gwen's whisper echoed through the stables.

"I would rather Lord Nicholas not have any further insight into our troubles," Isabel said. "It is bad enough that we are stuck with him for the evening."

Particularly bad for her.

"They seem to be good men," Lara said, drawing the attention of the rest of the group.

Gwen said, "Do they?"

"Well, I have not spent any length of time with Lord Nicholas . . ." Lara hedged, "but Mr. Durukhan . . . seems charming."

"Charming," Kate repeated.

"Yes. Charming. Well, nice. Nice enough, at least."

They all studied Lara for a long moment, until she turned away to give her attention to one of the large horses that had arrived with the objects of their discussion. The movement betrayed her, and the women looked to one another, each confirming the others' suspicions.

"Lara," Isabel teased, happy for the distraction from her own troubles, "has the giant captured your attention?"

Lara looked back at them, wide-eyed. "I did not say that!"

"You did not have to," Kate said. "It's clear from the rose in your cheeks."

And it was. Isabel watched as Lara opened her mouth then closed it, and immediately understood her cousin's struggle. She knew precisely what it was to be so turned around by a man she had met merely a day earlier.

"I heard Lord Nicholas call him Rock yesterday," Kate said. "It seems an apt name for such a massive creature."

Lara thought for a while before responding, simply, "He has kind eyes."

Isabel grinned at the description of the enormous Turk, wondering how long it would be before her guests had ensorcelled every woman in the house. After all, these were not the same kind of men that the residents of Minerva House were accustomed to—they were charming and handsome and intelligent. . .

And superior at kissing.

No. She would not consider the positive aspects of the man. In order to retain any semblance of sanity while he was in her house, risking everything for which she had worked, she must remember his overpowering arrogance, his flippant challenges, his absolutely unacceptable behavior in the attic.

Of course, she'd had no trouble accepting it at the time.

Her experiences with men were spare; aside from the shopkeepers in town and the vicar, there was little reason for her to interact with the opposite sex—particularly unmarried, eligible Londoners with wide shoulders and arms like steel and eyes bluer than any should be.

No.

She had spent her life eschewing wealthy, charming men-about-town who captured the eye of every female in the vicinity with their perfectly tied cravats and quick, easy smiles. Men who delighted in robbing others of their happiness.

Men like her father.

Men who ultimately ruined everything. Who made mockeries of their marriages, who turned starry-eyed women who had once loved them into desperate, self-loathing females who would do anything to find a reason for the loss of their husbands.

And then Lord Nicholas St. John had arrived, all handsome face and imperious arrogance, and she had expected him to be one of them. And, instead, he had agreed to help her, he had put himself in harm's way to ensure her safety, had assured her that her problems could be overcome—all in the span of a few hours.

No wonder he made her so nervous. There was nothing about this man that was normal. Nothing that even came close to what *normal* meant to Isabel.

Now he was stuck in her house. A guest. Among two

dozen women, hiding from any number of evils that might come down around them.

And, to make matters worse, he'd kissed her.

Not that she had stopped him from kissing her. Or even considered doing so.

For years, she had dreamed of what her first kiss would be like. She had considered it in countless places, with any number of faceless, nameless men, each one a hero in his own right, as part of professions of love, proposals of marriage, and other fantasies that plagued young, innocent girls.

And all the while, she'd known there was no point in the dreams. Because heroes did not exist. And there was no truth to the idea that love completed women. Indeed, in her experience, love only lessened women—made them pained and desolate and weak.

She did not want that.

And yet, in Lord Nicholas's arms, she had glimpsed that ephemeral promise—that temptation—that came with being the focus of all his attention. And in that moment, she had been a girl again, dreaming of her first kiss.

She had never imagined, however, that her first kiss would be with a virtual stranger, in the musty attic of her ancestral home, after nearly toppling off a roof.

To be fair, she also hadn't imagined her first kiss would be quite so very wonderful.

And she was certain that in all her fantasies, no matter how secret, she'd never imagined her first kiss would be with a man who was so . . . well . . . male.

She gave a little sigh, drawing the attention of the other women. Jane's eyes narrowed on her. "Isabel? Is there something you would like to share?"

Isabel looked down, making a show of adjusting the cuffs of her breeches, drenched in rain. "No, why should there be?"

"What happened after I left you on the roof with Lord Nicholas?"

"You were *alone* with him? How wonderful! *Pearls and*

Pelisses tells us that you must remain in his mind . . . and in his eye!" Gwen was thrilled.

One side of Isabel's mouth kicked up. "Yes, well, since we've trapped the poor man here, I think he's about to have more than enough of me in his mind and in his eye. Whatever that is supposed to mean."

"Well, either way, leaving them alone on the roof was a capital idea, Jane! Well done!"

Jane rolled her eyes. "It was not entirely my idea. Had I stayed, I think he might well have noticed that I am not a man. I was saved by the fact that he could barely tear his gaze from Isabel."

Isabel snapped her head up to meet Jane's gaze. "That is not true!"

Was it?

"Really?" Kate said. "That *would* explain his strange reaction to you on the roof yesterday."

"It was not a strange reaction!" Isabel protested. "It isn't every day that a lady is on the roof of her home, Kate."

"I noticed it, too," Lara chimed in, apparently past her discomfort with the women's earlier line of questioning. "In the statuary yesterday. He is intrigued by her."

"He is not!"

She was not at all intriguing. *Was she*?

"What happened after I left the roof?" Jane asked, her tone deceptively casual.

"Nothing happened. It started to rain and we came in." Isabel bit her tongue. Perhaps the others had not noticed the nervousness in her words, which had come too fast.

They noticed. Four sets of eyes were upon her, so intent that she had to remind herself that kisses did not leave a mark. "We were wet."

Kate's gaze narrowed. "Were you?"

"And then what?" Gwen's words were breathless with excitement.

Their rapt attention was disconcerting. She looked up and spoke to the ceiling, frustration in her words, her voice an octave higher than usual. "And then nothing! Then James called and said Kate needed me, and I rushed out of the room because I was terrified he would reference the stables or something else that would give away the fact that the entire house is populated with a motley crew of *nearly*-servants who only *appear* to be men!"

A heavy silence fell, and Isabel looked back to the other women, registering their identical, wide-eyed looks, focused on a point beyond her left shoulder. An immediate sense of dread came over her as she turned to look in the direction of their singular gaze.

Of course.

Standing in the doorway of the stables was Mr. Durukhan, mouth slightly ajar, looking from Jane to Kate, taking in their masculine attire, the tightly fitted cap that hid Kate's hair from view, the stark, old-fashioned queue that Jane preferred. His gaze took in every little feature that they could not hide: unstubbled chins; Kate's high, arching brow and long neck; Jane's stunning cheekbones and wide mouth.

They were caught.

He cleared his throat and gave a little mock bow in their general direction. "Lady Isabel, Miss Lara," he said, ignoring Isabel's breeches quite well, "I had come to speak with your . . . stable master to discuss our departure."

There was a beat of silence, punctuated only by Rock's horse, stomping in his stall at the sound of his master's voice. The women had been rendered mute. If she were not so horrified, Isabel would have been amused.

None of them was willing to be the first to speak—to acknowledge what he had so obviously overheard.

Isabel swallowed nervously. She was the mistress of the house. It was her responsibility to speak. To manage this. To do what she could to protect their secrets . . . the ones that she had not carelessly revealed. "Mr. Durukhan—"

"Please," he interrupted, a half smile slicing across his bronzed skin, "Rock will do."

"Oh . . . I . . . we couldn't."

The smile became a full-blown grin then. "Prior to this particular moment, my lady, I would have agreed. However, it appears that we all have a much more . . . familiar . . . relationship now, do you not agree?"

Gwen snickered and received one of Kate's elbows in the ribs for her trouble. Isabel ignored the cry of pain and the furious whisper that came from their direction, instead watching with a looming panic as the enormous man's dark, knowing gaze returned to Kate and Jane, tracing first one, then the other's body from cap to boot—as if again confirming the information he had overheard.

Oh, Isabel. She closed her eyes briefly. *How could you have been so foolish?*

She'd been distracted and flustered, all the result of Lord Nicholas. If he hadn't insisted on causing such complete upheaval. . .

Oh, no. Lord Nicholas. Surely Rock would tell him everything. Which meant it was only a matter of time before everyone in London knew about Minerva House. . .

Dread settled in the pit of Isabel's stomach. If he found out, everything would be ruined.

Perhaps there was a way to keep it from him. Perhaps the man in front of them would. . .

"I assume you have a very good reason for such a masquerade?"

Isabel blinked at the words, deceptively casual. "Sir?"

Rock turned dark eyes on her. "Your stable master, my lady. And your butler. I assume that their . . . uniforms . . . they serve a purpose?"

Isabel's gaze narrowed. What was he getting at? "We . . . yes."

He nodded once, firmly. "I did not doubt it."

"I—" she started, not knowing what to say. "We—" She looked to the others for assistance, but none of the women seemed eager to enter the discussion. "That is . . ." *Oh, for heaven's sake, Isabel. Out with it.* "I hope you will keep our secret, sir."

He considered her for a long time, the steady fall of the rain on the roof of the stable the only sound. Isabel worked very hard not to fidget under his focused gaze. "You want me to keep it from St. John."

This was it. The moment of truth. "That is precisely what I would like."

He went silent, and Isabel felt sick at the idea that he might refuse her. Her mind began to race, cataloguing the locations and the people where she could send the girls quickly—to disperse the occupants of Minerva House before anyone from London discovered their whereabouts. She would not let her foolish outburst cause any one of them harm.

"It is done."

She was so wrapped up in her panic that she almost missed the words. "I—I beg your pardon?"

"We all have secrets, my lady."

"We do?"

One side of his mouth rose in a crooked smile. "I certainly do. And I would not like to think that you would give them away if you discovered them."

"Certainly not." She shook her head, vehement.

"While I do not understand it, I imagine you have a very serious reason for this"—he considered the other women—"unorthodox arrangement."

She nodded. "I do."

When it appeared that she was not planning to elaborate, he nodded once, apparently content with her answer. Perhaps Lara was right. Perhaps he was a nice man after all. "You do realize, however, that he will discover it for himself."

Isabel's brows snapped together. *No, Lara was wrong. He wasn't at all nice.* "I see no reason why he should. Plenty of men—including *you*—have been inside Townsend Park and never noticed."

"Isabel . . ." Lara's voice was filled with caution.

Rock ignored it. "St. John is not like other men. He is keenly aware of his surroundings. I would venture to guess that if he were not so distracted by the other . . . peculiarities . . . of the house, he would have already discovered that which you are hiding beneath his nose."

"There is nothing peculiar about Townsend Park!" Isabel protested.

Rock's gaze flickered from Isabel to Kate to Jane—lingering on the masculine attire that all three wore. "Of course not." Returning his attention to Isabel, he said, "He will not like to be the last to know."

"He shan't be the last to know," she said, feeling incredibly peevish. "He shan't *ever* know."

Rock made a noncommittal sound deep in his throat before saying, "Yes. Well. In any event, we are through in the statuary for the day, so you have at least the evening to decide how you will continue your charade tomorrow." He turned to Kate and, as though the whole situation were perfectly normal, he said, "Our mounts are required."

A crack of thunder sounded then, loud and ominous, startling the women into action. "Of course," Kate said, taking several steps toward the stall where Rock's horse was stabled, before stopping short. She spun back, eyes wide, to meet Isabel's gaze. "Oh."

"Is there a problem?" Rock asked.

"No!" Lara, Kate, Gwen, and Jane all spoke in unison, looking from one to the other awkwardly.

"It's simply that—" Jane started, then stopped.

"You see, sir—" Gwen tried, unsuccessfully.

"The road is flooded," Kate blurted out.

"It's not as bad as it sounds . . . quite common in a summer storm . . . it should be passable soon . . ." Lara rushed to make the situation seem better.

Of course, the situation wasn't better.

"But, for now?" Rock looked to Isabel. *Was that a glimmer of amusement in his eye?*

Isabel replied, defeated. "You cannot leave."

There was a beat as Rock processed the information. "I see. Then this will all be much more interesting than I initially thought." There was a beat. "May I escort you ladies back to the house?" He offered Lara an arm.

Lara stilled, uncertain of how to behave, until Gwen elbowed her in the side and she jumped forward with a soft "Thank you, Mr. Durukhan."

He settled her hand in the crook of his arm. "Rock. Please."

She blushed and giggled.

Isabel's brows rose. *She'd actually giggled!*

Of the many reasons why they kept men away from Townsend Park, giggling was top of the list.

The entire group began to exit the barn, leaving Isabel behind to consider her options. The men would have to spend the night, and Lord Nicholas would soon know all their secrets—whether told by his friend or not. The girls were not skilled at playing men. Their positions, clothing, everything was designed as a ruse in a passing moment—not in the long term. It was only a matter of time before one of them revealed her disguise.

And they would be beholden to Lord Nicholas.

And it wasn't simply during the evenings. If he was here, working closely with them for two weeks . . . they'd never be able to keep the secret.

She sighed. It wouldn't do.

Hopelessness surged. Nothing had changed. She hadn't solved any of their problems. Instead, she had brought more down upon them. She'd invited a *lord* into their house. Someone who could ruin them all with a single word.

He didn't seem the type to do so, but he *could*. And that was enough to set her on edge.

She had to devise a way to win him to their side. So that when he did discover the truth about them, he wouldn't give them all up.

But how?

"Isabel?"

The sound of her name interrupted her thoughts. She

looked up to meet Gwen's curious gaze. "Is everything all right?"

No. "Yes. Perfectly fine."

Gwen gave her a look of disbelief. "It shall be all right, Isabel."

Isabel couldn't help her little, panicked laugh. "He's going to find out."

The cook nodded once. "Yes."

Her agreement opened the floodgates, Isabel's words coming fast and furious. "And what shall happen to us? At least with my father there was safety. No one cared enough for Townsend Park to care about Minerva House. No one came near us. No, we didn't have money. We didn't have protection. But we were safe nonetheless." She paced across the floor of the barn as she spoke, unable to keep herself still. "And, as though my father had not done enough, deserting us all and setting us up for failure, then he had to *die*. And he couldn't leave us anything. Not money, not safety, not even the care of someone we could trust."

Gwen came toward her. "Isabel—it will be all right."

The words sent Isabel over the edge. She covered her face with both hands in frustration. "Stop saying that!"

Gwen paused, and the air went heavy between them.

"Stop saying that," Isabel said again, quietly. "You don't know that."

"I know you will find a way—"

"I have been trying, Gwen. I have been looking for a way. Since I received the news of his death, I have been trying to think of a way to make it all right." She shook her head. "But nothing has gone right: The house is falling apart; James is no more ready to be an earl than he is to fly; we haven't the money to pay our bills; and I've brought a fox into the henhouse." There was a beat. She huffed a little, self-deprecating laugh. "Oh, how apt a metaphor *that* is."

She sat heavily on a bale of hay, hopeless. "Suffice to say, I am out of ideas. And it appears that, with the arrival of this rain, our time is up."

She could no longer keep them all safe.

She could no longer hold the house together.

She'd always known this day would come. That it was one silly mistake, one change of luck away. She'd never been strong enough to protect them all.

It was time she admitted it.

Tears pricked. "I cannot save us, Gwen."

There was comfort in the whispered words—words she'd thought dozens, hundreds of times before, but never said. Saying them aloud helped.

There was a long stretch of silence as Gwen considered her words. Then: "Perhaps he is not such a danger to us. I have not met Lord Nicholas, but it seems that his friend is a good enough sort."

"You couldn't possibly know that."

"You forget, I have known enough bad men to have formed something of an expert opinion."

It was true, of course. Gwen had been raised the daughter of a country vicar with, from what Isabel could surmise, a penchant for fire and brimstone. While she did not speak often of her childhood, she had revealed early in her time at Minerva House that her father had always believed her to be closer to sin than her brothers—who had taken pleasure in agreeing with their sire. Gwen had escaped her house at the very first chance—marriage to a local farmer, who had been far worse than her father or brothers ever could have been. She'd borne his beatings for less than a year before defying the law and finding her way to Isabel.

On her third day at the manor, Gwen had woken and found her way to the kitchens, her bruises already beginning to fade. With the wide grin that had come to be her most recognizable characteristic, she had proclaimed the residents of the house "a battalion of Minervas . . . all goddesses of war and wisdom."

Minerva House had been christened.

And Isabel was about to lose it.

"He's a stranger. We cannot trust him."

"I am the first to question the nature of men, Isabel. But I don't believe they are all bad. And I don't think you do, either." She paused before repeating, "Perhaps this one is not out to get us."

Oh, how she wished that were true.

"He's very distracting," Isabel said.

"Handsome men often are," Gwen replied. "I have read that his eyes are impossibly blue . . ."

"They are."

Gwen smiled. "Ah. You have noticed."

Isabel blushed. "I did not *notice.* I merely . . ."

"He kissed you on the roof, didn't he?"

Isabel's eyes widened. "How do you know that?"

Gwen's smile became a full-blown grin. "I didn't. I do now, however."

"Gwen! You mustn't tell anyone!"

The cook shook her head. "I'm afraid I cannot agree to that. Did you enjoy it?"

The blush flared higher. "No."

Gwen laughed then. "You're a terrible liar, Isabel."

"Oh, fine. Yes. I enjoyed it. He seems a very skilled kisser."

"You had better be careful. If you fall for this lord, you shan't know what has happened to you."

Isabel considered the words, turning them over and over in her mind. Everything was tumbling out of control. She was at risk of losing everything she cared for . . . everything she held dear.

And she was kissing strangers on the roof.

Gwen was right.

She did not know what had happened to her.

Eight

"All of her servants are female."

Inside the Townsend Park library, Nick leaned against a long, low table where he had spread his notes on the collection of marbles and subsequently forgotten them. He had tried to immerse himself in the manor's marbles—the one thing about the house that he felt he understood—after supper, but deserted the work after mere minutes, distracted by the truth of the manor house. And of its owner.

Rock looked up from his book, unperturbed. "Yes."

"You've noticed."

"Yes."

Nick's brows rose. "And you did not feel that you should mention it?"

Rock shrugged. "I was waiting to see how long it would take you to detect it."

"Not long."

"They don't seem to do a very good job of hiding it."

"No. Did you notice the footman at dinner?"

"You mean did I notice the footman's breasts at dinner?"

Nick turned an amused smile on his friend. "You shouldn't be looking at servants that way, Rock." Nick stalked to the window and looked out into the darkness. He spoke to the pouring rain. "What would one need with a houseful of women?"

Rock set his book aside, leaning back against his chair and looking up at the ceiling. "There isn't a single reasonable answer to that question."

"I've known Lady Isabel for only two days, but I can tell you that *reasonable* is not a word I would ascribe to her actions." He turned back to his friend. "A school of some kind? A finishing school?"

Rock shook his head. "She would have no reason to hide it. Its secrecy makes it more likely that it's something villainous."

The idea put a foul taste in Nick's mouth. "I doubt that."

"If she's doing something illegal, she's dooming her brother," Rock said. "London will never accept him if his father *and* his sister were involved in questionable activities."

Nick considered the possibilities. "She hasn't got any money. If she's a procuress, she's not a very good one." He thought for a long moment. "Is it possible that it's a bordello?"

"Not without men."

Nick thought for a moment. "Maybe it was some kind of harem. For the earl."

Rock gave him a look of disbelief. "You think the Wastrearl had a harem. And he never announced it to the world?"

The idea was preposterous, of course. "No. Of course I don't. But what the hell is this place? There aren't any men here for a reason."

Rock sat straight in his chair. "Unless."

"What is it?"

"It's a houseful of women."

"Yes . . ."

"Perhaps it is a houseful of women with no interest in men. But rather . . . interest in women."

Nick shook his head. "It's not that."

"Nick. Consider it. They could easily be—"

"Some of them, perhaps. But not Isabel."

"You can't be sure."

Nick leveled his friend with a look. "Yes, Rock. I can be. Isabel is not interested in Sapphic pleasures."

Understanding dawned. "Already?"

Already. And she was soft and stunning and he wanted more.

Nick moved back to the place where he had been working earlier. He did not speak.

"Why, St. John," Rock drawled, "may I say well done."

With a growl, Nick sat back at the low table, considering his notes on the statuary, ignoring his friend's amusement. He should not have admitted it. Kissing Isabel had been an extraordinary mistake. The only solution was to put the entire event out of his mind.

Of course, he had been attempting to do just that since it had happened. To no avail.

Instead, every time he thought he might have succeeded in forgetting Isabel and their interlude in the attic, he was snapped back to the memory of her—soft and willing in his arms.

The woman's sigh was a weapon, for heaven's sake. How was a reasonable man to resist her?

It was enough to drive him to drink.

Which was another problem, as there appeared to be no worthwhile alcohol in the damned house.

He and Rock had received a small carafe of wine with their supper that evening, which they had eaten alone. The ladies had sent their apologies, Isabel declaring that her state of mourning made it impossible for her to entertain, thereby making it impossible for Lara to join them in light of the breach of propriety that came from a young woman dining with two unmarried men.

One wouldn't guess it, but apparently propriety was an issue in a house filled with women in men's attire.

So Nick and Rock had eaten alone—a perfectly acceptable meal of cold beef and warm vegetables—and when the plates were cleared, a young, quiet footman, no, foot*woman*, had escorted them to the manor's library.

Which would have suited Nick perfectly well if he were able to concentrate on anything but the mistress of the house, who was a distraction of the very worst kind.

He shuffled his papers—considering his notes on Voluptas once more. *She is in the throes of climax*, he had written earlier in the day about the luscious statue—before he'd begun to imagine the statue's owner in a similar state.

After that, he hadn't done much work at all.

It was then, preoccupied with the image of Isabel splayed before him in the height of pleasure, that he had finished his work and gone looking for her. He'd known it would be more punishment than anything else—and their interlude on the roof had only proven as much.

Nick had not wanted that kiss to end. Rather, he'd wanted nothing more than to lay her down in the musty attic and show her precisely how welcome summer storms could be. If not for the interruption of the young earl, Nick could not guarantee that he would not have done just that.

He shifted in his chair at the thought, the tightness in his breeches reminding him of his location—of his mistake.

He had never been so frustrated in his life: frustrated by his inability to understand the situation into which he had been thrust; frustrated by the compelling female who had turned him inside out earlier; and frustrated by the godforsaken rain that was trapping him in this house.

"She's got to be in some kind of trouble." He stood again, returning to the window before smacking his palm against the wainscoting and turning back to Rock. "This incessant rain does not bother you?"

One side of the Turk's mouth kicked up in a ghost of a smile. "Even men of our ilk cannot move mountains, Nick."

The words rankled. "I do not want to stop the rain, Rock. I simply want to be able to leave this house."

"Do you?"

Nick's eyes narrowed on his friend. "Yes. You doubt me?"

"Not at all." Rock returned to his book, refusing to rise to Nick's bait.

He'd always been difficult in that way.

After a long moment, Nick threw open the window and leaned out into the darkness. There was only the storm beyond the house, nothing but a black, yawning emptiness.

He had wanted her that afternoon.

And now that he could not understand her, he wanted her more.

He gritted his teeth.

A drink would do him a not insignificant amount of good.

He pulled himself back inside, ignoring his wet hair, and moved to the sideboard, tearing open the cabinets there. "There has got to be some kind of liquor in this house."

"You are doing it again, you do know that, don't you?"

Nick snapped to attention, turning to face Rock. "I am afraid I do not follow."

Rock's mouth twisted in a wry smile, and he went back to reading his book. "Of course you don't."

Nick's gaze narrowed at the words. "What does that mean?"

Rock did not look up. "Only that, for as long as I have known you, you have been an easy mark for a mysterious woman. Even easier for a mysterious woman in trouble. Do you deny it?" Nick stayed silent. Rock continued. "I pulled you from a prison in the heart of Turkey, barely able to move from the beating you had received because of a woman. We've been in more fights than I can count because of your desire to save every girl you've deemed mistreated. But, leaving aside the fact that we came to Yorkshire to save some girl you've never met, of course . . . you are right. We are not at all trapped in this room, with nothing but books to entertain us, because of your misplaced sense of duty to every female that you meet."

Nick scowled. "Did you not just advise me on the immovable essence of nature? If it were raining any harder, we would be required to build an ark. I did not summon the weather, Rock."

The Turk's black gaze cut across the room. "You did not. But if *Lady* Isabel were *Lord* Reddich, would we have become trapped here in the first place?"

Nick did not like the question.

When Rock silently turned a page, he crouched low, hunting for a bottle. At this point, he was not willing to be picky. He'd drink what he could find.

Ordinarily, he would have enjoyed a night like tonight—the weather prohibiting him from leaving the house, from having to see or be seen.

Not tonight. Not while he was under this roof. Under *her* roof.

Not when thinking about this particular storm made him think about auburn curls dripping with rainwater, the lovely swell of a breast slick with the remnants of the afternoon storm.

He gave a short, harsh laugh—devoid of humor. He was in a strange house, in a strange library, with Rock and his notes on an orgasmic Roman statue. He was lusting after the most perplexing female he had ever met—who happened to be the mistress of the most perplexing house he'd ever visited.

And he was expected to do it all without a drink.

The universe was clearly conspiring against him.

He wanted out of this room.

Turning on one heel, Nick headed for the door, the quick movement attracting Rock's attention once more.

"Where are you headed?"

"I am returning to the statuary. I cannot concentrate here."

"Interesting."

Nick stopped at the dry tone, throwing a wicked glare in his friend's direction. "Is there something you would like to say, Rock?"

Rock smirked. "Not at all. I am merely amused that we fled the clawing masses of women in London only to land ourselves here—with an even more dangerous mass of women."

"That is something of an overstatement. They are harmless."

"Are they?"

Annoyance flared at the casual question. One day in this house and Nick was spoiling for a fight. "I am going to work."

He continued across the room and yanked open the door, determined to put Isabel from his mind.

If only she hadn't been in the hallway, he might have had a chance at doing so.

But she was there, frozen in movement, only the swirl of her skirts indicating that he had startled her. Nick felt a pang of disappointment at her attire—appropriately feminine, but far too conservative for the bold, exciting woman from earlier in the day. The dress was black, so black that, with her back to him, she might well have faded into the darkness if not for his keen awareness of her.

After a long moment, the tension between them became too much and she turned her head slightly, the light spilling from the library catching the angle of her jaw, the line of her neck, and Nick was mesmerized by the alabaster skin there.

She spun back, and the scent of orange blossoms surrounded him. He ignored the snake of pleasure that wound through him at the surprise in her wide eyes, the rapid rise and fall of her chest.

He relaxed into the door frame and spoke. "Lady Isabel. Was there something you needed?"

It was her library, for heaven's sake. And her hallway. Well, James's library and hallway, more accurately, but the point was, it *wasn't* Lord Nicholas's library.

And so there was absolutely no reason for Isabel to feel as though she were an errant child, caught skulking about. She had a viable claim to the space.

She could skulk if she liked.

Except . . . the way he was leaning lazily against the doorway, as if he had nothing better in the world to do but watch her . . . and smirk at her . . . made her feel as though he knew that she had been standing outside the door to the library for nearly a quarter of an hour, trying to gather the courage to enter the room.

She had decided to visit them in the hope that she could distract them from sharing their information. It had taken the combined efforts of Gwen and Lara to get her here, once the decision was made.

Every moment she had stood staring at the immense door, she had told herself, was a moment during which Rock could be regaling his friend with tales of his discovery in the stables. Or a moment during which Lord Nicholas could be regaling *his* friend with tales of his rooftop adventure earlier in the day.

She had been about to knock.

She really had.

Until she had decided that she really should make certain that he received a proper breakfast in the morning. And she had headed for the kitchens.

He had chosen that exact moment to open the door.

And he'd been so casual about it! Infuriating man.

Well. She, too, could sound casual.

"Lord Nicholas! Just who I was hoping to find!"

Hm. That did not sound at all casual. Rather, that sounded like a startled piglet.

Isabel quashed the little voice in her head.

"I am glad that I could accommodate your wishes," he drawled.

He was backlit by the light from the library, the flickering candlelight from the dark, dim hallway barely enough to illuminate his strong features, but she could see the small smile play across his lips.

"You are teasing me."

"Only a little," he acknowledged, holding the door wide to allow her entrance.

She stepped inside, just barely over the threshold, and he closed the door, trapping her.

Isabel paused, a foreign pang twisting in her gut as she considered the warm room, taking in the papers scattered across the unused writing desk on one side of the space. Regina had checked in after she had seen them safely ensconced; it appeared that they had made quick work of making themselves comfortable once the footman had left.

In one corner of the room, Rock was closing a window. He turned when he heard the door and offered Isabel a friendly smile and a short bow. "Lady Isabel," he said, "I was just checking the force of the rain."

"It has started to abate," Isabel said, eager for the safety of the topic. "I should think the roads will be passable tomorrow."

"How frequently do you find yourself without access to town?" Nick asked.

"It is not uncommon. Part of Townsend Park's charm is its seclusion from the outside world. There are worse things than being flooded—or snowed—in." At his noncommittal grunt, she added, "Of course, our belongings are not in town. I am sorry that you are so very inconvenienced."

He watched her closely for a long minute, and Isabel resisted the urge to reach up and check the state of her hair. Instead, she willed herself to meet his gaze and remain as calm as he seemed. The silence stretched between them, and she took in his wet hair, the lone drop of rainwater making its way down his nose. *Had he been outside?*

The thought had barely formed before Nick took a small step toward her. When he spoke, the words were low and liquid, setting her nerves instantly on edge. "Was there something you needed from us?"

Why was she there?

To keep him from discovering their secrets. And ruining everything.

Well. That was not an appropriate response.

For a brief moment, she was paralyzed, clutching the bottle she held tightly in her hands. Finally, the amusement flaring in his blue eyes propelled her into speech.

"I brought you drink," she announced a touch too loudly, holding the dusty bottle aloft. At the blank stares of the men, she pressed on, the words coming altogether too fast. "I haven't any idea what it is—we've a crate of it downstairs—in the cellars—there are other things down there, too—but this seemed most useful at this moment." She paused, then dug herself deeper. "Well, not for me—I certainly don't need to drink—but I understand that men—like you—well, perhaps you'd like it." She stopped then, taking in their surprise, their raised brows, their utter stillness in the face of her flood of words. *Shut up, Isabel.*

She flattened her lips into a thin, tight line and held the bottle out toward Nick, a peace offering of sorts.

He took it, his cool blue gaze focused on her. "Thank you."

The words, low and quiet, shot straight to the core of her, turning something there to liquid. A blush rose on her cheeks, unbidden and without cause. She looked away from him, to Rock—larger, darker, and, somehow, infinitely safer. She took a steadying breath. "You are welcome."

Nick's hands worked at the wax seal on the neck of the bottle, and Isabel was drawn to the movement. She noted the care, the certainty of his fingers—the same fingers that had caressed her that afternoon. They were bronzed from the sun, perfectly manicured, but strong and capable—nothing like the feminine hands of the wealthy men from aristocratic families whom she had met in the past.

They were quite lovely, really.

She was thinking about the man's hands. When she snapped her attention away from them and returned her gaze to his, she noticed the knowing gleam there, as though he could read her thoughts. As though he knew that she was admiring his hands.

How very embarrassing.

For a fleeting moment, Isabel considered escaping the room—running and never looking back. When Rock tilted his head in her direction, however, she was reminded of the reason that she had disturbed the men in the first place.

She must stay and entertain them. And keep Rock from revealing the secrets of Minerva House, and Nick from revealing the secrets of its mistress.

If she were not the subject of such intense scrutiny, she would have stomped her foot. *Men were trouble, indeed.*

Masking her frustration with what she hoped was a cordial smile, she said, "You will need glasses, of course."

Nick nodded once, and headed for the sideboard on the far end of the library, crouching low and retrieving three crystal tumblers.

Isabel did not conceal her surprise. "You have made quick work of making yourself at home. I see that you already know the location of our barware?"

He offered her a sheepish grin, a dimple flashing on one cheek, and she had a glimpse of the troublesome, charming child he must have been.

She found she liked that idea.

"Just a cursory reconnaissance, I assure you. Rock was watching me the whole time—he shall vouch for my behavior as entirely aboveboard."

Isabel looked to Rock, who, in mock seriousness, announced, "Lord Nicholas is ever the perfect gentleman."

Isabel couldn't help her smile when she returned her attention to Nick and said, "I am afraid I find that very difficult to believe."

The words were out before she could think better of them, and she was immediately aware of the possibility that Rock would read some clandestine event into them. Not that such a leap would be incorrect. Wide-eyed, she quickly shifted her attention back to Rock, uncertain of her next step. When the Turk laughed, big and brash, she let out a little breath that she had not known she had been holding.

"I am sorry that we haven't anything better than . . . whatever that is," she said, eager to change the subject, waving one hand in the direction of the dusty bottle in Nick's hands. "We do not have much cause for liquor, I am afraid."

Nick poured two fingers of amber liquid into each of the

glasses, then crossed the room to offer the drink to Rock and Isabel.

"No, thank you," she said, moving closer to the paper-strewn desk at the far corner of the room. She waved one hand in the air as she added, "I should like to know what it is, though."

Nick took a drink, then leaned against a low bookshelf, watching Isabel with a heavy-lidded gaze. "It is brandy."

Her head snapped up from the desk. "Really?"

"Yes. Rather spectacular brandy, I might add."

Isabel looked to Rock for confirmation. When the Turk nodded his agreement, she said, "I confess I am surprised. I cannot imagine that my father would have allowed a case of spectacular brandy to languish away in the caverns beneath this house. Not when he could have put it to perfectly good use in his own belly." She returned her attention to the table. "I am very impressed with the quantity of work you seem to have accomplished in a mere afternoon."

Nick moved toward her, glass in hand. "I am eager to get back to the work once daylight arrives." He paused, considering her for a long moment before returning the conversation to her father. "How do you think your father came into possession of a case of French brandy?"

Isabel considered the crystal tumbler in his hand, the wash of amber liquid beneath his strong fingers. She remembered the trip when her father had brought the liquor home. It was the last time she had seen him. The time he had tempted her with a trip to London, with the promise of a season. The time she had thought he had changed . . . until she discovered his plans to marry her off to the highest bidder.

She'd gone to her mother, begged her to help. To come to her defense. And her mother, desperate to regain the love she had lost, had refused to help her. Had called her selfish.

The earl had left within a week, anyway, apparently realizing that an unwilling, dowry-less daughter wasn't worth very much on the marriage mart.

He'd never returned.

And Isabel's mother had never forgiven her.

Well. She certainly could not tell Lord Nicholas the truth.

Isabel did not look up, willing her voice to remain steady. "I learned long ago, my lord, never to question my father's actions. I imagine the brandy arrived by the same means as everything else in this house—nefarious ones."

"Perhaps not." She could hear the care in his tone.

"Yes, well. We shall never know now, shall we?"

She was no longer focused on the papers at which she was looking, but Isabel reached out, moving one page to the side, nonetheless. Her gaze ran, unseeing, across his words, until she registered the strong, fluid lines of the word *orgasm*, and started.

What was he writing about?

She tilted her head to gain better access to the words on the paper before he interrupted, amusement in his tone. "Lady Isabel?"

She looked up with a too-bright smile, ignoring the heat that spread across her cheeks, and met Nick's smug, amused gaze. The infuriating man knew precisely what she had read.

He was wicked.

Well. She would not let him get the better of her.

"Please. Do not stand on my account. Shall we all sit?" She waved one hand at the cluster of chairs where Rock had set aside his book, and said, "Did you find something of interest to read on this horrid night?"

It was the Turk's turn to look sheepish at her question. He moved quickly to the book, lifting it into his enormous hands before she had a chance to see it. "As a matter of fact, I did."

One side of Isabel's mouth lifted in anticipation. "Oh? What is it?"

Nick's snicker attracted her attention for a brief moment, but when she looked at him, he lifted his glass to his mouth and, with a shrug, said, "I haven't any idea what he's reading."

She looked back at Rock, and the look he tossed in Nick's direction could only be described as violent.

What had started as a means to redirect the subject from her father now became a matter of utmost importance. Was the Turk blushing? "Rock?"

"*The Castle of Otranto.*"

Isabel gave a little laugh at the title—she couldn't help it. The gothic novel was one of the girls' favorites, the convoluted story of a doomed lord, a forced marriage, and the rise of a prince. It was decidedly *not* the type of book one would expect to find in the hands of a giant.

At her laugh, Nick said dryly, "I would not take it personally, Rock. Lady Isabel almost certainly would judge anyone who reads such gothic drivel."

"No!" Isabel exclaimed, "I am not passing judgment, Rock, not at all!"

"All is well," Rock offered in the face of her rush to reassure him. "Hang Nick. It is certainly a compelling story."

Nick chuckled, and Isabel shot him a quelling look before she rushed to correct the misconception. "It is! When the others read it . . ." Rock's eyes widened at her words, and she rushed to correct her mistake. "By *the others* I mean Lara and our—friends. From town, of course—they enjoyed it."

"And you, my lady?" Rock's question covered her awkwardness.

"Oh. I have not read it. Well, not all of it."

"You could not finish it?"

Isabel shook her head. "I never started it. I did not care for the ending."

Nick leaned forward. "The ending?"

Isabel nodded. "I always begin with the end of books."

Rock's brows went up. "Whatever for?"

She shrugged. "I like to be prepared."

Nick laughed, and she turned to meet his smiling eyes. Was he mocking her? "You find that amusing, Lord Nicholas?"

He was not embarrassed by her insinuation that he had offended her. "I do, indeed, Lady Isabel."

"Why?"

"Because it explains a great deal."

What did that mean?

Isabel resisted the urge to press him on the subject, instead redirecting her attention to her other—more likeable—guest. She moved to a nearby bookshelf and busied herself with looking for the book, willing herself to ignore Lord Nicholas.

"We have *The Mysterious Mother* here somewhere, as well. Let me find it for you!"

"Lady Isabel," Rock said, amusement in his tone, "while I am grateful for your offer, I do not need another book tonight. This one will do quite well."

She turned back at the sound of his calm voice. "Oh." She smoothed her skirts. "Well. If you decide you would like to borrow it, I am happy to lend it to you."

Rock dipped his head in a gracious gesture and said, "I thank you. But for now, I think I shall take myself off to read more about the doomed Lord Otranto and his very unlucky son."

Isabel blinked as he began to move toward the door. *He was going to leave her alone with Nick.* This was clearly punishment. She would never mock the gothic novel again. Never. *If only Rock would stay.*

Apparently, the gods had little interest in the good name of the gothic romance.

She made a last-ditch effort to keep him in the room. "Oh! But wouldn't you prefer to read here? The light is so fine. And we could discuss the . . . nuances of the text!"

"At least, the end of the text, Rock," Nick said dryly. Isabel wanted to hit him in the head with a text. A large one. The Gutenberg Bible.

Rock smiled at her. "That sounds wonderful, my lady. Perhaps tomorrow?"

She could not press him without appearing utterly inhospitable to Lord Nicholas and drawing attention to the tension building between them. A halfhearted "Of course. Tomorrow" was all she could manage as she watched him retreat from the room.

At the sound of the door closing, the air in the room seemed to thicken, and Isabel was suddenly keenly aware of being alone with Nick. With a shaky breath, she turned to him, uncertain of what would happen now.

He lifted the glass of brandy that she had refused earlier and moved toward her, reminding her of a large cat on the hunt. She met his gaze, marveling once more at the vivid blue of his eyes. "I should be off myself—I have interrupted your work for long enough."

Nick paused, considering the words. "Indeed, you have. But I would never dream of exiling you from your own library. Why not sit? We shall talk."

She did not notice that he had backed her up against one of the chairs in the corner until she felt the seat against the back of her skirts. "Talk?"

One side of his mouth kicked up at the disbelief in the word. "I am capable of conversation, Isabel. At least, I am told it is so."

It was not easy to focus on his words with him so close.

She sat, taking the proffered glass from him.

"Excellent." He followed suit, relaxing into the chair across from her. "Now. Tell me your secrets."

Lesson Number Three

Do not be afraid to share little gems of yourself to entice your lord.

When he inquires after your inner thoughts, be sure to share small and compelling parts of your mind—nothing too intellectual . . . we would not like him to think you a bluestocking! But small, interesting tidbits of your wonder: your favorite color; your preference for embroidery over oils; the name of your childhood pony.

Master the art of remaining forthcoming, yet not overpowering.

Pearls and Pelisses
June 1823

She froze at the words, uncertain of how she should respond. "My . . . my what?"

"Your secrets, Lady Isabel," he repeated, his voice low and coaxing. "If my instincts are correct, they are considerable in number."

"What an absurd idea," she said. "Why, my life is truly an open book."

He watched her from under heavy lids for a long moment—long enough to give her the real sense that he knew something she did not want him to know. *Was it possible that Rock had betrayed her confidence? The confidence of a houseful of women in need?*

It didn't seem very gentlemanly, but who was to say the enormous man was a gentleman? Indeed, his companion had not acted in accordance with any particular code of chivalric conduct earlier that afternoon.

Isabel shook her head. She would not think of the events of the afternoon. Not when she was here in her cozy library.

With a cad.

One of Nick's eyebrows rose and he leaned back in his chair—stretching out as if he owned the place—the arrogant man, crossing one leg over the other. Isabel made a show of moving her skirts out of the way of his boots. He watched, a smirk playing over his lips. His boots were nowhere near her skirts and they both knew it.

Still. He could have been more courteous.

"Forgive me, my lady, if I say I do not believe you."

Her eyes widened. "I beg your pardon?" she said, her tone as haughty as that of any queen. "Are you calling me a liar?"

"I am accusing you of withholding the truth."

"Well! Of all the—" It did not matter that he was right. That she was hiding several rather immense secrets from him. A gentleman did not question the veracity of a lady's words. "Need I remind you that, as a guest here at Townsend Park, you owe me a modicum of respect?"

"Need I remind you, my lady, that as my hostess, you owe *me* a modicum of generosity?"

Isabel leaned forward, no longer cozy. "What are you saying?"

"Only that you would do well to tell me the truth about your situation. I'm bound to discover it soon enough."

"I—" She stopped. To which situation was he referring?

"I know you're in financial straits, Isabel."

"Lady Isabel." He did not correct himself. "And I fail to see why this is at all a matter of concern to you, Lord Nicholas."

"St. John. Or Nick. Very few people call me Lord Nicholas." She did not correct herself. "And it is a very serious matter to me, Isabel. After all, you brought me here to value your collection of marbles."

"I—" She had to tread carefully. "I released you from that request."

"Yes, but it seems that nature has other plans for us." He paused. "How much do you need?"

Really. The man was impossible. Gentlemen did not simply plop themselves down across from ladies and ask about finances. The conversation was more than crass.

She could not imagine why any woman would want to land this lord, after all. She certainly did not want to.

That made everything easier.

"Lord Nicholas—"

"For every time you call me Lord Nicholas, I shall bring up an additional inappropriate question."

"There aren't many more inappropriate than this one."

"On the contrary, Isabel, there are far less appropriate topics that I would be happy to discuss with you."

For example?

He seemed to read her thoughts; his piercing blue gaze glittered with an unnerving knowledge, and in that moment Isabel wanted for nothing more than a list of all those dark topics. She felt her cheeks grow warm at the thought. To cover the blush, she took a pull of brandy, the fiery liquid burning her throat. She coughed once, then twice, desperate to keep the action delicate and not draw attention to her discomfort. When he did not look away, her blush flared higher.

She must not allow him the upper hand.

"Two can play at that game, my lord. For every inappropriate question you ask, I assure you I shall be able to find one myself."

"Yes . . . but will you be able to ask it?"

It was a test. They both knew it.

"Where did you—" She stopped.

There was a long pause while he waited for her to finish the question. She looked down at the glass in her hands, keenly aware of the feel of the heavy crystal, the amber liquid swirling along its walls. *She could not finish the question.*

"Where did I—?"

Isabel shook her head, not looking up. There was a droplet on the very top edge of the glass and, in her nervousness, Isabel touched her finger to the spot, watching the liquid disappear into her skin, wishing she could do the same—to disappear from this room, from this conversation that was so very beyond her experience.

His voice was low and liquid. "I am disappointed in you. I had hoped you would be a formidable opponent. And it seems you shan't be a foe at all."

Her gaze snapped up at the words, softly teasing. She watched the hint of a dimple in his cheek flash and decided then and there to put an end to his teasing.

"Where did you get your scar?"

The words were barely out when she desperately wanted to take them back. *What was she thinking?*

He grinned wide and took a sip of brandy. "Good girl. I knew you could do it. You know, no woman has ever asked me that question before."

She was instantly eager to dismiss the question. "I'm sure they barely notice—"

He raised a lone eyebrow, and the movement stayed her words. "Do not ruin my newfound view of you, Isabel. I acquired the mark in Turkey."

She shook her head once, as if to clear it. "I—I didn't mean—"

"Of course you did." He held up his glass in a toast. "Now that we've settled that, how much do you need?"

Isabel's thoughts were racing with additional questions.

He *had* opened the door. . .

"I'm not sure. More than we make off the estate. When?"

He did not pretend to misunderstand. He dangled his glass haphazardly from one hand, the liquid inside casually forgotten for the moment. "Nine years ago. Are you saying the estate cannot take care of itself?"

Isabel drank again. She leaned back, pressing herself into the soft chair. "Some months, it can—when we have the livestock, the crops to be self-sustaining. But there is nothing left. Nothing for school for James. No new clothes . . ."

"You would like new clothes?"

"No." She shook her head. "I'm talking about new clothes for James . . . for—" She stopped. *For the girls.* She met his eyes. "Did it hurt?"

"I've had worse."

"Worse than a four-inch-long gash on your cheek?"

He shook his head slowly. "It's my turn. For the record, I would like you to have new clothes. I'd like to see you in bright, bold colors. I think they would suit you—certainly better than the colors of mourning. I'd like to see you in red. A deep, welcome rose." Whether from the brandy or his thoughtful tone, Isabel felt warmer all of a sudden. She waited for him to speak, wondering what he might say next, eager for him to continue the conversation even as she feared the topics he might broach. "Why haven't you married?"

The question was not at all what she had expected. "I . . ." She paused, uncertain. "What does that have to do with anything?"

One side of his mouth twitched in a crooked, knowing smile. "Ah. I see we have found a topic of interest."

"I assure you, my lord, I am not at all interested in it."

"No . . . but I am." He stood, moving across the room to refill his glass. She tracked his movements, wide-eyed, and when he returned with the bottle and offered her more of the brandy, she did not refuse. "Marriage is the answer to your problems, Isabel. Why not marry?"

She hadn't thought there was a topic she wanted to discuss less than the estate's finances. It seemed she had been wrong. "It's never been an option. How did it happen?"

He sat again, facing her once more. "Wrong place at the wrong time. I do not believe that marriage has never been an option. Try again."

"The only men who have ever expressed an interest were friends of my father. If you knew my father, you would not consider marriage to any of his acquaintances an option, either." She drank again, the liquor smoother—more pleasant—this time. "I do not believe that you were merely in the wrong place at the wrong time. Try again."

A smile flashed as he recognized his own words. "A palpable hit, my lady." He leaned back in his chair. "I shall tell you, but then you shall have to be honest with me. Are you certain you are up to the challenge?"

No. But, in that moment, there was nothing she would not promise to hear his story. "Of course."

He raised one eyebrow, but spoke, nonetheless. "By a stroke of immensely atrocious luck and a fair bit of bad judgment, I landed myself in a Turkish prison while in the Orient." She sucked in a short breath as he continued, "I was there for twenty-two days before Rock found me and brought me to safety. The fact that I walked away with a single visible scar is rather impressive, I think."

How horrid. How lucky he had been that Rock had found him. What if he had not been saved? What if he had gone a month? A year? What other, more sinister scars might there have been? *Might there be?*

He leaned forward then, reaching one arm out toward her. She started when his long fingertips brushed the space between her brows, smoothing the furrow there that she had not noticed. "I can see your imagination running away with you."

She shook her head at the words, pulling back from his warm touch. "Nonsense. I am only happy that you were able to escape your captors. How horrible that must have been. How lucky you were to have Rock."

"Do not romanticize it, Isabel," he said. "I assure you, I deserved the scar." The words fell like stone between them. *What did that mean? How could this man, this lord, this . . . antiquarian . . . have done something worthy of such a wound?* Isabel's mouth opened, but Nick continued before she could ask any of the questions racing through her head. "It's your turn."

She blinked once, twice. *What had he wanted to know?*

"Marriage."

She must tread carefully here. "I . . . I never wanted to marry."

He waited. When she did not say anything more, he prompted, "But?"

She shook her head. "You are right—marriage would solve any number of my problems . . . but I imagine it would cause a fair number of new ones, frankly."

He gave a little laugh, and when she looked at him curiously, he said, "I beg your pardon. It is only that I have never met a woman who feels so about marriage."

She immediately understood that he was thinking of *Pearls and Pelisses*. "No, I don't suppose you have."

"You have no desire for wedded bliss?"

"If wedded bliss were an honest option, perhaps I would . . ." Isabel gave a little snort at the words, looking into her glass for a long moment before drinking the last of her brandy. The truth was coming easier now. "But wedded bliss never seemed viable for me."

"No?"

She looked up, meeting his curious gaze. "Not in the least. You did not know my father?"

"I did not."

"How lucky for you." For a moment, she thought he would say something in response to her acid words. When he remained silent, she continued, "He did not spend much time here—my mother was very much in love with him for some reason . . . although I could never see why. He was handsome enough, I suppose, and certainly the heart of any party. He was a carnival of a man. But when we needed him, he was never here."

There was more to say—much more—but Isabel stopped herself. Lord Nicholas St. John, however easy to talk to, however compelling a companion, was a danger to her—to all of them—and she needed to keep him at arm's length. "Suffice to say, the idea of a marriage like theirs has never sat well."

He nodded once, slowly, as though he understood. "Not all marriages go the way of theirs."

"Perhaps," Isabel allowed quietly before looking back into her empty glass. "I suppose you have a warm, loving, wonderful family. You're probably the product of a love match."

Nick gave a little laugh at the words, and the sound drew Isabel's curious attention. "You could not be farther from the truth." He did not elaborate, instead changing the topic. "And so you are selling the collection."

The pain of it flared. When she spoke, she could not keep the regret from her voice. "Yes."

"But you do not want to."

There was no point in lying. "No."

"Then why do it? Surely there was a guardian named in your father's will who is able to help?"

"Our *guardian*, if one might call him that, has not been found. As usual, my father has left it to me to keep food on our table and a roof over our heads." She paused, then flashed a smile. "Literally."

He smiled at her joke, and in that moment of shared amusement, something changed in his eyes, the warm summer blue shifting with awareness, and Isabel knew precisely where his thoughts had strayed—to the roof, the rain, and their earlier encounter. Her cheeks warmed, and she fought the urge to press her fingertips to her face and chase away the color there.

"Perhaps you know him?"

"Your guardian?"

She nodded. "Oliver, Lord Densmore."

Nick's brows shot up. "Densmore is your guardian?"

She did not like the sound of that.

"You do know him, then?"

"I do."

"And what is he like?"

"He is . . ." She watched Nick intently as he searched for the appropriate adjective. "Well, he certainly is entertaining."

"Entertaining." Isabel tested the word on her tongue, deciding that she did not care for it.

"Yes. How was it that you described your father? A carnival of a man?"

Isabel nodded.

"Like follows like. But he is not a man I would choose to protect my family."

Of course he wasn't.

Isabel had known the truth, but a small part of her had hoped that in this, his last act, her father might have been a father to her. And if not to her, at least to James.

Instead, at Nick's words, an immense pressure built in Isabel's chest. All of a sudden, she could not breathe, so unsettled was she at the thought of yet another man, irresponsible and nevertheless so powerful, holding sway over her . . . over James . . . over the girls. She could feel the panic rising, pure and unfettered.

She had to get the girls out. Now. Before they were trapped.

Before they were found.

Before everything she had so carefully built was torn down by a man just like her father.

She tried for a deep breath—but the air wouldn't come.

"Isabel."

The sound of her name came from far away as she closed her eyes and willed herself to breathe. Nick was next to her then, his strong hand on her back, running along the bones of her corset. "These things are torture devices," he muttered as he lifted her chin with one finger, forcing her to meet his gaze. "Look at me. Breathe."

She shook her head, "I am . . ." She paused, trying again. "I am fine."

"You are not fine. Breathe."

The firm calm of his voice settled her, and she did as she was told. She took several deep, shaking breaths under the guidance of his liquid gaze and the warm stroke of his hand at her back.

When she had returned to normal, Isabel squeezed back against one arm of the chair, desperate to get away from his unsettling touch. He released her, but did not move from his position, crouched low, at the side of her seat. She looked away from him, guilty, embarrassed by her actions. Her gaze fell on the door at the far end of the room, and she considered the myriad reasons she could fabricate to flee.

"You aren't leaving this room."

She could leave if she wanted. It was her room, for heaven's sake. He needn't be such a lion about it. She gripped the edge of her chair, her knuckles turning white. "There is no need for you to be concerned."

His eyes flashed as he shifted his weight to one knee and took both her hands in his. "You are weighed down with secrets, Isabel. At some point, you are going to have to share them."

She looked at the man across from her—this man who seemed to be good. And strong. And rich. And she realized that he was, indeed, her best hope.

If only she didn't feel so guilty about it.

"Why not start with your father?" She pulled back, physically resisting the idea of opening up about the man who had started her down this path. He squeezed her hands then. "Why not speak what you cannot stop thinking?"

Isabel caught her breath at the words, so soft, so coaxing.

What if she told him?

What if she let some of her secrets go?

They hovered there, on the brink of something more powerful than either of them, and Isabel felt the silence as if it were a physical weight. Neither of them had worn gloves that evening; the casual nature of the manor house had not required it.

He rubbed her hands between his carefully, tracing his broad, wonderfully roughened fingertips down each of her fingers in turn. She watched the movement, wondering at his calloused skin—how had one of London's most coveted lords developed the hands of a workman? She was so distracted by the feel of his warm bare hands on hers that she nearly gave in to his request.

Nearly.

But somewhere, deep within her, she knew that if she opened up to this man, it would be the most dangerous thing she ever did.

He made her want to believe that she could share her burdens.

When the truth was that she was alone.

And she always would be.

In the beginning, she had thought that was best. Because every woman she'd known who had chosen to share her life had regretted it. She learned from her mother, from the women of Minerva House. Sharing life with a man would ultimately lead to being half a woman. And she never wanted to feel that way.

No matter how much his warm hands and encouraging words tempted her.

She swallowed, willing her voice to come out strong and firm. "There is nothing to say. You know his reputation as well as I. Better, I would imagine. We did not know him. He did not care to know us." She lifted one shoulder in a small shrug and tugged at her hands, eager to be free of his grasp.

Nick did not respond, releasing one of her hands, but keeping the other in his firm grip, turning it over and baring her palm to his gaze. With his thumbs, he began to rub slow circles across her hand. The sensation was instantly overwhelming.

When he spoke, it was in a whisper. "You do not have to tell me . . . but believe me when I tell you that you cannot allow him to turn you against life. Do not let him rob you of its pleasure."

Her eyes flew to his, but he was not looking at her. Instead, he was watching his ministrations, the press and stroke of his thumbs that sent the most marvelous waves of pleasure through her. She sighed and fell back against the cushion of her chair, knowing she should stop him, but unable to muster the energy to do so. Whatever he was doing to her hand . . . it was *lovely*. Far lovelier than anything she'd experienced in a very long time.

Except maybe his kiss.

That had been rather lovely, as well.

She really should remove her hand from his.

But something that he was doing to her—the way his fingers seemed to find the most sensitive spots on her hand . . . she'd never noticed the pleasure one's fingers could experience.

Her gaze slid from where she watched the play of his hands up to his neck, where the corded muscle slipped beneath his shirt collar in lovely, sun-kissed lines. She had never noticed anyone's neck before, and, as she followed the length of his throat up to his jaw, she wondered why.

Necks were quite magnificent, actually.

He shifted the pressure on her hands, rubbing the base of her thumb with the strong pads of his fingers, and she turned liquid at the touch, sinking further into her chair. Nick continued his ministrations, pressing and stroking in the most marvelous way, sending waves of pleasure through her. She sighed, knowing she should stop him, but unable to muster the energy to do so.

Instead, she raised her eyes to his face, taking in the sharp angle of his jaw where it met the lines of his throat, his strong chin and firm, soft lips. She did not linger on that mouth . . . or the unsettling memories it wrought; instead, she turned her attention to the slight, nearly imperceptible bend in his nose.

It had been broken at some point. Perhaps at the same time he was scarred?

Who was this man, at once gentleman antiquarian, mysterious prison escapee, and infuriating kisser?

How did he seem to understand her so well?

And, more importantly, why did she want so very much to know him?

She braved a look at his eyes then, and was relieved to discover that he was focused on her hands rather than her face. She watched his intent gaze. The brilliant blue that she had noticed from the start—that every woman in London had noticed at one point or another if the silly magazine was to be believed—they were not simply blue. They were a stunning combination of grays and cornflowers and sapphires . . . framed with lush, sooty lashes any courtesan would envy.

He was beautiful.

The thought broke through, and Isabel sat up straight, yanking her hand from between his and pushing aside the immediate sense of loss that came over her as she did so. She swallowed once, collecting herself. "You are too familiar, Lord Nicholas." She managed not to cringe at the shaking of her voice, and was quite proud of her restraint.

Without missing a beat, Nick set his hands to his thighs, not moving aside from the slight lifting of the corner of his mouth in a small, wry smile. "I heard your sigh, Isabel—your body did not find me at all overly familiar."

Her eyes widened at the words. "Of all the arrogant . . . ungentlemanly . . . things to say!"

He gave a small, almost unnoticeable shrug. "I did warn you of what would happen if you called me Lord Nicholas again."

Isabel opened her mouth to retort, but found she had nothing to say. She closed her mouth. How frustrating. In novels, the heroine always had something witty to say.

She was no heroine.

She shook her head to clear it of the thought, then stood, squaring her shoulders and pushing past him, taking pleasure in the sound of her skirts brushing against his shoulder where he crouched.

When she was far enough away from him, she turned back.

To find him standing altogether too close.

She froze, immediately nervous as he lifted one hand to her cheek, running his fingertips over the skin there, sending a tremor through her. She was surrounded by the scent of him, a heady combination of brandy and sandalwood and something wonderful that she could not place. She resisted the temptation to close her eyes and breathe him in—to lean into the light touch and encourage him to take the moment further.

What if he did? What then?

Would he kiss her again?

Did she want him to?

She remained utterly still, transfixed by the softness of his touch.

Yes. She wanted him to kiss her.

Her gaze flickered to his, and she willed him to move closer—to repeat his actions from the afternoon.

He could read her thoughts; she knew he could. She could see the flicker of masculine satisfaction in his gaze as he registered her desire . . . but she didn't care. As long as he kissed her.

He was so close; it was maddening. She couldn't bear the waiting—the intense anticipation of a caress that might not come—and she closed her eyes finally, unable to maintain the contact with his intense, knowing blue gaze. Without the benefit of sight, Isabel felt herself begin to sway toward his heat. She knew it was brazen, but there was something about this man that made her forget herself . . . her past. Everything that she had ever promised she would not become.

"Isabel . . ." He whispered her name and she resisted the urge to open her eyes for fear of breaking this warm, intimate spell that had been woven around them. Instead, she reveled in the sound of her name on his deep voice as her hands rose of their own volition, just barely touching the coarse fabric of his topcoat—itching to explore the wide expanse of his chest.

He had spoken of life's pleasures. She wanted him to show them to her.

The light touch seemed to spur him forward, and Isabel sighed as he settled his lips to hers . . . and she was overcome with a mix of pleasure and relief.

The kiss was softer, less urgent than the one they had shared that afternoon, an exploration of a caress. His hands slid into the hair at the nape of her neck as his lips passed over hers in a feather-light touch once, twice . . . intoxicating her with sensation. Isabel sighed, her lips parting, and he rewarded her by deepening the kiss, aligning his mouth to hers, and sliding his tongue along her full bottom lip, leaving a path of fire in its wake.

Isabel spread her fingers wide, passing her hands over his broad shoulders and pressing herself against his chest, willing him closer. He understood, wrapping his arms around her and pulling her closer, into the cradle of his arms, and stroking his tongue against hers before breaking off the kiss to trail his lips across her cheek to her ear where he whispered her name—more sensation than sound—and took the soft lobe between his teeth, worrying the skin there until a shiver of intense pleasure sent her arms around his neck.

She could feel his satisfied smile against her skin as he pressed his lips to the soft spot behind her ear, where her pulse beat in a mad, unbearable rhythm. He rained soft, irresistible kisses down the side of her neck, pausing to scrape his teeth against her skin until she whimpered her pleasure and struggled to remain standing.

He lifted her in his arms then and, without removing his mouth from her neck, returned himself to the large winged chair by the fireplace, and settled her on his lap. He lifted his head, capturing her gaze as if to confirm her willingness to continue. She sighed her approval as he tilted her chin up and returned his mouth to the soft skin where her neck met her shoulder, licking softly, the roughness of his tongue making her wild.

She gasped, and the sound brought his attention back

to her mouth. He took her lips again, stroking his tongue past her lips as one hand slid up her side to the edge of her breast. Once there, his hand stilled, and the lack of movement proved to be Isabel's undoing. Her breast felt infinitely heavier than it ever had, full and wanting in a way that made her desperate for his touch. She wanted his hand on her in a way she had never dreamed of prior to this moment—to this man.

She squirmed then, willing him to move, to touch her, and he lifted his mouth from hers, opening his brilliant blue eyes and capturing her gaze.

"What is it, beauty?" His thumb moved, just barely, but enough for her to know that he knew precisely what she wanted. He was teasing her.

"I—" She couldn't say it.

The heel of his hand—that wicked hand, so close to where she wanted it—pressed against her and he set his lips to her ear. "So beautiful . . . so passionate . . . my very own Voluptas." The words, more breath than sound, sent an explosion of heat through her. "Show me."

The demand unleashed something inside her. She slid her hand down his arm to where his hand lay. She pulled back, meeting his gaze with more courage than she'd ever known she had, and moved his hand to capture her breast. When the heavy weight settled in his grasp, they both watched as he stroked his fingers across her breast, running the edge of his thumb over the place where her nipple pebbled beneath the fabric. She gasped at the sensation and their gazes collided.

"Tell me how it feels."

She blushed. "I—I cannot."

He repeated the caress and she sucked in another breath. "You can."

She shook her head. "I have never—it is too much. Too good."

He rewarded her with another long kiss as he slid one finger under the edge of her gown, running the back of it against her heated, straining skin. She cried out then, breaking the kiss, and he set his forehead against hers, a ghost of a smile playing across his swollen lips.

"It shall only get better." The words were filled with heated promise.

He lifted her again, surprising her with the movement as he rose, then returned her to the chair with the utmost of ease. He leaned over her, bracing himself on the arms of the chair, and stole her lips once again, until she was left unable to move.

He pulled back then, and she opened her eyes to find an intense desire in his—quickly replaced with something she could only describe as determination. Confused by the change, she could only watch as he whispered, "I don't know what you are hiding from, Isabel, but I will know soon enough. And if it is in my power to change it, I shall."

Her mouth fell open at the words—so unexpected.

He pulled away from her then, and, even as she longed for more of his touch, he left the room, his movements as confident as his words had been.

Ten

Nick knew before he opened his eyes that someone was watching him.

Keeping his breath even, he considered his options.

He could hear soft, steady breathing coming from a few feet away. The intruder was close to him, near the bed, and not at all nervous. If this were a decade ago, and Nick were in Turkey, he would be unsettled by that fact—but he was in Yorkshire, stranded in a rainstorm, which left a rather limited group of possible visitors.

He did not smell orange blossoms, which meant that it was not Isabel who had joined him in his room that morning—unfortunate, that. He would have liked to have woken to her by his bedside. The events of the prior evening had only served to increase his curiosity about her; he'd never known a woman so passionate . . . and so mysterious. He wanted to discover everything there was to discover about her.

Yes, he would have liked to have woken to her in his bed, warm and lush, next to him, her honeyed gaze sleepy and welcoming. There was nothing in the world worth leaving a bed so well filled.

He snapped his attention back to the matter at hand. His visitor was not dangerous—that much he could tell—but now was not the time to fantasize about the lady of the manor. In fact, fantasizing about Isabel at all was a very dangerous task, indeed.

He opened his eyes and met a serious brown gaze, not altogether unlike the one he had been imagining.

"Good. You're awake."

Of all the possible intruders, Nick had not expected to find the young Earl of Reddich crouching low beside his bed, unblinking.

"It would seem so."

"I've been waiting for you to wake up," James announced.

"I am sorry that I have kept you waiting," Nick said dryly.

"It's not a problem, really. I don't have lessons for another hour."

Nick sat up, the linen sheets falling to his bare waist as he ran one hand over his face to chase the sleep away. "Hasn't anyone ever told you that sneaking into guests' bedchambers is bad manners?"

James tilted his head to one side. "I thought that was only girls' rooms."

Nick smiled. "Yes, well, it's even more true for girls' rooms."

James nodded, as though Nick had just imparted some great secret. "I shall remember that."

Hiding his amusement, Nick swung his legs over the edge of the bed, pulling on the too-small dressing gown that had been offered to him the prior evening. Standing, he pulled the belt of the robe tight and turned back to the boy considering him from the opposite side of the bed.

The boy had an air of seriousness about him—a wariness in his brown eyes that was far beyond his years—Nick noticed as James tracked his movements, unable to keep his thoughts from going to Isabel; the seriousness was hereditary, it seemed.

"What can I do for you, Lord Reddich?"

James shook his head. "No one calls me that."

"They should start doing so. You are the Earl of Reddich, are you not?"

"Yes—"

"But?"

James chewed on one side of his lower lip. "But I don't really do the things that earls do. I'm not old enough."

"What things are those?"

"Things my father did."

"Yes, well, I'm not certain that *I* am old enough to do the things your father did," Nick said, crossing to the opposite side of the room and splashing cold water from the basin set there onto his face. He pulled a linen cloth from the nearby towel stand and dried himself before turning back to the boy, who was now seated at the foot of the bed, watching him.

"I shall learn soon enough, I suppose," James said, and Nick noted the lack of eagerness in his tone. "Isabel says that when you are through with your work in the statuary, we shall have enough money to send me to school."

Nick nodded once before making a point of lifting a shaving pot that had been left beside the basin and soaping his face. He turned to the looking glass in the corner of the room, aware that the boy was watching his movements, fascinated. "How old are you?"

"Ten."

The age he had been when everything had changed.

Lifting a straight razor from the table, Nick pretended not to notice the boy's intent stare. He set the blade to his cheek carefully and said, "My brother is a marquess, you know."

It took a moment for the words to reach James, so focused was the boy on the movement of the steel blade across Nick's skin. When they did, the young earl's eyes widened. "Really?"

"Really." Nick focused on his task for a few seconds before adding, "And he learned most of the things he knows about being a marquess at school."

Silence fell between them, with only the sound of water on Nick's razor in the room as James considered the words. "Did you go to school?"

"I did."

"Did you like it?"

"Sometimes."

"And the others?"

Nick paused, using the delicate task of shaving his chin to buy time to consider his answers. He had much in common with this boy—a strange history that set him apart from his peers, an uncertain future, an unfortunate past. Nick considered his mother's desertion, the maelstrom of gossip that began soon after her leaving, the way his father had shut down and packed Nick and Gabriel off to school without preparing them for the way others would talk . . . the way they would tease. As the second son, without a title, Nick had received the brunt of the teasing; and on those days he had thrown himself into his schoolwork.

That was before he'd learned to retaliate with his fists. Before he'd realized that his size and stature and physical power could open the door to a life that was more than the one he'd expected to live as second son of the Marquess of Ralston.

No, he had not liked school much. But it would be different for James. He was not the son of a weak marquess and his marchioness of questionable morals. He was an earl, and due the respect of the title.

"Sometimes men must do things they do not enjoy. It is what makes us men."

James considered the words. Nick watched him closely in the mirror, wondering what the young earl was thinking. Finally, the boy lifted his head. "I should like to be thought a man."

"Then I am afraid school is a must."

"But what about . . ." Nick did not press the boy, instead drying his now clean-shaven face and waiting out the long silence. "What about the girls?"

Something burst high in Nick's chest then—a warm tightness that spread at the plaintive question. The boy was worried about his sister. And, considering the woman's recklessness over the past two days, Nick did not blame him for it.

Not that he would say that.

"Your sister seems to do quite well on her own, don't you think?"

James shook his head. "Isabel hates being alone. She would be sad if I left."

Nick resisted the image that flashed of Isabel sad and lonely. He did not like it.

"I think she would understand your duty."

The boy was back to chewing on his lip—an endearing habit of which Eton would break him immediately, Nick thought, a pang of disappointment flaring at the thought.

"What of my duty here? To the girls?" James asked.

"Isabel and Lara shall be here when you return, James. And they shall be better for all you will have learned of being an earl."

James shook his head vehemently. "They are not—" He stopped, collected his thoughts, and began again. "I cannot protect them when I am away at school."

Warning flared in Nick at the words. "Protect them?" he repeated, keeping his voice casual even as he moved closer to James. "Protect them from what?"

The boy looked away, out the window of the bedchamber at the acres of green land beyond. "From . . . everything."

Nick knew immediately that James was not referring to a general, overarching worry, but to a specific concern. He also knew the boy would not share it easily. "James," he said, not wanting to scare him away, "if there is something worrying you—I am able to help."

James looked back and his gaze fell to Nick's scar, surprising him—not because the boy was looking, but because he was looking for the first time. James's attention shifted away almost as quickly as it had landed there, this time to Nick's shoulders, where they strained the fabric of the too-small, borrowed dressing gown. "I think you might be able to help," the boy said softly, finally. "I think you are big enough to help."

If he weren't so disturbed by James's words, Nick would have smiled at the words. He knew his size—knew it was overwhelming to those who were unused to it. "I have never met a danger I could not overcome."

The arrogant words were only a half-truth, but the child need not know that.

James nodded once. "They will need someone to protect them. Especially . . ."

Isabel.

The name whispered through Nick's mind as he registered the obvious worry on James's face.

Was it possible that she was in serious danger? Was it possible that someone was after her? That she was in hiding? Nick gritted his teeth, a flash of protectiveness overwhelming him. He wanted to rush from the room, to find her and shake the information out of her. What the hell had the girl gotten herself into?

Finally, James whispered, "Especially Georgiana."

Awareness flashed. *Georgiana.*

"Who is Georgiana?"

"My governess."

They had found her.

The pleasure of the hunt surged, and Nick tamped it down, keeping his voice casual. "And how long has she been your governess?"

"Only a few weeks. But she's a good one. She speaks Latin. And she knows a great deal about being an earl."

Knowledge that comes from being the sister of a duke.

"What if she needs me and I am not there?"

The innocent question distracted Nick from his discovery. How many times had he asked himself the same thing when he was James's age? What if his mother had needed him and he had not realized it? How could he protect her when he had no idea where she had gone?

He shook his head once to clear it. This was a boy infatuated with his governess—a different thing altogether. "I know it is difficult to imagine being away from the manor, but I am sure that she will be all right without you." James seemed to want to disagree, so Nick continued. "She is well now, is she not?"

"Yes—but . . . what if someone comes for her?"

Guilt flared. *Someone is here for her already.*

"She will be all right." At least he could promise the boy that.

James wanted to say more—Nick could see it. But he instead dipped his head to the floor and said, "I suppose. Perhaps . . . if I left . . . you could stay? Just to be certain that they are safe?"

Nick considered the young earl, registering the concern in his eyes, recognizing it as the same concern he had seen in Isabel's eyes the evening before.

What in the hell were they involved in? Who were these girls? Were they all aristocracy?

He sucked in a deep breath. If she had a houseful of daughters of the aristocracy, Isabel was breaking a dozen different laws of the Crown. She was in enormous trouble. More trouble than he could help her out of.

Nick moved to where his clothes had been pressed and a fresh linen shirt laid out for him. Lifting the garment, he turned back to James, who was eagerly awaiting his reply. "I shall stay long enough to make sure you are all safe. Is that sufficient?"

"You give your word?"

"I do."

James's face split in a wide, relieved grin that reminded Nick of Isabel.

He couldn't help but find pleasure in the boy's happiness. "Now wait outside while I dress and you can show me your schoolroom. I should very much like to meet this governess of yours."

* * *

A quarter of an hour later, Nick was following James through the upper corridors of Townsend Park toward the schoolroom.

"It's on the way to the statuary—perhaps you could visit for luncheon. If you think you would like to, that is." The boy had been chattering since Nick had met him in the hallway outside his bedchamber; it appeared that their earlier conversation had comforted James, and, while Nick had little experience with children, he was happy to provide a distraction for the child's obvious concern.

Rightful concern.

Nick swallowed back his guilt. "Perhaps. We shall see how much work I have completed by then. But I will try."

The answer seemed to satisfy James, and he nodded once, turning his attention to a nearby closed door, its dark wood making it barely discernable from the dim hallway. James placed his palms on the wide panel and pushed, revealing a bright, welcoming schoolroom beyond.

Nick followed the boy inside, intrigued. It had been many years since he'd had cause to set foot inside a schoolroom, but the space registered at once both foreign and familiar—from the Latin words posted around the room to the telltale scent of chalk dust playing in his nostrils.

In the corner, Isabel leaned over a large glass rectangle, a young, fair-haired woman looking on. *Georgiana.* Even if she had not held herself as the daughter of a duke—straight and true as though she were untouchable—Nick would have known her. She had Leighton's coloring, the fair curls that sent women fawning over him and those honey-gold eyes that marked the Leighton line. She turned at James's cry of good morning, her gaze instantly settling on Nick. He made a point to hide his recognition, but he saw the flash of fear in her eyes and immediately knew that Townsend Park was not snatching girls—but saving them. Georgiana was terrified of him. She knew who he was—if Isabel had not told her, his scar would have given away his identity—and she likely knew that he was a friend of her brother's.

With a whispered excuse, she was gone, skirts flying out behind her as she rushed through a nearby doorway into an adjoining room. He watched her go, a strange emotion twisting in his gut.

Guilt.

He did not like it.

With conviction, he turned his attention to Isabel, garbed in gray muslin, reaching deep into a clear glass box, her head and one long arm submerged in the clear case. "Of all the— Why did I ever agree— The damned creature is, of course, as far from me as it can be."

"Izzy!" James rushed over to pull on her free hand. "What are you doing? You'll hurt him!"

"I will not." The words carried up, out of the box, and Nick moved farther into the room to gain a better look at the structure, filled with rocks and greenery, like a tiny forest. There, through the glass, he could see the tips of Isabel's fingers brushing aside leaves and pebbles and, finally, a thick branch. He watched as she turned a large stone until she could get a decent grip on it, clasping it tight. "I've got you!"

She righted herself with a triumphant grin, several long auburn strands of hair having escaped their moorings, giving her the look of an excited young country girl. Nick was immediately reminded of the evening before, of her kisses—so fresh and willing and eager. He watched, a smile playing across his lips, as she held her prize aloft, her height placing it far out of James's reach.

The young earl stood on his toes, reaching for the item in question. "Izzy! Give him to me!"

"Why should I?" Nick heard the teasing in her tone—was drawn to it. "I'm the one who saved him. By all rights, he belongs to me now."

"You don't even like turtles!"

"And for that, brother, you should be eternally grateful."

She looked past him with a laugh then, and noticed

Nick. He knew the moment that she registered his presence. Her smile vanished and she immediately looked around the room. *For Georgiana.* She was hiding her from him. Anger flared, fleetingly, at the discovery—that she did not trust him.

Not that she should. He was about to reveal their location to the world.

One hand went to her hair in a movement he was coming to recognize as the product of her nervousness. Distracted, she lowered her arm, delivering the item she had so proudly procured into James's grasp.

Nick felt a keen sense of loss at her change in demeanor. He wanted to know the smiling, happy Isabel. He'd had enough of this serious one.

He dipped his head. "Lady Isabel. Once more, we meet under . . . peculiar . . . circumstances."

She gave a quick, almost imperceptible curtsy, more to avoid meeting his gaze than for anything else, he guessed. "Lord Nicholas. If you would stop turning up uninvited, I assure you I would seem less peculiar."

"I never called you peculiar. Unique, yes. Intriguing, certainly. But never peculiar."

Color rose on her cheeks, and Nick felt a wash of pleasure at the sight. Even as he considered acting on the feeling, however, he was reminded of James's presence. Turning his attention to the boy, he crouched low. "I very much like turtles, Lord Reddich. Yours appears to be a fine specimen. May I have a look?"

James proudly held his pet out for inspection. Nick made a show of looking the turtle over. "Good-looking, indeed."

James beamed. "His name is George. After the king."

"I am certain the king would be very proud to have such a namesake."

"I found him in the spring. Izzy and I built the vivarium for him. It took us several weeks to make it perfect."

Nick looked up at Isabel, curious about a young woman who would spend such time developing a habitat for a turtle.

"Did you?" His gaze did not leave her. "What an excellent project."

Isabel huffed her irritation with the conversation, deliberately looking away and crossing her arms, pulling the fabric of her dress until it stretched tightly across her breasts.

He willed himself not to notice.

She had lovely breasts.

"Yes, well, if we do not move this vivarium, George shall lose all of his land," Isabel said, drawing Nick's attention back to the matter at hand. "The leaky roof has taken aim at the turtle."

James and Nick followed the direction of Isabel's finger, pointing at the ceiling. There was a leak in the roof and George's habitat was, indeed, under siege.

"You might as well stay, Lord Nicholas," Isabel said, and Nick noted the dryness of her tone. "We could use your brute strength."

Nick felt a primal satisfaction at her words—a recognition of the most basic of differences between them. The unrefined response was not something of which he should be proud, he knew. "I shall take it as a great compliment that you think me useful at all, Lady Isabel."

He noticed a small smile played across her lips as she turned back to the giant glass enclosure. She was not the unflappable female she wished to be.

"Put George down over there," she said to her brother, indicating a low table in the far corner of the room, "then come over here and help." She looked up at the ceiling again, considering her options.

Finally, she looked back at Nick and, indicating the far corner of the room, said, "I think over there is our best bet."

With a nod, Nick took his place at one end of the vivarium. "I do not suppose you would allow me to fetch Rock to help instead of doing this yourself?"

Isabel matched his stance at the opposite end of the enclosure. "If I needed help, St. John, I would call for a footman."

"Of course you would," Nick said dryly, wondering which of the motley crew of footwomen she would summon. It was not worth the argument. He put his shoulder to the container and pushed. Good Lord, the thing weighed a ton. He did most of the work of moving the vivarium, Isabel lending her strength to guide it into its new home, James looking on, clutching George.

And then the sky fell.

One moment, he was catching his breath, waiting for Isabel to indicate that she was satisfied with the new location of the enclosure, and the next, there was an ungodly crash behind him. He whirled around at the sound to find that an enormous piece of the ceiling plaster had fallen, landing in the exact place where they had all been standing not a minute earlier. A cloud of dust marked the path of the chunk of wet ceiling, heavy with rainwater that had soaked through the roof overnight.

There was a moment of stunned silence as they all took in the damage before Isabel let out a long sigh. "I suppose it was only a matter of time before that happened. Now you see why I was repairing the roof yesterday, Lord Nicholas." She turned to James. "You might as well go find your governess. I cannot imagine you'll be using the schoolroom today."

James blinked up at his sister, considering his options. Apparently, an afternoon with his governess somewhere other than the schoolroom was too enticing. Returning George to his home, the boy tore from the room, leaving Nick and Isabel to the mess.

Nick watched as the turtle emerged from his shell and tore a chunk from a nearby leaf, chewing leisurely, unaware of any external upheaval.

Oh, to be a turtle.

He turned back to Isabel, who was staring up at the hole in the ceiling. And then he saw it. One lone tear tracked from the corner of her eye down her cheek. She brushed it away immediately, so quickly that it was almost as though it had not happened.

But he had seen it.

Hell.

"Isabel—" he said, the uncertainty in his tone sounding foreign to him.

With a deep breath, she turned to him. "There isn't much we can do about it now, is there? We shall just have to hope that the rain stops before we must build a bathing room here."

And, in that, he recognized how much he admired this woman. Every other female he had ever known—from his mother, to the women he took to his bed—used tears to manipulate.

This one hid them.

And that made her even more remarkable.

He wanted to pull her to him. To give her a chance to let down her guard. She had an immense amount of responsibility. He did not blame her for feeling overwhelmed. But he knew implicitly that she would not want him to mention the tears, so he didn't. "All the very best houses in London are installing bathing rooms. They're spending small fortunes to do so. You would be the very height of fashion."

There was something in her eyes when she met his gaze—something between relief and gratitude. "Well, how lucky are we, then, to have such an accommodating roof?"

She chuckled then, a ripple of sound that teased his senses. He allowed himself to join her, and they laughed for a long moment, enjoying the companionship and the release.

When Nick's humor ebbed into silence, it gave way to a realization. He liked this girl. Far more than he would like to admit, frankly.

A sobering thought. One that inevitably led to pain. Or shackles.

He cleared his throat. "I wondered at James's nervousness about your safety, but now I see that he is not wrong to be concerned. Danger does have a way of seeking you out."

Her brows snapped together. "James is nervous about my safety?"

"Yours, his governess's, Lara's . . . 'the girls,' as he refers to you." She looked away instantly. "Isabel, is there something you should tell me?"

Tell me. He willed her to confess everything. If she did, he would do everything in his power to keep them safe. But she had to trust him.

She didn't say anything, of course, instead moving across the room to fetch a pail in which to put the large chunks of plaster that had shot across the room upon impact.

"Isabel . . . I can help you." He heard the words come out even as he knew he should not speak them.

"What makes you think that we need help?" Her tone was light, but Nick heard the thread of tension there. He was too aware of her to miss it.

He crouched low, across from where she had stooped to clean up the plaster. He put one hand out, settling it on her wrist, letting his bare hand linger on the band of skin between her glove and her sleeve. "Do not push me. I can tell there is something amiss."

She looked at the place where they touched, then farther, to meet his eyes. There was steel in her gaze. "It is not I who is doing the pushing, my lord. All that is amiss is a leaky roof and a visitor who will not leave well enough alone. Stop attempting to understand us. We are not your problem, Lord Nicholas. You would do us both well to stop pretending that we are." Silence fell in the wake of her tirade. She pulled her hand from beneath his, and resumed her cleaning. "I can take care of us. I always have."

There was a wealth of pain in the words.

"I never suggested that you couldn't."

She turned on him then, her voice rigid. "Yes, you did. Everyone does. But I've been here for years. Alone. Keeping the house together. And I shall be here long after you leave. Leaky roof and child earl and all."

The wicked rise and fall of her chest underscored her frustration, and he said the only words he could think. Words that were utterly wrong. "Let me help you."

Her gaze narrowed on him, the rise and fall of her chest

violent in the still room. "You want to help? Appraise the damned marbles."

She turned away again, and he watched her, fists clenched in irritation.

There was something going on in this house. He had faced enemies too vicious to recount—men who could inflict pain with scientific precision. Women with cold hearts to rival any of their male peers. Villains with more wealth and power than any evil man should have. He knew with an unwavering certainty that he could conquer whatever demons Isabel faced—that he could save this girl. This earldom. Without question.

But he did not know why it was so important that he do it.

What was it about this woman, this house, this place . . . that made him want to stay when his whole life, even a hint of permanence, of responsibility, even the threat of remaining too long in one place, had sent him running for the next adventure?

He wasn't leaving her. Not until he was certain they were all safe from whatever evils they were facing.

He simply had to convince her to let him do what he did best.

One of them had to stop lying.

And so he told her the truth.

At least, part of it.

"For God's sake, Isabel. I know about the girls."

Eleven

Lesson Number Four

Enlist allies.

Wooing your gentleman is waging a war. You will need superior strategy, time-tested tactics, and a trusted company of men (or women) to ensure victory. Strategic alliances will be necessary—nay, critical to your success! Consider friends, family, servants, and others who might help to bring you together. Do not discount the power of a willing host or hostess; a true gentleman will never ignore a hint to waltz, and it is a small step from a waltz in a ballroom to a walk in the gardens . . . And from gardens filled with strains from a ball, chapel and aisle are no distance at all!

Pearls and Pelisses
June 1823

There was something rather calming about his discovery of Minerva House.

She wouldn't have expected it to be so . . . She would have expected to be panicked, or to feel compelled to deny what he had seen—to scoff at his discovery and move on as if nothing had changed.

But what she felt when he'd looked her right in the eye and, as though he were announcing the weather, proclaimed his knowledge . . . it was more akin to relief than to panic. She was tired of hiding from him . . . of waiting for him to discover their secret in one way or another. In hindsight, it had been silly of her to imagine that she could keep the truth from him.

"You've a female butler, female footmen, and a female stable boy."

She stood at his words, removing her gloves, which were ruined from the plaster she had been cleaning. "I've a female stable *master*."

He ignored the correction. "You've a houseful of women."

"Not entirely."

"How many, entirely?"

She paused. "All but one."

He turned away from her. She noticed the scar on his cheek, white and stark with frustration. She watched his hands cup the back of his neck as he looked up at the ceiling. "Your brother."

"The *earl*." It seemed imperative that she underscore the title.

"The ten-year-old earl."

"What does it matter? He is still the earl!"

"It means there is no one to protect you!" The words shook the room, surprising Isabel with their power. All at once, she was angry. Angry at the truth of the words. Angry at the universe. Angry at this man—who had known her for less than three days—and his insistence that she must be protected. That she could not care for herself. For her brother. For her girls.

"You think I do not understand the straits in which we are? You think I do not see the risks we take? You think that if there were another way, I would not have found it?" Tears came fast and furious. "I never asked for your help, Lord Nicholas. I never asked you to protect me."

He met her gaze, frustration flaring in his blue eyes. "I know, Isabel. You wouldn't dare ask me for help. You are too afraid of revealing your weakness."

"Perhaps I do not ask you for help because too often it is men from whom we need protection. Did you consider that?"

She immediately regretted the words, which fell between them like a stone.

He did not deserve them. He was not like those other men. She knew that.

Even as she knew he was infinitely more dangerous.

"I am sorry."

He searched her eyes for a long moment. "It was easy enough to discover that they were female, but who are they? Why are they here?"

She shook her head. "You cannot really believe that I would tell you that."

"Are they criminals?"

"Some of them? I'm sure you would think so." She knew she wasn't being fair. But she could not stop herself. She was transfixed by the movement of his hands, clenching and unclenching slowly. "Some are just girls who needed an escape."

"If you are harboring criminals, Isabel, you could go to gaol."

She did not answer.

"People may come looking for them. That is why you keep them secret."

He was putting it all together, but she would not give him the pleasure of acknowledging the truth.

"The marbles. Your concern about finances. It isn't just for James. It is for them."

"I never denied that I needed the money for more than James's school."

"No. You merely omitted the whole truth."

"It is not your truth to bear."

"It seems I bear it nonetheless."

"I never asked you to do so."

He did not respond, instead turning back to the window, looking out over the wet, stormy land beyond. She could see only the scarred half of his face, the white line stark in the gray morning light, whiter still for his stony silence. He stood there for long minutes, unspeaking, until Isabel thought she might go mad from it. Finally, he spoke. "You can trust me."

Trust. What a lovely word.

There was something about this man, about his strength, about the way character virtually seeped from him, about the way he looked at her with patience and honesty and *promise*, that made her desperate to believe him. That made her want to place her faith, her trust, her girls, her house . . . everything she had . . . in his grasp and ask him to help her.

But she couldn't.

She knew better.

Oh, certainly he thought he could help them. He thought he could be their protector. Certainly the idea appeased some kind of masculine desire within . . . but she had seen what happened when men with pretty words and strong arms grew bored of their surroundings. Of the needs of the women in their lives. She had watched as her father had deserted her mother, leaving her with nothing but a crumbling estate and a broken heart.

If she leaned on him now, she would not survive it when he left.

"You have brought me into your world, Isabel, like it or not. I deserve to know."

There was no room to trust him. No matter how badly she wanted to do so. No matter how much his strength and his certainty—and his kisses—beckoned to her.

This man was more dangerous than legions of men like her father.

She shook her head.

"So you will not tell me."

She held her ground. "No."

"You do not trust me."

I want to!

"I—I cannot."

Something flared in his eyes—something dangerous—and Isabel wished she had not said the words.

He took a step closer to her, his voice low and dark. "I will find out on my own, you realize. I am an excellent hunter."

She did not doubt it. But she would not let him see that. "Oh, for heaven's sake. This is not a collection of marbles. You cannot expect them to simply open up and tell you all."

One side of his mouth kicked up. "They would not be the first women to do so."

She did not like thinking about other women opening up to him. She remained silent.

"So it's to be like that, is it . . . Izzy?"

There was something in the sound of her childhood nickname that made her feel laid bare. She did not like it. Not one bit. She squared her shoulders. "So it would seem."

"Excellent. Then let the hunt begin."

"This makes everything easier, doesn't it?"

"The girls will certainly be happy that they do not have to be so careful around him."

Isabel looked from Gwen to Jane, certain that the pair had lost their minds. "I don't think you understand. This is not a good thing. Lord Nicholas knows that we are hiding a houseful of women. He knows that Minerva House exists. This is not good."

She removed a sheaf of papers and an inkpot from a small kitchen drawer and sat at the large table in the center of the room. "I've got to find space for you all. I'm moving you from Townsend Park until all is settled. I'm sure I can find half a dozen households willing to take in a girl or two."

Silence fell at Isabel's words, only the sound of the nib of her pen scratching across the paper in the room. Gwen and Jane looked to each other, then to Kate, urging her to speak. "Isabel . . . perhaps you should reconsider such a drastic action."

"It's not drastic at all. It's the only *intelligent* course of action. Lord Nicholas knows that we've a household of women and it is only a matter of time before he discovers just how you all came to be here. Then what? Do you think that Margaret would take a girl or two?"

"Margaret used to live here. Of course she'd take some of the girls in. But is it necessary? Why not just wait for the marbles to be sold and move everyone?"

Isabel shook her head. "It's too late for that."

"You cannot believe that Lord Nicholas would reveal our location," Kate said in disbelief.

"I can, indeed, believe it," Isabel argued, not lifting her gaze from the paper in front of her. "Why would he side with us?"

"No," Kate said, "I cannot believe it."

"It's nonsense!" Gwen agreed. "It is clear that he is a good man . . ."

Isabel stopped writing to stare at Gwen. "How could you know that? You haven't even met him!"

"Well, I've *seen* him. And heard him with you. Between that and his willingness to help us, that seems enough."

Isabel blinked. "It seems nothing of the sort."

"I think that what Gwen is trying to say is that he seems like a good sort of man," Jane said cautiously. "After all, he came out to value your marbles on nothing but a random invitation. Such a level of generosity is rarely nefarious."

"Such a level of generosity is nearly *always* nefarious! Why, he could be anybody! He could be . . ." Isabel paused, searching for the very worst possible identity. The girls looked on as she struggled, smiles tugging at their lips.

"Yes?" Jane prompted.

"He could be a procurer of women!" Isabel announced, one finger in the air to punctuate her words. "A whoremonger!"

Jane groaned.

Kate rolled her eyes. "He's not a procurer, Isabel. He's a man who happens to be interested in helping us. And we just so happen to be in need of some help."

"He also happens to be one of London's Lords to Land, don't forget," Gwen added.

"And that," Kate agreed.

Isabel groaned then. "Oh, how I wish I'd never heard of that ridiculous magazine. Then I wouldn't be in this situation to begin with!" She looked from one girl to the next, each looking more sheepish than the last. "My God. You think I should be pursuing him."

"Perhaps you could *try* following one of the lessons. Number three, maybe?" Gwen was hopeful.

"Wooing Lord Nicholas St. John is not a reasonable solution to this problem!"

Jane spoke then. "For heaven's sake, Isabel. You've a generous, wealthy gentleman—"

"Handsome, too," Gwen interjected.

"Fine. A generous, wealthy, *handsome* gentleman who seems to want to be kind and helpful to you—despite your attempts to dissuade him of such—and who just so happens to have taken an interest in our situation, which, I might add, is precisely the kind of situation that could well be solved by a wealthy gentleman's interest. As far as I can tell, wooing St. John is the very best solution to our problems."

"Not to mention that you haven't much choice anymore, Isabel," Kate said. "If you're going to keep Minerva House solvent and secret, this is your best chance."

Isabel looked from her butler to her stable master and back again. "I thought neither of you wanted a thing to do with this silly magazine and its silly rules!"

They at least both had the grace to look sheepish.

"That was before it seemed to be our best bet of keeping a roof over our heads," Jane said.

Isabel scowled. "He is a wealthy gentleman who happens to be acquainted with the lion's share of London! What if he knows your father, Kate? Or the man from whom you stole, Jane?"

Kate shook her head, rejecting the threat. "First, I highly doubt that your handsome lord knew my brute of a father. And, second, I think that if this all goes in the direction we're expecting it to go, I won't have anything to worry about."

Isabel's gaze narrowed. "He is not my handsome anything."

"That's not what Gwen says," Kate teased, setting Jane and Gwen snickering.

Isabel considered throttling the lot of them. Why couldn't they take this seriously? How could they *not* take this seriously? It was for their safety that Minerva House had been so carefully protected for so long. It was for them that Isabel had worked to keep their location and their identity so quiet.

Kate spoke first. "Isabel. We know you have spent a large part of your life attempting to keep us safe. You've given us more than safety—you've given us courage—and faith in ourselves and in the world. We are not discarding your feelings—but you must realize that it would take more than one man knowing—"

"Two men," Isabel corrected.

"—more than two men knowing about Minerva House's . . . unique character . . . to bring us down."

"Not much more."

"We shan't leave you," Kate said.

"You shall." Isabel was not interested in debating the point.

Kate stiffened. "Well, I cannot speak for the rest of them, but I'm not leaving you."

The words were straight and true, and Isabel met Kate's green gaze across the table. Kate had been the youngest girl ever to arrive at Minerva House. She'd been barely fourteen when she'd marched up the wide, stone manor steps, mangy dog by her side, and knocked on the door, proud as could be.

Isabel had opened the door that morning, and one look at the defiant set of Kate's jaw had convinced her that the girl should stay.

Five years later, Kate was an invaluable addition to Minerva House. It was her strength that gave the girls their courage. It was her work ethic that set the tone for the rest. None of the girls were more loyal than Kate—jaw set now the way it had been when she was fourteen—who would walk through fire to save any one of them.

Isabel put down her pen.

"Now," said Kate, "why don't you tell us what you really think of this Lord Nicholas?"

The question echoed around them as Isabel looked down at the scarred table around which they were gathered. She traced a particularly deep gash in the wood, wondering absently where it had come from as she considered the answer to Kate's weighted question. "I—"

What *did* she think of him?

Truthfully, he'd done nothing to warrant her mistrust.

Nothing but saving her life twice, agreeing to value her marbles, befriending her brother, and offering to keep them all safe.

And then he'd kissed her.

Indeed, in three days he'd done more to warrant her trust than any other man had done in all her twenty-four years.

She sighed.

She did not know what to think.

"I suppose I rather like him."

Isabel was saved from having to elaborate on her statement by the arrival of Rock and Lara, laughing and stumbling into the kitchen from outdoors. Lara was wrapped in Rock's immense cloak, and she removed it as Rock closed the door firmly behind them, shutting out the wind and rain that threatened never to relent.

Looking around the room, Lara registered the seriousness of the other women.

"What has happened?"

Jane answered, "Lord Nicholas has discovered Minerva House."

Lara pushed her hair back from her face, wringing the rainwater from its sodden strands. "How?"

"He's known since yesterday," Rock said, removing his hat.

Isabel supposed she should have been surprised, but she wasn't. "This is all my fault. If I hadn't invited them here . . ."

Lara shook her head. "No, Isabel. If you hadn't invited them here, we wouldn't have any chance of saving Minerva House."

"He wants to know everything," Isabel said.

"And? What shall you do?" Lara asked.

"I don't know."

"She's decided she likes him," Kate announced.

"Kate!" Isabel blushed, looking at Rock, who did his best to ignore the announcement.

"But that's wonderful!" Lara said, breathy excitement in her voice. "The rain makes it ever so much easier to catch him!"

Rock coughed then, and Isabel had the distinct impression that he wanted to disappear. "I have not decided to catch him," she assured him.

"I did not ask," he said, half smiling.

Isabel cringed.

Silence fell, and she wondered if everyone in the room thought her a fool. She'd never been so uncertain of her actions before. She did not like this newfound doubt that came with men.

"If I may?" Rock spoke then, and had Isabel not been so caught up in her own thoughts, she would have been amused by his tentative tone.

She waved one hand idly in the air, pointedly. "By all means. No one else seems to mind interjecting an opinion."

"I assume that he did not take your secrecy well."

"That is correct. In fact, he threatened to seek out the truth himself." Isabel took a biscuit from the plate. "I do not understand why he cannot leave well enough alone."

Rock gave a little laugh. "Nick has never been able to leave well enough alone. Particularly when it comes to beautiful women." Isabel started to protest, but he pressed on. "He is irritated because you will not share your secrets. If he does not know them, he cannot protect them."

"How do I know he'll protect them?"

He pulled back as if he had received a physical blow. "Did you suggest such to him?"

She hedged. "I may have."

"Well. I don't imagine he responded well to that."

"No."

"There are few things I know with certainty, Lady Isabel. But this is one of them: If Lord Nicholas St. John vows to fight on your side, so he shall."

She was immediately chagrined. "I did not . . ."

"It sounds as though you did, Isabel," Lara said. "Mr. Durukhan, would you like some tea?"

Rock turned to Lara, giving her his undivided attention. "I should very much like some tea, Miss Caldwell. Thank you."

Isabel watched as Lara poured a cup of tea for Rock, peering up from her task with a soft smile. When he matched it, Isabel felt something flare in her chest. A longing for such a moment—filled with sweetness. There was something quite enticing about the obvious tentative interest between the two.

The moment was gone in an instant, and Rock had returned his attention to Isabel. "You must, of course, do what you think is best for your home and your staff, Lady Isabel. But you would do well to remember that Nick is a great ally. And he understands the seriousness of secrets. He would not like me saying so, but he is not without several of his own."

Isabel was not surprised by the words. There was something deeply compelling about Lord Nicholas St. John—a mystery that seemed to lurk beneath the surface, a darkness that she had witnessed firsthand when she was in his arms.

It was something that felt familiar. Something that made her believe—after all these years of thinking that the world was against her—that there might be someone who understood her. Who could help her.

Perhaps she could trust him.

That was, if she had not completely alienated him.

"I made him rather angry, I think."

There was encouragement in Rock's smile. "Nick is not one to stay angry for long."

"I am going to tell him everything." Her audience watched her carefully, no one speaking. "You realize that this will change everything. Once he knows, I cannot take it back." Isabel took a deep breath, as though steeling herself for battle. "I am not doing it for me. I'm doing it for Minerva House. For James. For the earldom. Not for me."

She had to believe that. For sanity's sake.

Lara reached across the table to take Isabel's hand. "He can help us."

Isabel looked at her cousin for a long moment, then turned to Rock, meeting his dark, serious gaze. He was watching her carefully, as if assessing her character. Finally, he nodded once. "You are precisely the kind of woman that he needs."

She blushed. "Oh . . . I am not . . ."

"Maybe not," he agreed, "but you are it, nonetheless."

Her stomach roiled at the words, and she was immediately nervous. But she could not back down now. She squared her shoulders and headed for the door, ready to search until she found him.

"Isabel?" Gwen called after her. When she turned back, the cook said, "Show interest in his work. Gentlemen like ladies who share their entertainments."

Isabel gave a short laugh. "*Pearls and Pelisses*? Still?"

Gwen smiled. "It has worked so far."

Sarcasm laced Isabel's tone when she replied. "Oh, yes, it's working brilliantly."

"Well, it would do, if you were following it more carefully. Also, do not be afraid to be close to him!"

Isabel looked to the ceiling for patience. "I am leaving now."

Gwen nodded once. "Good luck!"

Isabel spun on one heel, wishing that *Pearls and Pelisses* had offered up *Ten Ways to Apologize to London's Lords to Land.*

Unfortunately, in this, she was on her own.

Twelve

Lesson Number Five

Cultivate interest in your lord's interests.

Once your discreet first meeting has successfully garnered the gentleman's attention, it is time to offer thoughtful and unwavering companionship for his pursuits. Any great man will have masculine interests, but remember that there is always a way for you to remain relevant despite your womanliness.

Does your lord love his horseflesh? Perhaps he would like an embroidered blanket upon which to find his seat!

And do not be afraid, Dear Reader, to be close to him!

Pearls and Pelisses
June 1823

Isabel stood at the entrance to the statuary, watching Nick work.

The storm had cast the room in an unearthly green pall, and the thunder and howling wind outside had hidden her arrival from him, so she could watch him unheeded. Whether from the light, or from the tension in his frame, or from the contents of the room, he seemed immense, even as he bent over a notebook, scribbling notes on a nearby statue.

She had never met a man like him. He was broad and firm, and his surroundings made it impossible for an onlooker not to compare him to the marbles—these great, ancient sculptures designed to honor and celebrate the perfect form.

He put them to shame, all wide shoulders and long legs and sinewy power. She watched as one thick lock of hair fell across his forehead, catching between his brow and the silver rim of his spectacles. This was the first she had seen of the glasses—an incongruous addition to this daunting man, an addition that served only to make him even more tempting.

She caught herself at the thought. When had spectacles become tempting?

When had this *man* become so tempting?

She was instantly nervous about what was to come. He so confused her—one moment, she wanted him gone, and the next, she wanted him here. For as long as he could stay.

She sighed, and the sound, soft and barely heard, turned his head.

He met her eyes, his gaze unwavering, and waited, unmoving, for her to take the next step. She hovered in the doorway, unable to look away.

And then she stepped into the room, and closed the door behind her.

He straightened as she approached, removing his spectacles and placing them on the pedestal of a large black statue nearby, before he leaned against the base and folded his arms across his wide chest, waiting for her.

Show interest in his interests.

She could do that.

She stopped mere inches from him, looking up at the statue. "This is a fine marble. Have you identified it yet?"

He did not follow her gaze. "It is Apollo."

"Oh?" The high-pitched squeak grated on her ears. She cleared her throat delicately. "How do you know that?"

"Because I am an expert in antiquities."

He was not going to make this easy.

"I see. I suppose I owe you the answer to a question now."

He turned back to his notebook. "I find I've grown tired of that game."

"Nick." The sound of his name on her lips surprised them both. He turned back to her. Waited. She stared for a long minute at the place where his collar met the tanned skin of his throat. She spoke to the spot. "I am sorry."

The only sound in the room was his breathing, slow and steady in the wake of her words, and there was something in its evenness that spurred her on. "I have never told anyone about Minerva House—" She met his curious gaze. "That's what we call it. The house. The girls."

She paused, waiting for him to ask questions. When he didn't, she began speaking—always to the notch in his throat—unwilling to meet his gaze, unwilling to look away entirely. "We had nothing. My father had left and my mother had gone into a . . . decline. She took to her bed and would go days without eating—without seeing us. And when she did—" She swallowed. *No. She couldn't tell him that.* "The servants were not being paid. I'm fairly certain that they were stealing from us. And then, one day, they were gone."

"How old were you?"

"Seventeen." She shook her head, lost in her thoughts. "Jane was the first to arrive. She needed work. Shelter. And I needed someone to help keep the estate running. She was intelligent. Strong. Willing. And she had friends who were in similar straits. Within months, there were half a dozen girls here. All looking to escape something—poverty, family, men; I suppose I was trying to escape something, too.

"If they were willing to work, I was willing to have them. They kept the estate afloat. They tended goats and mucked stalls and tilled land. They worked as hard as the men we'd had before. Harder, even."

"And you kept them a secret."

She met his eyes then. "It wasn't hard. My father was never

here. He paid for his life with his winnings when he was flush, with the contents of the house in town—ultimately the house itself—when he was down on his luck." She stopped, then laughed bitterly.

"And your mother?"

She shook her head, pressing her lips into a straight, thin line as she remembered. "She was never the same after he left. She died soon after Jane arrived."

He reached for her then.

She did not resist, even as she knew it was wrong—that she should not allow him to hold her. But how could she resist his warm strength and the way it enveloped her? How long had it been since she had been the one held? Since she had been the one to be comforted?

"Why do you do it?"

She turned her head, placing her ear against the crisp wool of his jacket. She did not pretend to misunderstand. "They need me."

And . . . as long as they need me, it's easier to forget that I am alone.

He made an encouraging noise deep in his chest, and it spurred her on. "There are a dozen of them out there—seamstresses and governesses, mothers and wives. One owns a pie shop in Bath. They had nothing when they came to me."

"You gave them something."

She was silent for a long while, ultimately pulling out of his arms. When he let her go, she felt a small pang of remorse that he did not resist. "It is all I have ever done well." She looked up at the statue of Apollo. "I couldn't keep my father from leaving—and taking my mother with him. Couldn't keep the estate afloat. But I could help these girls."

He understood. She could see it in his clear, open gaze.

"I am scared," she added softly.

"I know."

"I cannot expect Densmore to support us. I cannot expect him to keep our secrets."

"Isabel—" He stopped, and she could see that he was choosing his next words carefully. "Who are these girls that you live in fear of their discovery?"

She stayed quiet.

"Are they married?"

"Some of them," she whispered. "They've broken the law to come here."

"And you break the law to hide them."

"Yes."

"You know you risk James's reputation. He's got enough of a scandal to overcome."

Frustration flared. She did not like to think that it was James who would ultimately suffer for her choices. "Yes."

"Isabel," he said, his tone a mix of exasperation and concern, "you cannot shoulder this burden by yourself. It is too much."

"What do you suggest I do?" She wrapped her arms around herself, defensive. "I will not abandon them."

"You do not have to."

"What, then?"

"There are ways."

She gave a little laugh. "You think that, in seven years, I have not considered every possible avenue? Who will risk themselves to take in a woman who has deserted her marriage vows? Who will stand up to an aristocratic father coming to fetch his runaway daughter? And even if they might, who would take such a risk on nothing but the word of the daughter of the Wastrearl?"

"Let me help you."

She was silent then. She'd never wanted to trust someone as much as she wanted to trust this man—this man who reeked of strength and power and safety. It had all seemed so simple in the kitchen. But now, faced with him, could she do it? Could she place her faith in him? Could she place their future in his hands?

His blue eyes glittered with something she did not quite understand as he thrust both hands through his hair and turned away from her, his frustration sending him stalking several feet away before he spoke again. "You are the most infuriating female I have ever met." He turned back to her, and his words came fast and furious. "You take pride in the fact that you've done this alone, don't you? It's *your* house. They're *your* girls. It's *you* who have saved them. This is *your* work.

"You should be proud of it, Isabel—Lord knows you should be. But you are intelligent enough to know when you are in over your head. You've got nothing to protect you from whatever is outside these walls. I'm offering you help. Protection."

Isabel was at the edge of a precipice, a monumental change that would alter everything. She looked up into his blue eyes—eyes that promised everything she dreamed of, safety for her girls, support for James, security for the house.

He was a good man. She believed that.

But relinquishing her hold on the house—trusting him with everything—it would not be easy. Her doubts came on a whisper. "I don't know . . ."

He sighed. "I think you should go. The sooner you do, the sooner your damned collection will be valued and the sooner I shall be out of your life."

He turned away, dismissing her.

She didn't want to leave him.

"You don't understand. These are my girls."

He exhaled a harsh breath. "Nothing about that would change if you let me help you."

"I have nothing else!"

There. The words were out. And then she could not stop them.

"This is all I have ever had! All I have ever been! If I need you to help me keep it intact . . . what does that make me? What do I become, then?"

"It's not true." He moved toward her, his words hypnotic. Taking her face in his hands, he flooded her with heat, with need. "I know what it is to think yourself alone in the world, Isabel. It is rarely the case."

She hated feeling alone.

And she had been alone for so very long.

She closed her eyes against the thought, unwilling to show him her sadness.

Her weakness.

Yet, when he spoke again, she could not stop herself from meeting his firm gaze. "I've never met anyone like you. I've never met anyone—man or woman—with such strength. Such courage. You are not alone. You will never be alone."

She didn't know who moved first—which one of them closed the distance between them. All she knew was that when he was kissing her, she didn't feel alone at all.

She gave herself up to the feeling.

For a long moment, he was still, his lips soft and settled against hers, underscoring his presence, his strength, his control. She reveled in those things at first, until his nearness—his scent, his heat, his size—overwhelmed her, and she thought she would go mad if he did not move.

And then he did.

His warm hands tilted her face up to his, to better align their mouths, and his lips played across hers, demanding that she meet him in kind. And she did. He took everything she offered, stroking, sucking, loving her mouth with a relentless kiss that stole her sense of balance. That stole her sense altogether. She grasped his arms, reveling in their size and their strength, and she turned herself over to him, sighing into his mouth and matching him stroke for stroke, caress for caress.

When he finally pulled back and met her heavy-lidded gaze, a ghost of a smile crossed his lips before he lifted her into his arms. She gasped at the movement, and he stole her open mouth for another quick, intoxicating kiss before he spoke, his voice a dark promise. "Shall I show you how very far from alone you are?"

What a marvelous thing for him to say. "Yes," she whispered, the words barely sound. "Please."

He moved then, carrying her on a winding course through

the statuary, until they reached the far end of the room, where a wide, low bench sat beneath an enormous rose window. He sat, then, and settled her into his lap, running his hands up to her hair, deliberately scattering the hairpins, bringing her hair down around them. She watched him as he took in the mass of auburn curls, closed her eyes as he ran his hands through it in long, magnificent strokes. She tilted her head back, leaning into his caresses. The movement bared her neck to his gaze, and with a low groan, he bent over her, settling his lips to her skin, sending rivers of pleasure through her with the soft strokes of his tongue. She gasped at the wicked scrape of his teeth over the delicate spot where her neck and shoulder met, felt the way his lips curved in a private smile at the sound, then softened against her pulse and sucked at the spot until she thought she might die from the pleasure of it.

She cried out, wrapping herself around him, eager to touch him, to kiss him, wherever she could. Her lips met the corner of his eye and, without thinking, she touched her tongue to the rough-smooth line of his scar. The caress turned him wild, and all at once, his hands were loosening the ties of her bodice, freeing more skin as he dropped hurried, wet kisses across the slope of her. He ran his tongue along the edge of the fabric in a trail of fire, pulling it low and spilling her breasts into his waiting hands.

She opened her eyes at feel of him against her, knowing that she would find him watching her—wanting to see him watching her. Lightning flashed, untamed, in the sky behind him, casting them in a wicked white flash as Nick traced one finger across the straining skin of her breast, circling the tip once, twice, with reverence. She exhaled on a shaking breath, and he looked up, his blue eyes glittering.

"So beautiful," he said, circling her nipple again and again, watching her response as they grew hard and aching. "So passionate, so eager." He lifted his gaze to hers. "You are here, Isabel. As am I."

She was not alone.

She saw the desire in his eyes then, and the recognition sent a wave of feminine pleasure through her. He wanted her. She did not know where the words came from when she spoke. "Touch me."

She watched as his surprise flared in his gaze, quickly replaced by something darker, more intense. "With pleasure." And he set his mouth to her breast, sucking gently, working the hardened tip with his mouth and tongue and teeth until she cried out and clasped his hair, holding on to the one stable thing in her existence.

She squirmed against him, unable to keep herself from pressing closer to him, and he lifted his head, staying her movements with one hand as he hissed his pleasure against her straining nipple. With a feminine knowledge that she did not know she possessed, she rocked against him again, deliberately, and he lifted his mouth from her to meet her gaze. Putting one hand to the back of her head, he whispered, "Wait . . ." and took her mouth in a searing kiss as he lifted her and moved her to straddle him, pulling her closer. "That's better, don't you think?"

She tested the position, rocking against him once more, this time with her skirts bunched between them. When he groaned at the movement, she said, "Oh, yes. Much better."

He laughed at her words, the sound sending a jolt of pleasure to the core of her. "Shall we see what else is better in this position, my Voluptas?"

She smiled shyly. "Yes, please."

"Well, since you asked so politely . . ." He settled his lips to one breast, and Isabel called his name, the sound echoing in the room. She moved in time to the lovely pull of his mouth on her, to the way his fingers played at the tip of her other breast, sending waves of pleasure pooling deep within.

He shifted, his hands were smoothing up her legs, pressing her against him, guiding her movements, sliding over her linen pantaloons and pulling at the tapes there to gain access to that place where she hadn't known—but now knew without doubt—that she so desperately wanted him. With one hand, he cupped her gently, sending a dart of pleasure through her. She gasped at the feel of him, and he lifted his head, his smile a wicked promise in the room, their labored breathing and the rain pounding against the windows the only sounds in the room.

He took her mouth again, consuming her, making her forget everything but his hands, his lips, his body beneath her. She plunged her fingers into his heavy, soft hair and reveled in the deep, satisfied sound he made as he rocked the heel of his palm against her, giving her what she wanted but had not known to ask for. She pulled back with a little breath, unsure of the sensations he was rocking through her. "Nick . . ." His name came on a mix of passion and confusion.

"Yes, beautiful . . . I am here." His mouth was at her ear now, his teeth playing over the lobe and scattering her thoughts. She sighed at the feel of his tongue against her sensitive skin. His hand stilled against her. She moved again, but he did not give her that for which she had asked. "Isabel." Her name was a dark promise. "What do you want?"

She opened her eyes and turned her face to his, meeting his glittering blue gaze—those gorgeous eyes that threatened her sanity—"I want . . ." She shook her head. "I need . . ."

"Let me . . ." He slid one finger through the soft curls that shielded her, parting the folds there and pushing inside her heat. "Is this what you need?"

She closed her eyes at the soft caress and let out a low moan of pleasure.

"Mmm . . . I think it is precisely what you need . . ." He began to move against her, circling the secret folds of her, his words at her ear, a soft, sinful sound that sent heat coursing through her. "Do you ever touch yourself here, Isabel?"

She bit her lip. Shook her head.

"Oh, but you should . . . so soft . . . so wet . . . so wanting . . ." He stroked against her pulsing flesh, giving her precisely what she wanted, one finger delving deep into the core of her as his thumb worked a tight circle at the center of her pleasure. She cried out at the feel of him there, and his voice grew darker, roughened with his own desire. "You are made to come apart here. Do you feel it, love?"

She nodded, eyes tightly shut as he pushed her further and further toward the thing she so desperately wanted, but could not name. The movements of his thumb came faster and firmer, and she pressed against him, forgetting everything but the sound of his voice, the feel of his hand on the most secret part of her. "Take it, Isabel. Take your passion. I am with you."

She tensed as it came rushing toward her, and he took her lips in a rich, soul-stealing kiss. A second finger joined the first inside her, thrusting deep, in time to the rolling of her hips, to her silent demand for everything he could give her. He pressed long and hard against the core of her, where she most ached . . . where she most needed him. He pulled back, meeting her unseeing gaze.

She cried his name, desperate.

"Let go, beauty. I have you."

And because he did have her, she let go, exploding in his arms, writhing against him, begging for more even as he gave her what she wanted. And when he had wrung the last, pulsing movement from her, had captured her last, keening cries, he held her in his strong arms as she regained her senses.

Slowly, he began to right her appearance; she allowed him to refasten the tapes of her pantaloons, to lift her to restore her thoroughly wrinkled skirts to some semblance of normalcy, to deftly retie the bodice of her gown. When he was done, he held her to his chest, stroking her back and arms and legs gently.

This was what it was like not to be alone.

After several long minutes, he tightened his arms around her and placed his lips softly to her temple. "I think that it might be best if we got up before someone comes searching for us."

The words roused her from her daze, crashing her back to reality. She sat straight up, extricating herself from his embrace and nearly leaping from his lap. She dropped to her hands and knees immediately, grasping for the hairpins that he had scattered.

He sat forward, watching her for a moment before saying, "Isabel. It is all right."

She sat back on her heels at that, looking up at him. "It is not at all all right, my lord."

He sighed. "We are back to *my lord* again? Really?"

She had already turned away to collect more pins. When she had the last, she stood, moving to a nearby statue to set them down and restore her hair to some semblance of decorum.

In her most indignant tone, she spoke to the room at large. "I never should have . . . *you* never should have!"

"Yes, well. I am not going to apologize for it."

She turned back to him. "That's not very gentlemanly."

He met her gaze with a heated one of his own. "Nevertheless, Isabel . . . I enjoyed myself. And I think you did, too."

She blushed.

One brow rose. "I see I am not wrong."

Her gaze narrowed, but she feared her censure lost some power while her hands were high above her head attempting to restore her coif. "You are an incorrigible man."

"You can admit it to me, Isabel."

She gave him her back and muttered, "No. I can't."

He laughed then, leaning back in his seat. "You just did, beauty."

She spun back. "You mustn't call me that!"

Even though I like it.

Too much.

"Why not?"

She lowered her voice to a whisper. "You know perfectly well why not."

"Tell me you enjoyed yourself, and I'll stop."

"No."

He straightened his jacket sleeves. "Suit yourself. I rather like calling you a beauty. Since you are."

"All right. I enjoyed myself."

His grin was wicked. "I know."

She had to turn away to hide her own smile at his arrogance.

Dear Lord. What had she gotten herself into?

She looked over her shoulder at him. "This is an entirely inappropriate conversation. I must insist it end."

He barked with laughter at her imperious tone. "Isabel, I'm sure you will agree that it is rather late for such haughtiness."

She blushed. "You are too much!"

He leveled her with a liquid gaze. "I assure you, darling, I am just enough."

She did not fully understand the words, but his tone was enough to give her a general sense of his meaning. Her cheeks flamed. "I must go."

"No!" he called after her, standing finally. "Don't go. Stay. I shall endeavor to be the perfect gentleman."

One of Isabel's brows rose in an imitation of the look he had so often given her. "I shall believe that when it comes to pass, my lord."

He laughed again. "A hit, my lady." She could not help but join him in his laughter, and when it waned, it left them in a companionable silence. Nick spoke first, filling it. "Why have I never heard of you?"

"My lord?" Isabel's brow furrowed in confusion at the question.

"I did not travel in the same circles as your father, but you are the daughter of the Earl of Reddich, who cut something of a wide swath across London. Why did I not hear of you?"

Thank God you never heard of me.

Isabel swallowed once, uncertain. "My mother never wanted me to go to London—thinking back, I imagine she felt that way because she did not want me to witness the truth about my father. Perhaps she did not want to witness it herself." She met his eyes and registered the understanding in their depths. *He had a story, as well.* The knowledge pushed her forward, compelling her to reveal more. "My mother spoke of my father—as though he were a marvel. Her tales of him, I know now, were mostly fabricated—memories scrubbed clean of the scarlet ink he had spilled on them, rendered anew to be something more powerful, more magnificent than any real history could have been.

"But I believed her. And, as such, I believed in him. My earliest memories of him must be some perverse combination of fantasy and reality, because I can see them smiling together, loving each other . . . but I am not certain that was ever true."

Nick nodded, and she could not help but continue.

"But you asked about London," she reminded them both.

"Yes. Your mother may not have wanted you to go—but you must have had a season."

She stiffened at the memory. She'd been promised one, of course, on that fateful trip home, when her father had announced his intentions of using his only daughter to gain funds. Embarrassment flared. She could not tell him the story. She did not want him to think so cheaply of her. Instead, she shook her head. "No. I did not have a season."

His gaze narrowed on her, and she recognized disbelief there. She willed him not to ask any further questions.

"You did not want to take your rightful place in society?"

One side of her mouth kicked up in a wry smile. "Tell me, Lord Nicholas, do they often clear a spot at Almack's for the daughter of the Wastrearl?"

His gaze darkened. "Hang Almack's."

"Spoken like a man who is at liberty to avoid it."

He shook his head. "Not at all. My family is not without its fair share of scandal, Isabel. Indeed, my sister was recently denied entrance to Almack's."

Her eyes widened. "You jest."

"I do not."

"But she is the sister of the Marquess of Ralston!"

"Half-sister," Nick said wryly, "But until mere months ago, my brother was welcome in society under severe duress. His was not the most pristine of pasts."

"What happened to change it?"

"He married a woman with an unimpeachable reputation and connections to the most powerful families of the *ton*."

"An excellent strategy."

Nick smiled. "It would have been if Gabriel had strategized to win her. He did not. Instead, he fell in love. Quite accidentally."

Isabel's brow furrowed. "Such a thing happens?"

"Apparently. They're rather sick over each other."

Isabel ignored the tug of envy that came with his tale—so unfathomable. "How nice."

He smiled. "My point is, with or without Almack's, you could have come out. You could still take your place there."

Isabel considered the words. It had been a long time—years—since she had even thought of the trappings of society. She would not even know where to begin to enter society, and the idea of having to learn all the rules and regulations of the *ton* was enough to set panic loose within.

No. London was not for her.

"I think you overestimate the skills with which women of the aristocracy are born."

He tilted his head, a question in his eyes.

She gave a little sigh before turning away. She ran her hand along the edge of a nearby pedestal and confessed, "I would not know how to begin to be a society lady: I am certain that my conversational style is entirely wrong; I would certainly embarrass myself and everyone around me during my first social situation; while I am a competent seamstress, I have no knowledge of needlepoint; I don't have any understanding of fashion; and I cannot dance." She winced as the words flooded out of her. Certainly he would not find them at all flattering.

Not that she cared if he found her flattering or not.

Liar.

Isabel ignored the little voice in her head.

"You cannot dance?"

Of course he would latch on to that. "Not really."

"Well, that seems like it would be easy to fix."

She gave a little laugh. "In case you had not noticed, my lord, there are not very many dance masters this far north."

"Aren't you lucky that I am here, then? I would very much like to teach you to dance."

She swiveled her head toward him in disbelief. "I beg your pardon?"

"I think we should begin tonight. There is a ballroom in this house, is there not?"

"Yes." Surely he wasn't serious.

"Excellent. After dinner then?"

She blinked. "After dinner?"

"I shall take that as resounding agreement."

"I—"

"You aren't afraid, are you?"

Well, now he'd thrown down the gauntlet.

She cleared her throat. "Of course not."

He smiled. "I did not think so. Now, if you would stop distracting me, I will see you at dinner."

"I—yes, of course." In a daze, she began to move through the statues toward the door.

"Oh, and Isabel?"

The sound of her name on his lips was a wicked promise, even from a respectable distance. She spun back, suddenly breathless. "Yes?"

"Just for tonight . . . shall we pretend you aren't in mourning?"

The words sent a thrill through her, and she had an immediate sense that if she were to agree to his request, it would change everything.

She took a deep breath, hovering on the brink of an answer for a long moment. No matter what she told herself, she was not immune to this man and to his charms. He was the ultimate temptation. And she wanted to give in.

She took a deep breath.

"That sounds like a lovely idea."

Thirteen

Nick had just tucked in his shirt in preparation for dinner when the knock sounded on the door to his bedchamber. He snapped around at the sound, immediately on edge, then shook off the response.

If he were honest with himself, he would admit that he had been on edge since his afternoon with Isabel . . . and that he was eagerly awaiting the evening ahead.

But then he had little interest in being honest with himself.

A second knock sounded, and he turned in time to see James poke his head through the narrow space between the door and its seat.

"I hear you are joining us for dinner."

Nick raised a brow in response. "I had planned to, yes."

James nodded solemnly. "Good."

The boy did not move from his position, half inside, half outside the room. Instead, he watched as Nick turned back to the looking glass and lifted a comb to tame his sable curls.

For a few moments, neither of them spoke, until, finally, Nick said, "Would you like to come in, Lord Reddich?"

The words unfroze the boy, and he scurried into the room, closing the door firmly behind him. "I would. Please."

Nick hid his smile, instead watching his visitor in the mirror as he finished his toilet. He adjusted the sleeves of the linen shirt he wore before he smoothed its body along his torso. Lifting his cravat from where it lay on a nearby chair, he said, "Was there something you wanted?"

James shook his head, distracted by the sure, strong movements of Nick's hands as he began the intricate collection of movements that would result in an elaborately knotted cravat. "How do you know how to do that?"

Nick paused. "I've known how to do it for a very long time."

James crept closer, transfixed. "But . . . how did you learn?"

Nick thought for a moment. "I suppose my valet taught me."

"Oh." There was silence as James considered the answer. "I shall have to learn to do that before I go to school, I would think."

Nick turned. "Would you like me to teach you?"

The boy's eyes lit up. "Would you mind very much?"

"Not at all." Nick removed the strip of linen from his person and placed it around James's neck. Turning the boy to the looking glass, he walked James through the movements until the cravat was a fair approximation of the knot Nick had created earlier.

James leaned into the mirror, considering the neckpiece from several angles as Nick moved away to don the rest of his dinner attire. "It looks very well."

There was something in the boy's pride that tugged at Nick's memory. While he might not remember how he learned to tie a cravat, he did remember the powerful desire for approval, for acceptance as a man.

When Nick had been James's age, his mother had deserted them—absconding in the middle of the night with little but the clothes on her back, leaving twin sons and a desolate husband in her wake. In the weeks following, his father had disappeared, as well, pulling further and further into himself, leaving Nick and Gabriel to fend for themselves—to survive the crushing blow of the loss of two parents. They'd been shipped off to school within a month, thanks to the intervention of a committed aunt who had been aware of the devastation their mother had wrought.

Nick had spent the first year at school working as hard as he could—eager to impress his father, convinced that if, when he and Gabriel returned home for the summer holiday, he had received top honors at school, somehow he could convince his father that his sons were enough.

He had learned quickly that nothing would ever be enough to assuage his father's pain and guilt at losing his marchioness. But looking at this boy, the young, resilient Earl of Reddich, he remembered what it was like to try. And to believe that he might succeed.

And he wanted to give this boy what he had never had.

"Indeed, it does. You will have to practice to get it perfect, but it shouldn't take you long." Nick buttoned his waistcoat, watching the boy's eyes light with pleasure as he unwrapped the linen from his neck and practiced in the mirror once more. When the tip of the earl's tongue emerged at the corner of his mouth, and he screwed up his face trying to recall the movements he had just learned, Nick laughed and came forward to help. When the cravat was tied once again, James grinned up at him.

Who would have guessed that here, out on the Yorkshire moors, he would find such satisfaction as he did when he made the Townsend children smile?

Of course, there was nothing childlike about the elder Townsend.

As James destroyed his handiwork to try his new craft once more, Nick allowed his thoughts to turn to Isabel. One moment, she was pushing him away, telling him that she wanted him gone from her house and her life, and the next she was confessing her past, and her secrets and coming apart in his arms, sweet and sensual and splendid.

He'd never met a woman like her.

The way she had laid herself bare, confiding the story of

her father's desertion, of her mother's desolation, of her own commitment to keeping what little family she was left with together, of keeping Townsend Park working despite the devastating blow of the loss of its master—Nick was entirely intrigued by this enigmatic female.

"Around the other bit once more," he coached James as he reached for his topcoat.

James followed the instruction carefully. "I have been thinking."

"Yes?"

"I think you should marry Isabel."

Nick froze, coat halfway up his arms as he considered the boy's serious countenance. "I beg your pardon?"

"It is logical, really."

"Is it?" Of all the things the boy could have said, this was not the one that Nick had expected.

James nodded once. "Yes. Isabel would make an excellent wife. Shall I tell you why?"

"By all means."

The boy took a deep breath, as though he had been practicing his words. "She is very good at running a house. She knows her sums better than anyone I've known. Also, she can sit a horse as well as a man. Perhaps when it stops raining you will see for yourself."

"I shall look forward to it." Nick was surprised by the truth in his words.

"Also, she is excellent at charades."

"A quality any man should look for in a wife."

"There are other things, too." James tilted his head, thinking. "She is not ugly."

Nick felt a smile tugging at his lips. "No, she is not. But may I suggest that you not say it in quite that way to her?"

"I shan't. But perhaps you could say it. Girls like compliments."

"If you have learned that at such a young age, you shall be fine when it comes time for you to interact with the fairer sex," Nick said. "I shall happily tell her that she is not ugly."

He faced his reflection in the mirror, noting his young companion, watching him carefully in his irredeemably wrinkled cravat.

"I think you would make a good husband."

Nick looked to James, decided to tell the truth. "I am not so certain."

James's brow furrowed. "Why not?"

Nick did not speak. What could he say to this boy that would make sense?

"Is it because you are not titled?"

"No. I do not think a title makes a good husband, always."

"Nor do I. My father was not a very good husband."

Nick nodded. "I am sorry to hear it."

James shrugged. "I do not remember him."

"Do you wish that you did?"

The boy thought for a long moment. "Sometimes."

Nick drew in a deep breath at the word, so honest. He knew what it was to be a ten-year-old boy with no one to look to for guidance or help or advice. And he understood the confusion James was feeling with the man they called his father gone without ever having been more than a mystery. "What would you say if you could meet him now?"

James shook his head once. "I cannot meet him. He is dead."

"It does not matter. What would you say?"

James looked out a nearby window for a long minute before turning back to Nick. "I would tell him that I plan to be a much better earl than he was."

Nick nodded solemnly. "I think that is a fine thing to say."

James was silent for a moment, considering his words before adding, "I would also ask him why he did not want us."

Nick did not like the tightness in his chest at the boy's words, so familiar. Had he not asked himself the same thing for years after his mother had deserted them? "I cannot imagine that he did not want you."

James's large brown eyes were clear and forthright. "But you do not know."

"No. I do not." Nick felt the heavy weight of importance this boy would place upon his answer. "But I can tell you that if I were in his position, I would absolutely want you."

"And Isabel?"

"And Isabel." The truth of the words was rather startling to him, and he moved away to run a comb through his hair once more.

James tracked his movements. "Then you *would* consider marrying her?"

A ghost of a smile crossed Nick's lips. The young earl had clearly learned his tenacity from his sister. He set his comb down and turned back. He'd never seen anyone look as hopeful as James did in that moment, as though a proposal from Nick were all that it would take to make everything right.

What James did not know was that Isabel would want nothing to do with Nick when she realized the truth about him.

The thought grated. "I think that Isabel might not like the idea of us negotiating her marriage without her in the room."

"I am earl, you know. This is the business of men."

Nick barked in laughter. "And as a man who has a sister nearly as obstinate as your own, I suggest you never say *that* again as long as you would like to remain alive."

James sighed. "Well, if it matters, I choose you for her."

"I am flattered by your endorsement." Nick raised a brow. "Has there ever been another man in consideration?"

He should not be asking such questions.

James nodded. "Men come to collect her sometimes."

Nick's jaw went slack briefly. "To collect her?"

James nodded. "Mostly, they come because they've won her."

"They've won her? As in, her heart?"

He did not like the idea of that.

The boy shook his head. "No. They've won her in a wager."

Anger flared. Surely Nick had not heard that correctly. "They've won her in a wager with whom?"

James shrugged. "With our father, I expect."

Nick clenched his teeth. The idea that the former Earl of Reddich would have gambled away his only daughter—would have gambled away Isabel—was simply too much. Nick wanted to pummel something. Immediately. He clenched his fists tightly, imagining the pleasure he would take in putting his fist into the face of the smug aristocrat who had taken that bet. And the dead aristocrat who had suggested it.

He wanted to ask more, to gain more insight into this insane world where Isabel and James had been raised, but he could not. He forced himself to relax the muscles that had gone instantly alert at the boy's revelation. It was not his place to ask about such things. At least, not right now.

Right now, he was going to dinner.

And then he was going to teach Isabel to dance.

Isabel had been about to go abovestairs to check on James and Nick when she heard them coming down the center staircase just outside the dining room. Her pulse quickened at the deep rumble of Nick's voice in the hallway. Despite straining to do so, she could not make out his words; but the simple tenor of his deep, dark voice was enough to set her on edge.

She smoothed the skirts of her gown, immediately nervous about her appearance—it had been a long, long while since she'd had cause to wear an evening gown, and the one she had rescued from the depths of her wardrobe and had quickly aired that afternoon was embarrassingly out of style. Certainly the women with whom he socialized regularly in London were utterly *au courant*; they were surely beautiful and poised and would never dream of being seen in a dress more than a month old, let alone several years past its prime.

She winced as Nick and James shared a laugh in the hallway outside the door. She should not have agreed to his silly request. She felt like a complete imbecile.

And then he entered.

Without a cravat.

The collar of his shirt was open, leaving a wedge of warm bronzed skin, framed by white linen and the dark green topcoat he had been wearing when he had arrived the previous day. When he and James entered the dining room for dinner, Isabel's attention was drawn immediately to that tantalizing triangle of chest, and it took her a second or two to recover from the surprise of it.

When she raised her attention to his face, she realized that he was staring intently at her, his eyes raking over the bodice of her gown, lingering on the spot where its edge gave way to the slope of her breast before traveling up to meet her gaze. She recognized the masculine admiration there, and, blushing, she redirected her attention to her brother.

Only to discover that he was wearing an equally unlikely dinner ensemble: short pants, a dirty linen shirt, and an elaborately tied—if hopelessly wrinkled—cravat. *Nick's cravat.* He'd taught her brother to tie a cravat.

Warmth spread through her and she smiled at her brother. "What a fine knot!" The boy preened beneath her praise, and she met Nick's eyes. "Thank you."

He was making it very difficult not to like him.

Rock noticed his friend's missing neckpiece and laughed, a great booming laugh. "You seem to have forgotten something, St. John."

Nick grinned. "I hope you will forgive me my strange attire, Lady Isabel," Nick said, teasing in his tone as he stepped forward and lifted her hand to his lips, the caress scorching through her glove. "You see, I found that I had an avid pupil in neckwear this evening."

An image of James and Nick working together to tie the cravat flashed in Isabel's mind, and it was a powerful fantasy—in which James had a man to guide him through these complex and uncertain masculine hoops, and in which Isabel had a partner to help her navigate the challenges of raising a young earl.

A partner.

What a lovely word.

She met Nick's eyes for a long moment, lost in the idea of him here, able to help. Shaking her head of the thought, she said, "Not at all. I am certain we can find you another cravat now that yours has been . . . appropriated."

"Given freely, my lady."

He had a remarkable smile. One that made her feel as though there was too little air in the room.

"Well, there is no reason for us to stand on ceremony this evening. I am happy for you to go without the neckwear if you are." Isabel held her breath, considering this man and her brother and the charming portrait they made. Nick was instantly more accessible. More endearing. More attractive.

Too attractive.

Clearing her throat, Isabel said, "Shall we eat?"

They moved to the table, which had been elaborately set—at Gwen's orders, Isabel would wager—and the gentlemen helped the ladies into their seats. There was an intimacy to the movement as Nick held Isabel's chair for her, the way he leaned in, bombarding her with heat and the scent of sandalwood. She turned her head fleetingly in his direction to thank him, and his whispered, "It is entirely my pleasure," barely loud enough for her to hear. She felt the soft touch of his breath on her bare shoulder as he added, "I knew you would be stunning in red."

A flood of pleasure shot through her.

He was a dangerous man.

She shook herself of the thought, entirely inappropriate, and was rewarded by the arrival of dinner. Gwen had outdone herself tonight—creating a meal of simple, hearty food that had come almost entirely from Townsend lands. It was not extravagant—certainly Lord Nicholas had had more sophisticated meals—but it was well seasoned and well cooked, and a feast by the standards of Townsend Park.

As she surveyed the mutton and jelly that had arrived as part of the second course, Isabel was overcome with uncertainty. This meal was far too simple to entertain these men—

men who had traveled the world developing sophisticated minds and palates. What could they possibly find enjoyable about a quiet evening meal in the wilds of Yorkshire? What could they possibly find entertaining about the company of two uncultured young women and a ten-year-old child?

The thought festered as the meal went on, and Isabel drifted into silence, shutting out the conversation around her.

As Rock and Lara quizzed James on his lessons and the events of his day, Nick leaned close to Isabel. "You are not with us."

She straightened at the words. "I was thinking about the meal."

"It is an excellent meal," Nick offered, and Isabel's uncertainty grew.

"I am sure it is rather less extravagant than that which you are used to."

"Not at all."

"Certainly not as sophisticated as you have had."

Nick gave her a serious look, one that did not tolerate self-deprecation. "On the contrary, Isabel. This meal is the ideal end to an . . . extraordinary day."

And there, in the deep, welcome tenor of his voice, was the thing that chased Isabel's doubts away. His words were a dark promise that conjured images and emotions from their interaction in the statuary, making her wish that he would kiss her again. Making her wish that they were alone once more.

But they were not.

They were at dinner.

With people.

With children, for heaven's sake.

She dipped her head, hiding her blush in her plate. "I am happy that you are enjoying it, my lord."

" . . . and then Lord Nicholas and I had our meeting."

Isabel looked up at her brother's words, meeting Lara's surprised gaze. "Your meeting? What kind of meeting?"

James seemed to remember that she was there. "A meeting of men."

She sat back in her chair. "I beg your pardon?"

"We had something to discuss," James said, simply.

She looked to Nick. "To discuss."

He lifted his wineglass, making a production of drinking. "Quite."

"I—" She turned back to James. *What could they possibly have been discussing without her?* "About what?"

"It's really none of your concern, Isabel. I asked Lord Nicholas for a moment of his time, as earl."

As earl?

Her eyes widened at her brother's words. Mutely, she turned back to Nick, who was having obvious difficulty refraining from smiling. "I could not refuse, Lady Isabel. He is, indeed, the earl. And my host, no less." He paused, then added, "This mutton is superb, the jelly in particular is excellent. Don't you think, Rock?"

"I do," the giant said, and Isabel did not miss the humor in his tone.

She would like to see both of them doused in jelly.

She looked to Lara, noted the amusement dancing in her cousin's eyes, and scowled in her direction. Unmoved, Lara turned back to James and said, "And you have learned to tie quite an impressive cravat!"

"Oh, yes," James said eagerly, reaching up to touch the neckwear in question. "Would you like to see me do it again?" Before Lara could answer, James had tugged on one end of his creation, destroying it in an entirely inappropriate display for the evening meal.

As he began his lesson in the proper method of cravat tying, Isabel leaned toward Nick. "As you can see," she whispered, "my brother may be the earl, but he is in no way able to act as such on his own. I should like you to tell me what it was that you spoke about."

Without taking his eyes from James, Nick replied, "You."

Surely she had not heard that correctly. "Me?"

"You."

"What of me?"

He took his time cutting a sliver of mutton and combining it with a piece of parsleyed potato. He chewed thoughtfully for a long moment, until Isabel's frustration grew to the point where she could no longer remain silent. "Oh, for heaven's sake. Swallow!"

Nick turned with mock surprise. "Why, Lady Isabel, what forcefulness! You should be careful—you will give me a case of indigestion."

"And what a sad situation that would be, Lord Nicholas." He laughed, low and quiet, and warmth spread through her at the sound, audible only to her. "You are enjoying this."

He met her eyes, and there was no mistaking the heat in his blue gaze. "I confess that I am. In fact, I find that I enjoy all of my time with you."

Isabel blushed at the words, and the pleasure they brought.

What was he doing to her?

She could not allow him to reduce her to a simpering miss every time they spoke. Clearing her throat, she said, "I must insist, Lord Nicholas. What is it that you and James discussed?"

"You needn't worry, Isabel," Nick said. "Your brother is simply concerned about your welfare once he leaves for school."

Isabel looked to James, awkwardly craning to see his cravat as Rock helped him to complete the elaborate knot. "And why would he think that speaking to you would help?"

Nick sat back as their plates were cleared, leveling Isabel with a frank look. "He has devised a proposal to keep you safe, and was asking for my input." He turned back to James, across the table. "Well done, James. That is certainly the best knot you've tied yet!"

James grinned his pleasure at the compliment, and turned to receive additional praise from Lara, who was heaping it upon both the young earl and Rock, for his assistance.

Isabel was unable to appreciate the tableau. Brow furrowed, she whispered to Nick, "What kind of proposal?"

Waiting until Regina had cleared his empty plate, Nick finally leaned in close to Isabel. "He thinks we should marry."

Isabel opened her mouth, closed it, and repeated the action.

One side of Nick's mouth kicked up in amusement. "Why, Isabel. I do believe that I have rendered you speechless."

"I—" Isabel stopped, uncertain of what to say.

"He has contemplated it quite thoroughly," he said. "He believes that your ability to run a house and calculate your sums makes you an excellent candidate for a wife."

Surely this was not happening. Not here. Not at her dinner table.

"He is eager for me to see you sit a horse, as well. I am told your equestrian prowess will win me over. I am looking forward to that."

"I—"

"Also—and this is critical—you are not ugly."

She blinked.

Nick's eyes danced with amusement. "Remember, Isabel. It was your brother who said it. I would not dare to take credit for such pretty words. I would have said something much more pedestrian. It takes a great orator to come up with—"

"Not ugly." She gave a little shake of her head. "What a lovely compliment."

"Ah. You have recovered your voice." He smiled then, full and winning, and she could not help but match it.

"It would seem so." She paused, "Tell me, my lord, will school help my brother to learn prettier words with which to woo his future countess?"

"One can only hope," he replied, "else we should be very concerned for the Reddich line."

Isabel could not help but laugh at the bizarre turn of events, drawing the notice of their dinner companions.

"James did say one thing about Lady Isabel during our conversation that has me very intrigued."

He had the attention of the entire table now, and Isabel felt a thread of nervousness uncoil. Surely he would not repeat anything embarrassing, would he?

"What was that, Lord Nicholas?" Lara prompted.

"He claims that she is a champion at charades."

"Oh, she is!" Lara agreed. "I've never seen her equal."

"I should like to see proof of that." He leveled Isabel with a contemplative look. "But first, I believe that we have an appointment for dancing."

Within moments, they had agreed to adjourn to the ballroom, and Isabel's anticipation had set her on edge.

Nick held her chair as she stood, and Isabel turned to thank him, only to find him watching her thoughtfully. Distracted from her observation by his intensity, she dipped her head and said, "Thank you."

He offered her his arm. When she took it, the heat of him rising up from the thick fabric of his coat, he leaned down and said, "I think you should know, I would have used a different phrase altogether to describe you."

Isabel felt her heart quicken, but attempted a light air. "You mean, other than 'not ugly'?"

He did not smile, and all of a sudden, there seemed to be less air in the room than there had been previously. Isabel caught her breath in anticipation.

"I would have described you as magnificent."

The ballroom had been transformed.

Isabel stopped short as she entered the enormous room, shocked. She had discussed the plans for the evening with Jane immediately after leaving Nick that afternoon, letting her know that the drop cloths needed to be removed from a section of the ballroom and suggesting that they dust the pianoforte in preparation for the evening.

Instead, Jane had worked a miracle.

The far end of the ballroom glowed in the soft, golden light from several dozen candles, unmatched and clearly pilfered from around the house and installed on tall candelabras. The lights had been strategically placed to create an intimate area of usable space, cordoned off with two low chaise longues on either end, and several comfortable chairs set off to one side.

There was a table of refreshments also, with a large crystal bowl of lemonade, a bottle of brandy from the cellars, along with several snifters and a platter of petits fours that James immediately pillaged. Isabel could not help but smile at the addition—she would wager that Gwen had spent much of the afternoon working on the tiny pastries.

Every surface gleamed with fresh polish, and Isabel wondered how many of the girls it had taken to turn the unused space into a little mini-ballroom, fit for an evening of dancing. "It is beautiful," she whispered, forgetting her audience for a moment.

"You seem surprised," Nick said, quietly.

"I am." She laughed, a small, delighted sound. "It's been a decade since this room has been used for its intended purpose. We clean it periodically and use it rarely, but never for balls . . ." She trailed off, one hand waving absently in the air as she searched for the rest of the sentence. "We don't have much cause for balls at Townsend Park. We are severely lacking in dance partners."

He smiled as she laughed again, and bowed low in an exaggerated way. "You have several willing ones this evening, my lady."

She met his smile with her own. "So we do."

An interior door to the ballroom opened then, and Georgiana entered, head down, moving quickly, as though she was not interested in the activities of the inhabitants of the room. Isabel opened her mouth to ask if there was something wrong, so surprised was she that the governess—who had been so terrified of being spotted by Nick—would choose to join them. She was stayed from speaking, however, when the young woman sat down at the dimly lit pianoforte, her back to them, and began to play a waltz.

James went to sit with her as Rock bowed to Lara, inviting

her to dance. Within seconds, she was in his arms, and the two were floating across the room, Lara's pale blue silk glittering in the candlelight. Isabel watched them with a mix of curiosity and nervousness, wanting to consider their obvious connection, but altogether too aware of Nick's nearness.

After an interminably long wait, she was rewarded with his low, deep voice. "Isabel . . ."

"Hmm?" She tried desperately for a tone of distant interest.

She heard the smile in his words when he said, "Would you care to dance?"

"Yes, please," she replied, her voice barely a whisper.

And then she was in his arms, and they were twirling across the room.

"James's governess has a gift for the piano."

"Minerva House boasts many talents, my lord." Isabel did not want to talk about the girls. She did not want to hide from him. Not now. Not while she was in his arms. "You are an excellent dancer."

He dipped his head, spinning her around a tall candelabrum and heading off toward the far end of the dance floor. "How it is that you think you cannot waltz?"

"I . . . I never do . . ." He turned her again, and she closed her eyes to enjoy the movement, the sheer strength of him, the way that he managed her weight so gracefully, swaying in time to the music.

"You should. Your body was made to be held like this." The words were soft and lush at her ear, and she knew that he was holding her much too closely. That she should tell him to stop.

But she couldn't.

They turned once more, and she opened her eyes to face the far wall and the door through which Georgiana had come. It was open again, and a row of curious faces peeked through the space between door and jamb, Gwen, Jane, and Kate all focused on the events inside the ballroom. Isabel could not contain her surprised laugh.

Nick looked down at her. "What is it?"

She looked up, amused, to meet his questioning gaze. "Do not look now, my lord, but it appears that we have an audience."

He grinned, immediately understanding. "Ah. Yes, if I know ladies, I can imagine we do."

"To be fair, they are attempting discretion."

"They are better at it than the women in my family."

The words, spoken with teasing admiration, made her curious. "Tell me about them."

He thought for a moment before he spoke. "My half sister, Juliana, is Italian, which makes her everything you would imagine. She is opinionated and infuriating and has a penchant for saying entirely inappropriate things at entirely inappropriate times."

She was drawn to the laughter in his voice. "She sounds wonderful."

He gave a little snort of laughter. "You would like her, I think. And I know she would like you—she has no patience for London, or the *ton*, and she has a particular distaste for simpering females and foppish gentleman. Which is going to make it virtually impossible to find her a husband. But really, that's Gabriel's problem."

She smiled. "Ah, the benefits of being the second son."

"Precisely."

"And your sister-in-law?"

"Now, Callie will love you."

She laughed at the words. "I find it difficult to believe that the Marchioness of Ralston will 'love' a country-raised northerner who wears breeches when it is practical and has spent most of her life with women who have done entirely inappropriate things."

Nick grinned. "That is precisely why the Marchioness of Ralston will love you."

Isabel gave him a frank look. "I do not believe you."

"Someday, Isabel, I shall take you to London, and you will hear the truth from my brother and sister-in-law themselves."

Isabel warmed at the promise inherent in the words—the assurance that there would come a time when they would be together in London. When she would meet his family and they would have reason to discuss the private history of one of the *ton*'s most talked-about couples.

She wanted it to be true.

It was strange. Here, in this darkened room, with the magic of the waltz, and the candlelight, and this strong, wonderful man, she wanted it to be true. She wanted to be tied to him. To be his partner. To have the life that peeked out from behind his words. Here, as she lost herself to the feel of the dance, to the sway of their bodies and the warmth of his arms wrapped around her, she let herself have the dream that she had shut away so long ago.

The dream that let this, her first waltz, be a waltz with a man who would care for her, and protect her, and shoulder her worries, and, yes . . . who would love her.

Isabel closed her eyes once more and gave herself up to the movement, aware of the place where his hand, unhindered by gloves, spread warmth through her gown to the curve of her waist. She could feel his long, muscled thighs where they brushed against her own as he guided her across the floor in an endless, curving journey. After several long moments, she opened her eyes, meeting Nick's searing blue gaze.

"Are you enjoying yourself, Isabel?"

She knew she should be coy. She knew that if he were in London, the woman in his arms would have something brilliant and witty and flirting to say in response. But Isabel had none of those things. "Very much."

"Good. You deserve to have pleasure in your life. I think you do not allow yourself enough of it."

She looked away, embarrassed. How was it that this man knew her so well, so quickly?

"Why is that?" The question was soft, a mere breath at her temple. "Why won't you take your pleasure?"

She closed her eyes, shaking her head. "I—I do."

"No, beauty. I don't think you do." He pressed closer, the warmth of him crowding her thoughts. "Why not dance and laugh and live the way you dream?"

Why not, indeed?

"Dreams are for little girls with no worries," she said, resisting the words even as she spoke them.

"Nonsense. We all have dreams."

She opened her eyes, met his brilliant blue gaze. "Even you?"

"Even me."

"What do you dream?" The question was exhaled—so breathy that she barely recognized her own voice.

He did not hesitate. "Tonight, I think I shall dream of you."

She should have found the words silly and teasing. Instead, she heard the promise in them, and wanted nothing more than to believe him. "Tell me what you dream of, Isabel."

"I should dream of school for James. Of safety for the girls. Of a repaired roof and an unlimited supply of candles."

He gave a little laugh. "Come, Isabel. You can do better than that. This is not their dream. It is yours. What do *you* dream? For yourself?"

For a long moment, her mind was blank. How long had it been since she had considered her own desires?

She smiled up at him. "I should like to dance more."

His teeth flashed. "I am happy to oblige." He spun her in circles in time to the music, and the smattering of candles about the dark room gave the illusion of dancing in starlight. The moment made her believe that if she spoke her desires aloud, they might actually come true.

After a long while, he probed, "What else?"

"I—I don't know."

His eyebrows rose. "Nothing? You can think of nothing that you wish?"

"I would not want to be thought of as selfish," she whispered.

He captured her gaze in his, arresting her attention. He

twirled them to a stop then, and she realized that they were at the far end of the room, where a chaise sat in near darkness.

"Selfish?"

She stared at the indentation on his chin and nodded.

He gave a little huff of laughter, disbelief in the exhalation. "Isabel, you are about the least selfish person I have ever known."

She shook her head. "It's not true."

"Why would you think that?"

She pressed her lips together, afraid of the answer.

But the desire to share it was too much.

She spoke to his chin. "I— My father gave me a chance to fix it all once. To save the house. The earldom. Everything." She had never told anyone this. "All I had to do was go to London. And let him arrange a marriage for me."

"How old were you?" The words were cold, and Isabel felt a sick feeling of dread—imagining that he was judging her actions. As her mother had done.

"Seventeen."

"You refused."

She nodded, unshed tears clawing at her throat. "I didn't want—didn't want the same marriage my mother had. I didn't want to be half a woman. Half a person. He left, and never returned. My mother—she died soon after. She blamed me for his desertion."

He was silent. Unmoving.

She should not have told him. "I am sorry if I have disappointed you."

His sharp inhalation drew her attention.

One finger beneath her chin, he lifted her gaze to his. She gasped at the emotion there.

"I am not disappointed, love." The whisper was low and close, so close that she felt more than heard the words. "I am furious." Her eyes widened as he cupped her face in his hands, turning them to ensure that they were entirely out of the view of the others in the room. She felt the trembling in his fingers. "I wish I had been here. I wish I could have—"

He stopped when she closed her eyes.

I wish you had been here, too.

He traced his fingers down the side of her neck to the place where her pulse was beating out of control.

She did not want to think of the past. Not now. Not when he was so close.

"I wish you would kiss me."

The raw confession surprised them both.

He lowered his voice to a whisper. "Ah, Isabel, if we were anywhere but here . . ."

She dipped her head at the words. "I know."

"Do you? Do you know how much I want you?"

She could not look at him. "Yes."

She felt his thumb run over the soft skin of her wrist, the maddening touch setting her pulse racing. "How do you know?"

The whisper, dark and coaxing, gave her the courage to look up at him. His eyes were dark—too dark to make out their color in this light—but she could read his thoughts. "Because I want you, as well."

He growled then, low in his throat, and Isabel felt the noise cut a path right through her, sending pleasure pooling at her core. She started to turn her face away once more, but he stayed the movement with one finger under her chin. "No, beauty. Look at me."

How could she deny such an urgent demand?

"I am not perfect. I cannot promise you that I will not do things that will hurt you." He paused, his scar a pale line against his darkened skin. "But I will do everything in my power to protect you and James and these girls."

He stopped, and she held her breath, waiting for his next words.

"I think you should consider your brother's proposal."

Fourteen

Lesson Number Six

Once you have captured his attention, do not waver.

Lord landing requires tenacity of purpose, Dear Reader! It is not for the weak-willed or the faint-of-heart. Once you have chosen your Knight and he has recognized you as his Maiden Fair, you must resist any temptation toward quiescence! Now is not the time to grow comfortable!

You do well to remember that battles are won and lost in their final stages. This time requires constancy, determination, and endurance!

Pearls and Pelisses
June 1823

Isabel was seated in a great copper bathtub, flushed from the steam coming off the near-scalding water. She lifted a hand absently, considering the wrinkled tips of her fingers. "He said he would use the word *magnificent* to describe me."

Lara looked gleeful from her place on Isabel's bed. "And he wants to marry you!"

The words sent a flood of nervousness through Isabel. "He did not say that. He said I should consider James's proposal."

"Which was marriage! To Lord Nicholas!"

"Yes, but that does not mean that he would *like* to marry me."

He likely thought her a sad, pathetic case in need of saving.

Lara gave Isabel a look. "Isabel. I think that is precisely what it means."

"No. It means that I should consider marriage. Not necessarily to him."

"Isabel. I think you are being deliberately obtuse. It is clear that his statement referred to marriage between the two of you."

"You cannot know that."

Neither of us can.

"Indeed, I can! And I shall tell you why. We haven't seen another marriageable man at Townsend Park in two years! Who would you have him suggest you marry? *And . . .*" she added, "I *saw* the way he was looking at you. The way you were dancing. He wants you."

"Maybe he does *want* me," Isabel said, peevish, "but I cannot imagine he wants to *marry* me."

Lara lifted herself up on her elbows to look her cousin in the eye. When she spoke, her words were rife with offense. "Whyever not? You are an ideal candidate for Lord Nicholas's bride! One might argue that, as daughter of an earl, you are well above marrying a second son!"

Isabel laughed at the idea. "Perhaps if my father weren't quite the lowest form of aristocratic life, that would be true. As it is, I think Lord Nicholas could do a fair bit better than me."

"Nonsense." Lara's words shook with irritation. "You are lovely, capable, intelligent, amusing." She ticked the qualities off on her fingers. "Any gentleman would be lucky to have you."

Isabel's lips twisted in a wry smile. "Thank you, coz."

Lara's brow furrowed. "It was not a compliment. It was fact. You must know a man like that would not consider marrying you if he did not find the idea more than palatable."

Palatable. What a horrible word.

Isabel did not reply, instead setting her head against the high back of the tub and closing her eyes.

Not twelve hours earlier, hearing that Lord Nicholas found her palatable would have set Isabel on edge—sending her fleeing his company and vowing never to return for fear of his opinions of her growing more committed. Now, she rather detested the very idea that he might have such ambivalent feelings for her.

How was it possible that she was beginning to care for this man? How had he invaded her thoughts in less than two days? How was it that she was actually considering placing her trust in this complete and utter stranger? She knew nothing of him, for heaven's sake.

Nothing but how he made her feel.

She sighed. She did not like the way he made her feel. She did not like the way his words made her pulse race, or the way his wicked smiles made her skin flush, or the way his simple, honest gaze made her want to tell him everything and give him access to her entire world. To her past. And her present.

And now he tempted her with a promise of the future by going and mentioning marriage. And for the first time in her life, Isabel was actually considering the idea. It did not seem that the marriage he meant was anything like the marriages she had experienced in the past—traps, battles for power, struggles for self-preservation.

A marriage to Nick would not be any of those things.

And, suddenly, marriage did not seem so bad.

Except. . .

"He has not offered to marry me."

Lara rolled her eyes. "Of course he has."

"No. He did not say the words."

"Which words?"

Isabel looked down into the bathtub, noting the way her body disappeared in the darkened water, hidden by the flickering candlelight bouncing like starlight across the surface—reminding her of the darkened ballroom and their waltz . . . and her confession. "He did not say, 'Marry me, Isabel.' "

Lara waved one hand. "A semantic issue."

Semantics seemed rather vital, suddenly.

"Nevertheless."

Lara stilled, leaning forward over the edge of the bed, squinting in the dimly lit chamber. "Oh, my."

Isabel turned at the breathy words. "What is it?"

"You."

"What about me?"

"You are . . . enamored."

Isabel looked away. "I am not."

"You are!" Lara's words were triumphant. "You are enamored of Lord Nicholas!"

"I've only known the man for three days, Lara."

"After last night . . . the dinner . . . the dancing . . . three days is enough," Lara said, as though she were an expert in all things romantic.

"Oh, how would you know?"

"I know. In roughly the same manner that I know that you are enamored of Lord Nicholas St. John."

"I do wish you would stop saying the word *enamored*," Isabel grumbled.

"How did this happen?"

"I don't know!" Isabel cried, lifting her hands from the water to cover her face. "I don't even know the man!"

"It seems you know enough of him," Lara teased.

Isabel looked up. "It isn't funny. It's awful."

"Why? He wants to marry you!"

"Not for any rational reason."

Lara tilted her head. "I am not certain that there has ever been a rational reason for marriage, Isabel."

"Certainly there has been!" Isabel insisted. "He could marry me for money, or land, or to appease society, or to add respectability to his name. But . . . no, he cannot be doing it for any of those reasons, because *I* decidedly cannot *provide* any of those things!"

Lara giggled at the words. "Isabel."

"It isn't funny, really. Well, not outside of a dark, macabre sense of humor."

"You are being dramatic. Can you really say that you aren't the smallest bit intrigued by the prospect of marrying Lord Nicholas?"

The frank question fell into the silence, and Isabel looked to the ceiling with a frustrated sigh.

She had spent twenty-four years telling herself that she did not want marriage. That she did not want children. That she did not want a mate. She had had a clear vision of her future—of helping James to restore the dignity of the earldom, of securing the future of Minerva House, of aging with the not inconsequential knowledge that she was impacting the world in some small, positive way.

Until tonight, she had been perfectly satisfied with her life as she knew it.

Mostly.

And now . . . all of a sudden, her whole world—everything that she had believed to be true and right and certain—was turned upside down.

Had she dreamed of the rest? Of marriage and children and waltzing and love?

Yes.

If she was honest with herself, yes. In the darkness, late at night, as she lay in her bed and worried about the future, about the girls and about James and, yes, about herself, she had dreamed of what could have been. She had dreamed, quietly, of how it might have been to have gone to London and filled her dance card and ridden in Hyde Park and been well and truly courted, and found herself a man who would be her partner, and her protector.

But that dream had never come to fruition.

Because it was unattainable.

Until now.

When she could imagine reaching out and taking it.

When she could *almost* imagine what it might be like to love him.

Love.

It was a strange and foreign word; a fantasy that had tempted her as a child and then terrified her as she grew—as she watched her mother torn apart.

No. She would not love him.

She knew better.

But. . .

"I like him," she said, the words barely sound.

Lara heard. "I know."

"I've never thought that would happen."

Lara nodded. "I know."

And now that I do, I'm frightened of what will happen next.

"It's rather terrifying."

Lara smiled. "I know that, as well."

Isabel raised her eyebrows. "You do?"

"I rather like his friend."

"Yes!" Isabel sat up quickly, water sloshing over the edge of the bathtub. "And it seems that he feels similarly to you! How did that . . . ?"

"I do not know! One moment I was showing him your marbles, and then I was accompanying him to feed their horses, and then . . . he was . . ." She stopped, dipping her head in embarrassment.

"He was doing something he should not have been doing, it seems!"

"Isabel!" The flaming red on Lara's cheeks gave everything away.

"You have kissed him!" Isabel accused.

"Oh! And you are one to judge!"

Isabel laughed. "No. I suppose that I am not."

"It's quite pleasant, isn't it?"

"Kissing? I'm not sure I would use the word *pleasant*. Thoroughly unsettling, entirely vexing, and altogether—"

"Wonderful."

Isabel smiled. "Precisely."

Lara grinned. "We are a pair."

"After years with no men in sight, we find ourselves made utterly silly by the first two that happen along."

"Not the *first* two. You avoided Mr. Asperton."

Isabel recalled the reedy, snakelike man and shuddered. "It was a challenge, to be sure, but yes, I did avoid Mr. Asperton."

Lara stacked her hands on the bed, setting her chin to them as Isabel made to exit her bath. "So . . . you will accept Lord Nicholas's suit?"

Isabel stepped out of the bath, wrapping herself in a long length of linen to ward off the chill that threatened. She approached the bed, perching on the edge of it as Lara turned to face her.

She considered the question. He was the answer to their problems. The handsome, intelligent, entertaining, good-natured answer to their problems. "Yes. If he asks, I will accept. For all of our good."

As the words left her mouth, she knew that they were a lie. That as much as she would like to believe she would accept for Minerva House, she would also accept for herself, despite the risk that came of tying herself to this man for whom she could so easily see herself coming to care.

For whom she could so easily see herself coming to. . .

No. She would not make the same mistakes her mother had made.

But Nick seemed nothing like her father. He was honest and forthright and kind, and he seemed precisely the type of man who would make good on his promises.

Which made everything much easier.

She simply had to ensure that, if she married him, it would be on her terms. Yes, she would care for him. Certainly she would enjoy his company, and his wit, and his superior touch—for his touch was most definitely superior, and enough to send all rational thought flying from her head.

But she would not love him.

She turned to Lara with a smile. "Perhaps it would not be so bad, after all."

As it began, rain ended quickly in Yorkshire. There was no gradual waning of water, no silent mist to ease the way from heavy drops to dry skies. Instead, there was a simple change, like the snuffing of a candle. One moment, there was pounding rain, and the next . . . silence.

And, after three days of the constant sound of rain on the windows, the silence was deafening.

Nick looked up from his cards and met Rock's gaze.

"Finally."

Nick grinned. "Longing for The Stuck Pig, are we?"

"Not at all," Rock said. "I'm simply growing tired of seeing you in that coat." He dealt a card, and Nick, recognizing his losing hand, tossed the handful of cards he had onto the table. Rock collected his winnings. "One would think that you would grow tired of losing to me after all these years."

Nick leaned back in his chair, taking a drink of brandy. He leveled his friend with a look and said, "I'm going to marry her."

Rock began to shuffle the cards again, casually. "Are you?"

"She needs me."

"That does not seem to be the appropriate reason to marry a girl, Nick. Particularly not when the girl in question is harboring a houseful of fugitives."

Nick narrowed his gaze on his friend. "I don't think it's a houseful. And I don't believe that she's doing anything wrong. Neither do you."

"No. I don't."

"Then?"

"I thought marriage was not for you?"

Nick did not pretend to misunderstand. He had said the words dozens, hundreds of times over the last years, certain that marriage would ruin him. He'd never seen a marriage that was a success. And he knew better than to believe that he could make one from any of the options that had presented themselves. He would not bind himself to some woman for a mere strategic alliance, he had no need for a daughter of the aristocracy, no need for a boost in finances.

But he would not mind a partnership.

And when they were together, they would find pleasure in each other.

Immense pleasure.

Yes, a marriage to Isabel could be ideal.

"I have changed my mind. I quite like the idea of aligning myself with her."

"Aligning yourself? Is that what it will be?" Rock raised a brow. "And what will you do when she discovers that you came here looking for one of her girls?" Nick did not respond. It was precisely the question he had avoided answering for the last two days. Rock dealt the cards again, and Nick considered his hand absentmindedly. "Marry her for the marbles. Marry her because you want to bed her. But don't marry her because she needs you."

"I don't need to marry her for the marbles. I would buy them anyway. And I'm not entirely certain she does need me."

"I note you don't deny the desire to bed her."

Nick signaled for another card. He wanted her. With a visceral intent. The events of the afternoon, the way she had given herself so freely, the way she had tilted her head back as she had fallen apart in his arms had made dancing with her—touching her—sheer torture. It had taken all his control to keep from kissing her in the darkened ballroom in the face of her confession, and when she'd finally taken to her bed, he'd had to force himself to remain belowstairs instead of following her into her bedchamber and showing her every conceivable pleasure.

He shifted uncomfortably in his chair, ignoring Rock's knowing smirk.

"I can tell you that I do not care for your phrasing." Nick tossed a coin onto the table. Rock matched the bid, turned over a card for himself, and swore under his breath. "What was it you were saying about my losing to you?"

"What is it you Englishmen call them? Red-letter days?" Nick began to shuffle as Rock continued, "The girl doesn't need you. She needs money. Buy the marbles."

"She needs more than money." He paused. "And she doesn't really want to sell the marbles."

Rock snorted. "Then what are we doing here?"

"Until five minutes ago, we didn't have a choice." Nick met his friend's dark gaze. "And you were enjoying yourself, reading your effeminate novels and quietly fleecing me of my fortune. What has changed?"

Rock reached to pour himself a new snifter of brandy. "Nothing. I am simply ready to leave."

"Has something happened with Lara?"

"Miss Caldwell, to you." Rock scowled.

"I beg your pardon. Has something happened with Miss Caldwell? You seemed thick as thieves earlier." Nick stopped, the words sinking in. "Ah."

Rock looked up sharply. "What does that mean?"

"It seems I am not the only one with a female predicament. Is yours as infuriating as mine?"

Rock threw a coin onto the table. "Deal the cards."

Nick did as he was told, and the next few rounds passed in silence. Finally, Rock said, "She's quite lovely."

Nick nodded. "She is."

"Not simply lovely. Perfect."

The words were so unexpected that it took Nick a few seconds to register their meaning. "I do not understand. What is the problem, then?"

"Nothing can come of it."

"Why not?"

Rock leveled Nick with a frank look. "Look at me, Nick."

"I am looking."

Rock threw his cards down on the table. "She's a gentleman's daughter. I am a heathen, born in the back alleys of Turkey."

"She lives in a house designed to harbor fugitives. She cannot be entirely beholden to the rules of society. At least, not in the way you suggest." Nick paused. "I assume that your intentions are honorable?"

Rock stood, unable to remain still. He moved to the window, throwing it open and letting in fresh air, still heavy with the recent rain. "If anything were to happen between us . . . she would be exiled."

"Farther than Yorkshire?" Nick said dryly.

Rock did not look back as he said, softly, "Her current exile is self-imposed."

Nick watched his friend for a long moment before standing and moving to join him at the window. "You overthink this. You have dozens of friends who are wealthy and titled, plenty of whom would happily accept your interactions with her."

Rock shook his head. "You know that isn't true."

"I know no such thing," Nick scoffed. "Not one of them would care."

The Turk turned away from the window, meeting Nick's eyes. "You only think that because you would not care. But they would. When I descended from the carriage in London with a beautiful blond Englishwoman by my side, they would care. And I would no longer be a friend. I would be a dark-skinned enemy, robbing them of their women."

Nick held Rock's gaze for a long while, the truth of his words sinking in. Finally, Nick swore quietly and clasped his friend's shoulder. "You care for the girl?"

"I do."

"Well, that seems to me that it should be enough. Hang the rest of them."

A small smile crossed Rock's lips. "It is easy for you to say such things. Second son of a marquess, planning to marry the daughter of an earl."

"She hasn't said she'll have me."

"She will have you. She would be mad not to. But promise me something. Promise me you are marrying her for more than your own insane desire to save her."

Nick considered the words. He knew what Rock was asking. *Was Isabel his way of repairing the damage that Alana had wrought?* Could this brave, unmatched Englishwoman erase the memory of her wicked Turkish counterpart?

He recoiled at the comparison of the two. "It is not the same."

"I am not certain you could survive at the hands of another woman whom you cannot help."

"What makes you think I cannot help this one?"

"Only that you have never been able to help them, Nick. Not in all the time I have known you."

There was a long moment of silence before Nick gave a self-deprecating laugh. "Not in all the time before that, either."

"You can help the girl without giving up your life. That is all I am saying."

Nick considered the words, playing them over in his mind. Was that all he wanted? Simply to help Isabel? Certainly that was a part of it—certainly he wanted to ensure her safety, to give her the peace of mind that came with knowing that her house would stand, that her girls would thrive, that her brother would succeed. But Rock was right, of course, he could give her all of those things without marrying her. He could leave here and go back to London, track down Densmore and convince him to turn over the guardianship of Townsend Park to him. If he guessed correctly, Densmore would happily relinquish the responsibility.

So why was it that marriage was there, looming so large in his thoughts?

What was it about this woman that had him tied in knots and willing to sacrifice everything for her?

What made him want to help her so very much?

An image of Isabel flashed, fresh and beautiful and relaxed—happy and certain that her world was not going to come crashing down around her. He had never seen her that way. He had seen her beautiful and teasing, beautiful and bold, beautiful and concerned for those around her, beautiful and coming apart in his arms, but never beautiful and sure of herself. Of her future. Of him.

He wanted to give her that.

Perhaps it was his weakness for women. Perhaps this was Turkey all over again. Perhaps Nick was destined to be trapped by this woman in the same way he had been trapped by his mother, by Alana. But he found it difficult to believe that Isabel was anything like them.

She seemed infinitely more honest.

She threatened to become infinitely more dear.

This was more than his history.

It was his future.

He met Rock's eyes. "I am going to marry her. We would make a good pair."

Rock nodded once. "Fair enough." There was a long silence as they both looked out the window, into the darkness beyond. "You know you can't do it without telling her the truth."

The words fell like lead between them. Of course Nick knew. He had known from the beginning that he would have to confess his relationship with the Duke of Leighton. He would have to tell Isabel that he was looking for Georgiana. And he would have to bear the full weight of her anger and interrogation.

But there had been a small part of him that had hoped that he might convince her to marry him and get the deed done before he had to admit his less than honest actions.

He was not entirely certain that it was not still possible.

There was something very tempting about wedding her, tying her to him, and only then, when she could not leave him, telling her everything.

Rock read the thought. "Your telling her is far better than her discovering it for herself sometime in the future."

"I know."

But he did not like the sound of either option.

Fifteen

The next morning, Isabel found Nick in the statuary, working.

She had gone looking for him after breakfast, telling herself that she was doing the gracious thing by seeking him out to inform him that the roads were once more passable after the rain. The excitement she felt when she saw him bent over his notebook in the brightly lit statuary, however, indicated a slightly different motivation for her coming to find him.

His hands flew across the paper, strong and sure, and she felt a fleeting envy at the complete attention he was giving his work. She watched as a lock of midnight hair fell, catching in the frame of his spectacles, and her breath hitched.

He was really very handsome.

And she was becoming an utter ninny.

The thought brought her back to reality, and Isabel cleared her throat delicately, gaining his attention. He turned his gaze on her, and she felt his scrutiny; she clasped her hands in front of her skirts to refrain from smoothing either her dress or her hair.

"I did not want to bother you, but I thought you might

like to know that Rock has returned to town—to fetch your belongings. We are happy to host you here . . . at Townsend Park . . . for as long as you need lodging."

He removed his eyeglasses, and Isabel felt a pang of remorse. There was something about the spectacles that she found compelling—something that underscored the intelligent, honest man beneath the handsome, overwhelming façade.

He smiled, a warm, welcoming smile that weakened her knees. Yes. She much preferred him with the buffer of the eyeglasses.

"That is very generous of you, Isabel. Thank you."

She did not know what to say at that point, so she hovered in the doorway, her uncertainty clear.

One of his brows rose in obvious amusement. He knew she was nervous. He was enjoying it. "Would you like to come in?"

She took one step into the room, keenly aware of the fact that only yesterday, he had kissed her here. More than kissed her.

Perhaps she should close the door.

Her pulse sped at the thought. Surely, if she did, he would take it as an invitation to repeat the events of the prior afternoon.

Close the door, Isabel.

She couldn't. What would he think?

Did it matter?

Surely it was too early for such activities.

They had only just had breakfast.

She met his glittering blue eyes, and saw that he knew precisely what she was thinking. There was a dare in the way he looked at her, as though he were willing her to close the door and take that which she had been unable to stop thinking of since yesterday.

She moved further into the room, leaving the door open, ignoring the pang of disappointment that flared. Her attention flickered to a nearby statue. She grasped for a safe topic. "How did you become so interested in antiquities?"

He hesitated before answering, as though choosing his words, and in that moment's pause, she found herself desperately curious. "I have always liked statues," he said, "from when I was a boy. In school, I found myself fascinated by mythology. I suppose that it is no surprise that when I left school and headed for the Continent—I was drawn to the ancient cultures."

Isabel perched on a pedestal nearby. "So you spent your time in Italy and Greece?"

He looked away briefly. "Italy was difficult to get to, considering there was a war on. It was easier to go east, and so I did, through the Ottoman Empire and deep into the Orient. The art there is unparalleled; their history is more ancient than anything on the Continent. You would never imagine such paintings, such ceramics . . . the art they have passed down through generations is like nothing I have ever seen. And not just painting or sculpture. Their whole bodies are their art, their spirits."

She was transfixed by the reverence in his voice. "How so?"

He met her gaze, and the excitement in his eyes set her pulse to racing. "Things are sacred in the cultures of the East—those who study music and dance and theatre do so with their entire being. In China, there are warriors who spend years learning the art of their combat. In India, dance is a ritual, the beginning and end of the world is held in a single movement of the female form."

His words had grown softer, drawing her in. "It sounds wonderful."

"It is. It's exponentially more sensual than the dance we shared last night."

Isabel found it difficult to believe that anything could be more sensual than their waltz the night before. There was something dark and liquid in his eyes when he continued, "I would like to teach you the things I learned in India."

She wanted to learn them. "What kinds of things?"

"Unfortunately, things that good English ladies do not learn."

"I find I have never been very good at being a good English lady."

There was a long silence then, during which she was flooded with embarrassment—where had those words come from? Should she apologize?

"I—"

"If you are going to apologize, I would prefer you not. I find I like this bold Isabel quite a bit."

Her gaze skidded to his, and the flash of his wicked grin transfixed her.

She could not help but match it, enjoying the feeling of sharing a secret with this intriguing man. She wanted to know more about him. She wanted to know everything about him. "How did you come to learn about Greek and Roman antiquities if you were whiling away your days in the Orient?"

He thought for a moment, then said, simply, "After a few years in the East, I returned to Europe."

"To Turkey."

He did not answer. He did not have to. "My recovery took place in Greece. I had months to learn about Greek antiquities . . . to learn their secrets. The Romans came last, before I returned to London."

She wanted to ask more about his time in Greece. In Turkey. But she knew instinctively that he would not share more than he already had. She searched for a new topic—something that could return them to the friendly conversation they had shared earlier, before she had resurrected his dark memories. Her gaze settled on the statue that he had been scribbling notes on when she had entered. "You are still working on Voluptas?"

"I find myself unable to leave her."

"She is beautiful."

"Indeed, she is." He indicated the statue. "Do you see how she is different from the others?"

Isabel considered the face of the goddess, the half-closed eyes, the full lips just barely parted. She recognized the emotion on the goddess's face—one she had always considered somnolence. She knew better now. She felt her skin heat.

"Ah. I see you do." His voice had changed; it was liquid now, warm and soft and private—sending a thrill up her spine. "It is not just her face, however. What makes this statue different from the others is the care the sculptor took to make every part of her so clearly Voluptas."

She was mesmerized by his voice, and when he moved his hands to the statue, she could not look away. "You can see her passion in every inch of her . . . in the angle of her neck, in the way that her chin is lifted, as though she cannot deepen her breath for the sensation coursing through her."

Isabel watched, transfixed, as his strong, tanned hands caressed the angle of the statue's jaw, his fingertips tracing the line of her neck. He kept talking, his hands following his dark, lush words. "Her pleasure is articulated in the way her shoulders are thrown back, the way one arm reaches up to absently touch her hair, the way the other crosses her rounded stomach, as though to still the trembling there."

Without thinking, Isabel's hand mirrored the action of the statue. His words, the way his hands stroked softly across the marble, it was enough to shake her to her core. She looked to him then, meeting his fiery blue gaze, seeing the knowledge in his eyes, the passion there. He knew what he was doing. He was seducing her.

When he turned back to the statue, Isabel sucked in a long breath. "But perhaps the most telling indicator of her emotion is here." He ran a hand across the smooth white marble to cup one of the statue's breasts in his hand. "Her breasts are fuller than those of other Roman statues of the time . . ."

How could he remain so unmoved?

"And she is anatomically perfect. You will note the hint of a hardened nipple . . ." Isabel bit her lip as she watched the circling of his thumb, resisting the urge to mimic his motions.

She wanted his hands on her.

She released the breath she had been holding on a long, shaking sigh, barely audible. But he heard it. His head snapped toward her, and he released Voluptas. He met Isabel's gaze, and she noted that his eyes had darkened to a lovely, promising blue. "Shall I continue?"

She took a step toward him, coming as close as she could without touching him. She noted the tension in his shoulders then, the muscle that twitched in his cheek in a motion that she was learning to recognize as restraint. He wanted to touch her, but was waiting for her move.

Well, she was through restraining herself.

Isabel set her hands to his chest, then used him as leverage to stand up on her toes, to get as close to him as possible. When she answered, she was not certain where the words came from. "Not with the statue."

She kissed him.

There was an exhilaration that came from taking one's own pleasure, Isabel discovered. He remained still under her kiss, not touching her, not moving against her lips, and Isabel realized that he was allowing her to take the reins.

She found she liked that idea very much.

She wanted to laugh at the heady sensation of her newfound power. But that did not seem at all appropriate.

She slid her hands up, wrapping them around his neck, pressing her body fully against his. He set his hands to her hips, holding her steady, and the feel of his warmth there through the layers of her dress sent a heady wanting through her. She opened her lips against his, softening, making it known that she was willing to be here, in this room, in his arms. When he did not take her mouth, she ran her tongue tentatively along his full, firm bottom lip.

And discovered the key that unlocked the lion.

He groaned against her, parting his lips and allowing her access to his dark, wicked mouth. She was nervous at first, unwilling to take what it was that she had asked for, but when his arms wrapped around her, all warm steel, and pulled her tight against him, caution was lost. Their tongues met, stroked, tangled, and it was long moments before he broke the kiss and lifted her to stand on the low pedestal with Voluptas.

Breaking the kiss, he commanded, "Stay," and moved away to close the door that she had agonizingly left open. When the task was completed, he approached her, and she was struck by the way he stalked her, like a lean, powerful predator. Her heart was pounding in her ears as he came closer, finally stopping in front of her, appraising her as he had the statue.

Her position made her several inches taller than he was, and when she could no longer resist, she reached out to run her fingers through his hair, tilting his face up so she could look at him. His eyes glittered with unspoken promise, and she watched as his scar turned white under her gaze. She placed one lingering kiss on the end of the mark, just at the corner of his eyebrow, then took his mouth again in a heady kiss.

His hands spread over her body, encouraging her boldness, running up the side of her bodice to the place where fabric gave way to skin. Pulling away, briefly, he set his mouth to her neck, scraping his teeth along the rigid tendons there as she tilted her head back from the pleasure of the caress. He tugged at the top of her bodice, pulling until one breast came free of its bindings, and he paused, marveling at the straining tip, in line with his mouth. "My real-life Voluptas," he whispered, the heat of his breath causing her nipple to harden even more before he set his lips and tongue and teeth to her breast and feasted upon her.

She clutched his head to her with a cry of pleasure, and lost herself to the powerful sensations that coursed through her at every knowing stroke, every magnificent tug. When he finally lifted his head, they were both breathing heavily, and she was leaning on his shoulders to remain upright.

"Before we go further," he said, his words coming in harsh breaths, "I think we should discuss the matter of our marriage."

She did not want him to stop. Could they not discuss this later? She reached for him. "Yes."

He kissed her again, tugging her head down for a drugging caress that left her barely able to think. "Yes, what?"

What had they been discussing?

"What?"

He smiled, and the full force of his pleasure twisted something deep inside her. "Isabel. I think we should marry."

She smiled back at him. "I agree."

"Good girl." He rewarded her with another long kiss before lifting her arms above her head placing her hands around the neck of the statue, her back bare and elongated against the cool marble goddess. Once he had positioned her to his liking, he returned his attention to her breasts. She gasped when his teeth scraped along the edge of her nipple before his tongue soothed the ache there, and again when she felt cool air beneath her skirts, his hands chasing up her legs to find the place where she ached for his touch. He lifted his head. "Shall we do it soon?"

If he did not touch her soon, she was going to perish.

Isabel opened her eyes at the question. Utterly distracted by the path of his hands, caressing her thighs in the most maddening of ways. "Yes. Let's." He made quick work of the tapes on her pantaloons and slid one hand inside, widening her legs and brushing his fingers over the heated core of her.

"Good. I do not think that I can wait much longer to have you here."

"No—" The word was exhaled on a breath as he slid one finger into her.

"I am so glad you feel the same way." The words, so innocuous, coursed through her like liquid fire on the heels of a long, stroking caress that robbed her of intelligent thought. She let go of the statue and clung to him, and, without removing his hand, he lifted her in his arms and moved her to the bay window where he had shown her such pleasure the day before. This time, he did not sit, instead settling her into the seat and kneeling before her on the floor.

She was on fire. She craved his touch.

This was the emotion that marked the end of women. This was what ruined them.

She must resist it. Him.

She opened her eyes, meeting his molten gaze. "Wait."

His fingers stroked slowly inside her. "Yes?"

She flexed against the remarkable movement, taking a deep breath and willing herself to remember what she had been about to say. "I just . . . you should know . . . I cannot love you."

"No?" His thumb rubbed a wicked circle around the spot that she had only discovered yesterday.

She gasped. "I think I could grow very fond of you, though."

He laughed then, low and dark, his free hand sliding her skirts up her legs. "I think I could do the same."

"But really . . . I shan't . . ." He spread her legs wide then, baring her flesh to the air and the room and his gaze. "Wait . . . what are you . . . you cannot!" She struggled to close her thighs, capturing his hand between them, and clasped her skirts, trying to push them down to hide herself from him. He could not possibly want to *look* at her there.

"Isabel." He drawled her name in a lovely, rich caress.

She stopped. "Yes?"

He leaned forward then, capturing her lips in a deep promise of a kiss. When she grew weak in his arms once more, he pulled back, placing a soft final kiss at the corner of her mouth before whispering, "Trust me, darling. You're going to like me very much after this."

He gently parted her thighs again, running his strong, knowing hands along the soft skin there. When he dipped his head and placed a soft, wet kiss at the inside of her knee, and traced a path up the smooth, pale skin of her inner thigh, Isabel covered her eyes in embarrassment that he would be so close to such a private, secret place. His fingers played at the auburn curls covering the center of her sex, sending wave after wave of temptation through her with the merest hint of a touch.

Finally, she uncovered her eyes, and met the sensual promise in his heated gaze. "That's what I was waiting for. Never hide from me, beauty."

He parted the slick folds of her sex then, stroking one finger down the center of her, her pulse racing from the feel of him against her.

He leaned closer, and when he spoke, the words were a wicked lash against her heated, wanting flesh. "You are so beautiful here. I want to know every inch of you. I want to feel every bit of your heat." His finger circled the straining center of her, the perfect pressure of the caress wringing a cry from her.

"Do you know how much I want to taste you?"

Her eyes widened at the words. Surely he couldn't mean . . . surely he wouldn't. . .

And then he did.

His mouth was on her and her body was no longer her own, but entirely his. She gasped at the sensation, plunging her fingers into his soft sable hair, not moving, not wanting to push him away, not willing to pull him closer.

But he knew what she wanted. His mouth loved her in every possible way, his tongue stroking through the moist heat of her, licking at the very heart of her, teasing at her core in lush, brilliant circles that she was not sure she could bear. He pushed her higher and higher, opening wider, feasting upon her until she thought she might die from the pleasure of it. She lifted her hips toward him and he accepted the movement, bearing her weight as his tongue found the swollen, aching center of her pleasure in a series of firm strokes that stole her breath entirely.

She did pull him to her then, unwilling to give up this impossible, extraordinary sensation and the man who was sending it coursing through her body. The movements increased, the speed threatening her sanity as she cried his name.

He stopped then, for a long, unbearable moment, and she could not bear it. She squirmed, but his firm grip held her still, his mouth and tongue against her in excruciating stillness. He was killing her.

"Nick—" she whispered, "please . . . please don't stop!"

He rewarded her begging with blessed movement, closing his lips around the tight, swollen nub of her and sucking, robbing her of thought and breath and leaving her only with sensation.

The feeling was too much to bear. "No . . . Nick . . . stop . . ."

But his wicked, knowing mouth spared her no quarter, instead licking faster, stroking deeper, and, finally, he thrust one, then two fingers deep into her, coaxing her closer and closer to the unknown precipice that she was hurtling toward—the one that she both feared and desired.

And then she was there, at the edge, and his mouth and hands and the satisfied growl deep in his throat were everywhere—and she tumbled over the edge on a wave of pleasure like nothing she had ever known. She cried his name as the room spun around them, clenching her fingers in his hair, clinging to the one stable thing in the maelstrom of sensation.

She collapsed against her seat, and after a long, lingering moment, Nick lifted his head, meeting her eyes. She registered the pleasure and the passion there, and she took a deep, shaking breath, attempting to compose herself as he lowered her skirts and moved to sit beside her. He pressed a soft kiss to her temple, pulling her against him to recover.

She set one hand absently against him, and he hissed at the movement, capturing her hand in one of his. Her eyes widened. "Did I . . . Are you hurt?"

He gave her a crooked smile. "Not at all. Merely desperate for more of you."

Understanding dawned, and Isabel said, "Would you like for me to . . . do something?"

He laughed then, squeezing her hand in his. "More than

anything on this earth, I want that." He kissed her hand. "But now is neither the place, nor the time. I am, however, very happy that you have agreed to marry me. Because I fully intend to accept that request very soon."

She blushed at that, immediately embarrassed by the way that they had discussed marriage.

He had the grace to look chagrined. "I did not propose properly."

She shook her head. "We need not stand on ceremony. There is no one here who will have expected formalities."

"Nevertheless, I shall make it up to you."

She looked away from him, considering her hands in her lap. "I rather like the way you did it."

He put one hand to her chin, turning her to look at him. He searched her eyes, as though looking for something. Something cleared in his gaze, and he kissed her, a soft, generous kiss that made her more than satisfied that she had agreed to marry this man who seemed so very easy to like.

If only she could be certain that he was not easy to love.

She was spared from having to consider the thought when a knock sounded on the door. Isabel leapt from her seat, her heart in her throat. If they had been interrupted just minutes beforehand. . .

The door opened, and Lara stepped into the room. "Isabel?"

For a moment, she had trouble finding them, well hidden at the far end of the room behind a collection of tall statues, but Isabel took the moment to say, more loudly than necessary, "I do believe this is a statue of Apollo, Lord Nicholas."

Nick stood, slowly, and came around the back of Isabel to consider the marble to which she was referring. "I'm afraid you are mistaken, Lady Isabel."

Isabel was not paying much attention—instead watching as Lara hurried through the maze of statues toward them. "Why would you say that?"

"Well," he said dryly, "in the first place, this statue is female."

Isabel snapped her head up to look at the marble for the

first time. "Well. Obviously I don't mean *this* statue. But that one over there."

"Of course, my mistake." He gave her a small, knowing smile. "Which one?"

"That one over there." She waved a hand absently, distracted by Lara. "Lara? Is all well?"

Lara came closer.

All was not well. "Isabel."

Isabel knew at once what had happened. "Who is it?"

Lara stopped, catching her breath; she had clearly rushed the entire way. "Georgiana."

Isabel felt Nick stiffen beside her. She turned to him and was surprised to see the seriousness in him. Gone was the teasing charmer from earlier, replaced by a stone-faced man. "What about her?"

"She has gone missing."

He met her gaze. "What do we do?"

If she had had the time to consider his words, Isabel would have been happy with his use of the word *we*, yet more proof that they would make a sound team. But she was already heading for the exit, Lara on her heels.

"We find her."

Sixteen

Lesson Number Seven

Show appropriate awe in the face of his remarkableness.

There is nothing a lord likes better than to be reminded of his superior strength, intelligence, and power. Feign ignorance and allow your lord the right in all things, and he is yours. Give him little opportunities to support you; should you singe your fingers playing Snap Dragon, allow him to tend your wounds; encourage his superior skills in cards and other parlor games; and, when possible, laud his vast knowledge and particular might.

Pearls and Pelisses
June 1823

"Who saw her last?"

Isabel's question was short and efficient as she entered the kitchens of Minerva House, taking a large, rolled sheet of paper from Gwen and moving straight to the table at the center of the room.

Nick noticed Rock enter from the opposite end of the

room, back from his excursion to town. He met his friend's eyes and read the urgency in them before looking away, immediately distracted by the rest of the inhabitants of the kitchen. And slightly overwhelmed by them.

Here was Minerva House.

There were two dozen women there, each dressed in men's clothing, breeches, linen shirts, Hessian boots, hair tucked inside caps. They stood when Isabel entered, as though she were Wellington himself. And in that moment, she could have been. With the calm and ease of a lifelong general, Isabel unrolled the paper on the center table, holding it down with a large kitchen block, a saltcellar, and two wooden bowls. Nick took a step forward, recognizing it as a map of the manor, spread before her like a battle plan.

This was not the first time that something like this had happened.

"I saw her last," Jane said, facing Isabel across the table. "She was headed for the laundry with some of James's clothes."

Nick met Rock's gaze across the room. The Turk indicated the door to the outside, a question in his eyes. Nick shook his head.

He wanted to see her work.

"When?"

"A half an hour ago? Maybe forty minutes?

"And?"

"Meg found the clothes in a heap on the path," Jane said, indicating a woman nearby.

"When?" Nick stepped forward and spoke, unable to keep quiet, drawing the attention of the entire room. He might not be able to convince Isabel to trust him, but by God, he could help her find the girl.

Who had very likely been abducted because of him.

Damned if the woman called Meg didn't look to Isabel for approval before answering his question. When Isabel nodded her agreement, Meg said, "Not twenty minutes ago, milord."

"Where are the clothes now?" Nick asked.

Meg pointed to them in a heap on a stool nearby. "I hope I did right by bringing them in, Isabel."

"You did very well, Meg." Isabel moved to take them in her hands, checking each item quickly and carefully. She looked to Nick. "They're barely wet."

Admiration flared. She had understood the underlying direction of his questions. With the amount of rain that had fallen over the last two days, the fabric would have soaked water from the ground quickly. "She's not far."

Isabel turned back to the map, speaking quickly. "I would guess she's been gone twenty-five minutes, thirty at most. They must have come on foot, or Kate would have seen the horses." She looked to her stable master, who shook her head.

"They will not travel far with her by daylight," Nick interjected. "Not if they do not want to be caught."

Isabel looked up at him, considering his words. She nodded once. "Which means she's likely hidden on the estate."

Nick let out a slow breath. She was placing her trust in him.

A mistake.

He shoved the voice to the back of his mind as Isabel continued.

"Our knowledge of the Park puts us in a good position to find her. Kate, Meg, Regina, check the copse of trees in the east pasture. Jane, Caroline, Frannie, you take the west gate, through to the Marbury land . . . be certain to check the lean-tos where Marbury will have left his hay to dry."

She assigned the rest of the women to groups efficiently, marking the areas they were to search on the map as she went. Nick watched as the cook opened a small cupboard and passed hunting horns to each of the groups. "Take the horns. If you see anything that looks strange, sound the alarm. Don't do anything without the rest of us. I want you all back here right as rain. As ever, Gwen stays here. If you need anything, you tell her."

When she finished explaining the plan to the rest of the women, she stood, and Nick marveled at the way the other residents of the house straightened in her presence, shoulders back and spines as straight as any soldier hoping to impress his commander. Nick understood immediately that, like an army, they would follow her orders without question.

And he found himself willing to do the same.

"Lara and I shall search the area between the house and the main road. Any questions?"

He was not going to allow her to go searching for the girl without him. "Lady Isabel. I should like to see the place where Georgiana was taken."

She shook her head. "We haven't time."

He knew the risk of questioning her in front of her girls; he also knew that he could speed their process. He would have to prove it to her, and open himself to questions in the process. It was not a question. "I'm trained as a tracker."

From over her shoulder, he noticed Rock raise his brows in surprise. Nick ignored him. She met his eyes, and there was a long beat as she considered his words. She nodded once. "I shall take you there. Mr. Durukhan, would you be willing to partner with Lara to search the front grounds?"

Rock dipped his head. "Of course."

"Very well." She turned to the rest of the room. "Be quick. Be safe. Be back before nightfall."

Orders in hand, the women left the room like a well-trained battalion. Isabel gave last-minute orders to Gwen while Nick and Rock spoke quietly.

"There's no way they're headed for the road," the Turk said, pulling a pistol from his waistband and handing it to Nick.

"No."

Rock's gaze darkened. "Will you tell her why we are here?"

Nick shook his head, slipping the pistol inside his waistcoat. "Not if I can avoid it."

Rock nodded once. "I shan't be far behind."

They shook hands, and Nick turned back to Isabel. "Let's go then."

She opened the door, and they left the house.

The spot where Georgiana was taken was mere steps from the house, marked by a dirty vest that Meg had left behind in her haste to sound the alarm. Nick crouched low there, taking in the footprints on the muddy path.

Isabel watched for a moment, then looked out over the land. "Do you see anything?"

"Two men. It looks like she struggled." He turned away and swore under his breath, then pointed south toward a faraway cluster of trees. "That way. Is there shelter there?"

"There's an abandoned woodcutter's cottage. James likes to play there."

"That's where they will have headed. They will be waiting for cover of night to travel with an unwilling third." He paused. "Is there any chance I could convince you to wait here with Gwen?"

She was already walking, her long legs carrying her briskly across the land. "None whatsoever. How did you learn to track?"

He allowed her to change the subject, training his eyes on the trees in the distance. "When I was on the Continent, there was a war on."

They walked for a few long moments before she realized he was not going to say more. "That's it? There was a war on?"

"What more would there be?"

"Who taught you?"

"A very intelligent member of the British War Office."

"But you were not a soldier?"

"No." He changed the subject. That way lay danger. "How many times have you planned a search and rescue?"

She shrugged, walking faster. "Several."

"How many is several?"

"I don't remember."

"Try. One time? Fifty?"

"More than one. Less than fifty."

The woman reveled in trying his patience. "How often are they successful?"

She shrugged again. "More often than not."

"Even now, we are to be married, I am helping to get this girl back, and you don't trust me."

Clever girl. He willed the voice in his head quiet.

"It's not that."

It wasn't? "What is it then?"

She did not answer.

"Who is Georgiana that she has been abducted?"

Tell me, Isabel.

"I cannot tell you that."

"Isabel, I do grow weary of that answer."

"It is not my information to share."

"What can you tell me?"

She looked at him for a long moment, not breaking her stride. Turning her attention back to the trees in the distance, she said, "I can tell you that she is more than a governess, but you knew that already. I can tell you that she is worth a great deal to a great family. And I can tell you that when I took her in, I knew that it was only a matter of time until this day came."

"Then why take her in?"

Her answer was soft and serious. "I've never turned a girl away. I was not about to begin with her."

He let her walk several paces ahead of him then, watching her long, willowy frame move across the grounds toward the trees ahead. She had changed into men's clothing earlier, on her way to the kitchens, claiming that breeches allowed her a greater freedom of movement. He could not contain the appreciative smile that flashed as he watched her. She looked more beautiful this afternoon than she ever had before.

He considered the fact for a long moment before realizing why it was true. There was nothing tentative about her movement—nothing to indicate that she was nervous or hesitant about what was to come. Instead, she moved with a quiet, sure grace, ready for anything.

He had never known a woman like her.

And he realized, in that moment, that he was entirely drawn to her powerful combination of strength and vulnerability, this madwoman who spent entirely too much time on rooftops and traipsing across the Yorkshire countryside in pursuit of kidnappers . . . and still found time to doubt her actions and question her worth.

No wonder he was going to marry her.

She was remarkable.

Yes, he could keep her safe, protect Minerva House, send James to school . . . all of it. He had the money, the family, the history to do it.

And he found that he rather liked the idea.

It was going to be impossible to convince her that *she* liked the idea, however, if the reason for his being in Yorkshire was revealed.

They had reached the trees, and he glimpsed a small building several yards away. He reached for Isabel, capturing her arm and staying her movement. "I'd like you to stay here, and let me go in by myself." She shook her head and opened her mouth to protest. He held up one hand. "If they have weapons, Isabel . . . what then?"

"I've faced weapons before."

The words made him angrier than he had expected. "Of all the damned fool— Do you have a way to defend yourself?"

She paused. "No."

He made a mental note to teach her to use a pistol. "So? What do you plan on doing? Exasperating them until they turn her over? That might work on me . . . but I imagine this lot is professional."

She cut him an irritated look. "Usually all it takes is a few mentions of the earl, and they scatter."

"You jest."

She looked away. "No."

"Isabel. From what little you've told me about Georgiana, do you think that the people chasing after her will be afraid of your brother?"

She did not answer.

"Precisely." He set her back against a tree. "You will stay here. Do not move until I come to fetch you."

"What if something happens to you?"

He sighed. Did the woman have no faith in him whatsoever? "If I'm not back in ten minutes, sound the damned horn. And bring in your Amazons."

A little smile flashed. "They are rather like Amazons, aren't they?"

One side of his mouth cocked up at her amusement. "I'm happy I am able to amuse you." He removed the pistol from his waistcoat and checked its load.

"Nick!" He had turned away, but her whisper called him back.

"Yes?"

"I—" She stopped, transfixed by the gun. "Be careful."

In two long strides, he was next to her again, cupping her neck in one strong, warm hand and pulling her to him. He kissed her, quick and thorough, stroking deep and reminding them both of the pleasure they had found in each other's arms. Stepping back from the caress, he said, "There is absolutely no chance of my not returning. After this afternoon, we have unfinished business."

She blushed and looked away. "Go."

He pushed through the trees and approached the cottage. It did not take long to confirm his suspicions that there were two men holding Georgiana inside the shelter. The girl struggled against the ropes they had used to tie her up, and he could hear her angry, muffled cries through the linen rag that was supposed to silence her. One thing was true, the girl had well learned the first rule of surviving a kidnapping—remain loud and irritating. She was worth the most unharmed—and she knew it. Nick watched through the window, nearly amused, as one of her captors rubbed his temples at the noise.

"Gel," said the other in a thick cockney accent, "Ye'll only hurt yerself. We aren' takin' ye back. We're takin' ye *home*."

As he'd expected.

He made a mental note to lay Leighton out for not trusting Nick alone with the task of finding his sister.

The kidnapper's words only served to redouble Georgiana's efforts. She thumped her feet against the floor of the old cottage, and Nick fleetingly wondered if the old floorboards would hold such a violent beating.

He imagined the captors would not much mind getting rid of their difficult prize. For the right price. He sighed. *Amateurs.*

"What's happening?"

Of course.

He should have known that Isabel would follow him. But her whisper at his shoulder didn't make him any less angry. He turned to face her. "What did I ask you?"

"I—"

"No, Isabel. What did I ask you?"

"I'm not a child, Nick."

"Really? Because you seem to be having trouble following directions."

"That's not fair! You can't have honestly thought I'd let you come storming in here without my help?"

"Did you even consider the fact that my worrying about you would only make this more difficult?"

Her big brown eyes widened in innocent surprise. "Why would you worry about me? I'm perfectly capable of taking care of myself."

He shook his head. "I am tired of this conversation, as well. Stay here, if you must. But try to remain out of this, will you?"

He started around the corner of the cottage, toward the single entrance, ignoring her whispered "What are you going to do?"

He was going to put an end to this ridiculous exercise.

And likely bring Isabel's wrath down on his head.

He approached the door and knocked firmly three times. "Open this door, gentlemen. I want the girl and I'm not leaving without her. So let's have a chat, shall we?"

There was silence in the wake of his words, and Nick turned to find Isabel standing a few feet away, mouth wide open in shock. He raised a brow. "I prefer the direct approach."

She closed her mouth. "So I see."

The door opened, Isabel gasped, and Nick found himself at the business end of a wicked-looking pistol. He paused, considering the somewhat unsavory, wool-capped character who was holding the weapon. "I don't think we need bring pistols into this, do you?"

The man behind Wool Cap, inside the cottage, grinned a gray-toothed grin and nodded in the direction of Nick's gun. "Apparen'ly ye did, milord."

Nick looked down at his weapon, then back up. "Fair point. Well, let's try to make sense of it without bloodshed, shall we?" The man shrugged one shoulder. Nick took it as a positive sign. "How much is he paying you?"

"I don' know who yer talkin' 'bout."

Nick's gaze narrowed. "We neither of us are stupid, man. You do yourself a disservice to act as though you are. How much is the Duke of Leighton paying you to bring his sister back?"

He heard Isabel's gasp behind him. Tried to ignore it. Had to ignore it.

"An 'undred quid." Wool Cap looked to Gray Tooth, then back at Nick. "Each."

"I'm guessing that means he's paying you a hundred pounds together, but I'm not going to quibble. I'll give you both two hundred pounds right now if you leave the girl with me and take Leighton a message."

The two men looked at each other, then to Georgiana, then to Nick. They knew a good bargain when they heard one. "Wot message?"

"Tell him that St. John has her."

"'At's it?"

"That's it."

There was a beat as the man considered Nick's words. Then he motioned with his pistol, once. "The blunt?"

"Rock?" Nick called out, not looking away from the door.

There was movement in the trees behind him, and Rock was beside him in seconds. "Here."

"Free these gentlemen from their weapons and escort them to the edge of the property. Once there, give them their money and send them on their way."

Rock looked from one man to the other, each wide-eyed at his enormous size. He put out one mammoth palm, and Wool Cap placed his pistol there. Rock smiled. "With pleasure."

Nick grabbed Wool Cap and thrust him against the wall of the cottage, lifting the smaller man from his feet. "Hear me. If you return to this land, I will use my pistol. And I'm an excellent shot."

"F-fair enuf." The little man nodded his head, and Nick dropped him to his feet, pushing into the house and crouching low next to Georgiana to untie the linen from her mouth. She worked out her jaw and said, "Thank you."

He moved to the ropes on her hands. "You should be more careful, my lady."

She blushed. "How long have you known?"

He considered lying. Decided against it. "Since before I arrived."

"You came for me?"

Nick said nothing.

"Simon sent you?"

"He is very worried about you."

Her eyes welled with tears, and Nick knew in that moment that she was not afraid of her brother. He recognized homesickness when he saw it. He had too often felt it himself.

"I have a sister myself, Lady Georgiana. I would not like to lose her."

"Are you— Must you take me back?" There was palpable fear in her voice.

"No." Her hands came free, and he moved to her feet. "Your brother asked me to find you. Not to fetch you."

"Thank you," she whispered again, rubbing the raw skin on her wrists.

"You know you will not be able to hide from him forever?"

She nodded. "No more than you will be able to hide from Isabel."

He winced. "I don't imagine I am much in her favor right now."

"It does not appear so, no."

He followed her gaze over his shoulder to find Isabel standing in the doorway of the cottage. Rock and the two men were gone, and Nick wished, fleetingly, that he had left with them.

He did not like the look in her eyes.

The look that accused him of the very worst kind of betrayal.

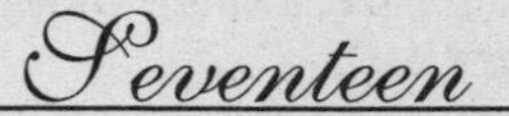

Seventeen

Lesson Number Eight

Learn to love the errors of his ways.

You will find it difficult to believe, we know, but even lords as landable as these will have a flaw or two. Perhaps he laughs a touch too loudly, or his eyesight is less than perfect! Perhaps he has a rogue lock of hair which falls distractingly despite all attempts to tame it!

Embrace these flaws, Dear Reader! For it is in these peccadilloes that we find the charm and joy at the heart of any deserved match!

These lessons, well used, shall ensure that he adore you despite your own failings!

Do you not owe him the same?

Pearls and Pelisses
June 1823

He had lied to her.

Isabel stood in her darkened bedchamber looking out the window over the heath—the land that had been owned by generations of Townsends before it had been slowly parceled off and sold until, ultimately, there was little left for the current earl. She watched as the last rays of sunlight disappeared and the sky turned a brilliant scarlet, then faded into a deep, inky blue.

She had been standing there for hours, her land changing beneath her unseeing gaze, a single thought repeating itself over and over in her mind.

He had lied to her.

She should have known, of course. Should have predicted that something like this would happen. Should have known that he was not what he seemed, but instead the final straw—the one that would break the back of Minerva House.

She placed one hand on the windowpane, watching as the cool glass fogged beneath her fingers.

He had asked her to trust him. He had coaxed her into caring for him.

And, against her better judgment, she had.

She had trusted him not to hurt the girls. Not to hurt the delicate balance of Minerva House.

Not to hurt her.

And he had.

He'd been their enemy from the very beginning. Sent by the Duke of Leighton to find his sister, to uncover their secrets. To betray them.

And he'd done it in the worst possible way.

By making her believe in him.

She took a deep breath at the thought.

What a fool she had been.

Tears threatened and she closed her eyes tightly. She would not cry over this man . . . whom she had known for only four days. Whom she never should have brought to Minerva House. Whom she never should have allowed into her life.

What a terrible mistake she had made.

She had let herself be wooed by his pretty words and tempted by the promise of his touch.

Just as her mother had been.

The girls would never forgive her.

She would never forgive herself.

She pressed her head to the window, feeling the cool pane of glass against her brow as she breathed deeply, willing herself to stop thinking about him. Urging herself to think, instead, about how she was going to save them all now that their secrets had been laid bare, now that it was only a matter of time before all of London—all of England—knew who and where they were.

For some reason, the fear of discovery was nothing compared to the pain of his betrayal—the keen awareness that everything she had let herself believe might come next. . .

Would never come.

There was a soft knock at the door that stayed the tears from welling again.

She had ignored several earlier attempts to gain access to the room, but she could not bear the thought of being alone any longer.

"Enter."

The door opened slowly, and Isabel was surprised to see Georgiana, her riot of blond curls glowing in the candlelight from the hallway beyond. It took the girl a moment to spot Isabel in the corner of the room.

She entered tentatively, stopping several feet from Isabel, considering her surroundings for long moments before she spoke, hands clasped in front of her. "I am sorry to disturb you . . ."

Isabel gave a humorless laugh. "If one of us should be apologizing, Georgiana, I assure you it should be me."

Georgiana's eyes widened. "Whatever for?"

"I brought that man down upon you."

The younger woman leveled Isabel with a frank look. "I assure you, Lady Isabel, you did no such thing."

"Oh? You think he would have found his way here if I had not invited him to come for a visit? You think he would have discovered you if I had not been so foolish as to trust him?"

"Yes."

Isabel looked away.

"You do not know my brother, Isabel. He is the most imperious, commanding person I have ever known, and he has never been denied anything in his life. He is the eleventh Duke of Leighton. Do you know how far back a family tree must stretch to make *eleven* dukes? Each one more arrogant than the last?" Georgiana shook her head. "Simon would have moved heaven and earth to find me. I am honestly surprised that we only had to deal with Lord Nicholas and two idiotic kidnappers. I would have expected my brother to force King George to send in his personal guard." Georgiana placed her hand on Isabel's arm. "You did not bring Lord Nicholas down upon me. I brought him down upon you. And for that, I apologize."

The words coursed through Isabel and she sank to the seat under the window where she had been standing for hours. Indicating that Georgiana should join her, Isabel said quietly, "I am sorry that you have had such a brother looming over you."

Georgiana smiled. "Do not be. I have never doubted Simon's love for me. He may be arrogant and domineering, but he protects his own."

"Then why—" Isabel did not understand.

"There is more to my story than a girl who ran away."

"There always is."

"I would like to tell you. I think you deserve to know why all this has happened."

It happened because I trusted a man I should not have trusted.

"I would like to hear it," Isabel said, silencing the nagging voice.

"I am . . ." Georgiana paused, looking at the window, where Isabel knew she could see nothing but her own face reflected in the dark glass. "I fell in love. It is not important with whom."

Isabel did not speak, waiting for the girl to find the courage to go on. "I made a terrible mistake. I believed that he loved me in return." She stopped, looked down at her hands where they wrung the fabric of her skirts. When she spoke again, it was in a whisper. "But he did not." She took a deep, stabilizing breath. "I suppose it is for the best . . . Simon never would have allowed us to marry. I was crushed. He left, without a word. And then—"

She stopped, unable to continue for the weight of her memories. Isabel leaned forward, clasping Georgiana's hands in her own. "You do not have to tell me."

"I want to," Georgiana whispered. "I want someone to hear me say it."

Isabel remained still, knowing what was to come.

"I discovered that I was with child. I could not tell Simon. I could not disappoint him. Weeks earlier, my maid had told me a story she'd heard of a house in Yorkshire. A place where young women went to start fresh. Run by Lady Isabel." She smiled, small and uncertain. "And so I came here."

She looked up, meeting Isabel's eyes, her gaze wide and innocent . . . little more than a child herself. "I knew he would come after me. I did not think he would find me so quickly."

Isabel squeezed the girl's hands. "I knew he would come after you, as well. It did not change the fact that you are welcome under this roof"—she smiled a small, wry smile—"what little is left of it . . . with my protection. And the protection of the Earl of Reddich."

"As much as I admire the earl, Isabel, I do not think he could do much in the face of my brother."

"Nonsense. It is clear that my brother has a special place in his heart for his governess. I think he would happily do battle for you."

The girl's smile grew into a broader grin. "I am very fond of him, you know. And whatever happens, I will always be proud to say I taught the young Earl of Reddich his Latin."

They shared a smile at the words before Georgiana continued. "There is something else. About Lord Nicholas."

Isabel sobered, shaking her head. "I shall send him away immediately."

"I do not think you should."

Isabel's mouth fell open. She could not possibly have heard correctly. "I beg your pardon?"

"He is a good man, Isabel. If I had not heard such for years from my brother and his friends—the way they spoke about St. John, as though he were a hero among us . . . If I had not heard such from ladies who sighed their longing for his return from the Continent, and who sighed their respect for him when his half sister arrived in London and he stood proudly by her side as the rest of the *ton* laughed at her . . . I would have known it today, when he could have turned me over to my brother, but he let me return here, with you, instead."

Isabel's heart ached at the words, so clearly a description of the man she thought he was. Perhaps he was loyal to his friends, and committed to his sister, and the best of catches for the vapid society ladies who saw only his handsome face and his fat purse. But he had proven today that he was not for her.

She felt tears prick and willed them away. "You are mistaken. It must be another St. John. For this one is a villain who deliberately preyed upon our trust."

Upon my trust. Upon my feelings.

"I think he was very likely trying to be a good friend to my brother."

Isabel shook her head. "It does not matter. He did everything he could to get close to me . . . to find you and reveal your location. I am afraid there is nothing about that man that even comes close to the noble St. John whom you describe."

And then, as though she had conjured him with her invective, he was there at the entrance to the room, in the doorway Georgiana had left ajar. "I am sorry that you think that."

Isabel caught her breath at the sight of him, silhouetted, tall and broad and overwhelmingly dark, against the small rectangle of light. His presence brought with it a flood of feeling—betrayal and anger and mistrust, but also sadness and something else that was nearly unbearable.

Longing.

She steeled herself, determined to keep her voice cold despite her roiling emotions. "I feel certain that I must be mistaken. You cannot possibly still be in my home after what you have done."

She could not see his face, but he stiffened at her words, and suddenly it felt as if there was less air in the room. "I came to speak with you."

"Well, that shall be something of a problem, I am afraid, as I have no interest in speaking with you."

He took a long step into the room, the movement obviously born of frustration.

"And now I see that you are committed to insulting me as well as betraying me. You will leave my bedchamber at once."

He turned his head slightly, focusing all his attention on the other woman in the room. "Lady Georgiana, I would very much like for you to leave us. Lady Isabel and I have things that we must discuss. Alone."

Georgiana pulled herself up straighter—displaying herself in all the manner of a highborn aristocratic lady. "I cannot do that, my lord."

"You have my word that I will not do anything to harm her."

Isabel gave a little humorless laugh. "And your word holds such weight here."

"I understand that you are angry, Isabel. I would like you to give me a chance to explain." He turned to Georgiana again. "I assure you. She is safe with me. We are to be married."

Georgiana's jaw dropped at the announcement, which sent a flood of anger and frustration through Isabel.

How dare he.

"We are to be no such thing," she protested.

He looked back to her again, and for a fleeting moment, she wished that she could see his face. Cloaked in shadow, he was more dangerous and unsettling than he had ever been before. Especially when he said, low and dark, "You said you would marry me, Isabel. I expect you to honor your promise."

"And you said I could trust you, Nicholas. What of that promise?"

A rigid silence fell, neither one willing to be the one to speak after such a gauntlet had been thrown. Finally, Nick gave in, again pleading his case with the younger woman. "Lady Georgiana—I have assured you that I will defend you to your brother, have I not?"

"You have."

"And I have given you my word—as devalued as it has become"—he paused, casting a long look at Isabel—"that I will not force you to return home."

"Yes."

"Please, allow me this."

Georgiana thought for a long moment, considering first Nick then Isabel. Her decision made, she said, "I shall give you a quarter of an hour, my lord. No more."

Isabel snapped her head in the direction of the girl. "Traitor!"

"Fifteen minutes, Isabel. Surely you can spare him that. I shall be just outside."

Isabel scowled as the girl left the room, pulling the door nearly closed behind her, leaving a sliver of light coming into the bedchamber. Isabel moved to the side of her bed and lit a candle, unwilling to remain in darkness with this man, who had so quickly gone from ally to enemy.

She made quick work of lighting candles around the room until they were bathed in golden candlelight, and Isabel regretted her actions.

He had changed into new, clean clothing. He wore black now, an elegant coat and waistcoat that underscored his handsomeness. She noted the perfect knot in his cravat, and was distracted for a fleeting moment by the memory of him with James.

James. Anger flared.

He'd even won over James.

She crossed her arms, warding off the chill of the thought. "I haven't anything to say to you."

"Yes. You've made that abundantly clear."

He was straight and still, entirely composed. She had never seen him this way, so unmoving. It was as though he were a different person from the man whom she had come to know over the past few days.

As though he had been lying to her.

Which, of course, he had.

She looked away, unwilling to show him how much his betrayal had smarted.

He saw, nonetheless. With a sigh, he spoke, his words softer, more cajoling than before. "Isabel. Let me explain. It is not how it appears."

"It appears that you were searching for us from the very beginning."

He paused. "That is correct, although not for you. Not for any of you but Georgiana."

"Georgiana is one of us!"

"Georgiana is the sister of the Duke of Leighton, Isabel. Did you really think you could hide her away forever?"

"No! I—" She stopped, uncertain of her words. "I simply did not expect *you* to come looking for her."

"I am rarely what people expect."

"Yes. I'm beginning to see that." She looked to the ceiling, frustration coursing through her. "It is my fault. I made it all easier by asking you to value the marbles."

"If it had not been the marbles, it would have been something else that brought me here."

"Maybe not."

"Isabel." The way he said her name captured her attention. "I am very good at what I do."

"And what is it that you do, Nick? Because it seems to me that what you are very good at is convincing women to tell you their secrets with your charming smile and your pretty lies and seductions and proposals of marriage—that was a particularly impressive way of gaining my trust, by the way—and then you betray them for your own gain."

"It was not a lie. It was all true." His whisper was tempting, so lovely and soft, with that hint of honesty that she had found so warm and welcoming. Well, now she knew better.

She closed her eyes. The conversation was growing exhausting. "Please, Nick. Don't you think you have done enough to us? Enough to me?"

"You do not understand!"

"What is there to understand?" she cried. "How many times did you ask me to trust you? How many times did you tell me I was wrong to doubt you? How often did you offer me your protection? To James? To the girls?"

"And here I am! The offer still stands!"

"Just go away. You have the information you came for. But tell the Duke of Leighton that he had better bring an army when he comes for Georgiana. For if she does not want to leave, I shall protect her with everything I have."

"And I shall be beside you."

"Stop it!" His words broke her. "You think you can convince me to forget what has happened? You betrayed us! You betrayed *me*. The things I told you—" She stopped, then took a deep breath. "You cannot honestly believe that I would place this house, these lives, in your hands after what you've done. Not when I know that your allegiance can be sold like cattle to the highest bidder."

The words fell like lead between them, and she knew immediately that she had gone too far. He could no longer remain still. He grabbed her by the shoulders and pulled her close to him, forcing her to look into his eyes. "No. I will suffer your accusations. I will bear the brunt of your anger. But I am through with your assault on my honor."

She opened her mouth to retort and he pressed on. "No, Isabel. You will listen to me. I came to help the girl. Not to hurt her. Had I known that she was here and safe, I would not have agreed to the mission. But I did not know those things. Instead, I knew that my friend was beside himself with worry. And I did what I could to help him. Yes. I found your little enclave of Amazonians. Yes. I discovered your secrets—not that they were very well hidden. But none of this is Leighton's business. Leighton's business is that girl"—he let go of Isabel's arm to indicate Georgiana beyond the room—"and the child in her belly. You know nothing of who I am or why I am here. I was never going to give you up. I gave you my word that I would protect you. That I would keep your secrets. And so I shall."

Isabel did not know what to say as he let her go and stalked to the door. As he set his hand to the handle, she found her voice. "How did you know?"

Only his head turned back to her, and not enough to meet her eyes. His tone was clipped. "How did I know what?"

"How did you know that Georgiana is increasing?"

There was impatience in his tone when he replied. "I have said before, Isabel. I am very good at what I do."

The words rankled. "As am I!"

"Yes. You are very good at hiding."

"I am very good at hiding *them*," she corrected.

He did turn back then, his lips twisted in a smile that she did not like. "You do it for them."

"Yes."

"I don't think so."

She blinked. "Of course I do."

"No. I don't think you do it for them at all, Isabel. I think you do it to keep yourself in hiding. To keep yourself from having to face the world beyond your little kingdom. And what might come with it."

She froze at the words.

They weren't true.

They *weren't*.

He waited for a long moment, as though expecting her to reply, before adding, "I will be gone in the morning. I find I am tiring of Yorkshire."

And, with that last parting shot, he left the room, closing the door firmly behind him.

Once he was gone, Isabel crawled onto her bed, exhausted from the verbal sparring and confused by the feelings coursing through her. He had seemed so honest—so true—so hurt.

But what of her?

How lovely had it been when they were rushing off to rescue Georgiana to have this strong, committed man by her side? How much had she adored the feeling of having a partner? Of being able to finally, after all these years, share her burden with another person? What of the comfort she had felt then, for the first time in so very long?

And what of the emptiness that came when he'd snatched it from her?

Perhaps he was right. Perhaps she was afraid.

She rolled onto one side, refusing to allow the thought quarter.

She must remain angry.

Because she did not think she could face the darkness if she allowed herself to think on the sadness that she could so easily summon.

Nick could not sleep, and so he headed for the stables, forcing himself into some kind of perverse penance for his betrayal of Isabel. He paced the floor, keeping the horses awake as he replayed the past days in his mind, thinking of all the ways he could have told Isabel the truth. Of all the times he could have confessed his part in this bizarre play.

But he hadn't—and, instead, he'd lost her.

And, all of a sudden, that mattered more than anything else.

The irony of the situation was not lost on him. He had agreed to Leighton's ridiculous mission because he had been so desperate to leave London and the silly magazine article behind. He'd been avoiding the mincing females who were immediately drawn to him for all the wrong reasons. He'd been eager to escape them and the drama that came with them.

And he'd landed here. In a houseful of females, so rife

with drama that they spent most of their lives in disguise, hiding from kidnappers and dukes and God knew whoever else was determined to find them at any cost.

If it weren't his life, it would be comical.

And at the center of their circus was Isabel—powerful, intelligent, strong-willed Isabel, his Boadicea. Beautiful, passionate Isabel, unlike any woman he had ever known.

There was so much about this woman to admire. To care for. To desire.

To love.

He froze at the thought.

Was it possible that he loved her?

Dread settled in his stomach at the thought. For so long, he had avoided love—a thing that was perfectly fine for others, but entirely wrong for him. He'd seen the way women wielded love as a weapon. He'd watched as his mother had destroyed his father. And, worse, he knew what became of him when he allowed himself to attempt to love. The way Alana had turned the emotion against him and, like a master puppeteer, maneuvered him through the deserts of Turkey and straight into prison.

If his past had taught him anything, it was this: If he allowed himself to love Isabel, there was no way it could end well.

He could take his escape. Here was his opportunity to leave her—and the insanity that came with her—behind. He could return to his normal, staid London life, to his antiquities and his club and his family, and forget the days he had spent here in Yorkshire.

Except, when he considered that life, which had so satisfied him before he'd arrived here, he found it sorely lacking. Lacking in Isabel's strong will, and her smart mouth, and her sweet lips, and her wild, auburn curls that clung to him whenever she was near.

He wanted her.

He turned toward the door of the stables and, for a fleeting moment, considered the lateness of the hour. He hovered there on the brink of movement, considering his options.

He should leave her.

Perhaps she had found sleep.

A vision flashed of Isabel soft and willing, eyes half open, watching him, welcoming him . . . and it proved too much to resist.

He wanted her.

And if he had to wake her to win her, all the better.

She was sleeping when he crept into her room, still in breeches and a linen shirt. She had not put out the candles after he had left, and several had burned out, leaving nothing but a pool of wax. Two remained burning, one by the door and the other by her bedside, casting her sleeping form in a pool of soft light.

He closed the door, knowing that he was committing the very worst of sins, entering her bedchamber without her knowledge or consent, but it did not stop him from slinking close to watch as she slumbered.

She was curved into a near ball, lying on one side, facing the door and the light. Her hands were fisted beneath her chin and her knees were pulled up tightly, as though she could protect herself from the beasts that threatened in the dead of night.

Beasts like him.

He resisted the words, instead focusing on her face, looking his fill at this woman who had wreaked havoc upon his life. She was beautiful, her full lips and long, straight nose combined with high cheekbones dusted with freckles. He paused there, marveling at those tiny brown spots that betrayed her time working in the sunshine—yet another example of how this woman was so very different from all others.

His gaze caressed her face, finally settling on her brow, where worry furrowed the space above her nose even as she slept. Nick felt a tightening in his chest as he watched the dimple there deepen; he had done this to her. He could not resist reaching out, smoothing one long finger softly along the wrinkle, willing it away.

The touch was enough to bring her out of her too-light sleep, and she came awake with a deep breath, her limbs extending as consciousness returned. He took a fleeting moment to remember her like this—warm and lush and barely aware of her surroundings.

Someday, he would kiss her awake and keep her abed for hours.

The thought did not have time to linger.

When she saw him, sleep gave way to surprise, then to outrage. She shot straight up. "Why are you here?" She swung her legs over the edge of the bed, and Nick resisted the instinct to put distance between them, somehow knowing that if she stood, he would lose any ground in this battle.

She immediately understood what he was doing. Her eyes narrowed. "Let me up."

"No. Not until you listen to what I have to say."

"You have already said quite enough, Lord Nicholas."

The sound of the honorific on her lips sent a river of distaste through him. Somehow, he had to convince her to hear him. He had to convince her that he was worth it. Desperation surged, and he did what came instinctively, crouching in front of her and capturing her hands in his.

She immediately tried to extricate herself from his grasp, but he held firm and after a few seconds, she gave in.

"I have not said that I am sorry." She did not respond, and his lips twisted in a wry smile. "If you knew me better, you would know that I do not apologize well."

"Well, perhaps it is time you learn," she said, simply.

"I never meant to hurt you, Isabel. Had I known what I would find when I came north, I would never have agreed to Leighton's request." He stopped for a moment, looking down at where their hands were entwined. "That is a lie. Had I known that I would find you when I came north, I would have come years ago."

Her jaw dropped, and he gave her a lopsided grin. "I see I have rendered you speechless. You see, Isabel, you are something of a marvel. I have met many women in my lifetime, all across the globe. And yet, I have never met a woman so strong, so vibrant, so lovely as you. And you must believe me when I tell you that I would *never* do anything to hurt you."

"But you did hurt me."

The words, filled with pain and barely a whisper, propelled him forward, and he lifted her hands to his lips, kissing them with reverence. "I know that I did. And you've every right to hate me for it."

"I don't hate you."

He looked up at her then, meeting her gaze, seeing the truth there. "I am very happy to hear it."

Her brow furrowed again, and he itched to kiss the fret away. "But I do not understand . . ."

"Someday," he promised, "someday I will tell you everything."

She shook her head. "No, Nick. No more someday. It is time for the truth."

He took a deep breath, knowing in his heart that she was right. That he must tell her everything . . . that he must lay himself bare for her if she was ever going to trust him again. And somehow, with that knowledge came strength. "Fair enough."

He stood, pacing the room as he spoke, unable to keep still as the words poured out of him. "My mother left us when I was ten. One day, she was there; the next, she was gone. We knew nothing of where she went—after a while, it was difficult to believe that she had ever really been there to begin with." He stopped by the candle near the door and turned back to her. "You would think that losing one's mother would be the hardest thing for a child—but it wasn't, really. The hardest thing was that I did not know what had happened. What had caused her to leave. The hardest thing was the worry that . . . somehow . . . it had had something to do with me."

She opened her mouth to speak, but he pressed forward, not willing to stop, not sure that he could start again if he did. "I became obsessed with her leaving. With the reason behind it. My father had had every one of her possessions disposed of within days of her disappearance, but I was dogged in my search for something that would point me in the right direction. I found a diary, and in it her plans for the future. She was leaving for the Continent. Going first to friends in Paris, then on to Italy. She called it her *adventure*." He gave a little laugh. "Apparently marriage and children and being a marchioness were not exciting enough for my mother.

"I never told anyone that I found that diary. Not my brother, certainly not my father. But I kept it for years, until I finished with school. By then, my father was dead and Gabriel was the marquess, and I was nothing." He shook his head. "And so I took to the Continent."

"To find your mother," she whispered.

He nodded at the words. "Of course, by then, we were in the thick of the war and any means that I might have used to track my mother had long disappeared. But I was young and strong and had a brain in my head, and a high-ranking official in the War Office—whom I've always thought Gabriel had paid off to ensure that I would be safe traipsing through a war zone—noticed my obsession and took me under his wing to teach me to track."

She watched him as he ran his fingers over the candle flame once, twice. He could tell that she was curious—desperate to ask questions. He waited out the silence until she could bear it no more and said, "Whom did you track?"

One shoulder lifted in a barely perceptible shrug. "Whoever needed finding. I specialized in people who went east. I cared little about what I was doing, and far more about where I was doing it. My work proved a means to a very satisfying end. I was seeing the world, and for the more than fair price of a few days' work whenever the Crown was seeking someone."

"Did you . . ." She paused, clearly uncertain of her next words. "Did you ever hurt anyone?"

He considered the question for a long moment. He did not want to lie to her. He did not want to lie to himself. He looked away from her when he answered, becoming lost in the words. "Never on purpose. My task ended when the missing person was found. They were no longer my concern after that."

"So they might have been hurt."

He looked to her. "They might have been."

She pressed on. "And you could have been hurt, as well."

"Yes."

She held his gaze for a long moment before she stood, crossing the room to stand before him. She faced him head-on, and Nick was struck once more by her strength. "Why did you stop?"

He was silent for a long while. He knew the answer would mean something to her—that she would find some measure of understanding in the words. He wanted them to make sense. But, more than that, he wanted them to be true.

"I don't know. Perhaps I stopped because I became too good at it, because I liked it too much. Perhaps I stopped because I did not care about the people I sought. About the ones whom I found." He met her gaze, wishing that he could make her understand. "Or perhaps I stopped because they did not care about me."

The words hovered in the air between them and he took a step closer to her, narrowing the distance between them. "I should never have agreed to this mission . . . but Leighton is an old friend, and I could not deny him. I swear, Isabel. I did not come to hurt you, or Georgiana, or James, or any of the other girls. If I had ever thought I might do damage to you . . . I would never have come."

He bent his head to meet hers, their foreheads nearly touching. "I want nothing but happiness for you. Nothing but pleasure. Please, give me another chance."

She closed her eyes at the whispered words, and he watched as the emotion played across her face. He held his breath, hoping that he had told her enough to win her over.

A ghost of a smile flickered across her lips, gone so quickly that if he had not been watching so closely, he would not have seen it. She opened her eyes, her lovely brown gaze honeyed in the flickering golden light. "I am scared and worried and not at all certain that I should trust you . . . but . . . I am rather happy that you did come. To Yorkshire," she qualified on a whisper, "and tonight."

He released the breath he had been holding on a rugged exhale and, in the pleasure that coursed through him, he reached out to pull her into his arms. And then he did the only thing he could think to do.

He kissed her.

Eighteen

She had vowed not to fall victim to his pretty words and his alluring promises.

But when he had confessed his past, she had been won again. Even as she berated herself for believing him, she could not stop herself from wanting to trust him again—to believe in him. And then he had kissed her, and her mix of emotion was distilled into a single, powerful thought.

She wanted this man in her world.

The words, combined with the irresistible caress, unlocked something deep inside her, the place where her most secret desires had been ferreted away never to be seen—never to be shared. But now, here was this man who seemed able to tear down her carefully erected defenses with a single word. A single touch.

She sighed against his lips and he deepened the kiss, claiming her mouth with a rough tenderness that sent a current of pleasure through her. His kisses came harder and deeper, each one headier than the last, punctuated by long, lush pauses during which he whispered her name like a benediction. She clutched his arms, strong and warm beneath his shirtsleeves, and held on to him—her rock in a storm of sensation.

His hands were everywhere, stroking across her shoulders, down her arms, finally lifting her until she had no choice but to wrap herself around him. He clasped her to him for a long moment, burying his face in her neck and making small, unbearable circles against the soft skin there with his tongue. Isabel cried out at the pleasure of the caress, and he lifted his head, his blue eyes gleaming in the dim light.

He set his forehead to hers. "Isabel, you should tell me to leave."

Her eyes widened at the words. "Why?"

"Because if you do not, I am going to stay."

The words, low and graveled with emotion, sent pleasure pooling deep within her. When she replied, she did not recognize the woman who spoke. "And if I say I want you to stay?"

He did not reply for a long moment, and she was mortified to think that she might have said the wrong thing. He took a single long step, and set her on the table by the door. He cupped her face in his large, strong hands and set his lips to hers again, robbing her of thought and breath in one long, lovely kiss.

When he lifted his head, they were both breathing hard. "If you want me to stay, it would take an army to get me to leave."

Isabel raised her hands then, plunging her fingers through his sable locks, drawing him down for another kiss. Before their lips touched, she said one word, more breath than sound. "Stay."

He growled his response, plundering her mouth as he tugged her shirt free of her breeches and set his hands to the warm, soft skin beneath. Not breaking their kiss, he stroked upward, pulling the linen with him until, finally, she lifted her arms above her head and let him remove the garment from her.

Immediately shy, Isabel covered herself.

"No," he whispered, dropping several soft, distracting kisses on her lips. "Don't hide from me. Not tonight." His hands traced down her arms, their fingers entwining as he lifted her hands away from her breasts. "Tonight, they are mine. To do with as I please."

He set his lips to one of them, and all nervousness was gone—lost to pleasure. He closed his mouth around the tip of one breast, tugging, licking, teasing until she cried out and arched toward him, desperate for more of him. At the movement, he clasped her thighs in his hands and tugged, pulling her flush against him, her legs wrapped around his waist as he lifted her up to gain better access and suckle harder.

She writhed at the movement, rubbing against him, his hardness sending a wave of feeling straight to the core of her. He growled his pleasure, and she pressed against him, rocking her hips once, twice, before he tore his mouth from her breast with a gasp. Meeting her gaze, he saw the feminine power there, and he took her lips in a bold, welcome kiss before trailing his mouth across her cheek and finally taking the lobe of one ear between his teeth and biting gently. "Minx."

Isabel whispered his name, half plea, half protest, and the sound spurred him on. She felt the shift in him . . . the change from man to something more primitive—and when he lifted her again, she knew precisely where they were headed.

He followed her down onto the bed, capturing her mouth once more in a desperate, rugged kiss—a lavish caress that left only passion in its wake.

His hands were free to roam her body, and he stroked down her torso, smoothing the heated flesh there until he reached the edge of her breeches, the palm of one hand flatting against the curve of her stomach. He stayed his movement then, and all feeling—all heat and touch and trembling pleasure—pooled there.

He lifted his head, waiting for her eyes to open and meet his, and when they did, she found him watching her intently, a wicked gleam in his gaze. "I have never had the pleasure of removing breeches from a lover."

Lover. The word echoed between them, a dark promise, and Isabel was struck with the intimate knowledge that, after tonight, that was what she would be. *His lover.*

His hand hovered, waiting for her permission.

"I think it is time," she whispered, timid and bold all at once, and it was all the freedom that he needed. Within seconds, she was naked beneath him, eyes closed against the truth of the moment, embarrassed, nervous, self-conscious.

"Isabel, open your eyes."

She shook her head. "I cannot."

"You can, darling. Look at me."

She took a deep, shaking breath and peeked up at him, aware of her position, bare to his sight, to his touch. She moved one hand, covering the thatch of curls between her legs, unable to remain entirely bare for him. His blue eyes flamed at the movement. "No, love, don't hide from me."

"I—I must."

He gave her a half smile. "You are so beautiful . . . and you don't even know it."

The words warmed her cheeks. "I am not."

"Yes, you are." He set one finger to her lips. "Here"—he trailed it down her neck to the tip of one breast—"and here"—down over the curve of her belly—"and here"—to the back of the hand that protected the very heart of her. "And here, Isabel . . . here you make me ache."

The words sent pleasure humming through her. No one had ever called her beautiful. And now, here, in the quiet cocoon of this place where she had slept for her entire life, this man was showing her precisely how beautiful she was.

"I should like to see you," she said, softly. "I think you might be very beautiful yourself."

His smile widened. "I do not think that is quite the word, love. But if you would like to see . . . far be it from me to deny you your whim." She giggled at the words and he kissed her swiftly. "I like to hear you laugh. I do not hear it enough." He rolled to his back then, stacking his hands beneath his head. "All right, beauty. I am yours for the taking."

Her eyes widened in shock at the words, as she considered him next to her, unmoving, a gleam in his eyes, waiting for her. "I . . . I couldn't."

He laughed, and the low rumble shook the bed beneath her. "I assure you, Isabel. You can."

She rolled onto one side, lifting one hand to touch him, but stopping just before she did. "I—I don't know where."

The laugh turned to a groan. "Anywhere, love. Anywhere is better than the torture of nowhere."

She settled her hand to his chest, the broad, firm mass of him overwhelming her. He seemed to sense it, and he moved one hand to capture hers and guide it, stroking over his chest and down the flat planes of his stomach to the place where his shirt tucked into his breeches. She eyed his waistband, wondering what she should do.

"We shall only do what feels good, Isabel. What feels right." Something in his words calmed her, made her want to press on. "What do you want?"

She met his eyes, blue and serious. "You always ask me that."

"I want to know," he said simply. "I want only to give you that which you desire."

I want you. She held the words back.

"I want to see you without a shirt."

Without words, he sat up, pulled his shirt over his head, and sent it sailing across the room.

Isabel swallowed.

He was perfect. He was like one of her statues.

She sat up, too, then, nervous again. "I—I don't think . . ."

He reached out, pulling her to straddle his lap. "Perhaps you should not think, beauty." And then he kissed her again, and they went tumbling back onto the bed, and he let her have control. This time, it was she who took, her tongue and teeth and lips that led the way as they explored each other. When she pulled back to catch her breath, he moved her to sit up above him and said, his words more begging than demanding, "Take down your hair."

She lifted her hands to do as he bid her, and he groaned, his hands and eyes raking over her. "You are a siren."

She smiled, enjoying the way he seemed to be transfixed by her. "Am I?"

He met her gaze. "I am creating a monster."

"Perhaps," she allowed, lowering herself until they were curtained by her auburn curls. She kissed him then, long and slow, letting her tongue stroke along his full bottom lip before she trailed her kisses down his neck and over the sloping planes of his chest. When she reached one flat nipple, she paused, lifting her eyes to his. He was watching her through heavy lids, and she could feel that he was holding his breath. "Does it feel as good for you as it does for me?"

He did not move. "Why don't we find out?"

She set her lips to the spot, licking delicately before she closed her lips around him and repeated his earlier actions, scraping her teeth lightly across him before she sucked him into her mouth. He gasped, plunging his fingers into her hair and whispering her name. After long moments, he could no longer bear it and he lifted her from him. She looked to him and said, "Did you not enjoy it?"

He laughed, breathless. "I enjoyed it too much, love." He took her mouth again, and their tongues tangled in a long kiss before she placed both hands on his chest and leveraged herself above him. "I should like for you to remove your pants now."

They were gone in seconds, and she gasped as he rolled her on the bed, settling himself between her long, slender legs and taking control once more. He kissed down her neck, stopping to scrape his teeth along her collarbone before he laved the spot with his tongue and sent her writhing against him. "Nick . . ." she whispered, "no . . ."

He stopped at the word, lifting his head to find her gaze. "What is it, beauty?"

"I want to touch you."

He went utterly still, and for a moment, she thought he would deny the request.

"Please . . ." she added.

He laid his head down on her breast for a long moment, as if shoring up strength, and he rolled back over, allowing Isabel full access to his naked body. She traced her fingers down the planes of his torso, discovering him—the lean muscle, the warm skin, the place where a long raised scar wrapped around his right side. She paused there, stroking the spot, grateful that he had survived the attack that had left such a mark.

When her hands moved again, their aim was true. She tentatively stroked the long, firm length of him; he sucked in a deep breath and she paused, uncertain. "Is this . . ."

He groaned at the words, punctuated with a tentative squeeze of her hand. "Yes, Isabel."

Feminine power coursed through her. "Show me."

His eyes flashed, and he set one hand to hers and did as she asked. Watching their joint movement, he guided her, showing her just how to touch, just how to stroke, until both of them were breathing heavily. Finally, he stopped the motion, lifting her hand to his lips and kissing her palm. "No more, beauty."

"But I want . . ."

He gave a harsh laugh. "As do I, love. But there is nothing that will keep me from you tonight. And if I let you continue your sweet torture, this night will end all too soon." He rolled over her again, settling between her legs, moving down her body, pressing soft, moist kisses across her torso before he paused at the opening to her and, with one finger, pressed deep inside her. "Ah," he said, his voice dark and languid, "you are so wet here. Can you feel it?"

She bit her lip at the sensation of his fingers delicately stroking, caressing. He added a second finger to the first and, with his thumb, began to circle the spot at the very center of her, where all her pleasure had pooled. Isabel writhed on the bed, clutching the coverlet and biting her lip to keep from crying out. He did not stop the torture as he asked, "Is this what you want, beauty?"

"Yes . . ." The word came on a low moan.

"Here?" His thumb circled faster, pressed harder.

"Yes, please . . ."

"So polite. So passionate. My Voluptas." He slowed the caress to an unbearable rhythm. "But that's not everything you want, is it?"

She opened her eyes, meeting the emotion in his. "I—"

"Tell me, Isabel. What is it that you really want?"

"I want . . . I want you."

"What part of me?"

She blushed, pressing against him, urging him to go faster. "No, Nick . . ."

He grinned, wicked and wolfish. "Oh, yes, Isabel . . . what part of me."

He stopped entirely then, his fingers high inside her, but unmoving, his thumb gone from the place where everything seemed to begin and end. She spread her legs, uncaring of what it might look like, of how it might seem. "Nick . . ." she cried, his name a plea and a protest.

"You have only to ask for it, Isabel."

He blew a stream of cool air against the heat of her then, and she thought she might go mad from the torture. "Your mouth," she whispered. "I want your mouth."

"Good girl." He was on her, his lips and tongue perfectly against her, caressing and licking in a lash of pleasure that robbed her of thought. Her fingers clenched in his hair as he worked her with fingers and tongue, and he growled his satisfaction against her. The rumbling sound brought with it the crest of feeling, a rolling wave of pleasure. She cried his name and he flickered across the peak of her sex, his mouth adoring her until she was gone, pressing against him, lifting her hips to meet his wicked, wonderful mouth, the pleasure rolling over her until she could do nothing but hold him to her, afraid to lose the one thing that was at the center of her world.

After she had returned to earth, he lifted his mouth from her and kissed his way up her body, stroking her breasts, playing with the tips of them until she sighed, then taking her mouth in another long, lush kiss. "You must never be afraid to ask for what you want, darling. Not with me."

She opened her eyes and met his gaze. "I want the rest."

The blue of his eyes darkened immediately at the words. "Are you sure?"

She nodded. "Entirely. And you said all I had to do was ask."

He shifted against her, and she could feel the hard, heavy length of him against her. She lifted against him, eager for the next part of this marvelous dance. He caught his breath, and she could tell he was trying to remain still. "Isabel—has anyone ever . . . spoken to you about . . . this?"

She shook her head. "I have seen animals."

He smiled, half grimace. "It is not quite the same . . ."

She pressed against him again. "Nick . . . please. I don't care." His scar had gone stark white, and she lifted one hand to smooth a finger along the mark, hoping to soothe the demons he was fighting. "I want it. I want you."

"It will hurt, beauty. Just the first time. But I shall make it up to you."

Her heart clenched at the words. *He was worried about her.*

And she knew, in that moment, that this man—so full of concern even in this moment when she could barely think of anything but the feel of him against her—had never meant her harm.

She smiled, running her fingers into his hair and pulling him down to kiss her. When they came apart, she whispered, "I trust you."

And the words seemed to make everything right.

He lifted himself then, pushing just barely inside her, allowing her time to stretch, to accommodate him. She tilted her head, considering the sensation. "It is strange."

He gave a hiss of laughter at the words. "It only gets stranger, darling. But we shall try for something more."

He rocked against her, traveling slightly deeper each time,

until she was sighing her pleasure with the movements. "That does not feel strange. That feels nice."

"Just nice?"

"Quite lovely."

"Good." He thrust deep, and she gasped, her eyes opening wide as he seated himself to the hilt. He stilled, holding himself above her, "Isabel? Are you . . ."

"Strange again," she said, her voice tight, pained.

He loved this woman. The thought came clear and fast at the entirely wrong time for him to address it. But he knew, without a shadow of a doubt, that it was true. He brushed his lips across hers in a soft, reverent kiss.

"I shall make it better, beauty."

He moved, pulling slowly out of her, and she grasped his arms at the movement. "Oh. Oh, that feels . . ."

He reversed his movement, returning to her. "Yes?"

"Nick," she sighed.

"I love the way my name sounds on your lips." He leaned down and suckled one nipple until she was panting with pleasure. He moved in earnest then, deep, smooth strokes that chased away her pain and left pure pleasure in their wake. When she lifted to meet his thrusts, he knew he had her. He read her movements, following where her body led, eager to help her find her pleasure.

"Say it again." He began to thrust deeper, faster, and the tension that had been mounting became unbearable.

"Nick," she whispered.

Finally, he reached down between them, placing his thumb against the rigid core of her; he stroked there once, twice. "Again."

"Nick!" she cried out.

"I am here, love," he said, capturing her gaze. "Look at me, Isabel."

"I can't . . . It is too much," she panted. "Please! I don't know . . ."

He lowered his mouth to her ear, speaking softly there. "I know. Take it. I shall catch you when you fall."

And she did as he told her, falling over the edge, convulsing around him, milking him with a heady, nearly unbearable rhythm. She cried out his name again, and he did catch her, finding his own pleasure only once she had fully experienced her own. He unraveled above her, thrusting a final time before he collapsed to her chest, their harsh breathing the only sound in the still, dark room.

He lay there for a long moment, trying to focus, to regain the power of thought before he stirred, lifting his weight from her even as she tempted him to stay with the little protest that she offered at the loss of him. Propping himself on one elbow next to her, he ran his hands over her flushed skin. She shivered and curled into his warmth.

He felt her lips curve against his chest in a smile and he pulled back to meet her gaze. "What is it?"

"It was not strange in the end."

He grinned. "No?"

"No."

"What was it, then?"

She tilted her head, considering the question. "I think it was rather remarkable."

He kissed her, quick and deep. When he lifted his head, he said, "It was that."

She drifted to sleep in the long moments that followed, and he watched as she slumbered, considering this woman who was so strong and soft and beautiful. Here was a woman who *lived.* She was filled with passion and pride, and she would take nothing but what she believed was right and fair. He reflected on the events of the day—the way she had so vehemently agreed to marry him. . .

The way she had so violently recoiled when he had proven to be different than what she had first thought.

She curled against him, sighing in her sleep, and the sound punctuated his shame. She had come to believe in him, to have faith in him and the life that he was promising her, and he had robbed her of her sense of certainty. And, while her body clearly trusted him, it would take time to win back her mind.

He would not stop until he had done just that.

He loved her.

It was in that moment, with the second admission of his feelings, that he realized the full force of the words.

And the terror that came with them.

"Isabel! Isabel, wake up!"

Isabel shot straight up in bed at the pounding on the door to her bedchamber. The sound was disorienting, and for a fleeting moment, she had no knowledge of where she was or what was happening.

When the events of the prior evening came flooding back, she gasped, one hand flying to her lips to hold back the sound, and she searched the room for any sign of Nick.

He was gone, along with all evidence that he had ever been there. She noted that he had even moved her clothes, which had been discarded without thought, and draped them over a chair by the fireplace. The care with which he had covered his tracks made Isabel at once grateful and disappointed—grateful that he would take such steps to protect her reputation with the other residents of Townsend Park, and disappointed that he would so easily slip from her room without a backward glance.

As though he had done it many times before.

She scoffed at the thought. She did not care if he had done it a hundred times before. His habits were not her concern.

One hundred did seem a few too many times, however.

The knocking began again then, distracting her—thankfully—from her thoughts.

"Isabel!"

"Enter!"

Lara came bursting through the door at the command, breathless and disheveled. "You must dress!"

With a sigh, Isabel threw back the covers and got out of

bed, heading for the wardrobe to fetch clothing. "I know that I have overslept, but it cannot be that late. What time is it?"

Lara had frozen in midstride across the room, her eyes wide as she watched Isabel.

Isabel turned back at the silence. "What is it?"

"Why aren't you wearing any clothes?"

Isabel looked down at herself, immediately covering the pertinent parts as she willed herself not to blush . . . unsuccessfully. "I didn't . . . that is . . . I . . ." She paused, irritated at her stammering search for a quick and reasonable answer. "I was hot," she ended simply, grasping the closest gown and hurrying behind her dressing screen to avoid further embarrassment.

She could hear the disbelief in her cousin's voice when she replied, "You were hot."

"Precisely. It is nearly July, Lara."

"In Yorkshire. At night."

"Nevertheless," Isabel said, willing Lara to accept the excuse. She peeked around the edge of the screen to find her cousin slowly looking around the room. *She must distract her.* "Lara." The word gained the other woman's attention. "Was there something you wanted to discuss? A reason you were hammering on my door, demanding that I wake and dress, perhaps?"

Lara's eyes widened. "Yes!"

Isabel stepped out from behind the screen, tying a long belt on the midnight-blue mourning dress. "What is it?"

Lara pursed her lips. "You shan't like it."

Isabel stilled. *Was it possible that Nick had left?* He had said he was leaving last night . . . but that was before . . . well, before things had changed. "What is it?" she repeated, tentatively.

"We have a visitor."

A feeling of dread settled deep within.

Everything was about to change.

"Who is it?"

Lara clasped her hands together tightly in front of her, hedging.

Densmore. The guardian was here. The house, the girls, James—their fate was in his hands now.

And Nick would leave. There was nothing to keep him here any longer. He was no longer needed for the marbles, or for anything else.

Except, all of a sudden, she seemed to need him quite desperately.

An ache started in her chest.

She would be alone once more.

"It's Densmore," she announced to the room, her voice emotionless.

"No." Lara shook her head. "It's the Duke of Leighton. He has come to fetch his sister."

Nineteen

Minutes later, Isabel was pressing her ear to the heavy mahogany door of the earl's study. She could detect the low hum of masculine voices from within, but their words were impossible to understand. She leaned closer, cursing the earl who had selected such a sturdy portal.

While she appreciated that had the ancestor in question likely had goings-on that he had not wanted overheard, the choice of two-inch-thick wood showed an obvious lack of foresight when it came to the requirements of future generations.

"Nick is in there with him?" she whispered.

"Yes," Jane replied, just as quietly. "He joined him almost immediately."

Isabel turned an irritated look on the butler. "And why was he given the opportunity to meet with him before I?"

Jane had the good grace to look chagrined. "He asked for you and Lord Nicholas and his sister when he arrived. Since I knew his sister was not an option, I opted for you and Lord Nicholas, not wanting to irritate the man any more than he already is."

"He seems irritated?"

"There's no seeming about it. The man is furious."

"Well, I suppose I should not be surprised to hear that." Isabel pressed her ear back to the door.

The butler whispered, "You shan't hear anything that way."

"Yes, Jane, I've discovered that, thank you."

What were they talking about in there?

Was Nick pleading their case?

Or was he betraying their trust once more?

Isabel quashed the thought. Surely after last night. . .

"Would you like to sneak around the outside of the house and see if we can hear from beneath the windows?"

Isabel considered the idea for a fleeting moment before she realized just how craven such an action would be. With a frustrated sigh, she turned her back to the door and faced the staircase at the center of the great foyer of the house, where Lara and Georgiana stood. "No. I shall go in." She set her hand to the door handle before Lara stayed her. "You aren't going to knock?"

"I am not. For two reasons. First, I appreciate the element of surprise. And, second, it's my house. The duke had better get used to that idea."

She ignored the three sets of wide, doubtful eyes watching her and entered the study, closing the door sharply behind her.

"Dammit, Leighton, you're not hearing me . . ." Nick trailed off as she entered, turning to give a short bow in her direction. Isabel noted the concern in his blue gaze and ignored the instant pounding of her heart at the sight of him.

He was too handsome for his own good, or hers.

She redirected her attention to the second man in the room.

Who was not much better.

It appeared that the Duke of Leighton was an angel. She'd never seen anyone like him—a man who could only be described as beautiful. He was tall and broad, with a mass of golden curls; high, angular cheekbones; and eyes like his sister's—the color of warm honey, fresh from the comb.

Surely a man this perfect was not the portrait of arrogant entitlement that everyone claimed.

"I assume you are the chit who is hiding her." His tone was flat and unemotional.

Apparently he was both arrogant and entitled. And rude.

"Leighton." Nick growled the name.

Isabel squared her shoulders and ignored the snaking pleasure she felt at his warning tone.

She did not need him. Would not.

"I am *Lady* Isabel."

If the duke heard her emphasis on the honorific, he did not let on. "I am happy that you were finally able to find time to join us."

Her brows rose at the sarcasm in his tone. What a loathsome man. No wonder Georgiana had run from him. "What is it that I can do for you?"

"I've already discussed the matter with St. John."

His imperious tone set her on edge. "Excellent. And what is it that you think Lord Nicholas will be able to do to help your cause, considering that it is I who run Townsend Park?"

His gaze narrowed on her. "As far as I understand it, *Lady Isabel*"—he said her name like it was poison—"you have absolutely no hold on Townsend Park, nor anything in it." She went cold as he continued. "Indeed, it seems to me that my speaking to you will succeed in doing nothing but infuriating us both." He leveled her with a cool look. "Do not make me seek out Lord Densmore to get what I want."

He was threatening her!

She opened her mouth to retort, but Nick entered the fray. "I should not have to remind you that we are in the lady's house, and you will treat her with the respect she is due."

The duke did not look away from Isabel. "She kidnapped my sister, St. John. What respect is due her for that?"

"I did no such thing!" Isabel protested.

"Yes, well, I imagine it will sound very like that when the magistrate hears of it."

Isabel gasped at the threat.

Nick's scar grew stark. "Leighton. Enough."

Isabel turned on him. "You call this cretin a *friend?*"

"Cretin?" Leighton's voice shook the walls. "I am a peer of the realm and a duke. You will refer to me with respect."

Isabel's eyes flashed. "No, I don't believe I will."

The duke lost his patience, turning to Nick. "You will control your female, St. John."

"I will say it once more. Treat the lady with the respect she deserves, or I will put you through a wall. Again. And there's no one here to expel me this time."

His voice was low and menacing, and Isabel was rendered mute by the angry threat she heard there. The duke watched her response, then said, "Well. That seemed to do it." Silence fell for a long moment before he added, "Lady Isabel, I should like to see my sister."

Isabel took a deep breath, finally moving to sit behind the desk. There was something about the position that filled her with confidence. Indicating the two chairs on the opposite side of the desk, she said, "Why don't we sit and discuss it?" She waited, feigning patience, until the two men sat. "Would you like tea, Your Grace?"

Leighton blinked once, surprised by the shift in her demeanor. "No I would not like tea. I would like to see my sister."

"And see her you shall," Isabel said, "but not before we have spoken."

Leighton looked to Nick. "Is she always this dogged?"

Nick smiled. "Yes."

"Of course you would find this amusing." He returned his attention to Isabel. "Lady Isabel. I am aware of what you are doing here in Yorkshire."

"Your Grace?"

"Not three minutes ago you called me a cretin. I feel confident that we can dispense with the formalities. I know you are running some colony of females here." Neither Isabel nor Nick confirmed the idea. "I do not particularly care what you're doing, as long as you don't bring my sister into whatever nefariousness in which you are involved. Am I clear?"

Isabel leaned forward, placing her forearms on the cool leather blotter atop the desk. "Not entirely, no."

"Isabel . . ." Nick's tone was edged with warning. "Do not incite him."

The words only inflamed her ire. "Do not incite him? Whyever not? What makes him think that he can barge into my house, threaten my safety and the safety of those who reside here, and simply expect me to turn over the poor girl?"

"She is my sister!" Leighton thundered.

"Sister or no, Your Grace, she arrived here of her own free will, scared and uncertain and desperate to be far from you! What would you have had me do? Turn her out?"

"You've been harboring the missing sister of the Duke of Leighton! I've turned London inside out to find her!"

"With due respect, she was not missing to me."

The impertinent words shocked the duke into silence. She looked at Nick then, not understanding the gleam in his eye. "Are you going to side with him?"

Nick took a long moment to consider his words. "I think it is best to remain Solomon in this particular argument."

"Well, I'm certainly not cutting the poor thing in half."

"A pity. That would have made it all much easier." Nick stretched out his long legs, crossing one ankle over the other. "Do you think perhaps you would be willing to give His Grace a moment with his sister?"

Isabel's gaze returned to the duke. "Assuming your sister agrees, I see no reason why we cannot arrange a meeting."

The duke dipped his head, the portrait of graciousness. "A noble beginning."

"If you lay a finger on her, I will have you exited from this house," Isabel said flatly, as though she were discussing the weather.

Leighton and Nick both stiffened at the words, so clearly an affront to the dignity and honor of the duke, but Isabel remained stoic under their surprised and offended gazes, standing and moving to the door.

She did not know him. Nor did she know Nick, for that matter.

A pang of sadness threatened. She set her hand to the door handle and turned back to the two imposing men standing side by side, waiting. "Georgiana is under the protection of the Earl of Reddich. The full weight of the title is behind her."

She left then, closing the door firmly in her wake, and Leighton turned to Nick, his tone icy. "The Earl of Reddich is an *earl*. I am a duke. Last I checked, the hierarchy of peerage is still in effect in Yorkshire, is it not?"

Nick felt a pang of sympathy for the man. "I think you should be prepared to forget everything you have ever believed about your power as a duke. Every resident of this house would swear fealty to that woman before they would King George."

As would I.

Leighton met his eyes. "Don't tell me. You're smitten with the girl."

Nick returned to his chair, allowing the words to flow over him. *Smitten.* The word did not do justice for what he felt for Isabel. Not after last night, not after this morning, as she had lorded from behind this great desk that had been the seat of men for generations, not after she had fearlessly taken on one of the most powerful men in England . . . and won.

"Suffice to say, she has earned my respect and admiration. And perhaps more."

Leighton's eyes narrowed. "You're mad to take her on, you know."

"I do."

"And yet?"

"I shall do it anyway."

The duke's nod was punctuated with the opening of the door. Nick stood again as Isabel reentered, and he was struck by her beauty; even dressed for mourning, the lovely shape of her was undeniable—tall and lithe and perfect. She met his eyes briefly, but her gaze skidded away before he could read her thoughts. *Was she as consumed with the events of last night as was he?*

He had been in his chamber, devising a plan to get her away from the house for the day when the knock had come and Jane had announced the arrival of Leighton.

As usual, the duke had damned terrible timing.

The thought was quashed by Georgiana, who stepped into view behind Isabel, hands clasped tightly in front of her, averting her eyes to the floor of the study.

Leighton stepped forward, and when he spoke, there was immense pleasure in his voice. "Georgie . . ."

Georgiana looked up and Nick was amazed by the pure emotion in her face—elation mixed with nervousness and sadness, yes, but also with love. When Leighton lifted her off her feet in a powerful embrace, she could not keep her happiness from her tone. "Simon!"

Something that had been tensed in Nick's chest since the previous day, when he had revealed his relationship with the duke to Georgiana, loosened at the portrait of sibling adoration that the two made—he was now entirely sure that Leighton had had nothing to do with driving the girl north.

Instead, when he set her down, Leighton took her hands in his and said, "I have been so worried, Georgie. You must tell me what has happened. I swear I will do everything in my power to make it right."

The words brought tears immediately to the girl's eyes, and she pulled her hands from his, taking a step back, away from him. Isabel was there, putting her arm around Georgiana in a gesture of comfort and solidarity. It was Isabel who spoke. "Perhaps I should have tea brought in."

Leighton's frustration—his inability both to understand and to repair the damage that was obviously devastating his sister, set him off again. "For the last time! I do not want tea! I want my sister! What has this place done to her?"

Georgiana looked up then, fiercely protective of Isabel and Minerva House. "This place has done nothing but take me in. And give me a home. And a purpose." Nick felt a wave of admiration for the waif of a girl as her voice rose to its full strength. "This place has done nothing but accept me."

Leighton raked his hands through his hair. "*I* accept you. Whatever it is, Georgie . . . whatever sent you running to Yorkshire, I can fix it."

She met his gaze with the firmness of a queen. "I do not think you can, Simon. I am very happy you came to find me. I am happy to have seen you, even happier that Lady Isabel and the rest of the residents of the Park need not live in constant fear of you coming to find me. But you must let me stay here. This is where I belong."

"Nonsense," Leighton scoffed. "You are the sister to the Duke of Leighton. You deserve to have a life that is worthy of a duchess."

A little smile played across Georgiana's lips. "And what makes you think that living here is not that life?"

"For heaven's sake, Georgiana. Look at this place."

Nick watched as Isabel opened her mouth to defend the Park before thinking better of it. She met his gaze and closed her mouth. He nodded his approval. *Good girl.* This was not her battle to fight.

"I like it here. And Lady Isabel has generously offered me a place."

Disbelief flooded Leighton's face. "A place?"

The girl nodded. "Governess to the earl."

The duke looked to Nick, then to Isabel, then back to his sister. "Governess?" he thundered. "You are *employed* here?"

Isabel stepped in then. "It is not, precisely, employment, Your Grace."

"Oh? What is it then, Lady Isabel?"

"It is more a question of each of the residents of the Park doing what they can for the good of the larger community."

Isabel trying to explain the reason behind the bizarre world that operated within the walls of the Park was an amusing thing, indeed. If the situation were not so serious, Nick might have laughed. But he had a very real concern that Leighton was in danger of throttling Isabel or his sister or both—which was not at all amusing.

"So if I were to pay for a governess for your brother, my sister would be allowed to go without working."

Isabel paused, pursing her lips. Nick decided the expression was rather darling. "No, not precisely."

"I would not want such a thing, anyway, Simon," Georgiana interjected.

The duke lost his patience. "This is ridiculous. You are coming home with me."

Georgiana looked to Isabel, who nodded once in a silent show of support. Georgiana took a deep, steadying breath. "No. I am not."

Leighton scowled. "I'm afraid you haven't a choice. I am your brother and guardian."

"Simon." The girl's voice grew soft, filled with sisterly love. "I know you are worried about me. I know you want me to come home. But please understand that I cannot. Not right now. I like it here. I feel that I belong here. I am safe here."

Simon bowed his head, and Nick felt a pang of sympathy for him, this man who had never been denied anything in his entire life. He was confused and uncertain and he wanted to make this situation, which he did not understand, better. Nick had come to understand that sense of helplessness most acutely over the last six days. It seemed that the women of Minerva House were rather expert in developing it in the men around them.

What the girl did not know was that, ultimately, her secret would out. Isabel could hide her for only so long. It was merely a matter of time before news traveled that the Duke of Leighton's sister was increasing in Yorkshire, bringing a scandal of epic proportions down on Leighton's head. And his house.

The duke should be prepared to face it.

But it was not Nick's information to share.

The duke lifted his head. "Tell me what has happened."

There was desperation in his voice, a bare emotion that Nick recognized as more human, more feeling than he had ever seen the man show. Suddenly, there was no place for him and Isabel in this room. Shifting his attention to Georgiana, he saw the tears well in her eyes, the subtle, uncontrollable trembling of her lower lip, and he was moved to act.

He met Isabel's discomfited gaze, saw that she, too, recognized the private nature of this moment. "It is time the two of you speak without an audience," he said, crossing the room to her side and ushering her to the door. "We will wait for you outside."

Neither sibling responded, remaining still as Nick and Isabel exited the room.

At the sound of the door finding its seat, Isabel spun toward him, concern in her eyes. "She is going to tell him."

"Yes."

She began to pace the foyer, lost in thought. He watched as she wrung her hands, the motion unlocking something deep within him. Here was a woman who cared deeply. Who loved powerfully. *What would it be like to be on the receiving end of such emotion?*

Finally, she turned to him again.

"What will he do?"

He took a long moment to think, leaning against the banister of the wide stone staircase that dominated the space. Leighton had always been proper. He'd always been staid and stoic and resistant to change or to anything that might sully his name. He'd always been the type to look down his nose at the baseness of others. When the St. John twins had received news of a half sister arrived from Italy earlier that year, it had not escaped Nick's attention that Leighton had distanced himself from them at society functions.

He did not like scandal.

And there were few scandals more devastating than a pregnant, unmarried sister.

Isabel was standing mere inches from him, brown eyes wide and worried and beautiful, and his heart ached for her.

"I don't know what he will do." He reached out and took her fidgeting hands in his own, clasping them firmly and commanding her attention. "But whatever happens, the girl will be safe. I swear that to you."

She searched his gaze for a long moment. "I want to believe you. So very much."

But she didn't.

She was not willing to trust him again. Not yet.

Perhaps not ever.

And that truth hurt him more than he could have imagined.

"Isabel—" He did not know what he could say to change her mind, and so it was likely best that the door to the study opened then, drawing their attention.

Leighton stood in the massive doorway, stone-faced.

He had not taken the news well.

Isabel was already moving toward the study, eager to get to Georgiana, to comfort the girl. Leighton's words stopped her in her tracks. "I should like to speak with you both."

Isabel—*strong, brave girl*—met the duke's cold stare. "Your sister, Your Grace. She needs me."

If possible, Leighton's face became more unmoving. "I have no sister. Not today. And the woman in that room"—he paused, and in that brief silence, Nick understood the powerful battle raging within his friend—"she can wait. If you wish to remain mistress of this place, Lady Isabel, you will hear me. Immediately."

There was an unpleasant, imperious threat in the words, one that Isabel knew better than to ignore. She squared her shoulders, not taking her gaze from the duke. With a firm "Certainly, Your Grace," she led the way to the library.

Once inside, Leighton moved to the fireplace, staring down into the darkened hearth. There was a long silence, then: "I imagine that mine is not the only family that would be rocked by scandal if this place were found."

Isabel took a step toward him. "No, Your Grace."

Nick admired her for her truth in that moment.

Leighton looked over his shoulder at her briefly. "There is a part of me that wants to bring this house to rubble."

She rocked back on her heels at the venom in his voice. She turned to Nick, and he registered the silent plea in her gaze. *He must defuse the situation.* He moved, leaning against a nearby pillar in an approximation of calm. "It is not the house, Leighton. And you know it."

"Without this house, she would have been—"

"Without this house, she would still have been in her predicament," Nick pointed out, drawing the duke's hateful glare. "She simply would have had nowhere to run. You should thank Isabel for taking her in."

"Yes, well, I don't think that is going to happen quite yet." The duke turned then, meeting Isabel's gaze. "The way I see it, Lady Isabel, I have two options. The first, I bring the magistrate down upon your head and take the scandal I have coming now." Isabel did not respond, remaining stoic under the angry barrage. "The second, I let her stay her. She bears the child. And the scandal comes later. At a time I cannot predict. Because you cannot reasonably protect yourself or your residents, and it is only a matter of time before everything is made public." He turned to Nick then. "If you were in my position, St. John, which would you choose?"

Nick felt Isabel's gaze on him, knew that she was willing him to choose the second option. He also knew that any reasonable person would choose the first. If scandal were to rock a family, it was best that it do so at a time of the family's choosing, so that they were prepared, so that they could arm themselves against the gossipmongers.

But there was nothing reasonable about this situation for Nick. He wanted Isabel safe. He wanted her girls safe. And there was only one way to ensure such a thing.

"I would choose the latter."

Leighton laughed, the sound humorless. "You would not."

"I would in this case. Because there is a factor that you have not considered."

Isabel could no longer remain quiet. "There is?"

He looked at her then, registering her uncertainty, her surprise, and behind it all, her fear. "There is. We are to be married. Which puts Lady Georgiana—and her circumstances—under my protection."

The duke crossed his arms and turned to Isabel. "Is this true?"

Isabel shook her head, her face pale. "No. I never said I would marry him."

Her denial cut Nick to the quick. The idea that she might not marry him after yesterday—after last night—was unacceptable. Anger flared, along with hurt and irritation. Years of practice kept them from surfacing.

Instead, he turned to cool humor. "Your memory is failing you, Isabel. You said you would marry me yesterday morning." He paused, waiting for her to meet his gaze. "In the statuary. Don't you remember?"

Of course she remembered. She gasped at the words. "That was before everything changed!"

"Indeed, it was. Before it became an imperative." The insinuation in the words sent a blush across her cheeks.

"That's not what I meant and you know it!"

"I know precisely what you mean. I also know I am not leaving here without marrying you."

"I don't need you. We are fine by ourselves."

I don't need you.

The statement set him off. "Yes, I see that. Because you've got a houseful of women in hiding with no protection for them and God only knows how many ruffians hunting for you after Leighton put out his call, a house, I might add, that is literally falling down around you, not to mention a child who needs more training than most pups I've met and has inherited one of the most troubled earldoms in the country, the sister of a duke about to bear a bastard child, and . . . you've been compromised! But you are *fine*.

"You think that asking for help makes you weak. What makes you weak is your naïve insistence that if you say you need no one, you will be able to hold everything together! Of course you need me! You need a battalion to keep this place out of trouble!" His voice rose to a thunder. "How can you possibly think that I *wouldn't* marry you, you madwoman?

His words echoed in the room for a long moment, and Isabel's eyes welled with tears. He immediately regretted his words. "Isabel," he said softly, reaching for her, wanting to take it all back.

She held up a hand, staying his motion. "No." She turned to Leighton, "If those are my options, Your Grace, then obviously I choose the one that is least likely to ruin Townsend Park."

The duke cleared his throat. "If what St. John has said is true, I must insist you marry, Lady Isabel, as a gentleman."

She nodded.

"I shall send for a minister."

She nodded again, her lips pressed in a thin line, as though she were holding back tears. And then she ran from the room, leaving Nick feeling like an ass. Frustration flared. "*I* shall send for a minister, dammit."

As if it mattered.

He moved to go after her, eager to explain himself.

To apologize.

To do what he could to win her.

"I would not, if I were you," the duke intoned.

Nick turned on him. "Oh, and your actions with women today seem so very on point, Leighton."

"She shall come around."

"Yes, well, I'm not so sure. She is not like other women."

"I had not noticed."

Nick moved to sit in a nearby chair, holding his head in his hands. "I'm an ass."

Leighton took the seat across from him and removed a cheroot from the silver case in his pocket, lighting it. "You shan't get an argument from me."

Nick looked up. "You're an ass, as well, you know."

"I suppose I am." The duke sighed. "Goddammit. Pregnant. She's only seventeen. Not even out."

"You can't ignore her forever."

"No . . . but I can give it some effort."

"She's a good girl, Leighton. She does not deserve your anger."

"I do not want to think on her." The words brooked no discussion. There was silence for a while, before he added, "So you are in love with the lady."

Nick sat back in the chair, staring up at the ceiling. *Of course he was in love with her. She was the most remarkable person he'd ever known.* "God help me, I am."

"In my experience, the path to a woman's heart rarely begins with announcing her being compromised to a roomful of people."

"It wasn't a roomful." Nick closed his eyes. "I am an idiot."

"Yes. But she's going to marry you."

"Because we've forced her hand."

"Nonsense."

Nick looked at his friend. "The Duke of Leighton has insisted she marry or he will destroy the thing she considers most dear. What would you do?"

"It is a fair point," Leighton allowed. He took several thoughtful puffs on the cigar. "Although I will say this . . . Your lady does not seem the type to run from adversity."

Nick thought of Isabel on the roof, and on the Dunscroft commons, and in the kitchens with her Amazonian army. "You are right about that."

The duke considered his cheroot for a long moment. "Is it possible she cares for you?"

"Not this morning."

"You should tell her you love her."

Nick shook his head. "That is a terrible idea."

"Afraid she will not return the emotion?"

Nick met the duke's serious gaze. "Terrified of it."

"The *bulan*. Terrified. How interesting." Nick resisted the impulse to put his fist through Leighton's face.

Leighton removed a watch from his pocket, checking the time. "As much as I would enjoy the fight you are so clearly itching to have, the girl is in mourning. You shall need a special license."

"Which means I shall have to go to York."

"Aren't you lucky that I happen to know the archbishop there?"

Nick scowled. "Oh, yes, Leighton. Your arrival has brought with it the very best of luck."

Twenty

It had not been the kind of wedding one imagined.

Nick had returned sometime in the early morning after traveling through the night to York for a special license, then back via Dunscroft to wake the town vicar and drag him to Townsend Park to perform the ceremony. He'd barely had time to change his clothes. If Isabel was to judge from his harried appearance, the deep circles under his eyes indicated that he had not slept since they had last seen each other—the graveled voice with which he spoke his vows serving as further proof.

They had married in her father's study, with Lara and Rock as witnesses. The ceremony had been quick and perfunctory, explained to the minister as a way they could marry without desecrating the memory of her father.

The minister had not protested, so impressed had he been at the special license inked by the hand of the Archbishop of York himself.

Isabel had not protested, either.

It was, after all, the only solution.

So they had sworn to love and honor; they had pledged their mutual troth. And when he had bent to kiss her, she had turned just enough for the caress to land slightly off-center, a blessed relief, for she did not think she could bear the feel of his lips on hers in that moment when they were marrying for all the wrong reasons.

She'd left the house as soon as the vicar had, sneaking out into the western fields of the Park. She had been walking for some time—hours, perhaps—thinking.

She had seen the many faces of marriage in her life: marriage for love that dissolved into desolate isolation; marriage for escape that had become a marriage of desperation; marriage of duty that never blossomed into anything more.

In those rare moments when Isabel had allowed herself to fantasize about marriage, however, she had dreamed of a marriage that was more than isolation and desperation and duty. It was ironic, she supposed, that hers was born of all three.

But if she was honest with herself, two days earlier she had believed her marriage to Lord Nicholas might blossom into love.

His name was Nicholas Raphael Dorian St. John.

It was the most she could claim to know with certainty about her new husband.

The wind had picked up on the heath, and the long grass lashed at Isabel's legs as she walked in a long, straight line out to the edge of the Townsend land—land that had been in her family for generations.

Land that would be saved for future generations because of what she had done that morning.

Not so selfish now.

She closed her eyes against the thought. When she opened them, the broken rails of the fence that marked the western edge of the property were in her field of vision. Another thing that would now be fixed.

She hadn't wanted to marry him for money. Or for protection. Or because the Duke of Leighton willed it.

But, of course, she had, in part.

Hadn't she?

"No." She whispered the word, and it was carried away on the wind, lost in the sway of the reeds.

She had wanted to marry him because she cared for him. And because he cared for her.

But it was too late for that.

A vision flashed from yesterday, long ago now—a distant past. She had refused his suit, and he had made it seem as though she desperately needed him. As though they would not survive if he had not come and saved them. As though their time was up.

And he had been right.

She brushed a tear from her cheek. She could no longer hold it all together.

And she was terrified of what that meant.

Who was she if she was not this? If she was not the mistress of Townsend Park, the keeper of Minerva House, the one with the answers, the one to whom everyone else turned?

Who would she become?

"Isabel!" The shout, punctuated by hoofbeats, pulled her from her thoughts, and she whirled to face Nick, high atop his gray, bearing down on her. She froze as he pulled up on the reins, leaping down before the horse came to a stop. He held her gaze as he advanced, his voice raised above the wind. "I've been looking everywhere for you."

She shrugged. "I took a walk."

"Rather a long walk for a bride on her wedding day," he pointed out. "Were you attempting an escape?"

She did not smile at the jest. "No, my lord."

There was silence as he searched her face. "You are unhappy."

She shook her head, tears welling. "No, my lord."

"I have heard tell of brides weeping on their wedding day, Isabel, but I had always considered them tears of joy." He paused, watching her carefully before pulling her to him in a warm embrace. "Call me *my lord* one more time and I shall not fix your fence. Which has something of a hole in it, if you had not noticed."

"I noticed," she said, the words muffled against his chest.

"Isabel. I am sorry. For the things I said. For the way I said them." He spoke the words against her hair, the warm breath of them a promise. "Forgive me."

Oh, how she wanted to.

She did not reply, instead wrapping her arms tightly around him. It was all she could give him right now. She let him hold her for a long time, enjoying the feel of his strong arms around her, the warmth of his chest against her cheek. For a moment, she imagined that this was a different kind of wedding day. That they had married for any reason but the one for which they had married.

That they had married for love.

She pulled back at the thought, and he watched as she smoothed her skirts and looked anywhere but at him. "Isabel." At the sound of her name on his lips, soft and lush, she looked up and met his eyes—saw the emotion there. "I am sorry you did not have the kind of wedding of which you dreamed. I wish we could have done it another way, with a church . . . and a dress . . . and your girls."

She shook her head, emotion making it difficult for her to speak.

He took her hand. "We left out an important part of the ceremony this morning. I assume the vicar thought that we could not fulfill its requirements, so he skipped over it."

Confusion marred her brow. "I don't understand."

He opened his hand, revealing a simple gold band that lay in his palm, "It's not what you deserve—I woke the first jeweler I saw last night in York. He did not have much of a selection. The first chance I get, I shall buy you something gorgeous. With rubies. I like you in red."

He spoke quickly, as though she might refuse him if he gave her the opportunity to speak. It was fine, though. She did not want to interrupt. Taking her hand, he placed the ring on her finger. With a crooked smile, he said, "I do not remember the exact words . . ."

She shook her head. "Neither do I."

"Good." He took a deep breath. "I am not perfect, and I realize that I have a long way to go to earning your trust once more. But I want you to know that I am extraordinarily happy that you are my wife. And I shall do my very best to make you an excellent husband. Let this ring bear the proof of my words."

He cupped her cheeks in his hands, his thumbs brushing away the stray tears that fell at the words. "Don't cry, darling." He sipped at her lips in soft, lingering kisses, so tender and caring that, for a moment, she forgot that they had married for a host of wrong reasons.

He lifted his head and met her eyes once more, and said, "For the rest of the afternoon . . . for today . . . can we forget everything else? Can we simply have a wedding day?"

He was buying them a day before they had to remember all those wrong reasons.

Perhaps to discover a right reason.

And, God help her, she wanted it.

She nodded. "I think that is an excellent idea."

He grinned and offered her his arm. When she took it, he said, "The day is yours, Lady Nicholas. What shall you do with it?"

Lady Nicholas.

What a strange thing to be this new, different person. Isabel played the name over in her head, her earlier concern resurfacing. Who was Lady Nicholas? What had become of Lady Isabel?

"Isabel?" Nick's question interrupted her thoughts.

Tomorrow. She would worry about Lady Isabel tomorrow.

She smiled. "I should like to show you the Park."

Within minutes, they were on his horse, Isabel seated in front of him, clinging to him as he trotted the gray across the heath toward the house. As they traveled, Isabel pointed out places that had mattered to her as a child—the copse of trees where she had hidden whenever she wanted to get away, the pond where she had learned to swim, the crumbled remains of the old keep where she had pretended to be a princess.

"A princess?"

She kept her eyes on the stone structure, set on the highest point of the property. "Yes, well, pretending to be a queen seemed too much. A girl must know her limitations."

He laughed, and stopped the horse. "Shall we tour your castle, Your Highness?"

She looked back at him, noting the teasing interest in his eyes. "By all means."

He lifted her down in an instant, offering her his hand and leading the way up the little hill to the piles of rubble that were left. Isabel took the lead then, running her hands across the worn stones. "It's been years since I've been up here."

Nick gave her room to explore, leaning against a low stone wall that marked a room of the long-destroyed building, watching as she wandered through the crumbled pillars. "Tell me what you used to pretend."

She smiled to herself. "The same things all little girls pretend, I would think . . ."

"I did not have the privilege of knowing many little girls," he said. "Elaborate, if you please."

She paused at a stone archway that might have been a window long ago. Looking out to the bold, sweeping landscape beyond, she answered. "Oh, that I was a princess in a tower, waiting for my knight . . . perhaps I was under a magic spell, or guarded by an evil dragon, or something equally fantastic. But it was not always so elaborate; sometimes I just came here to . . ." She turned, and noticed that he had disappeared from his place.

"Came here to . . . ?" He was at the other side of the archway now, leaning his forearms on the wide stone wall. She laughed in surprise at the picture he made, mussed sable hair and crooked grin in his formal wedding attire.

She matched his pose, her arms touching his on the sill. "Came here to imagine what my future might be."

"And what was that?"

She looked away. "The normal things, I suppose . . . marriage, children . . . I certainly was not planning for Minerva

House." She paused, thinking for a long time. "It is funny how those things push their way into little girls' dreams. I did not have a very good example of a marriage. I did not have proof that such a thing was worth having. And yet . . ." The words trailed off.

"And yet there was a time when Lady Isabel dreamed of becoming a wife," he said, his voice light, teasing. Precisely what she needed it to be.

She smiled, meeting his blue eyes. "I suppose so. Of course"—her tone turned impish—"she certainly never expected to marry one of London's most eligible bachelors. She was lucky, indeed, to secure such an eminently landable lord."

His brows shot up at the words, his jaw dropping in surprise, and she dissolved into giggles at the picture he made, so comical and clownish.

"You knew!"

She placed a hand dramatically to her breast. "My lord, how could you have imagined that there was a woman in this great land who did not know? Why, we need not have a subscription to *Pearls and Pelisses* to recognize such a "—she paused with great emphasis—"paragon of manhood . . . when we see one."

He scowled at the silly description. "You think you are very funny, Lady Nicholas."

She grinned. "I *know* I am *exceedingly* funny, Lord Nicholas."

He laughed and reached out to brush away an auburn curl that had come loose in the wind and landed against her cheek. When the task was completed, their laughter died, and with the barest of pauses he continued the caress, cupping the back of her head in his large hand and pulling her toward him, kissing her thoroughly on her warm, smiling lips. The kiss was deep and thoughtful, sending a river of pleasure straight to the core of her. She sighed into his mouth, and he moved to settle little, soft kisses on her cheek, the tip of her nose, and her forehead before pulling back.

"So you thought you might land me," he teased.

She shook her head with a laugh. "No. The girls thought I might land you. They urged me to use the lessons from the magazine to do so." She smiled at his groan of disbelief. "Needless to say, I was never very good at following instructions."

He chuckled. "And so? What was your plan?"

"I thought I might land your expertise in antiquities."

"Well . . . you seem to have received more than you had bargained for."

She made a show of considering him with a critical eye. "Indeed, it seems I have."

He barked in laughter. "Minx."

She laughed, too, and he left the window then. She leaned through to watch him make his way to a nearby entryway, her heart quickening as she realized that he was coming to be closer to her. Wanting to retain her illusion of calm, she hopped up to sit on the low sill, waiting for him to come to her. Excitement pooled in her belly as he approached, carefully navigating the stones that littered the inside of the keep, his blue eyes trained on her.

The magazine had been right. He was a remarkable specimen of a man.

And he was her husband.

The thought rocked her to her core.

He did not stop a discreet distance from her, instead coming as close as he could, his legs brushing her skirts, his body blocking the sun from her face. He lifted his hand, running the backs of his fingers along her cheek, leaving a trail of fire in their wake. His eyes roamed over her face, and there was something there that she could not identify.

"What are you thinking?"

Were they at any other moment in their time together, she would not have asked . . . but they were here, in this magical place, the rest of the world and the rest of their lives far away. Today, they were simply husband and wife.

As if there were anything simple about it.

His gaze found hers, and her pulse raced as she recognized the passion there. She held her breath, waiting for his answer.

"I am thinking that you are the most magnificent woman I have ever known."

Her jaw went slack at the words, so unexpected, and he pressed on, his hands cradling her face. "You are strong and beautiful and brilliant, and so passionate—it makes me ache to be near you." He placed his forehead to hers as he continued, "I don't know how it happened . . . but I seem to have fallen quite impossibly in love with you."

The words rendered Isabel speechless.

Was it possible that such a thing could be true?

He loved her.

The words echoed in her mind, making it impossible to think of anything else.

And then he was kissing her. And she could not think at all.

Professing his love to Isabel had unlocked something raw and powerful in Nick, and without removing his lips from hers, he lifted her from the low stone wall to move to a patch of soft green grass in a small square footprint of the keep. They stood there for a long while, their mouths and hands exploring, and Nick was keenly aware of the difference this moment had from all others . . . of the powerful, heady nature of making love to his wife.

To a woman he so thoroughly loved.

When her hands fell to the buttons of his coat and his waistcoat, Nick tore his mouth from hers, gasping for breath as she searched for skin. He shucked his layers as they kissed madly and Isabel tugged on his shirt, making space for her hands to explore the wide, warm expanse of skin beneath the linen. The feel of her fingers against him was torture, and he broke the kiss, pulling the shirt over his head and letting it flutter on the wind to land outside the walls of their sanctuary.

He reached for her, eager to resume their kiss, but she

danced away from his grasp, eyes locked on his chest. "No," she said, her voice filled with a feminine power that made him ache to have her, "I want to see you."

She came closer, blocking his hands from pulling her to him, instead running her palms over his chest and down his arms. "You're so broad . . . so bronzed . . . how does that happen?"

He struggled for words, mad for her touch. "I have an estate outside of London . . . I like to work in the fields."

Her heavy-lidded gaze met his, and he clenched his fists to keep from pulling her to him and taking her mouth. "You do not wear a shirt?"

He shook his head. "Not always."

"How wicked," she whispered, setting her lips to him and tracing moist, wet kisses along the rigid planes of his chest until he could no longer bear it.

He took control for sanity's sake, capturing her lips, then turning her to make quick work of the long line of buttons at the back her dress, loving the nape of her neck as she sighed her pleasure on the wind. When the fabric loosened, Isabel caught it to her breasts and turned, her brown eyes filled with a siren's promise as she let it go, the lavender fabric pooling at her feet.

Nick took a deep, steadying breath, reaching for her again, whirling her around, and tearing at the ribbons of her stays. "I loathe the woman who invented the corset," he growled.

Isabel laughed, looking over her shoulder at him. "What makes you think a woman invented the corset?"

"Because a man would never have made it so difficult to get to you." The undergarment fell away from her then, and he swung her back around, brushing the straps of her chemise from her shoulders until she was bared to him and the sky and the keep. His gaze raked over her beautiful body, flushed with a mix of excitement and embarrassment. "There you are," he said, his voice made barely recognizable by the wanting in it. "Come here."

He pulled her to him, her bare breasts pressing against

his chest, and he took her mouth in a thunderous kiss, stroking deep as his hands cupped her breasts, teasing their tips until they were hard, desperate points of flesh. She cried her wanting against his lips, and he rewarded the sound by setting his mouth to one tip, worrying the flesh with teeth and tongue and a gentle, maddening sucking that set her writhing against him. With one hand, he reached down to stroke the eager core of her, parting the soft curls that shielded her sex with one finger, finding the place where her passion pooled and circling there, pressing until her gasps became too much for him.

He shifted them, laying her down on the soft grass like a sacrifice, parting her legs to bare her to the sun and the wind and the sky as he added a second finger to the first, driving her to the edge of pleasure, watching her eyes glaze with passion.

He wanted to watch her come apart in his arms.

She arched her back against the ground, her hips circling, lifting, showing him where—how—to touch, to stroke, to circle. He leaned down and whispered in her ear, taking the lobe between his teeth, "That's it, my love. Take your pleasure."

He gave her that for which she did not know to ask . . . faster, harder, stronger, deeper . . . until she cried her pleasure to the ancient stones and clung to him as she spiraled out of control.

Afterward, she lay still for long minutes, and Nick drank his fill of her, naked and willing and *his*. When she finally opened her eyes, his breath caught at the wanton gleam there. She ran one hand down the length of his chest, sliding one finger beneath the waistband of his breeches, where he was hard and hungry for her.

"It is my turn," she whispered, plucking at the buttons of his breeches altogether too slowly.

He stepped in, disposing of his boots and breeches quickly, until he was as naked as she, hard and hot and desperate for her. He took her mouth in a long kiss before saying, "I would hate to be thought of as unfair."

She laughed, the sound low and wanton, and he hardened even more as she cupped him in her hand, stroking until he closed his eyes against the pleasure. What she lacked in skill, she made up for in eagerness; Nick opened his eyes to slits and watched her as she looked at him, fascinated as he grew in her hands, harder and longer than he had ever been.

As he watched, she leaned down to settle a soft, moist kiss on the tip of him, and he thought he might die from the pleasure of it.

At his groan, she stopped, lifting her head, concern flooding her face. "Did I hurt you?"

He closed his eyes at the innocent question, unable to stop his hips from moving, desperate for more of her touch. "No, love. No . . ."

She looked down at him again, skeptical. "Shall I stop?"

His voice shook. "Do it again."

She did, her lips soft and torturous against him. He held his breath, waiting for her next move, and when he felt the soft, tentative lick of her tongue there, he sighed his pleasure, "Yes . . . like that . . . God, Isabel."

The words spurred her on, and in moments, her innocent caresses, the soft sucking of her mouth, were threatening to kill him. If she did not stop—*she must stop.*

He lifted her from him then, his strong arms moving her to straddle him, and he pulled her down to take her mouth. She lifted from the kiss and he met the uncertainty in her gaze. "Did you not enjoy it?"

He gave a harsh laugh. "It was the most incredible thing I have ever experienced, love. I enjoyed it too much."

Her brow furrowed, and he realized that she did not understand. He took her mouth once more, long and deep and powerful until they were both panting, then set his mouth to the tip of one of her breasts, suckling until it was hard and aching and she was crying out. "I do not want to take my pleasure without you with me. Not today."

He moved her then, guiding her until the tip of him was settled against her. Her eyes widened at the sensation. "Can we? Like this?"

He raised a brow. "Let's find out."

He lifted her, lowering her onto him until he was seated to the hilt. "Is this all right?"

"Yes," she whispered with reverence. "Yes—" She rocked against him, testing their fit and his sanity. "It feels wonderful."

"Good." He lifted her again, showing her the movements, encouraging her to take control of their lovemaking—of their pleasure. She took to it immediately, as he had known she would, rocking against him, testing her movements, seeking her pleasure.

He watched, his hands stroking her lean, strong thighs, running up her torso, cupping her breasts, letting her find the rhythm that brought her to the edge.

It was torture.

She finally found the movement that brought her pleasure, rocking hard and fast against him, crying out as the wave of ecstasy threatened to break. He watched as surprise and passion passed across her face, as she looked down at him and spoke his name over and over—a litany of pleasure.

He reached down to where they were joined, setting his thumb to the peak of her sex, rubbing small tight circles there as he felt her tighten around him, about to shatter. Her eyes widened then, and he commanded, "Look at me, Isabel. Look into my eyes as it comes."

She put her hands to his shoulders, her eyes locked with his, blue against brown. "I cannot . . ." she panted. "Nick!"

"I know." He clasped her hips to his, the wave crashing over them, sweeping them both up in a maelstrom of passion and they were both crying out, the sounds echoing on the ancient walls as they found their pleasure together.

Isabel collapsed against his chest, and he held her there

until their labored breathing had calmed, and all that was left was the sound of the wind rustling through the stones.

He placed his lips to her temple and whispered his love again. She shivered at the words, pressing closer to him, and he wrapped his arms around her.

Perhaps there was a chance for them after all.

Isabel sat at her dressing table, wrapped in a linen towel, preparing for her wedding night, which was an odd sort of thing considering that she and her husband had spent much of the day outdoors, naked, having their wedding afternoon.

Of course, no one inside the house could know that, and so when Lara had forced her into a hot bath, she had said nothing—not unhappy to have some time alone with her thoughts before she had to face her husband again.

Her husband.

Who loved her.

Or who said he loved her, at least.

Oh, how tempting those words were. She understood how weak her sex could be, now, how—with mere syllables—a woman could be laid low with excitement and breathless anticipation.

There was a sharp knock on the door, and Isabel's heart immediately jumped into her throat with the thought that it might be Nick there before she realized that the sound had come from the wrong door. Earlier in the day, he had been moved into the adjoining chamber, their rooms now connected by an interior door. This knock had come from the hallway.

"Yes?"

The door opened, and Gwen and Jane entered. Isabel sat up immediately. "Is everything all right?"

Jane smiled. "It seems you are wound rather tight this evening, Isabel. Is there something on your mind?"

Isabel scowled. "No. What would be?"

Gwen laughed, sitting on a low stool by the bed. "Oh, Isabel. It's finally happened!"

"What has?"

Jane perched on the far edge of the copper tub. "You've gone and found yourself a husband."

"It's not as though I went searching, Jane. The whole thing happened somewhat without my consent."

"But you're not unhappy about it, are you?" Gwen asked.

Isabel considered the question for a long while. "Not exactly. He seems like a good man."

"Despite the confusion yesterday?"

Isabel nodded. "Yes. He's made it more than clear that he's willing to help to keep Minerva House safe." The women nodded, and she added dryly, "He doesn't have much of a choice if he's marrying me."

Gwen grinned. "Married. Past tense."

Isabel shook her head. "I am a wife."

"Indeed, you are," Jane said. "And may it bring you much happiness."

Isabel could not ignore the nervousness that came at the words. She did not know marriage as a happy thing. And there was no small part of her that believed that it was an impossibility.

But what a remarkable feeling it was to be loved.

And how terrifying. For it brought her one step closer to losing herself . . . if she were to reciprocate his feelings, who would she be then?

She took a deep, stabilizing breath, and Gwen and Jane shared a knowing look.

"What is it?"

"Well, we've been sent here . . . to speak to you . . ."

Dread flared. "Oh, no. About what?"

Gwen smiled. "About your wedding night."

Isabel's brows snapped together. "Whatever for?"

Jane shifted to face her more fully. Lowering her voice, she said, "We think you should be prepared. That is, you should know what to expect."

"And since your mother is no longer with us—" Gwen added.

Understanding dawned, and the purpose of their visit was so different than the myriad of other reasons she had been imagining that she began to laugh. Rather hysterically.

The two women looked at each other, each more dumbfounded than the other, and Isabel kept laughing, unable to stop herself. She set down the comb she had been using and attempted to breathe. "I'm sorry!" She raised a hand, waving it frantically. "I'm sorry! I just . . ." and she began to laugh again.

Perhaps she should tell them that she did not need any advice about the events of the evening . . . but their awkwardness was amusing, and there was a little part of Isabel that wanted to lead them along for a bit—if for nothing else than to distract from her earlier thoughts.

"I am sorry. Please, go on." She turned to face them. "What should I know?"

Gwen began. "Well, you have already mentioned that Lord Nicholas is a satisfactory kisser . . ."

"More than satisfactory."

A blush began to rise on the cook's cheeks. "Excellent. Then we have hopes that he will be an equally acceptable . . ." She paused, looking to Jane.

"Lover," Jane said bluntly.

Isabel turned back to the mirror and lifted her comb once more. "I certainly hope so."

"Yes, well," Gwen pressed on. "You might be surprised by the way that . . . things . . . happen."

Isabel grinned, trying to keep the laughter from her voice. "Things?"

There was a pause. Jane spoke first. "Well, as you know from your statues, Isabel, you have different . . . features . . . than does your husband."

"Yes . . ."

"We are not going to get into too much detail," Jane said, frustration edging into her voice.

Isabel willed herself not to smile. "But how will I know how to do it?"

"We feel confident that Lord Nicholas will know, Isabel."

It was too much. Isabel snickered. "Yes. I'm fairly confident of the same."

Both women's eyes grew wide. "You already know!" Gwen cried.

Isabel grinned, moving behind her dressing screen to don the night rail that she had selected for the evening—a deep rose silk that she hoped her new husband would enjoy. "I do. But thank you very much for your concern."

"You are a horrid, horrid woman," Jane said, laughter in her voice, "and he doesn't deserve you."

"Apparently he hasn't a choice, considering she's only been married for twelve hours and she's already had her wedding night," Gwen said, dryly. "So are we right?"

Isabel peeked out from behind the screen. "Right? About what?"

"Is he an acceptable lover?"

"Gwen!" Isabel blushed, slipping back behind the screen.

"Ah. It seems he is." Gwen teased.

When their laughter died down, Jane asked, serious, "Do you love him?"

Isabel paused at the question that had been playing over and over in her mind since that afternoon. Since before then, if she were truly honest. She caught a glimpse of herself in a long looking glass, noting her shape silhouetted beneath the silk negligee she had selected for him.

To make him happy.

To make him want her.

To make him love her more.

The truth was, she did love him.

And there was nothing more terrifying. She was terrified that, if she admitted it, she would somehow turn into her mother; that their marriage would somehow become that of her parents. How long had her mother pined for her father, how long had she waited at the window for a sign of his horses? How had she doted upon him when he was there . . . and told fairy tales about him when he was gone?

And hated her children for his desertion?

How could Isabel possibly risk repeating that terrifyingly desolate, despairing life?

No. Love had brought nothing but pain to this house, to her life.

She would not let love destroy her the way it had done her mother.

She would not live half a life.

And so, even as she admitted the truth of her feelings for Nick, she refused to speak them aloud.

"Isabel," Jane called from the room beyond, shaking her from her thoughts.

She took a deep breath and spoke to her image, ignoring the sadness in her face, the pain that tore through her at the lie. "I do not love him," she announced, willing her voice to stay light, to convince her friends that she was still as strong as she ever had been. *To convince herself of it.* "I married him for duty—for James and Minerva House and Townsend Park. I see no need to bring love into the scenario."

She pasted a bright smile on her face—one she did not feel—and came out from behind the dressing screen, only to find Gwen and Jane standing, eyes fixed on a different part of the room.

She followed their gaze, and her heart sank.

For there, in the adjoining doorway, stood her husband.

He had heard everything.

Her smile faltered as he bowed stiffly. "My apologies. I did not know that you had company."

"I—" She stopped. *What could she say?*

"We were just leaving, my lord," Jane said, and she and Gwen were gone faster than Isabel had ever seen anyone exit a room.

She was alone with the man who loved her.

And she had cheapened that love with her stupid words.

He turned away, retreating into the other room. She followed without thinking, crossing the threshold as he poured himself two fingers of brandy from a decanter that had been set out for him. He stared into the glass for a long moment before he drank deep, then sat in a large, low chair and turned his attention to her. His gaze was cool and devoid of emotion.

She stepped toward him, desperate to fix what she had broken. "Nick."

"You are wearing red."

She stopped, the words strange to her ears. "I—" She looked down at herself. "I thought you would like it."

There was silence as he stared at her, eyes shuttered from emotion. "I do."

She did not like this Nick. His stillness was unsettling. "I—"

I lied. I love you.

Fear stifled the words. She willed him to hear them anyway.

"Come here."

The command was imperious and dark—like nothing that she had ever heard from him—and there was a part of her that wanted to run from it. To close and lock the door between their chambers and hide from him until he had returned to normal.

At the same time, she wanted to submit to it.

He drank again, his blue eyes not straying from her.

Daring her to refuse.

Daring her to accept.

She wanted him.

The thought propelled her forward. Once by his side, she was transfixed by his gaze, by the cool gleam there. She wanted to shake him, to bring back the vibrancy that had been there all afternoon. The love that had been there.

He did not move for long moments, and she wondered if he might reject her, ultimately, sending her away and refusing to touch her again. The silence stretched into an eternity, devastating. And just as she was about to turn and leave on her own, he moved.

He leaned forward, reaching for her and pulling her to

him until she stood between his thighs. He put his face to the soft roundness of her belly, breathing deep, pressing his open mouth to the silk there. His hands stroked up along the outside of her thighs, around to cup her bottom, pulling her to him as he moved his mouth to the place where the core of her was covered by the fabric.

The feel of his hot breath was too much; she put her hands to his head, threading her fingers into the thick sable strands, and curved her body toward him, cradling him with her whole being.

He lifted his head then, running his hands up to cup her breasts, finding the darkened tips beneath the fabric, teasing them with his thumbs and fingers until they were hard and aching for him. And only then, when her breath was coming in harsh, shaking pants, did he give her what she wanted—taking one hard nipple between his lips and suckling through the fabric, alternately worrying with his teeth and licking with his tongue until the fabric was wet and plastered to her breast. He repeated the process with the other breast until she cried her pleasure.

The sound spurred him on. He stood, bringing the hem of her gown with him, lifting it up over her head, baring her to his pale blue gaze. He lifted her, and she wrapped herself around him as he carried her back to her bedroom. He dropped her onto her bed, following her down, covering her with his warm body. She clawed at his shirt, eager to have it gone, to have him against her, and he let her pull it from him as he slid down her body, placing hot, moist kisses along the center line of her, at the indentation at the base of her neck, between her breasts, down her torso and across her soft stomach.

He eased her legs apart and she did not protest, instead moving to accommodate his wide shoulders as he pressed her against the bed and spread the downy folds that protected the heart of her. When he set his lips to her, he gave no quarter, working his tongue and teeth in a rhythm that pulled her off the bed with the pleasure of it, and she was crying out within seconds. His tongue was wicked against her, fast and furious, unwilling to accept anything but all she could give.

She shattered beneath him, screaming his name as he thrust one, then two fingers deep within her, reaching a spot that she had not known existed, that sent her over the edge once more.

He was above her then and, with a single thrust, inside her, taking her, leaving nothing, his movements deeper and more intense than anything she had felt before. He pushed her to the edge again almost instantly, and she was begging for release, begging for the climax that only he could provide. He held her there for an eternity, until she was crying his name, pleading with him for resolution.

He took her mouth in a scorching kiss, deeper and more passionate than anything they had shared before, and he reached between them, setting his thumb to the place where everything seemed to begin and end. He thrust deep, spilling inside her, and she was lost, flooded with emotion, able to think only of him.

She whispered his name as she came apart in his arms.

After a long moment, he lifted himself from her. She reached for him as he moved to the side, wanting to share the aftermath of their earth-shattering event.

He was gone from the bed before she could touch him, lifting his shirt and pants from the floor and leaving the room.

She sat up, calling out to him as he closed the connecting door firmly, shutting her out.

Regret came quick and painful, and she realized that he had not spoken once during their lovemaking.

Twenty-one

Lesson Number Nine

Nurture your mystery.

Once you have piqued your lord's interest, consider spending time away from him to encourage his suit. One need only think of the annual foxhunts across our fair land to know the savage urge to hunt that even our most gentlemanly of gentlemen harbor deep within.

Be the fox, Dear Reader, and do not fear!

These skilled hunters will track you down!

Pearls and Pelisses
June 1823

Isabel barely slept, finally giving up on the idea and making her way to the kitchen. She was standing over the stove, watching the kettle, when Kate came in just after sunrise.

Isabel did not look up from the water, lost in thought, wondering what she could do to repair the damage that she had done to her marriage the night before.

What kind of a wife ruined a marriage on the first day?

Your kind.

She resisted the answer, watching the little bubbles form on the bottom of the pot. Perhaps she could convince him to take another ride today . . . perhaps they could try again.

Perhaps she could find the courage to tell him that she loved him.

"You know what they say about watched pots," the stable master said, opening a cupboard and pulling out a biscuit tin.

"Yes, well . . . I'm testing the theory."

Kate leaned against the table and watched her mistress for a long moment before saying, "One of the horses is gone."

That got Isabel's attention. "Gone?"

"As if it never was."

Her heart leapt into her throat. "Which one?"

"Your husband's."

"He's gone?"

"It seems that way."

She shook her head. "No. He was here. Last night."

"Perhaps he's just ridden into town for something." There was little confidence in Kate's tone.

Isabel rushed from the kitchen back upstairs, knocking on the door to his bedroom and barely waiting to enter.

She stopped just inside the door.

He was gone; his things vanished with him.

The bed was not even slept in.

He had left immediately after—

Isabel hugged herself, suddenly cold and unbearably tired.

She turned back to the door, where Kate stood. "Isabel. Is there something I can do? Is there something you need?"

Isabel shook her head, barely hearing the words.

He was gone. She had driven him away.

Just as her mother had driven her father away.

"I—I need . . ." She shook her head, a crushing sadness overwhelming her. "I need . . ."

I need him.

"I need to be alone," she whispered. "I've . . ."

I've ruined everything.

Kate did not speak, understanding even as Isabel did not. She stepped back into the hallway, leaving Isabel alone in the room.

Isabel closed the door, and climbed into the bed—the bed where her husband should have been sleeping. Where they should have been sleeping together.

But he was not here.

She was alone again, and worse for having had him there at all.

He had left her. Just as her father had done.

Just as she had feared he would.

She'd driven him away.

Turning on her side, Isabel pulled her knees up to her chest, and let the tears come. She wept, deep racking sobs that mourned her marriage and what could have been, if only she had trusted herself to love him.

And when there were no more tears, she slept.

It was late when she woke, the sun streaming into the warm room in long golden rays. For a moment, she did not know where she was, and she sat up trying to place the room. When she did, the memories came flooding back.

She stood, sadness and regret making the simple movement more difficult than she would have imagined.

She moved to the door and opened it to find a worried Lara standing outside. Her cousin turned at the sound, and Isabel said, "How long have you been here?"

Lara waved one hand in the air. "It does not matter. Oh, Isabel." She took Isabel in her arms, hugging her fiercely before pulling back to ask, "What happened?"

Isabel shook her head. "I don't know. One moment we were happy and I believed we might be a success, and the next . . ." *I ruined it.* " . . . the next, I was making a mess of it. And he was gone."

"I am sure you did not make a mess of it," Lara said, with a certainty born of love and friendship.

"But I did." Isabel looked into her cousin's eyes, recognizing the worry there. "I love him, Lara."

Lara gave a little supportive laugh and said, "But that is not a mess! That is wonderful!"

Tears sprang to Isabel's eyes. "No. It isn't. Because I told him I didn't love him. That I couldn't love him."

Confusion flashed on the other woman's face. "But why?"

Isabel was flooded with sadness. "I do not know."

Lara came forward, wrapping her arms around her. "Oh, Isabel."

Isabel clung to her, tears coming fast. "I didn't tell him because I was scared. I thought that if I loved him, I would turn into my mother. I thought I would open myself to heartache, and now . . . now it is too late. I hurt him. I hurt him and he left."

"Perhaps he will come back," Lara said, hopeful.

"Perhaps." But even as she said the words, she knew it would not happen.

How many times had he worked to regain her trust, to prove his worth? And how many times had Isabel rejected him? And then that last time—when the fire had gone from his eyes, leaving only a cool, calm aristocrat—that was when she had lost him.

Isabel cried for a long while, drawing comfort from her cousin.

Finally, the tears stopped, and she took a deep, calming breath just in time to face James as he came tearing up the stairs. "Isabel!" He stopped short, registering her tearstained face. "What has happened? Why are you crying?"

James slowly came closer, his face serious. Isabel noticed that he was wearing a waistcoat. And a perfectly tied cravat. He was a little man. The evidence of Nick's influence had tears near once more. She closed her eyes against them, refusing to reveal her sadness to her brother.

Isabel forced a smile. "It is nothing, James. What is it?"

James stared at her for a long while, his brow furrowed in concern. Finally, he said, "Jane sent me to fetch you. I think you will feel better when you see why."

I doubt it.

"What is it?"

He shook his head. "She told me I wasn't to tell you. You must see for yourself."

Isabel sighed. The Park still needed its mistress. Lovelorn or not. "Very well, lead the way."

As the trio descended the stairs to the second floor, Isabel became aware of the noise. It was a loud, raucous collection of chatter unlike anything she'd ever heard. They hurried to the top of the stairway leading to the grand foyer, and she paused there, frozen in surprise at the picture below.

The entryway to the Park was filled with men. Men with pails and crates and satchels, each more surprising than the next, each attempting to gain the attention of Jane, who, standing several steps up the staircase, was doing her very best to play the part of unflappable butler. Of course, it seemed that few butlers in the world had ever had to deal with half of the residents of Dunscroft in their main hall.

Descending, she came to Jane's side as the butler called out, "Good sirs, if we could all have a moment of quiet while we sort things out, perhaps it would make all our lives slightly easier?" She lowered her voice to a mutter. "Certainly it would help me to think."

Isabel asked, "What on earth?"

Jane turned to her. "It's about time you arrived."

"Who are they?"

"From what I can tell," Jane said, pointing out the men in question as she spoke, "that boy has three crates of candles and more on order; those two have been sent to repair the western fence; that one is here to tune the pianoforte—did you even know that the things required tuning?—the man in the topcoat is waiting to meet with you so you may select a coach to go with your new carriage horses, which are already in the stables—Kate is beside herself in elation; that one is delivering several casks of wine for the cellars; the two women cowering in the corner, poor dears, are here to outfit all of us in new clothes; that man with the spectacles is a banker, requesting an audience with 'the lady of the manor'; the circle of giants standing with Rock—Lord knows where they came from—are here to patrol the edges of the property; and—" She peered around the fencers. "Oh, yes. There are also a half-dozen roofers requesting access to the attic."

Shocked, Isabel blinked at the congregation, still not entirely understanding. "What are they all doing here?"

"Music man!" Jane called, drawing the attention of a quiet, wizened craftsman nearby. "The ballroom is through that door there." She turned back to Isabel. "They say Lord Nicholas sent them."

It took several seconds for the meaning of Jane's words to sink in.

"All of them?"

"It is my experience that merchants don't just show up with free wares, Isabel. Yes. All of them."

Mute, Isabel looked out over the collection of people in her foyer, overwhelmed. When she finally looked back to Jane and Lara, she could say only one thing. "He sent me roofers."

Jane was busy instructing the man with the wine to the kitchens. Turning back, she said, "It appears you've married a madman."

She laughed then. "He sent me roofers."

It was the loveliest thing that anyone had ever given her.

Lara smiled broadly. "He certainly knows the way to your heart, Isabel."

The tears threatened once more.

If only she had been brave enough to let him in.

Isabel took a deep breath, willing herself to remain strong. Smoothing her hands down her wrinkled skirts, she said, "What do I do?"

"I think you should set those roofers to work."

Just before dusk, Isabel stood on the front steps of the manor house, watching as the last of the workmen made his way down the long drive from Townsend Park. They had worked for several hours on the roof, promising to return the next day with the materials needed to repair the more significant damage.

As the tradesmen faded into the night, she sat on the wide stone steps, wrapping her arms around herself to ward off the cool evening breeze as she looked up at the darkening sky, wishing that everything were different.

Wishing that she were more courageous.

She had been so terrified of allowing herself to love him, so afraid that her relationship with Nick would mirror the relationship of her parents. She had been scared that if she were to love him, she would place herself at risk of becoming her mother—of pining away here in Yorkshire waiting, desperately, for him to return.

And so she had not allowed herself to admit to loving him. Yet here she was, pining away in Yorkshire waiting, desperately, for him to return.

It seemed that she had turned into her mother anyway.

But he was not her father.

He had, in one day, done more for Townsend Park than her father had ever done for them. And it was not just the roof, or the fence, or the carriage. It was the way he so clearly cared about the Park. About Minerva House. He'd known the land and the girls for less than a week, but was committed to their well-being. To their future.

Because he was committed to Isabel's happiness.

She understood that now.

She sighed into the night.

If only she weren't too late.

"It has been a rather remarkable day, hasn't it?"

Rock's voice came from the darkness, and she turned toward him as he came around the base of the stairs, making his way to her. "That is one way of putting it," she said with a forced smile.

"Your security team is in place. They seem a good group of men. I shall introduce you to them tomorrow. We've created a makeshift headquarters in the old woodcutter's cottage. It will need some basic repairs, but I will speak to Nick about that when next I see him."

Her chest tightened at Rock's certainty that he would see Nick again. She wished that she could be so sure of the same. "This all happened so quickly."

Rock did not speak for a long while, looking out to the dark grounds. Then, finally: "He began the process when the rain stopped. When I went into town to fetch our belongings, he bid me speak to the constable about honorable men who might be interested in work like this."

Isabel pressed her lips into a thin line. He'd begun the process before Georgiana was kidnapped. Before they'd been forced to marry. Before everything had changed.

They sat in silence for a long while, lost in their own thoughts. There were a dozen questions she wanted to ask Rock, her only link to the man she loved—to the man she had driven away—but she was embarrassed and uncertain, and the emotions overwhelmed her.

Ultimately, she asked what seemed like a safe question. "Why did you not leave with him?"

He paused, considering his words. "Because, unlike Nick, I know that leaving the thing I want most in the world is not the way to win it."

"Lara."

He did not respond for a long while, so long, in fact, that Isabel began to think that he would not acknowledge the name. When he finally turned to her, his dark eyes were black in the evening light. "Yes."

She nodded. "I am happy for you both that you have found"—she paused, the lump in her throat making it difficult to finish the sentence—"each other."

Rock breathed deep. When he spoke, his words were fast and clipped, as though he wished not to be saying them at all. "I know that she is a gentleman's daughter. That she deserves someone infinitely better than me—a Turk—who will never be fully accepted in her world. I am not a gentleman. Not a Christian. But I care deeply for her. And I will do everything I can to make her happy." He stopped. "I am very rich."

Isabel smiled. "I do not know why you think that any of us would care about your being Turkish, Rock. Nor do I know why you would think we require you to be highborn. Have you learned nothing about this motley crew in the week you have been with us?"

He matched her smile with a very dear one of his own. "I was simply pointing out my faults."

"Goodness, let us not start doing that, else we shall be here all night as I list my own."

"Never," he said graciously, pausing for a long while to choose his next words. "I should like to marry her. And, since you are her closest family, I suppose I am asking you . . ."

She met his gaze, tears filling her eyes. "Of course you have my blessing. If she will have you, then you are happily welcome at Townsend Park." Rock released a long sigh of relief, and Isabel laughed through her tears. "Did you really think that I would refuse you?"

He shook his head. "I did not know. It is one thing to accept me as a guest in your home. It is another entirely to accept me as your . . ."

"Family," Isabel said, placing one hand on his arm. "Cousin."

He dipped his head. "Thank you."

"Yes, well, it did not hurt that you are rich."

He barked in laughter. "Nick was right. Yours is a sharp tongue."

She grew serious at the mention of Nick. "Too sharp a tongue, I think." She sighed, turning to this bear of a man. "I ruined it. When I saw him last . . . he was so different. Cold. Unfeeling."

"He needs time, Isabel."

"I love him," she confessed, and there was something freeing about admitting her feelings to this man, her husband's friend.

"Did you tell him that?"

She closed her eyes. "No."

"Why not?"

"Because I was afraid."

"Afraid of what?"

She gave a little pathetic laugh. "Afraid of him leaving me here. Alone. In love."

He did not laugh. He did not reference the obvious irony from which she was suffering. He simply said, "I think it is time that you hear about Turkey."

Isabel looked to Rock. "What about Turkey?"

"I assume he told you that we were in Turkey together."

"Yes. He said that you rescued him from a prison there."

"Did he tell you how he landed in the prison to begin with?"

"No."

"There was a woman. Nick thought he was in love with her."

A painful image flashed, Nick in the arms of an exotic veiled female who knew all the ways to his heart.

He leaned back against the stone banister, eyes glazed over with the memory. "We had been camped just outside of Ankara for several weeks. The Crown was nervous about rumors of an army being raised in the Empire, and they asked Nick to track an informant who had disappeared without a trace." Rock's voice turned admiring. "Nick was a legend across the East. They called him the *bulan*—the hunter. It was said he could find anyone."

Isabel nodded. Finding Minerva House must have been a parlor game for him.

"Alana appeared outside his tent one night, bruised and bloodied from a beating she received at the hands of her husband, weeping for help. He took her in, fed her, tended her wounds, but she left him before morning, terrified that her husband would find her and beat her more."

Isabel winced at the words, immediately understanding

that Nick would not have been able to resist such a wounded dove.

"She was back the next night, lip split. And the night after that with some other wound. And then she disappeared. And he grew frantic, worrying over her. He had tracked her to a house inside the city, and he became obsessed with finding her—with assuring himself of her safety. After days of waiting for her, he was finally rewarded with her appearance. She was headed for market with several other ladies from the house. He found a way to speak to her there and she begged him to leave her alone. Assured him that she was fine."

She wrapped her arms more tightly around herself at the words. No wonder he hated it when she claimed that she was fine without him.

Rock continued, "That night, she came to him again. Unharmed."

He did not elaborate, but Isabel was no fool. She felt sick at the idea of him with the woman. "Was she very beautiful?" The question was out before she could take it back.

"Yes. Very."

Isabel hated her.

"Her beauty was overshadowed by her being evil incarnate." Rock pressed on. "He begged her to stay with him that night. Assured her that he would keep her safe. Promised her safe travels back to England. She agreed, but refused to leave immediately—gave him some excuse about possessions or some such. He believed her, and they arranged a meeting place and time when he would collect her. And they would run away."

Dread settled in Isabel's chest. She knew what was coming, but could not stop herself from listening.

"It was a trap, of course. The Empire knew that the *bulan* was there, that he was searching for the informant. And they'd somehow discovered that it was Nick for whom they were looking. I was nearby when they took him. I watched the whole thing." He stopped, lost in the past. "This is the part that I remember the most—it took six enormous Turks, bigger than me, to hold him. When he was subdued, Alana approached, removed her veil, and spat in his face."

Isabel recoiled at the image of the betrayal.

"He told me that he deserved the scar."

Rock nodded once. "He thinks he did. As punishment for falling victim to her womanly charms. For believing that she loved him."

They were silent for long moments as the truth of Nick's past settled between them. Isabel flinched at the pain he must have felt, having been laid low by a woman he loved.

No wonder he had left.

She had done the same thing.

Rock continued, unaware of the turmoil she was experiencing. "He swore off women then. I've never known him to tie himself to one since. Not until we came here. Not until you."

The words were a physical blow. He had opened himself to her, trusting himself to love again. Trusting her to accept that love. And she had rejected it. Rejected him.

She was going to be sick.

He leaned forward, recognizing her turmoil. "Isabel. He loves you."

The words made it worse. "I did the same thing she did."

His protest was immediate and unyielding. "No. You did not."

"He loves me. And I rejected him."

"Isabel. She *betrayed* him. She sent him to prison. She had him tortured. He would have died had I not found him." He paused, using it to emphasize his words. "You are the very opposite of what she was."

She shook her head. "He does not know that."

"Yes, Isabel. He does. He just needs time."

"How much time?"

"I don't know. He will not be able to stay away, though. That I can guarantee."

They were quiet for long minutes, the sound of crickets in the background. Isabel thought about Rock's story and her own time with Nick.

For her entire life, she had been afraid to take what she wanted for fear of failure. She was afraid to leave Townsend Park and face the gossip that her father caused; she was afraid to send James to school for fear that he might turn into her father.

And she had been afraid to love Nick, for fear of losing herself.

Now, however—without him—she was lost anyway.

But she had a chance to make it right. To make it better.

To have the life of which she'd begun to dream.

All she had to do was reach out and take it.

Take him.

She stood, looking down at Rock. "I want to go after him."

Rock's brows shot up. "Now?"

"Now. Where is he?"

"Halfway to London, I would imagine."

London.

She nodded. "Then London it is."

He stood. "I shall take you."

She shook her head. "No. I must do this alone."

He narrowed his gaze on her. "Isabel. Nick will have my head if I let you travel to London on your own."

"It will be fine. I shall go by mail coach."

Rock laughed at the ridiculous prospect. "He shall kill me without a second thought if I allow you to do that."

"Why? Plenty of girls come here by mail."

"Yes. Well, you are Lady Nicholas St. John now, sister-in-law to the Marquess of Ralston. *You* do not travel by mail."

The conversation was taking up valuable time. She acquiesced to speed the process. "Fine. How do you suggest I go?"

"*We* shall rent a coach and six tomorrow morning."

"We shan't be there for days!"

He sighed. "If we stop only to change horses, we shall be

there in two and a half days. Mail coach will take four at the least."

Isabel's face lit. "Then your escort would be much appreciated, good sir."

Rock looked up to the sky. "He's going to flay me for this."

She smiled. "Not if I succeed in winning him back. In that case, he shall be eternally grateful." She turned and headed up the stairs, eager to prepare for the journey. Several steps from the top, she turned back. "Wait. Where do we go once we are in London?"

Rock did not hesitate. "We go to Ralston House. You will need the assistance of the marchioness."

Twenty-two

"I should kill you for forcing me to do this."

"Probably. But you won't. It's your own fault for returning to London. If I were you, I would have stayed away for the rest of summer."

"How would I have known that Callie was hosting a summer ball?" Nick took a long drink from the tumbler of scotch he held, stopping to scowl at his brother. The twins sat in Ralston's study as the orchestra in the gardens beyond began tuning their instruments. In less than an hour, half of London's elite—the half that had remained in town for the month of July—would be in the gardens, as well. Nick fidgeted in his formal attire. "Who has even heard of a summer ball?"

"Callie thought it would be a good way of keeping Juliana in the public eye," Ralston answered, refusing to rise to his brother's bait. "I might remind you that our sister suffers from something of an unfortunate reputation."

Nick growled into his scotch. "For no reason other than because our mother was a—"

"Yes. Well, society seems not to care much for the hows and whys." Ralston leaned forward to add more of the amber liquid to Nick's glass. "Callie is happy that you are here, Nick. Juliana shall be, as well. Try to enjoy yourself tonight."

Enjoy himself.

As though that were possible.

It had been five days since he had left Isabel, and he hadn't enjoyed a moment of the time. He highly doubted that spending the night in a darkened garden with simpering London misses and their clamoring mothers would change that.

Indeed, he was fairly certain that spending the night in a darkened garden would make him think of Isabel. And he was entirely certain that spending the night dancing with women who were not Isabel would render him quite mad.

"There is something you should know."

Nick's eyes narrowed to slits. "What is that?"

"You are still considered to be a very valuable catch. I assume many of the women here tonight will be here for you."

"I am married."

"That information has not been made public, as you know. Indeed, one would have thought you would have told your brother of the change in your status sometime before you arrived back in London, ready to chew nails."

Nick told his brother precisely what he could do with that thought.

Ralston leaned back in his chair. "I will say that anyone who has ever considered you the good-natured brother will be in for a surprise this evening."

Nick stood then, irrational anger flaring. "Then perhaps I shall leave and save you all the trouble of having to suffer my company."

"Sit down, you ridiculous ass."

Nick towered over his brother. "Call me that one more time."

Ralston made a show of calmly swirling the scotch in his glass. "I am not going to fight you in my study, in my formalwear. Callie would have my head."

Ralston's unmoved response took the wind from Nick.

He sat again, leaning forward and putting his head in his hands, scrubbing his face as though he could erase his frustration. When he looked up, Ralston was watching him with complete understanding. "She has done a number on you, brother."

It was the first time that Ralston had referenced Isabel outside of the short, clipped conversation during which Nick had announced his marriage, and Nick knew that he could ignore the words and his twin would allow him the space he needed.

But he did not want to ignore them.

He wanted to talk about her . . . as though the words could bring her closer.

As though they could make her love him.

He ignored the pain that flared at the words. "She is . . . incredible."

Ralston did not reply. He simply listened.

Nick began to talk, more to himself than to his brother. "She has such strength in her, like no one I've ever known. When she believes in something, or when she fights for what is hers—she's a queen. She is nothing like the women we know. If something needs doing, she does it." He looked up at him. "The first time I kissed her, she was wearing breeches."

One side of Ralston's mouth kicked up in a smile. "There is something about them in breeches."

"But there's a softness to her, as well. A deep-rooted uncertainty that makes me want to protect her with everything I have." Nick scrubbed his jaw with one hand as he thought of her. "And she's so beautiful. With these brown eyes . . . eyes you could just lose yourself in . . ." He trailed off, thinking about her. Missing her.

"You love her."

Nick met his twin's knowing gaze. "More than I ever thought possible."

Ralston leaned back in his chair. "So why are you here, drinking scotch in my study?"

"Because she doesn't love me."

"Nonsense." The word came fast and frank.

Nick shook his head. "I appreciate your affront, Gabriel, but I assure you. Isabel does not love me."

"Of course she loves you," he said imperiously, as though he could make it so simply by being the Marquess of Ralston.

"She doesn't."

"They always love us."

Nick gave a little huff of laughter at the pronouncement. "Yes, well, perhaps they always love *you*. However, this one does *not* love me."

"Well, then you must make her love you."

Nick shook his head again. "No. I am through with trying to make women love me. I've spent my entire life chasing after women who were decidedly *not* in love with me. I have learned my lesson."

Ralston leveled him with a frank look. "This is not chasing after some woman. This is your *wife*. Whom you do, in fact, love."

God, he did love her.

He'd never felt anything like the pain that had exploded through him at her announcement that she had married him for duty and not for love, but that pain did not seem to diminish his feelings for her.

He raked his fingers through his hair. "She doesn't need me."

Ralston smirked. "You are laboring under the mistaken impression that it is their job to need us. In my experience, it is almost always the other way around." He checked his watch. "A wiser man than I once told me that if he'd been a royal ass and lost the only woman he'd ever really wanted, he'd get her to the nearest vicar and then get her with child."

Nick winced at the words, and the memory they brought with them. "I've already married her."

"Then you are halfway there."

A vision flashed of Isabel at her stone keep in the sunshine, surrounded by children. *His children.*

Raw desire flared and Nick scowled. "I hate it when you are right."

Ralston grinned. "As I am rarely wrong, I imagine it is quite a problem for you."

Nick considered his options. They were married, for God's sake. He could not stay away from her forever. Indeed, he did not want to stay away from her. He wanted to get on his horse and rush back to Yorkshire and grab her by the shoulders and shake her. And then he wanted to kidnap her to the old stone keep and make love to her until she took him back. And then he wanted to spend the rest of his life making her happy.

If she could not love him now, perhaps, someday, she would learn to.

But she would never love him if he stayed in London.

He needed her.

He looked up, determined. "I am going back to Yorkshire."

Ralston slapped one hand to his thigh. "Excellent!" he announced, standing. "But first, you must attend this damned ball, or my wife will never forgive me."

Nick stood, as well, feeling invigorated by his decision.

He would go to the ball. And then he would go to his wife.

"Nick!"

Nick turned from the refreshment table, where he was pouring himself a lemonade and wishing it were a scotch, to find his sister-in-law bearing down on him.

He made an elaborate bow. "Lady Ralston," he intoned, "What a crush! What a success! You are certainly the greatest hostess of the *ton.*"

Callie laughed and lowered her voice. "Do not let Lady Jersey hear you. She'll *never* invite us to Almack's then."

He raised a brow. "And that would be a terrible pity."

She smiled broadly. "I am happy to see you. Ralston told me you were in town, but little else." Her smile disappeared. "How do you fare?"

Nick considered Callie's serious tone for a moment before saying, "It appears my brother told you plenty." At Callie's telling blush, he smiled. "I am much better now than I was a few hours ago."

Callie's brows rose. "It is not the ball that turned you round?"

Nick laughed at the preposterousness of the statement. "No, my lady."

She joined him in laughter as his sister approached, a happy smile on her face. As he leaned down to place a kiss on the back of her hand, Juliana said, "I cannot believe I did not know you had returned to town! What kind of a brother does not seek out his sister *immediatamente*?"

One side of Nick's mouth kicked up at Juliana's sprinkling of Italian. "A very bad one, indeed."

"You must come and visit us tomorrow, no?"

He shook his head. "I cannot, I am afraid. I must leave town again at first light."

Juliana's mouth made a perfect moue. "Whatever for? You have barely said hello!"

He hedged, not willing to share news of his marriage with his unsubtle sister in such a public setting. "I have some extraordinarily important business to which I must attend," he said, "but I assure you that you will be very, very happy with the results once my trip is complete."

"Well. I hope it involves a lavish present," Juliana teased, her attention moving to a spot over Nick's shoulder. "Callie, who is that?"

"Who?" Callie stood on her toes, following Juliana's line of vision.

"Shh!" Juliana waved a hand. "I want to hear her announced."

Nick rolled his eyes and reached for a quiche, barely registering that the two women were grinning like idiots.

"Lady Nicholas St. John."

A hush came over the crowd and Nick froze. Surely he

had misheard. He turned slowly toward the stairway leading down into the gardens, where guests were entering the ball.

There, resplendent in the most stunning scarlet gown he had ever seen, stood Isabel.

What was she doing here?

He could not take his eyes from her; there was a small part of him that thought that perhaps he had conjured her up. That she was not actually here. In London. In his brother's garden.

Juliana poked him in the side with one long, bony finger. "Nick. Do not be *un idiota*. Can you not see she is terrified? You must go to her."

The words unstuck him, and he was moving toward his wife, first walking, only to find that that was taking entirely too long. And so he began to run. Which was almost certain to cause a scandal, but he did not really care. He would apologize to Callie later.

Because all he wanted to do was reach Isabel.

And touch her.

And confirm that he was not, in fact, mad. That she was really there. That she had really come for him.

There was a benefit to running through a ball; a shocked crowd tended to move out of one's way, and he was at the foot of the stairway in seconds, bounding up the stairs to meet her. She watched him the whole way, her brown eyes wide with nervousness and surprise and excitement and something that he dared not name.

Once there, mere inches from her, he stopped, drinking his fill of her.

He watched as she took a deep breath, her breasts rising beautifully beneath the edge of the flowing silk gown she wore. "My lord." She dropped into a deep curtsy and whispered, "I have missed you."

When she finally met his gaze, he saw the truth of her words. "I have missed you, as well." He reached for her, but before he could touch her, a firm, pointed throat clearing stayed his movement. "Nicholas," Gabriel said from nearby, his words quiet but clear, "perhaps you should escort your wife inside?"

Isabel blushed and looked down, away from the crowd staring up at them with unabashed curiosity. He clenched his fists to keep from touching her and said, "Yes, of course. My lady?"

They entered the house, unspeaking, moving past a line of curious guests waiting to be announced and who would certainly be disappointed that they had missed what was surely the most exciting portion of the evening.

Pulling her into the first room they reached, he closed the door behind them and threw the lock to ensure their privacy. They were in the library, a single candelabrum burning from the fireplace mantel.

He guided her into the pool of light and kissed her, hard and desperate for the taste of her—the feel of her—which he had gone too long without. He ate at her mouth, stealing her breath. She met him stroke for stroke, caress for caress, and when she sighed her pleasure he groaned his. After long, intense moments, his lips gentled, and he softened the kiss, stroking her bottom lip with his tongue, ending the moment in an infinitely softer way than it had begun.

He put his forehead to hers and said, "Hello."

She smiled, shy. "Hello."

"God, I missed you. I missed the feel of you. I missed the smell of you . . . all orange blossoms and Isabel. But more than that, I missed *you*."

She touched his lips, stemming the flow of words. "Nick," she whispered. And in the one word was an ocean of healing.

"You came to London."

"Yes."

"How long have you been here?"

"Three days."

Three days and no one had told him. "Gabriel will pay for keeping this from me."

"I begged him not to tell you. I wasn't ready. I wanted to be beautiful for you."

He shook his head. "You are always beautiful for me." She dipped her head, and he lifted her chin with one finger. "Always, Isabel. In mourning, in breeches, in silk . . . in nothing at all. You are always beautiful for me."

"There is something I must say." She paused, and he waited. Finally, she took a deep, steadying breath. "I love you."

He closed his eyes at the words, words he had so desperately wanted to hear. When he opened them, she was watching him, nervous. "You don't have to say that."

Her eyes widened. "Yes. I do."

He shook his head. "No, love. You do not."

She took a step back, her voice firm and unwavering. "Nicholas St. John. Hear me. I love you. I love you more than I ever thought it was possible to love someone. I loved you the day of our wedding. And the day before that. And the day before that. I said what I said because I was afraid that if I told you the truth, you would leave me someday, and I would be sad and alone and heartbroken because you were not with me."

Tears welled at the words, and she dashed them away as she continued. "But not telling you that I loved you did not make me love you any less. And you left anyway. And I *was* sad and alone and heartbroken. So I came here. Because I cannot survive without you knowing that I love you. Because I never want you to think that you are less than what you are. Which is a man who deserves someone far, far better than me."

She stopped, breathing heavily, overwhelmed by emotion. She met his gaze, and there, in the depths of his blue eyes, she saw the Nick she thought she'd lost in her bedchamber with her silly words. She did not know what to say to win him back. And so she said the words that were in her heart. "I came to London to tell you that I love you. Please. You must believe me."

He stepped toward her, one finger lifting her chin, tilting her face up to his, and said what was in his heart. "I will never leave you again, Isabel. I am so very sorry that I did. I was coming back. I swear it." The kiss he settled on her lips was soft and stunning, and it echoed the promise in his words.

Tears came again when he lifted his head. "You left before I could fix it."

He pulled her into his arms. "I know. I am sorry."

She spoke, her words muffled against his chest. "I wanted to fix it, Nick."

"I know."

"I thought you might have decided that you do not love me anymore."

He pulled back to meet her worried eyes. "No, Isabel. By God, I love you more now than ever before."

She gave him a watery smile. "Good. I considered sending Voluptas as a peace offering, but she is too heavy."

He smiled. "I much prefer to receive the real thing." He kissed her again, stroking deep until they were both breathing heavily. When they stopped, Isabel wrapped her arms around his neck and he passed a wicked look over her. "This gown is incredible."

"Do you like it?" She stretched against him, catlike, and he groaned.

"Where did it come from?" He spoke the words at the place where her neck and shoulder met.

"Callie had her dressmaker send it over. I had only one request."

He was kissing across the tops of her breasts. "Mmm?"

She sighed as his thumbs found her nipples beneath the fabric. "That it be red."

He lifted his head, passion in his gaze. "It is gorgeous. I should like to remove it from your person so that I can better admire it."

She giggled at his teasing. "No, Nick. We must go back

to the ball. We've already caused an incredible scene." She gasped, pulling away. "Do you think Callie will ever forgive us? We've ruined her ball!"

Nick laughed at her concern. "Isabel, if I know one thing about my sister-in-law, it is that she will be eternally grateful to us for causing such a scene at her ball. It will set the standard for all future parties at Ralston House, Lord save my brother." He brushed a loose curl back from her cheek. "But if you want to return to the ball, we shall return to the ball."

She gave him a little smile. "I confess, I would like to return to the ball, my love. For two reasons, not the least of which is that I should like to dance with my husband."

"Now that is a very good idea." His eyes darkened. "I should like very much for everyone to see me dance with my wife."

With one final, clandestine kiss, they made their way back through the corridors and out onto the terrace, where scores of eyes immediately found them.

Isabel squeezed Nick's hand. "They're all watching."

He lifted her hand, kissing her knuckles through the silk of her glove before leaning over to whisper, "They are all attempting to calculate the length of time we were indoors."

She turned confused eyes on him. "Whatever for?"

He raised his eyebrows.

She gasped, covering her laughter with one hand. "No!"

He laughed, and she caught her breath at how handsome he was.

He was hers.

Just as she was his.

They descended the stairs to the back garden, hands entwined when someone called out to them. "St. John!"

Nick stopped, pulling Isabel close as a man approached. He was tall and lean and very handsome, his coat perfectly cut and his boots perfectly shined. He carried a silver-tipped walking stick and moved with a casual affect almost certainly designed to keep those around him from considering him more than a well-heeled dandy.

He stopped in front of them and Nick squeezed Isabel's hand. "Densmore."

Isabel's eyes widened. *This* was Densmore? This handsome, exceptionally well-tailored man with a silly smile was the Densmore about whom they had been so worried?

Densmore gave a short bow, turning to Isabel. "I say, Lady Isabel—"

It hadn't taken long for her identity to ripple through the crowd. *Her sisters-in-law had worked quickly.*

"Nicholas." Isabel corrected him.

"I beg your pardon?"

"If you are addressing me, my lord, I believe the moniker you seek is Lady Nicholas." She could feel Nick's approval washing over her.

Densmore looked from husband to wife, a wide smile on his face. "I was sure they were bamming me. But you *are* married."

Ah, yes. Her father's friend, indeed.

Isabel smiled her most brilliant smile. "I assure you that I am not bamming you."

Nick shook his head in mock seriousness. "My wife does not bam, Densmore."

"Well, at least, not strangers," she added, noticing her husband's dimple flash.

How she adored that dimple. She must tell him so.

Densmore rocked back on his heels. "Well," he said. Then: "Well! This works out splendidly!"

Nick squeezed Isabel's hand again. "I certainly think so."

"No, St. John. I mean—you can handle the Wastrearl's things now! I never wanted the ruddy responsibility anyway." He lowered his voice to a conspiratorial whisper. "Can't stand the stuff."

"We could not tell," Isabel deadpanned, drawing a grin from her husband.

Densmore shook his head, not entirely listening. "Capital!" He clapped Nick on the shoulder. "Say I send my man around tomorrow to discuss the particulars? How does that sound? Rather fantastic, I'd say!" He paused. "Bad luck about your father, Lady Nicholas. Er. My condolences."

And without waiting for a response, Densmore was gone, leaving Nick and Isabel to watch in surprise as he disappeared into the crowd.

She turned to Nick, amazed at the way the mysterious guardian, whom she had so feared, had simply wandered off.

"It seems I have inherited the challenges of Townsend Park."

Isabel grinned at his mock disappointment. "How will you ever survive?"

"It is difficult to imagine." He lifted her hand, brushing his lips across her gloved knuckles.

"Nonsense. You adore us."

His gaze softened on her, and she caught her breath at the emotion there in the depths of his lovely blue eyes. "Indeed. I do."

He was so close. She could just reach up and kiss him . . .

No. That would not be at all appropriate.

How long before they could leave this silly ball?

Understanding flashed in Nick's eyes. He leaned closer. "Soon," he whispered, the word soft and wicked and filled with promise. "For now, would you like to dance, beauty?"

She could not keep the blush of pleasure from spreading across her cheeks. "Yes, please."

He swept her into the crowd of dancers, waltzing across the grounds. After long moments of swaying and swirling to the music, he noticed the secret smile on her face and asked, "What are you thinking?"

"I am thinking about the second reason that I wanted to return to the ball."

He raised one brow. "Which was?"

"To show all these ladies who read *Pearls and Pelisses* that this particular lord has been well and truly landed."

His bark of laughter was entirely too loud, the way he pulled her to him entirely too close, drawing the attention of the couples around them.

They would be the talk of the *ton* for months after tonight.

And it would only grow worse when they had all discovered that Isabel was the daughter of the Wastrearl . . . and that she was supposed to be in mourning.

But as she laughed and danced in the strong arms of this man who loved her . . . she simply could not bring herself to care. And when he leaned down and whispered quietly in her ear. . .

Well, there were worse things in the world than the scandal caused by love.

Epilogue

Lesson Number Ten

It is most important, Dear Reader, for you to learn this final lesson.

Once your lord has been well and truly landed, it will be your duty to ensure that the nests of his life are properly and perfectly feathered, for singlehood is not for men of earnestness and respectable purpose. Indeed, it is marriage and children and the pleasures that come with both that are evidence of a life well lived.

And our lords—these pillars of men carefully selected and showcased for your benefit in these pages—will require brides able to love, to honor, and to cherish in all the ways they deserve.

Pearls and Pelisses
June 1823

"It was a beautiful wedding."

"Indeed, it was." Nick placed a soft kiss at the spot where Isabel's neck and shoulder met as he undid the long string of buttons on her gown, sending the garment pooling at her feet as he wrapped his arms around her and pulled her against him, one hand drifting up her body to capture a breast in his hand. "Not as beautiful as you were, however."

She laughed at the words, leaning into him with a sigh, allowing him the freedom to explore her. "Of course it was. Lara was glowing. And Rock . . . I've never seen him so happy."

Nick paused, considering the words before he set his lips to her neck once more. "Mmmm . . ." He took her earlobe between his teeth, nibbling on it until she shivered in his arms, squirming away with a laugh. He caught her to him, kissing her long and full before he lifted his head, concern in his gaze. "Are you sorry that we did not have a proper wedding?"

It had been two months since Isabel had traveled to London to fetch Nick and they had attempted marriage for a second time. And it was bliss. They lived at Townsend Park, though Nick had proposed that they visit his country estate in the autumn—it was close to Eton and would give Isabel a chance to be nearer to James during his first semester at school.

Before they had left London, Nick had assumed legal responsibility for the Park—much to the relief of the Viscount Densmore—so Minerva House was well taken care of and as protected as it could be. The women of the house flourished with the knowledge that their safety was well in hand with Nick, Rock, and the team of watchmen that had become a welcome part of the household. Even Georgiana had a modicum of contentment in the months following her brother's devastating departure. The duke was keeping their secrets—for now, at least.

Uncertainty about their future no longer plagued Isabel; she knew without a doubt that, no matter what the future held, Nick was as committed to the success of Minerva House as she was.

Content, she wrapped her arms around his neck and kissed him thoroughly. "I do not regret our wedding in the slightest. As long as you promise me that we shall have a proper marriage."

"A proper marriage it is," he said, lifting her in his arms

and carrying her to their bed. Once there, he slid one hand up the inside of her leg, bringing her silk chemise along with it. "How would you rate it so far?"

She pretended to think on the question, and he nipped at her shoulder in punishment. She laughed until his hand stroked up her thigh, playing at the soft skin there until the sound faded into a sigh. His gaze tracked her body and the chemise that clung to her curves, noting the absence of her stays. "I, for one, think it's going very well," he said. "I'm particularly happy that you've finally decided to see things my way and forgo corsets."

She smiled a small, quiet smile. "Not entirely because of your view of stays, Nick. I am going to have to go without them for a while. Several months, at least."

He paused as understanding dawned. "You mean—"

She nodded.

His hand slid higher, settling on the barely round swell of her belly. "A child," he said, and the reverence in his voice was undeniable.

She set her hand there as well, threading her fingers with his.

"I was rather surprised myself," she said, her tone dry. "It took Jane, Kate, and Gwen to convince me that it was true."

He chuckled. "As usual, the women of Minerva House know all before I do."

She joined him in private laughter. "Are you surprised?"

"Not in the least."

He kissed her, ending the conversation, the caress deep and thorough, rendering them both breathless. She ran her hands up, over his chest and shoulders, tangling her fingers in his soft hair and sighing her pleasure into his mouth as his hand moved lower.

"Nick," she whispered, "I love you."

He smiled against her lips. "I know."

She laughed at the certainty in the arrogant words as he captured her mouth once more.

And showed her just how much he loved her in return.

It has been said that idleness is the parent of mischief, which is very true; but mischief itself is merely an attempt to escape from the dreary vacuum of idleness.

George Borrow

Late August 1816
Blackwood Hall, outside London

The ancient hall was bustling with excited guests waiting for the presentation of the new Duke of Exeter. It was to be the bachelor's grand debut in London Society since ascending to the title—which, of course, brought everyone with a daughter even close to marriageable age to seek an invitation to the glittering event.

After all, a young, fit, unmarried man was all too quickly becoming a rare commodity in these turbulent war-torn times, but a duke . . . and a handsome one at that (or so it was rumored—for no member of the *ton* had actually reported *seeing* the man), well, he was a rare prize indeed.

Even so, the novelty of the evening had already worn gossamer thin for Lady Siusan Sinclair. She was very likely the only miss in the hall who did not wish to be there at all. "I daresay, we've waited long enough, Priscilla. No man is worth waiting about for four long hours—especially in this crowd."

Her younger sister's eyes went wide at Siusan's sacrilegious words. "An unmarried duke is entirely worth the wait!"

Siusan rolled her eyes as she dabbed her moist neck with her handkerchief.

"And do not dare perspire," Priscilla warned, critically studying the cerulean silk dress Siusan wore. "I only lent you the gown upon your solemn oath that you would not ruin it. That includes perspiring." She snatched up Siusan's wrist. "Come now, make use of your fan. Mine is keeping me sufficiently cool. A true lady does not perspire. Remember that."

"Aye, Priscilla, I know, however if we do not leave at once—"

"I am certain you can manage to refrain from glowing for a few more minutes." Priscilla narrowed her eyes at Siusan, then rose to her toes to survey the ballroom. "The duke will appear at any moment, I have no doubt. I shouldn't need to remind you of our predicament? His Grace is unmarried and from the country, some dreary old place in Devonshire. I am sure he has never even heard of the Sinclairs, and that fact works in our favor. Our chances of snaring his ring are as good as any other noble miss's."

Siusan stood on the tips of her toes as well and glanced about before returning her heels to the floor, pulling Priscilla down along with her. She moved her mouth close to her younger sister's ear, for as the daughter of a duke herself, Siusan was nothing if not well trained. Like her brothers and sisters, she simply did not always choose to adhere to the rules of propriety in the *strictest* sense. "Keeping us all waiting for his glorious presence, bah. I daresay, the duke is clearly very rude. Perhaps you are right, Priscilla. He may fit in with the Seven Deadly Sins nicely."

"Hush. Do not refer to our family so vilely. That others do does not make it acceptable." Priscilla glanced around them to be sure Siusan's assertion was not overheard. Convinced that it was not, she growled into Siusan's ear. "And besides, *my* future husband is not rude."

"*Your* husband, dear? Did you not just claim that *our*

chance for winning his ring were just as favorable as anyone else's?"

"Aye, but I meant that *my* chances are equal. Not yours. Do you not recall that I voiced my claim on the duke the moment we stepped down from the carriage?"

"Good Lord, are you still six years old?" Her sister's reliance on an old game might have been diverting at another time, but not tonight. "The wretched duke still hasn't had the courtesy to grace those waiting for him with his esteemed noble presence. Besides which, Priscilla, you cannot claim the duke unless you see him *first.* That is the primary rule of the game."

Priscilla suddenly looked very determined. "Then I shall ensure that I do see him first." She started off through the crowd, leaving Siusan to scurrying to catch up. Within a minute, Priscilla had climbed a step and positioned herself on the far edge of the musicians' dais.

"Priscilla, you are being a great goose. Come down. Please, let us find our brothers and away."

Priscilla's gaze swept the ballroom as she replied. "I have an elevated view of the ballroom from here, and I will signal you posthaste the moment the duke appears." She turned her eyes back upon Siusan. "That way you will know he has arrived . . . and that *I* saw him first."

Her sister was being ridiculous. Siusan swiped her cutwork fan before her face, hoping to coax the humid air into cooling her face. On another night, the prospect of meeting a strikingly handsome unmarried duke might have been sufficient incentive for Siusan to cram herself into a rented coach with her brothers and sister and ride eight dusty miles outside of Town.

But not tonight . . . of all painful nights.

All she wanted tonight was to be alone with her memories. But solitude wasn't a luxury she could afford. She and her wayward siblings, widely known within Society as the Seven Deadly Sins, had only accepted tonight's invitation for one simple reason—they were willing to do anything to earn back their father's approval. Not because they were truly ashamed of their wild and wicked ways, for indeed they were not.

Their motivation did not run quite so clear and deep. It was because the money their father, the Duke of Sinclair, provided them was only just enough to meet their most basic of needs, and even those funds were quickly dwindling. Their father's man of affairs had made it startlingly clear that no further pouches of coin were to make their way into the Sinclair brothers' and sisters' hands until they changed their wild ways and earned the respect the Sinclair name deserved. They all knew that time was fast running out.

And, well, there was an unmarried duke to be had. What quicker way for her or her sister to restore respectability than to marry a duke?

She glanced up at Priscilla, who was earnestly sweeping the dance floor with her gaze.

Well, her sister could have him. Tonight, Siusan just didn't care—about dukes, money, even her father's respect. With a sniff, Siusan raised her chin and surreptitiously dabbed a lace handkerchief to an errant tear budding in her eye.

Tonight marked one year. A full heart-breaking year without Simon. And despite her brother Grant's good intentions, no amount of whisky en route to the gala could lessen the aching heaviness in her heart this night. The spirits only made her head spin.

Gads, she wanted nothing more than to leave this place and to be alone. The moist heat emanating from the sweating hordes of ladies in pale silk gowns and gentlemen in dark coats thickened the air, adding to her irritation.

It was hard enough for Siusan to breathe in her overtight corset, but the stays were a necessary evil to fit into Priscilla's cerulean gown. *Simon had always favored her in blue, and this gown in particular.*

The backs of her eyes began to sting anew. Lud, the crush of perspiring bodies was unbearable! What benefit would the beautiful silk gown be to either of the Sinclair sisters if it became sodden with perspiration and ruined?

Nay, she had to remove herself from the crowd, if she could just slip outside into the unseasonably cool air for just a few moments, maybe she would be able to rein in her grief and mask herself with the composure expected of a Sinclair.

She made her way through the ballroom into a grand entry hall. The vaulted ceilings were higher there, but three small windows were no match for the body heat of hundreds below.

Och, where was the door? Like the other Sinclairs, Siusan was extraordinarily tall, and by standing on her toes, she barely managed to see over the shifting sea of guests to a darkened passage just ahead to her left. She made for it, but the crush of humanity was too great. She could not move through the crowd. And then she saw him. A tall officer with gleaming red hair . . . and God above, could she be mistaken, or was he wearing the uniform of the Royal Scots Greys? It was eerie how much he resembled Simon.

Her heart thrummed in her chest. *Simon*? Of course, it could not be . . . and yet—she had to get closer. She tried to follow him through the crowd. Aye, his tunic was scarlet with blue garter facings with gold trim with a gold-and-blue-striped sash around the waist. Simon's regimental dress uniform. The one he'd been wearing when he asked her father for her hand.

Gritting her teeth, she focused on the shifting sea of people.

"Sir. I say, sir!" she called out to him. A quartet of people parted to let Siusan through. "Please, wait for me. I see you." She pushed forward, squeezing her way down the hall. "Please do excuse me. He is just *there*. Thank you. Thank you ever so much." She edged her hip sideways through the next gathering, but she was losing sight of him. She raised her hand into the air. "Please wait. Just another moment."

But after a minute, he had disappeared. She had crossed the entire grand hall, but he was gone. Siusan started back, still scanning the crowd for any glimpse of the officer. Of course it was not Simon, but rather her mind playing tricks on her eyes, filling in Simon's features for those she hadn't seen clearly enough. Her eyes were stinging. Logically, she knew this, but still she kept searching. She had to see his face fully to tamp out this foolish fantasy that somehow Simon was here and had not died from his wounds.

Stop this folly, Siusan! Simon died, she reminded herself. *You saw him die.*

She spun around, unable to give up her search. Mayhap he knew her Simon, could tell more about what happened at Waterloo. After Simon returned from the battle, his mind was oft dull with laudanum. The words he managed to speak were sharp and cruel, likely coaxed between his lips from pain.

Suddenly, she spied a hallway she hadn't noticed before. Perhaps he went down the passage. It was possible.

The temperature of the dimly lit passage was somewhat cooler, but her head was whirling from the whisky and the heat of her rush through the grand hall. What she truly required was an open window and some time alone to calm herself. To evict this all-too-vivid memory of Simon from her head.

She hurried to the first door. After a wary glance behind her to be certain she had not been observed leaving the gala, she pressed down on the latch and peered inside. A wand of moonlight reached between the drawn curtains, allowing just enough light for Siusan to discern a snug library. She slipped inside and pressed the door back with her hip, closing it behind her.

She could smell the oiled books on the shelves lining the walls though she could not see them. But for the thin swathe of moonlight coming through a break in the curtains, the room was utterly black.

Siusan started for the window, but within her first three steps her knee slammed into something low and hard—*a table*? She bit into her lower lip to stifle a whimper. Her knee throbbed.

Reaching out, she felt for a place to sit down, her hand

finally finding a cushioned sofa. Limping around its arm, she sat down and hoisted her skirt up and pulled the ribbon at her thigh, then drew down her stocking to rub her barked knee. It wasn't bleeding, which was a good thing, since this was her last pair of silk stockings, and she hadn't the money to buy another if they were ruined.

Just then, she heard the door open. Her breath seized in her lungs.

Moonlight just barely touched the angular face of a large man. He was hardly two strides away.

Her heart pounded. How respectable would it appear for her to be found in a room meant for family, not guests? Thankfully, the library was cloaked in night. If she didn't move . . . barely breathed, the man mightn't even know she was in the library with him.

But then, his eyes shifted to her, and she saw a smile roll across his lips. She followed his gaze and saw that the lone shaft of moonlight was draped across her bare thigh.

"There you are. I couldn't recall if you said the anteparlor or the library," he whispered, striding unsteadily toward her. "Suppose I guessed right, eh?"

Siusan sat stunned, her mind all a jumble about what to do.

"I apologize for leaving you to wait. Went out for a long ride. Had to. I cannot endure the crowds and all of this meaningless fuss." He came and stood before her, his feet firmly positioned either side of hers. His hand shot out and one finger slid alongside her jaw, easing her head back against the sofa cushion.

Siusan's heart thudded harder in her chest. Panicked, she opened her mouth to tell him that she was not who he thought her to be, when suddenly his lips were moving over hers. She shivered as she felt his tongue ease into her mouth and began stroking the insides of her cheeks, twirling around her tongue. The peaty notes of brandy lingered on her tongue, and as she focused on the taste of his mouth, she didn't at first feel his other hand move between her legs and begin to caress her thigh.

When she did, Siusan clamped her legs together. He lifted his mouth a scant breath from hers and exhaled a short laugh. "Come now, it is not as if it is the first time." He nudged her knees open just a bit, then touched her bare thigh again, softly moving his fingers higher between her legs. Touching her just *there*. "And I know you like this quite a lot."

God, she did. A low moan slipped from her lips. *But how—* Siusan's eyes went wide—*how, pray, could he possibly know this*? Her mind spun like a leaf caught in a whirlwind. *No one else knew. Except Simon, of course—but he's—*

Suddenly, he was lifting her, and her back brushed the seat of the long sofa. He stood beside her as he shed his coat and his waistcoat, dropping them to the floor. Within an instant, he'd unwound his neckcloth and pulled his lawn shirt over his head.

She peered up at him. His face was obscured by darkness, but the shaft of moonlight cut across his muscled chest, scored his abdomen, and defined the hardness beneath his breeches.

Lord above. He was so very, very male. To her own embarrassment, moist heat began to collect between her thighs.

What was she doing? Aye, she was no longer a maid, but no one knew this. And it had only been Simon, her betrothed, the man she would have married.

Until Waterloo left him torn in shreds.

He hadn't been expected to survive the night, let alone his transport home. But somehow he did, if only to writhe in agony for weeks at her side, muttering the most hurtful things, untruths meant to drive her from his side. To spare her from seeing him finally succumb. One year ago . . . tonight.

He moved from the light, and she felt him part her knees. The cushion beneath her gave, and she felt him move between her legs.

She couldn't see him now, and she knew he couldn't see her face as he leaned over her and began kissing her again. She closed her eyes and remembered Simon. How she missed him. How she missed the feel of him. Tears welled in her eyes. She felt part of herself die alongside him that night, one year ago.

But in this man's arms, something miraculous was happening. She could scarce believe it, but there was no denying . . . she was beginning to feel again. As if . . . as if his tenderness, his kisses pressing down on her lips, her neck . . . my God, it was as though he was raising her from the dead.

And she did not want him to stop.

Aye, it was wicked, but her body and her mind needed this confirmation of life.

Her eyes snapped open. She could let herself have this. Reclaim her life.

Just one night.

No one would know. Even he thought her to be someone else.

Just one night of sin. That was all.

And in that moment, her decision was made. She raised a hand and ran it through his thick hair, holding him to her as she responded to his passionate kiss while she stroked his muscled chest.

"Mmm," he moaned, stealing one last kiss. He leaned back slightly and ran his fingertips over her breasts, making her arch into his touch. He moved lower and eased his hands over her belly, then beneath the rumpled skirts about her hips. He pushed up her silk chemise and petticoat. His mouth was searing as he kissed the insides of her thighs as he eased her legs wider, opening her sex to him.

Siusan closed her eyes. *Oh, God, this is madness.* But she wasn't going to stop him now. His touches and kisses had wound her body so achingly tight. He made her feel so alive again, the way she had when she was with Simon.

Aye, Simon. She would think of Simon.

His mouth centered on the heat between her thighs. He sucked on her core, flicking her, swirling his tongue with all-knowing surety.

Simon. Simon. She struggled to hold an image of him in

her mind. Only, Simon had never done *this*—so wicked a thing. Oh, God. *Oh, God.*

A warm shiver shook her. Simon never made her feel this way. Ever.

She trembled as his fingers spread her folds, then eased inside, slipping into her, curling up slightly as he circled her womanhood with his masterful tongue. She moaned and twisted as heat spiraled tighter and tighter inside her.

Her legs began to quiver uncontrollably. An urgency grew within her, one that she knew only a man could quell.

With both hands, she grasped his head and turned it up toward hers. When she felt him face her, she leaned down and caught his arms, dragging him back up to her.

In the darkness, she heard him laugh softly, and he moved and rose to kneel between her legs. She extended her arm until her hand felt his breeches stretched tight over his erection. With both hands she searched and finally found the buttons to his front fall. Against the strain of fabric, she fumbled to release the buttons.

His hands came down over hers, then moved them aside to release each button himself. At once the front fall opened, and she felt the heavy weight of his cock bounce down against her before rising again.

She grasped its long thickness and skimmed her fingertips up its shaft to its plump head the way Simon had once tutored her, hardening him to stone. In the wedge of moonlight, she saw a droplet pearl at his tip. She spread it over its crown, making it slick . . . for her.

The sound of the crowd in the ballroom swelled, and she felt his body twist. He was looking toward the door.

Nay, we've not gone this far only to stop now. Siusan pumped her hand once more, then boldly set his plum-shaped tip against the entrance to her wetness.

He groaned aloud and arched his body over hers, poised to take her.

Her anticipation was so great, she could scarcely catch her

breath, but when the musk scent of him filled her senses, her yearning grew ever more intense.

She thrilled at the sensation of his hot, muscled body between her thighs. She needed to feel him inside her. Needed to feed a hunger like no other she'd felt.

He eased his hardness into her moist folds, brushing past that place he'd made so sensitive with his skilled tongue. She shivered and brought her legs up and nearly around him.

In a low voice, he swore beneath his breath, then all at once, he grasped her wrists and held them on either side of her head as he thrust into her sheath. She gasped as her body stretched to him. Unbidden, her muscles gripped him, and she arched up, driving him deeper inside.

He slammed harder into her, filling her, almost to the point that she could not bear it. His fully aroused penis stroking her so forcefully created a mutiny of sensation, pushing her to the edge of sanity.

A whimper of carnal pleasure slipped from her mouth, drawing his attention. He kissed her again, hard at first, then slower and more gently, all the while pressing into her again and again, making her even wetter.

She gasped against his mouth, then again and again. He thrust into her harder and faster, until her muscles spasmed with an intensity she'd never known, overwhelming every inch of her with pulsing ecstasy.

With his last stroke, he swore again and tried to pull back, but her legs held him in place. Too long. His body suddenly arched and jerked into hers until his weight collapsed atop her. A sheen of perspiration broke over his back.

Panting, he rested upon her. "I'm sorry. I tried— Christ, I've always been able to stop. *Always*." He pushed up finally and came to his feet, busying himself with dressing.

Siusan slid to the corner of the sofa, her fingers scrabbling for the ribbon to her stocking. In the black of the room, she couldn't find it anywhere. So, instead, she rolled the top of her stocking to hold it in place, then, with a yank, she returned her skirts to her ankles. She sat still, keeping to the darkness, until she could make her escape.

He bent to retrieve what Siusan guessed to be his waistcoat. This was her moment. As quietly as possible, she rose from the sofa, slipped around behind it, and started for the door.

"Wait." His hand curled around her wrist. "I would be remiss if I allowed you to forget this." There was a clink of coins as he pressed a small leather bag into her palm.

She couldn't help herself. Siusan turned, her face catching the moonlight momentarily as she looked down at the bag, torn between her family's dire need of the money and feeling like she would have sold herself if she took it.

He released her wrist, and his hand dropped to his side. "You are not . . . oh God, you are not Clarissa."

"Nay, I am not." *Blast, I should not have said anything!* Abruptly, she dropped the bag on the floor, and when he instinctively bent to retrieve it, she opened the door and ran down the passage, chancing a hunted glance over her shoulder.

"Oof!" She'd slammed into a stocky, auburn-haired man rounding the corner into the passage just as she turned. She glanced back again as she twisted, and as she slid around him, she saw the man look down the passage toward the library.

Her secret lover stepped from the library at that very moment. Siusan lunged for the crowd. Suddenly the masses surged forward, and she was swallowed up into the swell.

She heard the bang of the liveried footman's staff on the floor behind her. "All hail, His Grace, the Duke of Exeter!"

Siusan pushed against the current of guests rushing forward to see the duke, just catching notice of her sister amongst their number.

"Priscilla!" She lunged forward and caught her sister's arm.

Startled, Priscilla turned to her. "There you are, Su! We've been looking everywhere for you. But here you are and just in time too. The Duke of Exeter has just been announced!"

"I am aware, but we have to find our brothers and leave at once." She tugged on Priscilla's arm.

"I daresay, I am not going anywhere." She furrowed her brow, annoyed.

Siusan grabbed her sister's shoulders. "Listen to me. We *must* leave."

A young woman bumped into Priscilla while blindly racing forward to join the crowd. This only raised her sister's ire. "I haven't yet met the duke."

"But Priscilla, *I have*, and if we do not quit this gala, the duke may recognize me and—oh God—Da will never forgive me for what I have done. Do you understand? He will toss me to the street before the week is out."

Priscilla's eyes rounded. "Gads, Su, what have you done now?"

Heat washed into her cheeks. "I-I will admit all to you later. I swear. Presently, though, I need for you to locate our brothers. We must away. I will meet you in the carriage." She pinned Priscilla with her gaze, hoping to impart the urgency of her words.

Priscilla nodded, then plunged into the crowd.

Siusan hurriedly descended the staircase. Budding tears stung her eyes as the liveried footman opened the doors, releasing her into the night. She could scarcely catch her breath.

She was such a fool. A damnable weak fool.

One night of sin . . . might well have cost her future.